KAREN MAITLAND is an historical novelist, lecturer and teacher of Creative Writing, with over twenty books to her name. She grew up in Malta, which inspired her passion for history, and travelled and worked all over the world before settling in the United Kingdom. She has a doctorate in psycholinguistics, and now lives on the edge of Dartmoor in Devon.

Writing as K. J. Maitland, *The Drowned City* is the first novel in a new series set against the spectre of the Gunpowder Plot – an historical thriller from an expert writer at the height of her powers.

By K. J. Maitland

Daniel Pursglove novels

The Drowned City

As Karen Maitland

The White Room
Company of Liars
The Owl Killers
The Gallows Curse
The Falcons of Fire and Ice
The Vanishing Witch
The Raven's Head
The Plague Charmer
A Gathering of Ghosts

Digital short stories

Liars and Thieves
The Dangerous Art of Alchemy
Wicked Children: Murderous Tales from History

K. J. MAITLAND

THE DROWNED CITY

REVIEW

First published in 2021 by Headline Review
An imprint of HEADLINE PUBLISHING GROUP

First published in paperback in 2021 by Headline Review

1

Cataloguing in Publication Data is available from the British Library

ISBN 978 1 4722 3598 5

Typeset by EM&EN

Printed and bound in Great Britain by Clays Ltd, Elcograf S.p.A.

Headline's policy is to use papers that are natural, renewable and recyclable
products and made from wood grown in well-managed forests and other
controlled sources. The logging and manufacturing processes are expected
to conform to the environmental regulations of the country of origin.

HEADLINE PUBLISHING GROUP
An Hachette UK Company
Carmelite House
50 Victoria Embankment
London EC4Y 0DZ

www.headline.co.uk
www.hachette.co.uk

'The [witches] can rayse storms and tempestes in the aire, either upon sea or land, though not universally, but in such a particular place and prescribed boundes, as God will permitte them so to trouble: which likewise is verie easie to be discerned from anie other naturall tempestes . . . in respect of the suddaine and violent raising thereof, together with the short induring of the same. And this is likewise verie possible to their master [the Devil] to do, he having such affinitie with the aire as being a spirite . . .'

Chapter V, Seconde Booke, *Daemonologie*, 1597 by
James R (King James VI of Scotland,
later King James I of England)

'Mighty hilles of water tombling over one another in such sort as if the greatest mountains in the world had over-whelmed the lowe villages or marshy grounds. Sometimes it dazzled many of the spectators that they imagined it had bin some fogge or mist coming with great swiftness towards them and with such a smoke as if mountains were all on fire, and to the view of some it seemed as if myriads of thousands of arrows had been shot forth all at one time.'

'Lamentable News', 1607, Anon

Author's Note

Dates in this book use the Old Style (Julian) Calendar. Under the old calendar, the year was not numbered from 1 January but from Lady Day, 25 March, which was regarded as New Year's Day. While some countries in Europe had adopted the Gregorian Calendar in 1582, England did not change over to the new calendar until 1752.

Prologue

THE BRISTOL CHANNEL

JANUARY 1606

THE OLD MAN, sitting, sucking on his pipe on the quayside, was first to see it, or rather he did *not* see it. And that was what puzzled him. He squinted up into the cloudless winter sky, trying to judge the angle of the sun, thinking he must have miscounted the distant chimes from the church. It was a little past nine of the clock. By his reckoning, the tide in the estuary should have been on the turn, racing and foaming up the Bristol Channel, barging against the brown waters of the River Severn and herding the flocks of wading birds towards the banks. But it was not.

The tide had started to flow in, just as it had twice a day ever since the first gulls had flown above the waters and the first men had cast their fishing nets beneath them, but now it had suddenly retreated again, as if the sea had taken a deep breath and sucked the water back out, a great blubbery beast pulling in its belly. In all his days, the aged fisherman had never known it to do that before. He half opened his mouth to say as much to the two lads trundling barrels towards the warehouse on the corner of the quay, but he kept silent, afraid they'd jeer that his wits were wandering.

The old man struggled to his feet and shuffled along the jetty, peering down into the mud of the harbour. He knew every drop of blood, fish or human, that stained the boards of that wharf and every spar of wood that poked up from the watery silt beyond it, but he didn't recall ever seeing the weed-covered ribs of the ancient cog ship which now lay exposed in the deepest heart of the channel.

But few other men hurrying around the quayside that morning had time to stop and gawp at old wrecked hulks, not at that hour, for it was as fine a day as any that could be expected in midwinter and no one could afford to waste such good fortune. The frost on the roofs of the cottages glittered in the sunshine and thin spirals of lavender-grey smoke rose from dozens of hearth fires as women began to bake the noonday's bread and sweep the dust from their floors, while their menfolk, rags wound about their hands, stirred vats of boiling tar or sawed planks for new boats, some standing in deep pits so that only the tops of their heads showed above the ground, blizzards of sawdust already covering their greasy coifs.

A flock of grey plover took wing from the mud flats and wheeled over the old man's head, their shrill cries piercing even the hammering and rasping from the boat builder's yard. He stared back down over the edge of the jetty. Maybe his eyes had deceived him, for the tide was coming in again now, a dark snake of water writhing swiftly back up to meet the river. The estuary was filling fast. There was nothing amiss, after all. And yet . . .

The old man shaded his eyes against the dazzling sun. Something was glittering far down the estuary. He couldn't make it out. He tottered further down the jetty. Was there a ship afire out there? Or were those not flames, but sunlight glinting off a forest of steel weapons? A Spanish invasion? It had been nigh on twenty years since those popish devils had last thought to seize the throne from Good Queen Bess, and rumour had it that King James had signed a peace treaty with them, but what Englishman would trust to a scrap of parchment? Maybe the Spaniards thought to try their luck again, knowing the new King had less stomach for a fight than the old Queen.

Three shrieking urchins rushed past the old man, almost knocking him into the water below.

'It's a huge whale, I tell you!'

'It's a sea dragon breathing fire!'

Alerted by their piercing yells, mothers were emerging from doorways wiping wet hands on their aprons. Men in the boat-yard glanced around, then abandoned their tools and crowded towards the water's edge, ignoring the bellows of the sawyers still deep down in the pits who were unable to understand the sudden commotion.

They all stood dumbstruck, staring at the monstrous thing racing towards them up the valley. Sparks and lights shot from it, like the giant wheels that soldiers set ablaze and sent rolling down a hillside towards an enemy camp. A haze of smoke hung in the air above it, keeping pace with it.

Somewhere in the gathering crowd, a little girl was laughing in delight, shouting that it was a magic castle and jiggling her rag doll above her head so that her poppet could see it, too. There was no doubt whatever was approaching had a strange and terrible beauty that was not of this world. Faster it came, growing ever higher, and still no one could drag their spellbound gaze from it.

Then a roar burst against their ears and a great blast of wind came out of nowhere, barging through the crowd with such force that people staggered against one another. And in that instant, the enchantment that had stupefied the crowd broke and now they saw the beast for what it was. A towering mountain of black water was bearing down on them, higher than the wooden crane that unloaded the ships' cargoes, higher than the tallest ware-house, higher even than the bells in the church steeple that had begun to toll a frantic warning.

But the warning came too late, far too late. Even as the little girl's laughter shattered into a shriek of fear, even as the crowd turned as one to run, trampling over each other in their frantic haste, the monstrous wave struck the wharf, smashing the wooden jetty.

Metal screamed as it was ground against stone. Splintered beams and boulders, iron hooks and tin ingots were plucked up by the water and carried off like feathers in a wind. The wave charged down the streets, churning the helpless bodies of men, women and children in its cauldron, their faces battered by rocks, their bodies impaled on jagged spears of wood and twisted shards of metal.

The old man was tumbled over and over in a whirlpool of icy water, dragged down till he was dashed against something hard beneath him. He had no way of telling if he was on land or sea, they had become one raging beast. The liquid that forced its way down his throat, up his nose and into his ears was as thick as soup and so impenetrable, he thought he must have been struck blind. Instinct made him claw his way to the surface. His face burst out into the blessed light, his searing lungs fought to gasp air, but even as his eyes opened, he glimpsed a great iron-rimmed wheel hurtling towards him. He tried to throw himself from its path, but it struck before he could even turn his head, smashing his face as if his skull was nothing more than a hollow eggshell.

The giant wave swept relentlessly inland. Nothing could stop it. Walls of cottages and smokehouses appeared at first to stand defiantly resolute under the attack, only to crumble and collapse minutes later. Those still alive in the water tried in vain to grab at tree branches and chimneys, only to be ripped away from them.

The stout oak doors of churches burst wide. Wailing infants in cradles were sucked from cottages. Stone bridges tumbled like sandcastles as screaming horses and riders were swept from their humped backs. Coffins, scoured from their graves, were smashed against grinning gargoyles and fishing boats sent crashing through the roofs of houses miles from the shore.

The sea would not be bribed. It granted no mercy to the rich or to the poor. Neither the meanest hut of a blind beggar nor the grandest house of a wealthy merchant was spared. The wave surged on like a fanatical preacher determined to cleanse the world from corruption, destroy the sinners and expose all that was hidden. A man's chamber pot hung upon a church cross; a bloodstained shift fluttered from a treetop; a forbidden holy relic was dumped on a drowned pig and the gold coins from the miser's chest lay scattered for all the world to steal.

Part of a wall of a warehouse, which had survived the first onslaught of the great wave, suddenly surrendered to the swirling black water, and as the stones slid beneath the sea, something tumbled out from between them and floated free. If there had been anyone to observe it, they might have thought at first it was merely a bundle of filthy rags. It twisted as the sea dragged it back and forth inside the warehouse. Only when the bundle was flipped over by the water was it plain to see that the rags were not empty; they clung to a corpse, a woman once, though whether young or old, it was now impossible to say. Only two things remained uncorrupted: the long tawny hair that floated out around her like seaweed, and a twist of vivid blue silk cloth tied so tightly around her throat it cut deep into the rotting flesh.

An exhausted rat paddled towards the drifting body, hauled itself up and tried to shake the water from its sodden fur. It dug its claws into its once-human raft, as another surge propelled the corpse towards the back of the warehouse with such force that the head and arm of the dead woman were driven between the rungs of a ladder that still hung from the loft. The body caught there, dangling like a child's rag doll. Even the rat abandoned it, leaping for the ladder and scrambling up into the darkness above. Rats always seek out the dark.

Chapter One

'YOU'LL HAVE TO FIGHT each other for it!' the turnkey shouted above the din of the crowded cell. He was standing in front of the only door at the far end of the long dungeon, dangling the last portion of bread between a decrepit old man and a skinny young boy. The turnkey grinned broadly, revealing his few remaining tobacco-stained teeth. Charity food was supposed to be shared equally between all the prisoners on the common side of the gaol, but they all knew the head gaoler kept the best of it to sell to those prisoners who were lucky enough still to have a few coins, and his turnkeys liked to have their sport with what remained.

One of the prisoners at the opposite end of the cell slowly lifted his head and turned to stare at the unfolding scene. He had not shared his name with his fellow inmates – not even a false name, as most offered. But dogs and men alike must be called something, so they had dubbed him Gallows on account of the scarlet firemark that twisted around his throat like a hangman's noose, and which even his matted black beard could not quite conceal.

A few of the other prisoners had begun to edge towards the turnkey, wolves slinking from the shadows, their eyes fixed on the half-loaf of bread. The turnkey's two assistants raised their halberds across their chests, gesturing for them to stay back. But most men were trying to shuffle well out of the way, those in irons dragging their heavy chains with them as best they could. When fights broke out, anyone unlucky enough to be too close could get their faces smashed or their legs broken.

Gallows sank down to his haunches, clutching his own ration of bread tightly to his chest. He pressed his back against the wall, ignoring the green slime oozing down the sharp stones. His shirt was already so mouldy and stinking, it scarcely mattered what else fouled it, but even after four months rotting in this hell pit – or was it five now? – he still hadn't grown used to the maddening itch of the lice swarming through his dark hair and beard. He clawed furiously at them.

'That's it, you have a good scratch while you can,' one of the guards called out. 'When they chop off your hands, what you going to use to rub your itch then – your pizzle?'

The men around him shifted uncomfortably. But it wasn't pity that prevented them from joining in the guard's mockery, or even fear of Gallows' fists – he'd never raised a hand to any of them. But they'd all heard the rumours about why he was here, and they had enough troubles of their own without baiting a man who could call down even more misery upon them, especially now that his iron shackles had been removed.

Gallows alone laughed at the guard's feeble joke. But he had watched the executioner's blade slice through the flesh and bone of others many times. He had heard the agonised screams, seen the humiliation and misery of the years that stretched out beyond, and it was all he could do not to heave his guts into the straw.

The long, narrow underground chamber was crammed full of prisoners awaiting trial and contemplating what lay in store for them. The Hole, as they called it, where the common men were caged – as opposed to the masters' quarters that housed the prisoners of rank and means – had no bed boards, no fires and no blankets, unless you could pay for them. The slime that dripped from the walls was only kept from freezing in winter by the heat from their bodies, and the air was clotted with the sweat of unwashed flesh, the fetid breath and farts from sour stomachs and the noxious clouds of tarry smoke expelled by those prisoners who could afford to buy the foul-smelling tobacco from the gaoler. That first night when Gallows had lain shivering on the floor listening to the snores, whimpers and groans, he'd been certain he would suffocate in that nauseous stench, but death does not come any more easily than sleep when you ache for it.

He should have seen it coming, should have got out of London long before. They say a violent wind rages when a great monarch dies. There may not have been a storm at the hour of the old Queen's death, but the wind had changed that day, and when the foreign Scottish king rode into London, cloaked in his fear and superstition, the mood in the city had begun to darken. People shrank into themselves, their shoulders hunched and their eyes lowered as they do when they hurry along the streets on a cold, wet evening. The summer of the Queen's reign was turning to winter under the new king. But Gallows had not understood just how keenly that winter wind would bite, until the night he'd been jerked from sleep by the hammering on the door of his lodgings, felt the gloved hands seize him and drag him, naked, down the narrow stairs, gagging from the iron bit they'd thrust into his mouth.

'Not hungry?' The turnkey was waving the bread in the faces of the two prisoners, as if he was taunting chained dogs. 'What about you, sirrah, I thought you used to be one of the Queen's men, killed a dozen Spaniards with your bare hands, didn't you? Why don't you show us how it's done?'

The older prisoner was white-haired, his back crooked as a gnarled apple tree. He seemed ancient to Gallows, but he probably wasn't. When Gallows had been dragged into Newgate, the gaoler had recorded his age as thirty or thereabouts, for the prisoner had never known the day or even the year of his birth. But he was certain he must look twice as old as that man now. What would he look like after four months had been dragged into six or eight or ten? Some men rotted in the Hole for years before they were brought to trial, if they ever were.

The old man rocked unsteadily on his feet. A glistening line of grey drool oozed slug-like from the corner of his mouth and trailed through his sparse beard. The other prisoners reckoned his wits had long since fled. The boy who faced him was a good foot shorter. His ribs stood out on his bare chest like those on a starveling greyhound. A single blow would surely snap them like kindling. In the coppery light of the turnkey's lamp it was hard to see the expressions of the two prisoners, but both were plainly trying to slink away.

Gallows lowered his head and tried to swallow the last of his own dry bread without coughing. Sometimes the pails of greasy, grey water would not be brought in until hours later in the day, and the men were forced to eat while their throats were raw from breathing in the foul night air, with nothing to wash the hard crumbs down. It encouraged those who still had money, or relatives to provide it, to buy beer and wine from the gaoler's tap. However stale or sour the ale was, if you were thirsty it was as welcome as the finest sack.

The only furnishings in the Hole were the rings embedded in walls, pillars and blocks to which neck and heavy leg irons could be chained. As many irons were fastened to a man as the head gaoler was inclined to load upon him, until the prisoner paid to have them removed. Those who had languished there for many months took a malicious delight in telling newcomers that a man had once been fastened so tightly to the wall by the neck, it had broken his back, while others had been forced into leg irons so small that they had lost the limb. Raw, weeping lesions around Gallows' ankles marked where the irons had bitten into his flesh and rubbed against his bone. And the rats always returned to gnaw on the same tasty sore.

Then, without explanation or warning, three days ago, he'd been dragged to the room where his irons had been struck off. The fee had been paid, the turnkey told him. But by whom? He hadn't a single relative living in this world that he knew of and no friend who would risk being associated with him after his arrest. But the turnkey only shrugged when he asked the identity of his benefactor.

'Gaoler gives his orders for them to come off, so off they come. And,' he added, jabbing his finger at the prisoner, 'you'd do well to bless your good fortune instead of asking pert questions. The gaoler can have them loaded on you again any time he pleases. You want to remember that.'

That night he'd lain awake, kicking at the rats, and wondering if his irons had been removed by mistake when the mercy had been bought for some other man. It certainly hadn't been done on the orders of that bastard Molyngton who'd interrogated him before he'd been cast into Newgate. Molyngton would gladly have seen him chained to a wall by a spiked iron collar, as would the spectators who'd been howling for his blood like a hoard of rapacious demons. There was only one who'd dared to meet his gaze, a woman who had smiled encouragingly from the gallery, as if she didn't care who saw her, but then she must have been a woman of some consequence, else she would not have been admitted to the interrogation. The delicate lace ruff that circled her slender neck and the ruby and pearl jewel at her breast were finer than any merchant's wife would wear. The wife of some official at the Royal Court, perhaps? Although the dark auburn hair piled high on her head had not been covered by a married woman's coif – but, these days, that did not always signify. It wouldn't be the first time a woman of rank had shown him favour.

The shouts from the other prisoners had settled into a steady chant of *Fight! Fight!*

'I'll wager my bread on the old cadger.'

'Two pence on the boy taking first blood.'

Fight! Fight! Fight! Prisoners started beating time with their irons. One who was chained to a pillar in the centre of the room began whimpering in fear, pressing his hands to his ears and rocking like a frightened child.

The turnkey's two assistants marched towards the two prisoners, their boots crunching on the lice and beetles that so thickly carpeted the flagstones it sounded as if they were walking over gravel. They jabbed the old man and the young lad in their backs with the points of their halberds, prodding them closer. A scarlet flower slowly blossomed on the man's shirt where the metal tip had pierced the skin. The young lad gazed wildly around, his eyes rolling like a terrified horse's.

A prisoner, crouching in the furthest corner of the cell, clambered to his feet, his fists clenched. He lumbered towards the turnkey. But Gallows' hand shot out, grabbing the man's ankle and digging his fingers into his leg iron sores until he sank down again.

'Not your fight, brother,' Gallows muttered. 'That bastard'll have you flayed to the bone and them alongside you.'

The turnkey was losing patience. He seized the lad by the back of the neck and cracked the boy's head against the old man's. Both staggered backwards, and the old man tumbled to the floor, but was swiftly hauled to his feet by two of the assistants. The turnkey, still holding the boy by the scruff, shoved him hard so that he collided with the old man again.

'Punch him, go on!'

The lad cringed in fear and humiliation. He raised his skinny arms to protect his head, leaving his belly exposed. One of the guards jabbed him violently in the guts and he doubled over. The turnkey reached for the lad's hair, intending to drag him upright—

A thump echoed from the stone as the door was pushed open with such violence that it crashed into the wall. The guards always flung the door wide and sprang back to ensure that they couldn't be ambushed. All heads turned. The head gaoler stood wrapped in the flickering red-orange glow from the torches in the passageway, looking like a demon risen from a stage trap-door, except that he held no pitchfork. Lifting a lantern, he peered at the tableau posed in front of him.

'So, this is where you're skulking, Lacy. What's keeping you?' He took pace inside, wrinkling his nose at the stench, for he seldom troubled to come down to the bowels of the prison him-self. 'There's a prisoner wanted up top in quick time, and no one to fetch him. No point in me keeping a hound, if I have to do my own barking. You want to remember that, if you want to stay turnkey here.'

'Went mad, he did, attacked this lad without any cause,' the turnkey protested indignantly, jerking his chin towards the old man.

'Should be in irons, he should,' one of the assistants muttered, twisting the prisoner's arm up his back, as if he was hoping to make him snarl like a wild man in a cage.

Lacy shuffled forward and seized the old man's shoulder, as if to prove it took three strapping men to restrain him. 'Don't you worry, sir, we'll flog the fight out of him. He'll not cause trouble after that, if he survives.'

'Aye, well, you'll have to wait for his hide.' The head gaoler held the lantern higher, peering down the long chamber. Finally, he pointed to Gallows. 'He's the man I've come for. Fetch him. He's about to get what he deserves.'

Chapter Two

'MOVE YOUR SCABBY ARSE. I've a hot dinner waiting for me,' the gaoler growled, as the prisoner stumbled ahead of him up the stone steps and down a long passageway. The blazing torches in the brackets along the walls guttered and smoked in the icy blasts that blew in through the narrow slits. He gulped greedily at the fresh air and tried to snatch a glimpse of the outside world, but the windows were too narrow to see more than a flash of watery daylight as the gaoler prodded him past.

'Where are you taking me?'

'You'll find out soon enough.'

Gallows was sure of one thing; he was not being led to the gate through which the felons were taken to the assizes. Nor was this the way to the room with the blacksmith's forge – and the head gaoler would not come in person to fetch a prisoner to be returned to irons.

Had Molyngton changed his mind or been persuaded to change it? Was he now determined not just to demand a confession, but to *extract* one by whatever means might prove expedient to loosen a stubborn tongue? The bastard would relish that.

When did you make a pact with the Devil?

What form does your familiar take?

There had been witnesses, or so Molyngton declared – though they had not been brought to Westminster to testify, for fear that the accused would take revenge on them – witnesses who had sworn they had seen him transform a mouse into a viper by sorcery and burn a doll with fire, before making it reappear whole and unmarked.

Do you dare to deny it?

Will you add to your manifold sins and crimes by lying before God?

The gaoler halted before a low door, thrust it open and jerked his head, impatient for his charge to enter. The prisoner edged towards the doorway, bracing himself for whatever might be waiting for him inside. The rough stone wall and the paved slabs of the floor seemed to undulate in the light of a candle burning somewhere beyond his sight, and his guts twisted into a hard knot. No window, then. That did not bode well. No one could hear you scream in a room like this.

'What are you waiting for? Get in there,' the gaoler growled. He seized the prisoner by the back of his shirt and thrust him violently through the doorway.

The door slammed behind him with a hollow echo that set the stones ringing, and Gallows found himself in a long and narrow chamber. Aside from iron rings set at intervals in the wall, the only furniture was a plain table at the far end on which a single candle burned on an iron pricket. The flame was so dim that the corners of the room lay in darkness, but the floor in the centre of the room was empty. He ran his gaze swiftly over walls and ceiling. No racks, or vices or whips. No chains or ropes dangling from hooks in the beam. It was said they always ensured prisoners saw the instruments of persuasion the moment they were brought in, for the sight alone was often enough to loosen a man's tongue. It was only as the shadow behind the table moved that he realised someone was already seated there.

'Come closer, sirrah. I've nae desire for my words to be heard by the whole of Newgate.' The man's accent was Scottish, thick as curds, but there was nothing to be learned from that, you couldn't take a dozen paces in London now without hearing it. Englishmen grumbled that so many men had followed their king south that the only Scots left north of the border were highland cattle.

A long, grimy hand snaked out of the shadows and lifted the

pricket to inspect the prisoner more closely, but in doing so the stranger briefly illuminated his own face. He was a broad-shouldered figure, plainly clad, with unfashionably short hair and a sparse though neatly trimmed beard. Drooping bags beneath his eyes seemed to suggest a man who slept but fitfully. He set the candle down on the table, plunging his own features back into darkness.

'You grow thin, Daniel. Prison does nae suit you, but I warrant you'll have even less flesh on your bones after a month dangling in a gibbet cage.'

Gallows' head gave a little jerk. No one had called him Daniel since he'd arrived in Newgate. 'You have the advantage of me, sir. The gaoler didn't tell me your name.'

The man snorted. 'It's not his business to do so. But I've been told ye canna contain your curiosity. We share that much in common, as do all men of wit and intelligence. So, I'll satisfy yours. FitzAlan's my name . . . Charles FitzAlan, a close confidant of the King. I like to think I am the King's most trusted adviser.'

Every fool at Court flattered himself he was that, Gallows thought.

FitzAlan rested his elbows on the table and leaned forward, pressing his long fingers together. The nails were rimmed with black, as if he had been clawing in the ground – at least, Gallows hoped it was dirt and not dried blood.

'His Majesty the King has lately received lamentable news of a disaster that has befallen his realm. Some days ago, a great flood swept in from the sea up the Channel of Bristol, destroying numerous villages and drowning many people and livestock. As yet, it is not known how many have perished. They say as many as two thousand souls are lost, but the waters still cover the land and it may be weeks before some places can be reached and the full extent of the damage discovered, for the lands are low-lying and the sea has invaded far inland, in places as much as fourteen miles.'

The prisoner looked up sharply. 'But the storm didn't reach London?'

'There was no storm,' FitzAlan said. 'The sea raged in without reason or warning. It was . . .' He seemed to consider the word. 'It was a most *unnatural* disaster and in that lies the rub.'

Unnatural – Molyngton had used that same word at his interrogation.

'The flood struck on the thirtieth day of January. Does that strike you as interesting, Daniel?'

'You can't tell night from day in this place, sir, save by the changing faces of the guards. I don't even know how many months have passed since I was brought here.'

'Come now, sirrah, that date is surely burned into the remembrance of the whole of London, indeed the whole of England,' FitzAlan said impatiently. 'It was the day that the first of the Gunpowder Treason conspirators received justice on the quartering block.'

The prisoner suddenly saw where this was leading. Was it really only a year ago? It seemed now like a dozen lifetimes. If it had been any other execution, he would have been there in the crowd waiting for the condemned, plying his trade among the piemakers and broadside sellers. But that day was not a day for magic, and he'd taken refuge from the biting cold by the warming fire of an inn. London was as agitated as a nest of angry wasps and even he'd had more sense than to risk being stung.

Thomas Bates, Everard Digby, John Grant and Robert Wintour, along with the three other prisoners who had conspired to blow up King and Parliament, had been tied to hurdles and dragged to St Paul's Churchyard, there to be hung and then cut down before they lost consciousness, castrated, disembowelled and quartered. And though most men in England had not actually watched the spectacle themselves, in the weeks to come they would be almost convinced they had, for the account of the barbarous deaths had spread faster than a fire in a field of dry corn. And for those who had not heard the tale as they drank their tankards of ale in London's inns, the broadsides detailed each brutal slash of the executioner's knife, every cry of agony, for those eager to lap up the last bloody drop of that play.

But rumours persisted that some, if not all, of the men who were dragged to the quartering block on that day and the next were innocent or, at the very least, had been deliberately drawn into the conspiracy by the Secretary of State, Robert Cecil, to harden King and country against the recusants.

'Well, Daniel, can you see what conclusions some might draw from the flood striking on the very anniversary of the executions?'

What manner of trap was this man baiting? Gallows had been raised in one of the great Catholic houses of England and although it had been fifteen years since Lord Fairfax had thrown him out of his household, fifteen years since he'd heard the words of the Mass murmured in low voices, he knew full well what Catholics would be muttering about this flood – and not just behind locked doors, and in the secret priest holes, but openly in the taverns and marketplaces, too.

'Speak up, sirrah! It will not profit you to play the gowk with me. Your wits were as keen as the eye of a hawk, and your tongue ready enough to answer, when Sir Henry Molyngton questioned you.'

The prisoner ran his tongue over his cracked lips, selecting his words with care. 'There may be some fanatical recusants who might be foolish enough to believe that this flood was a sign of God's anger . . . revenge for the executions.'

He waited for the King's adviser to press harder, but instead FitzAlan nodded gravely, as if that was the answer he had been seeking.

'Aye, some would say as much, and it takes but a wee pinch of yeast to make the whole vat ferment. I don't doubt you know, as does every Jack and Jill in England, that after the King and all Parliament had been blown asunder, the plotters intended to slaughter every Scot in London, kidnap the King's own daughter, the Princess Elizabeth, and install that young lass upon the throne.'

It may have been the flicker of the candle flame, but Gallows thought he saw a tremor convulse the man behind the table, as if he was seeing the bloody and mutilated remains of his Sovereign and friend lying before him.

The moment passed and FitzAlan resumed, fixing his gaze on the prisoner. 'But that threat has not receded. The Gunpowder Treason was not the first attempt to be made on the King's life, nor will it be the last. If the recusants take this flood as a sign from God, it might encourage the Catholics to rise up against their lawful Sovereign.'

Gallows knew this was no imaginary fear. As a boy in the Fairfax household he'd learned to hide in the shadows – curiosity always overcoming the threat of a beating – as he'd strained to hear the earnest conversations between the old chaplain and the young priests who oftentimes slipped into the house under the cover of darkness. He'd not understood much of what the young men had excitedly gabbled back then, but after the arrest and trial of the gunpowder plotters, the phrases he remembered hearing had taken on a new and chilling clarity.

Was this the reason for FitzAlan's interest in him? But even if he had somehow discovered he'd once been a member of that Catholic household, it had been over fifteen years since George Fairfax had ordered him to leave. Fairfax's old chaplain, Father Waldegrave, was probably long dead by now, and the King himself had banished all the zealous young priests from England.

Gallows' skin prickled, sensing that the trap was about to be sprung. He fought to keep his expression blank, glad of the guttering candlelight that masked any flicker of disquiet that might betray him. He held himself taut as FitzAlan hunched forward, studying him, as though trying to make up his mind about something. But his face, too, was cloaked in shadow and twisting flame. The stone walls undulated in the sickly yellow light as if they were dissolving. An unnerving silence filled the small chamber, amplifying the rasp of the prisoner's own breath and the relentless drip of water beating on hollow flags. Gallows waited.

Chapter Three

THE CHAIR BENEATH FitzAlan's backside creaked as he leaned back. 'This catastrophic flood has wrought much damage, not merely to those villages and towns it has destroyed, but to the whole realm. The ports along the west coast are almost destroyed, as are the King's ships and sea defences. If a single wall of a castle is breached, then the castle lies at the mercy of any who might seek to take it, and this flood has breached one wall of the mighty fortress that is England. I don't doubt news has already reached the shores of France and Holland, and it will speed swiftly enough to Spain.'

He held up his hand, casting a snake's head shadow on the wall. 'True, the King has made peace with Catholic Spain, but the Pope is not enamoured of that peace and with encouragement from the English Jesuits who have fled to Europe, there are some who might seek to break that treaty, especially if they thought there was a chance to install the Spanish Infanta as Queen of England. Twice before, enemies of the King have used witchcraft to try to destroy him through the conjuring of storms at sea. And twice they were defeated by the grace of God. But the King needs to know if his enemies have made a third attempt. Was this flood also conjured by enchantments? Were witches and sorcerers paid by the Jesuits to wreck the King's ports and ships, to open England's gates to an invading army?'

He rocked forward in his chair, as if about to impart a great secret. 'That is why I am sent here, Daniel. King James is an expert on witchcraft, doubtless you have heard of the book he has written on the subject, *Daemonologie*. You have read it?' For a moment, FitzAlan's tone was suffused with the youthful enthusiasm of a drinking companion eagerly inquiring if a friend has seen a play that he has found so amusing. 'The King takes a great interest in the questioning of those accused of maleficium. Full report was made to him of your interrogation. Your answers and, shall we say, your unusual skills have convinced him that you also have a knowledge of both those who practise enchantments and those who *feign* to do so.'

'I have never pretended to—'

FitzAlan cut through the prisoner's words with a razor-sharp tone. 'Kennel your tongue, sirrah. I am speaking. The King desires that you should travel to the west of England and make your own investigations as to whether the author of this flood is nature or the Devil.'

The prisoner almost laughed. 'Travel? Believe me, sir, if I really *was* a sorcerer, I'd have already made myself invisible to the guards and walked out of here. Or conjured one of the rats into a dog, and sent it to fetch me the keys.'

'You should have put that proof to Molyngton, it might have spared you both a keg of wasted words.' FitzAlan made an odd guttural sound, which might have been a snort of laughter. 'The King is no sorcerer, either. All the same, one word from him will magically unlock any door in this realm. You are detained at His Majesty's pleasure; therefore, it follows it may please him *not* to detain you.'

'Are you saying I am pardoned?'

Again, that strange growling laugh. 'I am certain I never uttered that particular word. But if you make diligent and discreet inquiries, and return in person to deliver a report which pleases the King, you will indeed be granted an absolute pardon. Furthermore, His Majesty might be persuaded to offer you some small remuneration, enough to keep you from the temptation of returning to your old ways for a few weeks at least.'

The prisoner had watched the battle between utter relief and mistrust play out on the faces of men reprieved on the scaffold.

Now he felt it. He would keep his hands! He would walk out of here a free man! Yet even as the door swung open, he saw it slamming shut before he could reach it. What exactly was FitzAlan asking of him?

'Is there someone you suspect, sir, someone I should watch?'

It may have been a trick of the guttering candle flame, but it seemed to the prisoner that he saw the trace of a crooked smile.

'Aye, you were well chosen,' FitzAlan murmured almost to himself. He glanced at the door behind the prisoner, as if to assure himself it was securely closed. 'Come a little closer.'

Gallows stepped forward till he was almost touching the table between them.

FitzAlan rested his chin on his hands. 'You'll recall there were four Jesuits complicit in the Gunpowder Treason, all smuggled into England some years before as missionaries for the Holy See. Henry Garnet, their leader, and Edward Oldcorne paid the price of their treachery on the executioner's block. But the other two, John Gerard and Oswald Tesimond, escaped our shores.'

The prisoner nodded wearily. For weeks you hadn't been able to walk down a street in London without someone trying to sell you a broadside crammed with fresh revelations about the Jesuit conspiracy in the plot.

'But what you will not know,' FitzAlan continued, 'is there was a fifth Jesuit conspirator, one who has never been found. The last time the conspirators all met together, in the Mitre Tavern in Bread Street, there was one man present who the intelligencer knew only as Spero Pettingar. After that night, he vanished. None of the conspirators questioned admitted to knowing his real identity and the intelligencer was able to furnish no description of him, for he never saw him. To have disappeared so swiftly and without trace means he must have been aided by the Catholic network, who doubtless hid him before smuggling him away. This priest has been biding his time, waiting to strike again.

'It was the King alone who was able to decipher the letter delivered to Lord Monteagle, warning of the Gunpowder Treason, when even Robert Cecil was blind to its meaning. And now, once again, only the King has had the wit to reason that if any man on earth called up this flood, it was Spero Pettingar. This Jesuit is more cunning than any of them, and he must be found.'

'But surely if Father Gerard and Father Tesimond were smuggled abroad, this man will also have fled to France or Spain. If the King's intelligencers cannot find him—'

'God damn you, fool!' FitzAlan pressed his hands down on the table, as if he intended to rise from his chair and walk away. He stared deep into the heart of the candle flame, but when he finally spoke again, his tone was quiet and measured. 'Bristol has become a nest of Jesuits. They use the trade ships to come and go as they please, spying on England for the Pope and their masters in Spain. The King has received many reports that the priests who were expelled are stealing back into his realm through that port. What better place could a man like Pettingar find to conceal himself, where he will find supporters who will shelter him? And there is another reason a man like Pettingar would be drawn to Bristol . . .'

FitzAlan paused, dragging his gaze from the flame and staring up at the prisoner to study his reaction.

'Not three months back, several women were brought to trial on charges of witchcraft. It seems that when a ship from Bristol was at sea, the quartermaster chanced to descend into the ship's hold and there he discovered a coven of naked women carousing and making merry. The women caught him watching and swore he would rue the day he had seen them, whereupon they promptly vanished. The quartermaster was struck with lameness and as the vessel entered the Bristol Channel it was stopped dead in the water as if an invisible anchor was holding it fast, though the tide was running in and a strong wind was blowing in its favour. The ship could not be moved until a blacksmith on the shore broke the enchantment and freed the vessel. The quartermaster who dwelt in Bristol recognised several of the women and laid charges against all those he could name, as soon as he reached port.'

'What became of them?'

'They confessed their guilt when questioned and were hanged,' FitzAlan said, with a shrug, as if remarking that his cook had plucked a chicken for dinner. 'But the quartermaster swore there were a great many more women down in the hold whom he could not name and who are still at liberty somewhere in the city. If a man wanted to conjure a flood by means of witchcraft, he would find there all the Devil's minions he needed to do his bidding. Jesuits and witches both are drawn to Bristol as rats and flies are drawn to a sewer. And it is a dark and dangerous alliance they form. The Devil's pact,' FitzAlan said, with great deliberation. 'You must discover if that flood was called up by witches. And if it was, then is Pettingar the dark spider who sits at the heart of that evil web?' He held Gallows' unblinking gaze. 'Speak your mind plainly, sirrah, are you willing to undertake this task?'

A witch hunter, a pursuivant, an intelligencer for the King! If such an offer had been put to the prisoner a mere two months ago, he would have walked away, shaking his head incredulously at the very idea. But a man's whole life can be flipped inside out by the single spin of a coin. *Are you willing . . . ?* At that moment, he couldn't think of a single thing he wouldn't be willing to do to get out of the Hole alive.

'So, to the practical matters,' FitzAlan said briskly. 'The King does not want it known that he has sent anyone to investigate this. If Spero Pettingar is in Bristol, we do not want him to be alerted by the faintest whisper that he is being hunted and to slip away before he can be apprehended. Equally, the King does not want Parliament to know that he is concerned about rumours that the flood was the work of witchcraft, should they prove false.'

The prisoner was not fooled by FitzAlan's carefully crafted warning. All London knew that there were many in Parliament –

and on the streets, too – who mocked the King's fear of the dark arts, and this would only hand them more dung to throw.

'Intelligencers hang about the inns and taverns of this land like ticks on a hound's arse, and every man at Court has his spies,' FitzAlan continued. 'If it reached certain ears that you'd been released, the blatherskites at Court would start speculating about who authorised it and what you're doing in a devastated city from which most men are fleeing. You'd be best advised to adopt another name. Let me see . . . *Sparrow*. That's a plain wee bird which few notice pecking for crumbs about their feet.'

The prisoner firmly shook his head. 'Won't do. People have a way of remembering names such as that. It's too easy for them to picture the creature and hang the image round the neck of the man, where it may tighten into a noose. I need a name that has a dozen cousins, so that they can't be certain they recall it correctly . . . Purlles, Pygott, Purslowe, Pursglove?'

'You've obviously had cause to give this matter a good deal of thought in the past. Now I wonder why that should be?' Again, there was the merest twitch of a smile. 'But, *Pursglove*, as you say, will do. It fits you like kid. You'll be conveyed to a house where your possessions, such as they are, have already been taken. Fresh clothes, money enough for food and lodgings, and a mount will be provided for you. You'll leave the city by noon tomorrow.'

FitzAlan cupped his black-rimmed fingers about the flickering candle flame as if he would pluck it and hold the fire in his palm. He did not look at the prisoner as he spoke.

'Let me offer you one word of caution, Master Pursglove. I said you'll be pardoned *if* you return and deliver a report which pleases the King. But should you find yourself tempted to scurry away and vanish, like one of the wee mice you're so fond of playing with, a notice will be sent to every town and hamlet in the land informing them that you are an escaped fugitive and the price that will be put on your head will be large enough to have all the men, women and children in the King's realm searching

26

every bush and barn, cave and crag for you. You'll not escape, Master Pursglove. The King has spies everywhere. And trust me when I tell you that *when* you are recaptured, your execution will be as long and agonising as any traitor whose head decorates London Bridge.'

Chapter Four

DANIEL PURSGLOVE

ALTHOUGH IT WAS not yet evening, darkness was already flowing into the coves and crannies of Bristol's twisting streets as I guided my horse, Diligence, around the deep potholes and piles of rubble. Eye-stinging smoke from frying blubber and burning refuse gusted in the sharp breeze. I had witnessed the devastation in the countryside outside Bristol, laid waste by the great wave, but even so, nothing could have prepared me for the sight of the mighty stone bridge that spans the River Avon in the city. Even from a distance, it was evident that the shops and houses that lined it lay half in ruins, shored up with wooden scaffolding. But the most curious sight was the bow of a sailing ship dangling in mid-air beneath one of the arches, its mast and rigging impaled through one of the shops on the bridge, as if it were as light as the toy boats that little boys fashion from twigs.

'Spare a bite, sir, for the children.' A woman shuffled towards me along the narrow street, barely glancing at me, her cry listless, habitual, like the call of the gulls, as if she had asked so often without any response that she no longer expected to receive any. A boy and two little girls trailed behind her, their noses running, their faces pinched with hunger and cold.

The trickle of people tramping away from the Channel had grown into an ever-greater stream, the closer I'd come to Bristol and the coast. A few of the lucky ones jolted over the stones and mud in horse-drawn carts piled high with boxes, wooden stools, iron tools, grizzling infants and old women who stared vacantly out at the alien hills. More often, men with ropes looped over their shoulders dragged handcarts, their wives plodding behind, steadying the carts, so they didn't tip over in the water-filled potholes. But most, like this woman and her children, hobbled past on the road, carrying little or nothing at all.

I tugged on the reins, guiding Diligence to the side of the street, away from them. The woman seemed to see me properly for the first time and, as I slowed, she took a few paces towards me.

'Just a bite, kind sir.' She tugged on the hem of my cloak, as the children suddenly broke into a run, jostling one another and reaching up to paw at me. Unnerved, Diligence skipped sideways.

'I've nothing. Keep back, the horse—'

As my mount swung round, I felt a blade graze my skin. In an instant, I'd dug my heels into Diligence's chestnut flank and bounded forward, scattering the children. I glanced behind me. A gangly, rat-faced lad stood in the street, hastily stuffing a knife back beneath his shirt as he screamed abuse and threats in his fury at being cheated of my purse. The lad had clearly been a professional nip long before the flood, but I'd earned my living on the road long enough to know all the thieves' tricks.

At first, as I journeyed, I'd caught only glimpses of the destruction caused by the wave as I crested the hilltops: the glint of water, which I'd taken for a lake or even the sea itself, until I saw the bare branches of trees stretching up out of it, as if begging to be saved; a church submerged to the top of the porch in swirling brown water; the bloated carcass of a pig caught in the roof beams of a cottage; sheep crowded together on slithers of mud, marooned in an ocean of water, their starving bleats carrying for miles. Once, I glanced up into a tree to see the face of a child peering down at me as if swinging upside down, the way they like to do. But this child saw nothing, nor ever would again.

The carcasses of horses, cattle, dogs and people lay strewn among wrecked buildings, floated in the swollen rivers or simply lay where the sea had finally dropped its playthings in sodden meadows of blackened grass. I was riding again through the desolation I had witnessed after the soldiers of an army to which I had once sworn allegiance had laid waste to a country not their own. But not even they had slaughtered every living thing as the merciless wave had. Here even the land itself lay slain, for pastures and fields would be poisoned for many months to come by the salt poured on to it by the sea.

My horse stumbled, almost pitching me over his head.

'Steady, sweeting, steady.' A woman's hand came from nowhere and seized the bridle to hold Diligence still, while she patted his neck. She glared up at me. 'Have you curds for brains? What kind of codwit rides a horse along these streets when you can barely see your own hand? There are holes under that mud deep enough to swallow a cart. If you've no regard for your own neck, then at least have a care for your horse. We've enough dead beasts in Bristol already.'

She was slender and small, but she tilted her chin back as if defying me to argue with her. In the twilight it was hard to see the colour of those piercing eyes, but I caught a flash in them as bright as steel. She looked no more than twenty. Since she gave no sign of relinquishing her grip on my bridle, I dismounted, my boots sinking ankle-deep in mud. In truth, it was too dark to be riding in these treacherous streets, though I wasn't about to admit that to this spitting grimalkin. But it was plain she knew her way around these parts and, as old Father Waldegrave used to say, guiding angels may take many forms, maybe even sharp-clawed cats.

I made a graceful bow. 'I have only arrived in your fine city in this past hour, mistress, and I'm sorry to find it in this state.'

'Darkness hides most of it. You'll see worse come daylight. But, day or night, you'd best be leading that horse and treading carefully yourself, there's metal shards and broken pots scattered all over . . . corpses, too, still buried in the mud—' Her voice caught. Then, as if angry with herself for faltering, she resumed her scolding tone.

'You should get yourself and that poor beast undercover before the evening grows much older. There's a curfew been declared after dark, to try to stop the looting, but that only serves to aid the band of thieves who nest up in the castle. They'll already be creeping out to steal what they may. One sight of that horse of yours and they'll be swarming over you like rats on a carcass. The night watchmen say they're trying to stop the robbing and looting, but while they're busy driving off the robbers in one street, others are already stripping a house to the bones on the next.'

She lifted her skirts, placing her feet carefully as she squelched away.

'Wait, mistress. As you say, I must find shelter for the night.'

As if to prove my words, a vicious sea wind gusted between the houses, slicing through my cloak as keenly as a fish gutter's blade. Diligence skipped sideways, trying to turn away from it, swishing his long, elegant tail in irritation.

'Do you know of an inn or any place I might find lodgings?'

She turned her head, but did not attempt to make her way back. 'Have you not eyes? Half the houses along the waterfront are washed away. Whole villages beyond were swept out to sea as if they were castles of sand built by children. You think there are lodgings to be had anywhere in the city?'

I glanced into the shadows behind me to ensure no one else was close enough to hear me. 'I can pay.'

'Pay? Can you indeed, my lord?' She put her hands on her hips, tilting her head, in a curiously impudent gesture. 'I reckon you can, too, by the looks of that beast you ride. But that's what is strange about you. Anyone with money is leaving Bristol and riding inland in search of a place where they can eat well and sleep without being up to their hocks in mud. So, what brings a man like you riding into the city not out of it? Lose your way, did you?'

'I've come to search for my mother's kin. My aunt and her children had journeyed to Bristol just a few days before the flood, to find passage on a ship. We don't know if they had already set sail, or if they were still ashore when the wave struck. There's been no word from them since they set out, so I've come to discover what news I may. My poor mother cannot eat or sleep until she knows what has befallen them.' I bowed my head, as if weighed down with grief. I fancied it was a good performance and darted a look at the girl. It was too dark to see her expression, but she took a few careful steps back towards me.

Her tone was gentler than before. 'Even that may not be possible. They're digging out more corpses each day from beneath the mud and rubble. But they say many people were dragged out to sea as the wave rolled back. They may never be found, unless the bodies are washed up down the coast. Even then, it may be weeks before anyone can reach them. And by then who will recognise . . . ?' Her voice cracked.

She gave herself a little shake and added, more briskly, 'But God grant your aunt and cousins are safe. Many survived, why shouldn't yours be among them? I work in an inn, the Salt Cat, two streets from here. My master has lodgings. Most are taken just now by Bristol folk who've lost their homes, but there is one chamber come free only yesterday, for a family left the city to go to their kin in the north. If you've money enough to pay . . .' She shrugged. 'There's a stable, too, for your horse, though there's precious little hay left in the city.'

'I'd sleep in the stables myself,' I said. My backside was numb, the muscles of my thighs and back were screaming from being in the saddle so long.

I followed the girl down a row of overhanging houses. A stream of oily yellow light poured out of a tavern towards the top of the street as someone opened a door. The light fell upon a woman pressed so hard against the wall by the man impaling her that it was a wonder her ribs hadn't snapped. A babble of voices rolled out before the door shut again, plunging the woman and her customer back into darkness. Somewhere a child screamed in terror, the cries cut off abruptly as if they'd been silenced for ever, but my new companion merely hurried on. A dog began to howl and, one after another, six or seven more joined in, until it seemed as if a pack of ravenous wolves were racing through the town, hunting their prey. With its streets as dark as the Devil's wings, and the flickering red glow of fires through the shutters, for a moment I almost believed that Bristol was haunted not merely by witches but by the very demons of hell.

Chapter Five

'THIS WAY.' The girl was standing in front of a low arch. Before I'd caught up with her, she'd vanished into the dark maw beyond. I tensed, drawing back against the wall, my hand sliding to the dagger in my belt. But she reappeared, holding up a lantern that gave off little light though a great stink of whale oil.

She jerked her head towards a long wooden hut at the back of the yard. 'There's the stable for the horses. I saw the master fill the water trough this morning for his own mare, so it'll be fresh enough.' She lowered her voice. 'I'll set a bite or two of oats in a sack on the lantern hook next to the door, but don't you tell the master. He'll sell you more, but you'll have to pay dear for it, it's as scarce as cock's eggs.'

I fed Diligence the handful of oats while I washed the mud from his legs and belly, then left him greedily drinking the water as I followed the girl across the yard towards a door that led directly into the parlour of the inn. It was like stepping into a thick sea fret, for the room was choked with the pungent tobacco smoke from a dozen pipes. A dingy mustard light filtered through the fog from candles on the walls. To amuse the customers these had been placed not in lanterns but in the bleached skulls of seals, or between the open jaws of dried sharks' heads, conger eels and even the skull of some kind of monkey or ape, which, but for its savage fangs, looked unnervingly human. High-backed winged settles huddled close around narrow tables, screening their occupants from both the draughts and sight of the door, and more were crammed into nooks and corners, so well hidden that only the murmur of voices and the occasional giggle or curse betrayed the fact that anyone occupied them.

A squat woman, plump and dumpy as a spiced bun, swung her pendulous breasts sideways through the door at the back of the parlour, a flagon in one hand, a platter of meat in the other, and a basket of bread hung over one arm. Her greying hair was tumbling from her cap, her face flushed and glistening with sweat. She scowled when she saw the girl.

'There you are, you idle trull. About time you showed yourself. I can't be expected to cook and wait on folks at the same time. Master's fit to boil your blood for puddings. You'll lose your place if you keep running off. There's plenty more wants work, if you don't.'

'Brought you a customer, Mistress Crugge, gentleman wants to rent the empty room.'

The woman's scowl melted into a black-toothed grin. 'Does he now? Well, what are you waiting for? By the looks of him, I'd say he's not had a square meal in weeks. Fetch him some vittles before he faints clear away. Meats and sack, is it, sir?'

'Ale,' I corrected. I didn't want to give the impression I'd money to scatter like chicken feed.

Mistress Crugge gave a great sigh. 'Like to oblige you, sir, but there's been no ale to speak of brewed here since the flood, and what there is would turn the stomach of a mariner. Spoiled it is, only a swindler would sell it. Best stick to the sack, sir, or wine, else you'll be shitting your guts into a bucket for a week. You take your ease, and Rachael will fetch it. As soon as you've had your fill, Master Crugge'll show you the snug little room that's ready for you.'

I slid on to the empty settle. In the shadowy corners of the parlour, small knots of men were engrossed in games of dice or cards. Gambling was, of course, forbidden at any season except Christmastide, but no one took much heed of that. Coins were scooped up and vanished almost as soon as they were slapped down upon the table, and I guessed the dice would vanish equally quickly if the constable or ward entered, not that there seemed much danger of that if they were busy chasing looters. Besides, in most towns the innkeepers ensured any constable's men suddenly turned deaf, blind and dumb, by slipping them a few coins each week or ensuring they were well supplied with free food and drink.

Other huddles of men leaned towards each other in earnest discussion, their voices low, their eyes constantly darting about to ensure that no one was paying them any undue attention. If the Salt Cat was anything like those inns I haunted in London, a man could glean a great deal by listening in to these murmured conversations. I might already have found the gateway I needed into the secrets of this city.

Rachael was threading her way back through the tables towards me. Men tried to grab her, demanding more wine or vittles, but she shook their hands off, telling them robustly to 'hold their wind and swallow a jack of patience' if they were thirsty. She set a wooden trencher of mutton and pickled oysters before me, then poured me a measure of sack, while extending her other hand for my hastily proffered coin. She didn't linger. Others were bellowing for her attention. I found myself gulping down every morsel like a starving prisoner, until I noticed some of the men were watching me curiously and forced myself to slow down. But most of the stares were cursory. I guessed those who frequented the Salt Cat had more pressing business of their own to attend to, and in a port such as Bristol, strangers must be as commonplace as gulls. I could pass without notice here.

Master Crugge, when he appeared, wiping his hands on the front of his stained and greasy tunic, was in appearance the exact opposite of his wife. He was as skinny as she was plump, with spidery legs and arms that seemed far too long for his body, and a pate as bald as an egg. *Jack will eat no fat, and Jill doth love no lean / Yet betwixt them both they lick the dishes clean.* The latter was certainly true for, as I soon discovered, between them, they set about plucking every coin it was possible to wrest from their customers.

'A private and commodious room commands a rich price, sir, what with rooms being so scarce. And a strapping young man, such as yourself, will surely be wanting a good wholesome breakfast and a generous supper. You'll find no better vittles anywhere in the city. Anyone can see a gentleman like you is used to his comforts, and for just a few shillings more I'd be glad to provide you with softer sheets for the bed and the purest wax candles, which give off not a particle of smoke, instead of those stinking oil lamps. Then there's the question of fodder and stabling for your fine horse. Would you be wanting your boots shining? We've a good woman comes every week to see to the washing. For a few pennies more, she'll willingly scrub your linens for you, and you won't find a maid in the King's palace who could get them whiter or sweeter smelling.'

But when you suddenly find yourself forced to make your own way in the world, after a childhood of plenty, you quickly discover how hard won every farthing is. I was not about to part with a single coin more than I had to, so it was a somewhat surly landlord who eventually led me across the dark courtyard to a flight of rickety wooden stairs that led up the outside wall of the inn to a room tucked beneath the roof.

It had probably once been an open loft for storage, but now a wooden partition formed one wall from which the roof sloped down to about a foot from the wooden floorboards on the other side. A large oak beam ran across the centre of the room at shoulder height. It must have been salvaged from an old ship, for it still bore the tunnels of seaworm. Master Crugge patted it as if it was a horse's flank.

'Now this is most convenient, you must agree, Master Pursglove.'

I was just thinking the exact opposite, for there was no way to cross the room except by ducking under it.

'See, you may set a lantern upon it, or your clothes to dry, and' – he flung out one of his gangling arms – 'you have a feel of this.' He caressed the bricks of the great chimney that ran up from the floors below. 'You'll not need any fire up here. Warm as a doxy's thigh – which I dare say you'd know all about, sir,' he said, with a conspiratorial wink and leer.

Getting no response from me, Master Crugge bade me sleep well and slithered out of the door, leaving me to explore what there was of the room. A narrow bed with a flock-filled mattress was wedged in the far corner where the heat from the chimney might best warm it. A stool had been placed in front of a long, rough table set with lamp, ewer and basin. There was a single small casement, which must in daylight afford some view of the street in front of the inn. A plain wooden chest served as the only place to keep clothes or possessions, and beneath the bed was a chamber pot that was relatively clean, though stained. I hadn't relished venturing down those stairs, half asleep in the middle of the night, to visit the jakes. Compared to the Hole, it was indeed a commodious chamber – in fact, a palace – but I wasn't about to mention that to Master Crugge.

A great weariness overwhelmed me. Before my arrest, I'd thought nothing of walking for miles in all weathers to reach a fair or a great house to seek work. I could march all day and entertain half the night, with as much energy as a skylark in summer. I hoped I was simply weakened from the foul humours, the damp and the wretched food in the Hole. I could not afford to fail in this task. I'd heard the steel in FitzAlan's voice when he'd warned me to bring back a report pleasing to the King, or pay dearly for my failure.

But there was a question that had begun to gnaw at me almost as soon as I turned in the saddle and saw the great city of London safely behind me. What exactly would *please* His Majesty? Spero Pettingar's head on London Bridge, clearly. Though I wasn't sure if I could help condemn a man – any man – to the torments of the rack and the agonising death that would follow, but if the alternative was my head on that bridge . . .

Then there was the question of whether witchcraft was at work. When Queen Bess was alive, the tavern joke used to be that the King of Scotland pissed his breeks if he so much as saw a black cock peering at him from some old crone's garden. No one dared make such jokes since he'd come south. And besides, of late it was rumoured that James had become more interested in uncovering imposters who feigned bewitchment, rather than witches. Yet the same could not be said for his attitude to the Jesuits. If anything, it was the reverse. Here was a king, born of a Catholic mother, who had begun his reign promising to tolerate the old faith for the sake of peace and order in his kingdom, but who was hardening against it by the day, and the Gunpowder Treason plot had only stiffened his hatred.

If that was not tangled enough, I knew that what might please the King would not necessarily please the King's advisers, and to reach His Majesty I had first to pass through FitzAlan. God's bones, this would take some unravelling. I was aching to lie down, but I couldn't rest until I'd made sure that old spider Crugge had given Diligence the fodder I'd paid handsomely for. *Diligence!* What a name to saddle a noble beast with – bad enough that the pinch-mouthed Puritans hung that millstone round the necks of their own miserable offspring, without imposing it on a fine horse.

I took the lantern from the table, crawled under the beam and pulled open the door. A blast of cold sea wind pierced my shirt. It was growing colder. A single poor torch burned on the wall of the courtyard, illuminating nothing much but itself in the smoky flame. As I descended the creaking staircase, thin shafts of light glimmered through cracks in the shutters of the rooms below mine. I could hear a babble of voices and the cat-like yowl of a newborn baby.

I was nearing the bottom of the staircase when something slid out from the dark cavern of the stable and crept along the far wall towards the archway of the courtyard. I raised the horn lantern but the dim light caught only the dark outline of someone swathed in a hooded cloak before they vanished into the street beyond.

Rachael had said there was a curfew in the city, so no honest man should have been leaving the inn at this hour. I slid the dagger from my belt and picked my way across the rough yard, slipping and stumbling over God alone knew what and cursing Crugge for his cheese-paring. The man was begging to be robbed if he was too mean to light more than a single torch. As it was, a dozen cut-throats could be hiding in the dark corners and door-ways.

I slipped through the open doorway of the stables, raising the lantern. A few chickens roosting in the rafters gave indignant squawks as the light fell on them. Two goats scrambled to their feet and stood eyeing me balefully. The stone-built stables in the Fairfax household had been divided into individual stalls where the valuable hunters and carriage horses could be fed, watered and groomed. This place was little more than a small barn, with a few tethering rings embedded in the sturdier beams. There was room for half a dozen small riding horses, but the only other horse occupying the space that night was a barrel-shaped beast more suited to pulling a cart than being ridden. I guessed it belonged to Crugge.

I'd tethered Diligence at the far end, furthest away from the doorway and the icy blasts of sea wind. I could hear him tramp-ling around, neighing and tugging against the ring that held him. The beast was obviously agitated. Was someone hiding in here? But there were no obvious places in which a man could conceal himself. Setting the lantern on a hook, I snatched up a pitchfork with two reassuringly sharp tines and edged slowly towards the frightened animal, prodding the makeshift weapon into the soiled straw as I went. A few startled rats leaped out and darted away. Rats wouldn't unsettle a horse though; they were constant stable companions.

It was too dark to see much more than the whites of Dili-gence's eyes, but they were rolled back. He was shifting restlessly and pawing the filthy straw. I ran my hands down the quivering neck, murmuring softly into his ear. He'd likely picked up a burr or thorn that was annoying him. I brushed my hands across his back and belly, then down each leg to check for any swelling or cuts, but it was only when I touched his hindquarters that I discovered what was wrong. I thought in the semi-darkness my eyes were playing me false. Gently, I touched the horse's dock. Diligence let out a shrill sequel, rearing as far as his tether would allow and swinging his hindquarters away from me. A warm, sticky fluid coated my fingers. I sniffed at it. Diligence's long flowing tail was gone. The thick hair had been chopped off so close to the tailbone that the poor beast was bleeding.

Chapter Six

THE COURTYARD WAS no less hazardous in the grey morning light than it had been the night before. Crossing from the stables to the door of the parlour, I was forced to edge around heaps of smashed wood and tottering piles of salvaged furniture streaked with salt stains, black mud and seaweed.

I pushed open the parlour door. The room reeked of strong tobacco, stale cooking and sweat, but at this hour few men occupied the settles. I slid behind one of the tables and glanced up as the door to the kitchen opened. Rachael nudged the door wider with her slender hip, frowning as she caught me watching her. She set a cold roasted pigeon on a platter and a flagon of cloudy cider down in front of me, then straightened up, tucking a strand of honey-brown hair beneath a patched cap. Her eyes, now that I could see them properly in the morning light, were slate-blue.

'Your horse, Master Pursglove, how does he fare? It was a wicked thing to do to a tethered beast that can't defend itself, wicked!' Her fists clenched as if she would gladly have thrashed the perpetrator with her bare hands.

'Mistress Crugge gave me a little salve to cover the cuts on the dock.'

Rachael raised her eyebrows. 'Gave it you? Never known her give anyone anything but a flea in their ear. She must have taken a fancy to you.'

'More likely she hopes to keep me from spreading the word that her customers' horses aren't safe in her stables. Though I can't fathom what profit any man could hope to gain from such an attack.' I'd lain awake half the night thinking about that. Was it intended as an insult? Father Waldegrave, my old tutor, had often recounted with glee that when the Bishop had sent out messengers instructing the people of Devon to use King Edward's new Reform Prayer Book, several had returned in shame and humiliation with their horses' tails cut off by the faithful, and the message that next time it would be the bishop's cods that would feel the knife. Could some Jesuit or recusant have already discovered why I was here? Was this a warning to me?

Rachael grimaced. 'Horsehair's worth a few pennies, but with so many beasts drowned after the flood, there's plenty to be taken from their carcasses without the need to go stealing from the living.'

'Can't tell you who it were,' a phlegmy voice said. 'But I reckon it's as plain as a pig in a patched gown why they done it.'

A wizened face, tanned to the colour of polished oak by the sea wind, materialized round the wing of the settle. With an eel-like smoothness that belied his age, the man's body followed, sliding into the seat opposite me.

Rachael's anxious expression melted into an urchin's grin. 'Might have known you'd be waggling your ears, Walter. Not as deaf as you feign to be when the mistress asks you to pay up, are you?'

'What's that you're saying, my little nymph?' He cupped his hand around one fleshy ear with so much hair sprouting from inside it that it was a miracle he could hear anything. 'How's about fetching me a tankard? Thirsty work, it is, talking.' He pointedly eyed my flagon of cider. 'Now, young master, you were asking why they'd take your nag's tail. Well, I'll tell you. Sorcery! Witches plait the hair, see, and make a magic bridle of it and then they put it on some poor wretch of a man while he sleeps, so he can't escape them. They ride him through the night sky to their witches' Sabbats, and he wakes in the morning back in his own bed. He can't recall a thing, save terrible nightmares that make no sense to him, but he's cold with sweat, and his back

43

and limbs ache so he thinks he's been racked. Can scarcely put a toe out of bed for that he's so weary.'

'That's what happened to you, was it, Walter? Some young witch ride you all night, did she? Is that why you're too exhausted to lift a spade?' Rachael had returned with an empty tankard.

Walter reached for my flagon and poured himself a generous measure. Then he tore a leg off my roasted pigeon, waving it at Rachael's departing back. 'She can mock, but there's more witches than gulls in this city. Saw them, I did, in the flood.'

I'd taken little notice of the tale so far. I'd heard old folks say such things before, and I believed them as much as I believed the stories of giants and of houses that flew through the sky from Nazareth to Walsingham. But this might prove useful.

'These witches, did you actually see them cast their spells? Did you recognise these women?'

Walter ripped the second leg from my pigeon and studied it thoughtfully before stuffing it into his mouth. He dragged the flesh from the bone through his teeth. 'How do you think I'd be recognising them,' he answered finally, 'when they were rats?'

I thought I must have misheard, for he was speaking through a mouthful of pigeon.

The old man gulped the meat down and took another swig of cider. 'Saw them with my own two eyes before the wave hit us. They knew, you see, because they'd called it up, stands to reason they'd be prepared. Sea went a longways out in the Channel, further than even a spring tide, so that's why I was staring at it. And then I saw it, a load of driftwood floating in the deepest gully where there was still a stream of water. Nothing strange in that, you'll say. Ah, but that's where you'd be wrong. There were rats clinging to every piece of floating wood, dozens of them, not a whisker of space between them, and not just on driftwood neither, even saw some floating by on a dead cat. They were waiting for the wave to surge back in so it would carry them inland to higher ground. And . . .'

He peered around as if he feared to be overheard, though there was no one else in the parlour. 'I heard about this man who was swept inland himself by the wave. Managed to grab on to the branch of a tree and haul himself out of the water. All day he sat up there and, come dusk, he felt something bump into the tree. It was an old door, floating like a raft, and every inch covered in rats. They all scrambled up into the tree, filled every branch. They pressed right up against him. He could feel their wet fur. But now here's the thing, three days and three nights he sat up in that tree with those rats and not a bite did he get, nor did they turn on each other. Now I ask you, would any natural rat sit starving and leave a man untouched? They were witches, I tell you. Turned themselves into rats so as they could survive, 'cause they knew that wave was coming. As for the real rats,' he waved a twisted hand towards the door. 'You go out there, young master, and you'll see the streets piled high with dead rats, drowned, the lot of them, but not the witches.'

I was painfully aware of the swollen rat bites on my own legs, which were not yet fully healed. If you were not chained in the Hole you could protect yourself, curl into a ball, sleep face down to shield your nose and lips, but if you were in leg irons, you were at their mercy. The corpses of those who died in the night often had their faces and bellies chewed up before the turnkey's assistants came to carry them out. If it was even half true that the rats had not attacked the man in the tree, it was strange indeed, but certainly no proof of witchcraft. And I would need more than a sackful of fanciful tales to satisfy FitzAlan.

Seeing Walter's fingers creeping towards the platter again, I scooped up what little remained of the pigeon and rose, surrendering the flagon of cider to the old cadger.

'I reckon the witch who stole your horse's tail means to come back to bridle you, young master. You be sure to hang a hag stone over your bed before you sleep, or a chaplet of bittersweet and holly to keep her at bay, else she'll ride you all night. Here,' he added, pouring himself more cider. 'You a gambling man?

Crugge is holding a cockfight here on the morrow. There'll be some good birds and a deal of money changing hands on them. With half the cocks drowned and most of the cockpits still under water, this'll be the first fight we've had in Bristol since the flood. And I'll give you this for nowt. Sam Harewell, the printer, he's the man to watch. Whisper is he's got himself a new bird that's worth putting a shilling on.' The old man winked and lifted his tankard to show that he considered he'd now repaid the favour.

And, indeed, he had. I wasn't much interested in watching cockfighting. Forcing two creatures to rake each other bloody had never appealed to me. But men from all walks of life, rich and poor, masters and servants, attended the fights. And when drink flowed and attention was fixed on the birds, they'd carelessly let slip all kinds of gossip. A cockfight would be a good place to catch any rumours of a fugitive Jesuit or where he might be hiding.

When I stepped out to explore the city that early morning in February, I became aware of a sound I had not heard the night before: the scream and squabble of hundreds of seagulls. The grey sky seemed to be full of them, rising and diving as they picked over the rotting remains of cats, rats, chickens and what might have been a porpoise. In streets that had taken the full force of the water, buildings lay in ruins as if they had been assaulted by a siege engine. Great heaps of rubble, twisted metal and smashed beams protruded from thick black silt. Here and there, the mud had been dug away, leaving deep pits in the debris as if giant moles had burrowed into it, where people had dug frantically in search of their belongings or their loved ones buried below.

The sea had brought with it a chaos of its own treasures from the deep, to mix with the debris of the land like the ingredients in a witch's caldron. Dead fish, starfish, seahorses, torn nets, seaweed and barnacle-covered timbers lay jumbled among smashed kegs and pots, sodden blankets and rusting tools. Inside the shell of one building, I glimpsed a flash of scarlet and, on stepping closer, saw that someone had set a little wooden doll clad in a red dress on the frame of a broken truckle bed. The dress was stained with the saltwater, and the face was battered, leaving only a painted mouth. Had it been dropped by a fleeing child and set there by someone who thought she might come back searching for it, or left there to mark the spot where its young owner had died?

Small knots of people in filthy rags huddled around fires, rubbing their hands and hacking in the cold morning air, their homes now pieces of sailcloth stretched between half-tumbled walls. But even on these streets, sometimes a single house, a church or a shop still stood, solid and defiant among the ruins, like a soldier on a battlefield with all their comrades lying broken around them.

Other streets remained almost untouched by the disaster. Shops were serving customers, men were sweating over their forges, stitching leather or hammering pewter dishes. I paused to watch a silversmith sweating metal with a candle in the window of his workshop. He was drawing a delicate pattern of the ship and castle, Bristol's emblem, in silver thread on to the polished surface of a copper brooch. It was a skilled art. He had to breath in through his nose, while at the same time blow continuously down a narrow tube with his mouth, directing the flow of air into the right part of the flame, so that the hottest part of it played on the metal he wanted to melt and fused it on to another. He glanced up, impatiently gesturing at me to step aside. I was blocking what little daylight seeped down the narrow street.

I stepped away and immediately sank knee-deep in thick, stinking mud from an overflowing open sewer, which had spilled out across the street. Crabs, some as big as a man's hand, others small and almost transparent, scuttled sideways among the stones. Black dots of eyes swivelled on their stalks as they plucked scraps of offal and rotting fish, as if they were grazing on the seashore.

A dozen or so traders had laid out their wares in a small square in front of a church that still stood, untouched, serving their customers from handcarts or from makeshift stalls. Some were selling chunks of meat rank enough to make even the most desperate prisoner in the Hole think twice before eating it, others displayed a few assorted pots, pieces of copper and pewter, iron tools and other goods salvaged from their own workshops or else looted from someone else's. But most of the customers were crowded round those who had brought goods into the city by packhorse, and the squabbles and fights among the women over small kegs of oil or flour, salt and dried peas, almost drowned out the screeching seagulls.

The door of the bell tower was open and a large weighing balance had been erected inside, from which a skinned and eviscerated sheep hung, head down, as a group of men haggled over the price. Watery blood dripped from the sheep's nose, splashing on to the church floor and trickling down the steps into the square. An emaciated hound lapped noisily at the scarlet stream.

A man climbed up on to the church steps, a sheaf of papers beneath his arm, and brandished aloft a broadside covered in black lettering. 'The warning of the strange and lamentable flood that went unheeded,' he bellowed, pointing to the title. 'Monstrous and wondrous signs sent by God to warn the people of his wrath. Ignore them at your peril, lest worse is to come.'

Even those busy haggling glanced in his direction. Some of the women stopped fighting long enough to clutch their neighbours, and I noticed one woman surreptitiously cross herself.

The pedlar held the sheet higher. 'See here, a child born with the head of a man and the tail of a fish, and flapping fins where he ought to have arms. Certain proof that the sea would shortly take the lives of men.' He flicked the broadside with his forefinger. 'A dozen worthy men and woman are named in here who will testify on oath that they saw the creature.

'And here is proof of the cause of this great drowning, a child who was born covered in scales like a serpent. And moreover, when its mother tried of her Christian compassion to give it suck, she discovered that though the babe was not an hour old, it already had a mouthful of teeth as sharp as any viper's, which did grievously wound its own mother's breast. A warning, plain as any man could wish for, that the papists would raise up a flood against our city, papists who are hidden among us like wily serpents.'

The broadsides in London had been full of these tales of monstrous births for the past year: twins joined by the chest and belly; goats with two heads; ducklings with four legs, and women who gave birth to kittens covered in fur or creatures too strange even to hazard a name. Half the Puritan preachers claimed these were a sign of God's anger against the sins of the parents, the other half declared that they were symbols of the canker of popery that the King still tolerated in England. And not to be outdone, the Catholic recusants swore that these aberrations were the sign of God's wrath against the twisted mockery that was the Protestant Church. But through all those months, neither Protestant nor Catholic zealot had thought for one moment it was a warning of an impending flood, until, that is, the wave had struck. Now they were claiming they'd known all along that that was what these births had foretold.

A few of these divine aberrations, both dead and alive, had even been exhibited in booths for the crowds to marvel at. Some months before my arrest, I'd heard one man in a tavern in Southwark telling the other pedlars that he had given the parents six shillings for a little boy whose legs were fastened to his body in such a way that his feet faced backwards and his spine was so twisted he faced his own rump. The man said his father was pleased to have the boy taken off his hands. But I had not parted with the pennies demanded to view such sights.

Even now, as I thought of it, my hand crept to my beard and I raked the curls down to cover the scarlet firemark which stained my throat. When we were growing up as boys together, Richard Fairfax used to tell everyone I should be exhibited in a fair – though he never said as much within his father's hearing, of course, only to the grinning servants. An elderly sewing maid had taken pity on me and told me my birthmark was a sign of good fortune, for it meant I'd never drown. But that malicious devil Waldegrave said the mark on my neck was a sure sign I'd end my days hanging on the gibbet, an observation he repeated every time he thrashed me, which was often, until I learned to reign in my temper whenever that little weasel Richard goaded me. Though if FitzAlan made good his threat, Master Waldegrave's prophesy about my ultimate fate might yet come to pass and wouldn't that delight the smug old bastard.

The pedlar on the church steps was still ranting his wondrous warnings. I was loath to encourage such pigswill by giving him even the penny he was asking for, but I had a Jesuit to find. One of the witnesses the pedlar had named in the broadside might have heard rumours of priests in hiding. Having proffered my coin to the pedlar, I deftly palmed it and slipped a live crab into his pouch. Now he'd really have a reason to cry witchcraft.

Chapter Seven

THE WIND FROM THE SEA had a raw, icy edge to edge it and I was glad to find a tavern with a crackling fire, and a bowl of stew to quiet the rumbling of my belly. It tasted of little but a salty pap of dried cod, but it was hot and filling. I read as I ate, but the broadside contained little of any use. There was a detailed description of the fish-child and a list of witnesses, their occupations and the streets where they could be found. There were reports of other omens, too, of how the night before the flood, the unearthly blue flame they call St Elmo's fire had been seen in the rigging of a ship that had sailed on the evening tide, a warning for the mariners to turn back, which went unheeded. It had foundered in the great wave, with all hands lost.

Then, that same night, at the darkest hour, the bells in some church towers, both inside and outside the city, had rung. Wardens and other townsfolk had hastened to the churches, fearing fire or invasion – or, more likely, that youths had broken in and were making mischief. But all the testimonies were the same, how when they'd crowded in, they'd seen the bell ropes still swaying as if the ringers had let go of them only moments before, but the towers were empty. Some swore that the spectral hands of the dead had pulled the ropes, others that swarms of witches flying through the night sky on their distaffs had struck the bells or even that the Devil himself had tried to land on the towers and had set the bells ringing.

Entertaining though the sheet was, it told me no more than that superstition and rumour were buzzing through the city like flies on a hot summer's day, and finding the truth was going to be as easy as discerning which of those flies had shat upon your supper.

My dish was empty. I left the broadside on the table, peeled myself away from the warmth of the fire and marched out into the grey afternoon. As I closed the door of the tavern, I saw that the broadside had already been snatched up by a young boy who was reading it out to a huddle of drinkers, all nodding sagely as if they had recognised the warnings all along.

I walked down towards one of the quaysides, or what was left of it, which was precious little. The wave had hit hardest here, ripping planks and tearing stout wooden piles from the wharfs and jetties, lifting iron anchors, huge wooden cranes, small wherries and even sailing ships as if they were toys and hurling the whole mass into the warehouses and city walls as if shot out of cannons. Forlorn wooden posts protruded from the mud; the planks of the jetties they had once supported had been stripped off like autumn leaves. Chandlers' yards and sailmakers' workshops lay buried beneath the smashed remains of boats and piles of silt and mud.

Fires were burning every few yards, sending dense plumes of foul black smoke into the wind as the carcasses of rats, water-soaked cloth, spoiled bales of wool and smashed kegs of spices and even the rotting remains of a shark which had been dragged up from the sea's bed were tossed on to the flames. Men lumbered through the gusting smoke, appearing and vanishing again like wraiths as they sorted through heaps of timber, hunting for planks that were still sound enough to fashion makeshift landing stages or repair any small boats that could still be salvaged.

Driven back by the acrid smoke, I edged my way along the quayside, to where a small church stood. The spire was gone, leaving a gaping hole in the roof, and the door had been smashed open by the force of the water. As I approached, a boy sidled out, a half-filled sack slung over his shoulder. As he caught sight of me, he fled around the side of the church, the plunder in his sack clanging as he ran.

I climbed over a heap of rubble and peered inside the church. Black mud, stones and weed had been washed the length of the aisle and piled against the far wall. Somewhere beneath the silt were the Books of Common Prayer that, for over fifty years, had cost the lives of hundreds of men and women, fighting with sword and pitchfork in their own streets or burning on a martyr's pyre, to defend or oppose that little book, each side proclaiming their right with equal bitterness and fervour. I gazed at a cross lying broken in the mud. If this flood was indeed an 'act of God', some men were bound to take this as proof that God had finally answered the prayers of the Jesuits and was waging war against the Protestants, and that would certainly not *please* either the King or FitzAlan.

Outside the church, the wall surrounding the small burial ground had been washed away. Headstones lay broken or tipped at crazed angles. Boulders, beams and iron bars had been smashed into the tombstones, and in one corner three mangy curs, one limping badly, were snatching at the yellow bones spilling from inside.

Where the earth had been washed away, broken coffins lay scattered. Bones and fragments of filthy cloth protruded from the mud and, from one, a rotted hand stretched out as if the owner, awoken by the raging sea and believing it to be Judgement Day, had tried to lift the lid and clamber up. As I stumbled backwards, I slipped over something round and slippery. At first, I thought it was a small boulder, then I saw that I had trodden on the dome of a skull.

There was a whimper behind me. I glanced around warily, thinking it might have been one of the feral dogs following me. The cry came again, but this time it sounded more human than animal, a hiccupping sob. I edged a few paces back towards the church. The noise seemed to be coming from one of the stone tombs. One side had fallen away but the other three sides and top remained intact. All I could see of the contents was a small blackened foot, and for moment I thought it was the mouldering remains of another body, until the toes twitched and the foot slid back inside.

I edged closer and crouched down until I could see into the tomb. The boy with the sack, who I'd glimpsed a few minutes before, was sitting inside, his knees drawn up to his chin. His feet and legs were coated in black mud and his hair was so caked with dirt, it was hard to tell what colour it might have been. There was no sign of the sack he'd been carrying, but crammed beside him in the small space was an assortment of muddy items – an iron ladle, a wooden bowl, a woman's shoe and a broken candle pricket. If this was what had been in his sack, they were hardly stolen valuables. The boy's face was buried in the crook of his arm.

'You hurt, lad?'

His head jerked up and I glimpsed a pair of startled blue eyes set in a face that was streaked with mud. The boy snatched an iron poker from beneath his blanket and brandished it in his small fist.

'Don't you come any closer, else I'll kill you. I swear it!'

I straightened up and took a pace backwards, holding up my hands. 'I'll not take another step.'

The boy looked about eight or nine years old, though children who've been hungry half their lives often appear younger than they are; but even so, I was intrigued to see a young lad on his own. Most street urchins band together or worm their way into a group of adult beggars, sheltering together for protection, sharing a fire and whatever scraps of food they can find to toss in the common pot. It took a brave lad, or a foolish one, to sleep alone when packs of savage dogs and desperate men were prowling the dark streets. Something in the boy's expression told me he wasn't a fool, and if he was fending for himself, he might be more willing than most to earn a few pennies. A street urchin, especially a small one, can pass unnoticed. Men who carry secrets guard their tongues when strangers are close by, but who pays heed to a beggar's brat sitting beneath a casement or lying curled up in a corner?

He was watching me warily, but when a boy or beast is afraid, you can usually win their trust by letting them think they have the upper hand.

'You must know the city well, lad. I'm staying at the Salt Cat, but the light will be gone soon and I'm growing hungry for my supper. I don't suppose you know a shortcut?'

I'd caught the expression of desperation on the boy's face when I'd mentioned supper. Just how long had it been since the lad had last filled his belly?

He peered up at me. 'Suppose I could show you, but it'll cost you . . .' He seemed to consider how much this stranger might be willing to part with, then finally added hopefully, 'It'll cost you sixpence.'

I laughed. 'That's half a day's wages. It's the quickest route I'm after, not a tour of the city.'

'A penny, then,' the boy ventured.

'Suppose, instead, I buy you supper for your pains, as much as you can eat?'

He nodded eagerly and scrambled from the tomb. He dragged two of the larger fragments of stone across the open side of the tomb, and piled a few smaller stones to cover the rest of the hole. Only when he had ensured his treasures were safe from prying eyes did he turn and lead me around the side of the church and back into the city.

It wasn't until we were sitting in the parlour of the Salt Cat and the boy had scraped his bowl clean of a third portion of stew, which Rachael had sneaked out to him, that he began to talk. His name was Myles, he confided, and he was the son of a tailor. He'd a mother and father, two younger sisters and a brother not long born. The morning when the wave came, his father had sent him to the far side of the city to deliver a doublet that was wanted in a hurry.

'There was this roaring like a great dragon, seemed to be coming from the sea, but I couldn't see anything for all the houses in the way, only smoke in the sky as if something was afire. Then there was a huge bang that went on and on like mill-stones grinding and blacksmiths hammering, all together, except louder, a thousand times louder. Then the screaming. They kept screaming . . .' Myles cringed, pressing his fingers to his ears as if he could still hear them.

He stared down at the scarred table. 'I couldn't get to our street, not for hours, but when I did . . . our cottage . . . it wasn't there. I thought it couldn't be our street. All the houses were there when I left, and when I came back, they was gone. How could they be gone?'

His head jerked up and he stared at me.

'And your family?' I asked. 'What happened to them?'

'I searched all the street, I asked everyone if they'd seen them. They said some people were buried under the mud, so I dug and tried to find them. I found some of Ma's things, and Father's, too. I'm keeping them safe for them. They wouldn't have gone without me, I know it. They'd have looked for me, searched everywhere like I did. Ma wouldn't have left me.'

For a moment, I almost envied the boy's certainty. I could barely remember my own mother. It was the first lesson I learned – mothers do not always search for their lost sons.

The boy's head drooped again and when he spoke his voice was dull, as if he was not allowing himself to feel anything. 'Some of the neighbours reckon they're dead, but if they were, there'd be bodies, wouldn't there?'

There was a small sigh and I looked up to see Rachael standing by the settle. I shook my head, cautioning her not to repeat what she'd said to me about the many bodies that would never be recovered. Her eyes flashed dangerously.

'Master Pursglove here is looking for his kin, too, just like you,' she said. 'You could help each other,' she added sweetly.

I glared at her. The last thing I needed was a brat trailing round after me. Rachael grinned at me triumphantly.

'Best be off now, though, and double quick, too. If the master sees a dirty-faced urchin like you in his respectable inn, he'll likely give you a dunking in the horse trough. Slip out that way.' She shoved Myles towards the door that led straight into the street. The boy did not wait to be told twice.

Rachael stared after him. 'There's a lot of orphans wandering the streets looking for their families or just sitting huddled in corners not knowing what to do or where to go. Folks say they're lucky to be alive, but I reckon it would have been better for some of them if they'd drowned with their families, at least that way they'd not know grief.'

I glanced sharply up at her, startled by the sudden bitterness in her voice. But before I could answer, she'd already bustled towards another customer, a smile appearing on her face like the sun bursting out from behind a dark cloud.

I was aching for my bed. Squelching for hours through Bristol's streets, clambering over rubble and slipping on rotting weed and worse, had set my muscles groaning. I threaded through the hazardous piles of broken furniture and carts that littered the dimly lit courtyard. Glancing towards the archway that led to the street, I saw the dark outline of a huddled figure crouching in the shelter, swathed in a cloak or blanket pulled down over his head. If he was intending to attack Diligence again, he would not get away with it this time! I swiftly slipped the knife from my belt and started towards the figure. I couldn't see his face, only a dark hollow beneath the hood, but he seemed to be staring up at the casement of my attic room. Was he watching to see when the lamp was lit up there?

I cursed as my shoulder caught the side of a ladder almost invisible in the darkness. It crashed to the stones, knocking down a piece of metal, which echoed across the yard like the peal of church bells. I was forced to look down to avoid tripping. I glanced back at the figure in the archway, convinced the noise would have sent him scurrying away. But the black outline hadn't moved.

Rigid with tension, I crept closer. I was almost at the archway before my mind registered what I was seeing. There was no one there, only a keg standing close to the wall, with a piece of sail-cloth bunched up over it, its edges stirring in the sea breeze. But I'd been so sure I'd seen someone. It couldn't simply be this. Someone must have been crouching in its shelter. I darted out into the street, peering up and down, but it was long past curfew and the street was dark and silent, save for some dogs snuffling around in the dirt.

I crossed swiftly to the stables, barking my shin on the edge of a wheelbarrow. But both horses were standing quietly at their tethers, their heads drooping, half asleep. They had clearly not been disturbed for hours. I rubbed my eyes, my relief turning to annoyance with myself for jumping at shadows, like some milk-sop clerk.

I dragged myself up towards my solitary attic chamber. The sounds of displaced families settling down behind their shutters drifted out on to the stairs: creaking beds, children whining, someone already snoring, and the raised voices of a man and woman arguing, people who had others with whom to share their joys and miseries, people who belonged to each other and cared what happened to each other. A cold cloud of desolation closed around me and I hurried inside my room, seeking the refuge of sleep.

I snuffed out the lamp and, when the room was in darkness, couldn't resist peering out into the deserted street. I was so sure someone had been lurking in the archway. FitzAlan had warned me that I would be hunted down if I tried to run. Was I already being watched by one of his spies? Had the severed tail of my horse been meant as a reminder of what would happen to me if I failed him?

Chapter Eight

THE TOWER OF LONDON

'My Lord, King James is . . . dead.'

'What!' The word exploded from Robert Cecil's mouth with the force of a cannonball, and the man standing miserably in front of him visibly jerked as if he had been struck. He was a full head taller than the hunchbacked Secretary of State, most men were, but today the unfortunate steward appeared to have shrunk to half his normal size.

'When?' Cecil barked. 'How? Yesterday, he was perfectly fit and healthy; you assured me of that.'

Grief and fear fought for control of the steward's features, and in spite of the chill, damp air, a rivulet of grimy sweat trickled down the side of his bulbous nose and into the silvery stubble on his chin. He stared down at the large iron key in his hand, twisting it over and over as if struggling to unlock a prison door that had suddenly slammed on him. The answer, when it finally emerged, was murmured so softly that Cecil was obliged to lean in to catch it.

'We think it poison, Lord Salisbury.' The steward's gaze flicked briefly to Cecil's large green eyes, which were bulging ever wider at each new utterance. 'Found him stiff this morning, in a pool of bloody vomit and flux. Must have been thrashing in agony before the breath left him.'

'Did you not hear his cries? Did no one attend to him in the night?'

The steward shrugged. 'He was always roaring and rampaging

at night, you know that, my lord. There've been complaints aplenty from all who live close by, not that the Tower's prisoners dare make any, of course. I dare say they're the only ones who welcome the clamour, for it drowns the howls of those being racked.'

'As you are in grave danger of discovering for yourself, sirrah,' Cecil snapped.

Fear flashed across the steward's face, for no one who had employment in the Tower could have failed to hear the cries and shrieks of those being invited to confess to treason, even if they had not actually witnessed their torments. Fear and anticipation, as Cecil well knew, were often more effective at loosening tongues than pain itself.

The steward swallowed hard, but his chin jerked up defiantly. 'But, my lord, even if we had found him earlier, there's nothing we could have done. He ate a haunch of venison last night with his usual appetite, and there were no signs anything was amiss when he was settled for the night. The poison must have been slow-acting, and once a powerful poison like that starts to show itself, it's already too late.'

'Who served him the meat?'

The steward hesitated, but his gaze momentarily darted sideways towards a low doorway.

Pushing him aside, Cecil barged through. Even in the heat of summer, a deathly chill haunted many rooms in the Tower of London, but this windowless chamber was colder and damper than most, for water ran constantly through the open drain that bisected the floor, carrying with it the blood that dripped from the butchering tables and from the carcasses of beasts that hung from the iron hooks in the ceiling as if they had also refused to confess their manifold crimes. The stench of bad meat, rotting offal and stale blood hung in the air, dense as a Thames fog. In the light of a single lit lantern, it appeared at first glance that the room was deserted, and Cecil thought he had mistaken the steward's glance. Then he heard the sound of a stifled whimper and, spinning round, glanced down to see a lad crouched in the corner on a heap of straw, his knees drawn up and head pressed between them, as if he was trying to make himself invisible.

'So, I take it you were the boy who prepared the poisoned meat.'

'I never poisoned it, I swear by the Holy Cross.' The voice was muffled, cracked with terror.

The steward took a pace into the room, dragged the lad to his feet by his ear and cuffed him so hard across the back of the head, he almost fell headlong into Cecil.

'Make your bow to Lord Salisbury, you addlepated maggot. You're in trouble enough without adding insolence to the brew.'

The lad bowed so deeply and for so long that he began to gag, and Cecil only just managed to take a pace back in time to avoid having his soft leather boots covered in a stream of vomit. He waited impatiently until the boy had wiped his face.

'Were the other lions fed meat from the same carcass? Are any of the other beasts dead? Sick?'

The lad shook his head, staring at the floor. 'Butchers' Guild delivered the offal for all the beasts by boat yesterday, same as always, and that's what I fed all the others, like I always do. But His Majesty sent half a stag's carcass for his namesake. Killed it with his own hands, according to his servant. He said a beast named for a king should dine royally. Been feeding it to James these past three days. He never came to any hurt till last night.'

'Is there any left?'

The boy flung out a bony arm towards one of the tables. Cecil stepped across the gully of running water and peered at what remained of the mangled carcass on the table.

He sniffed. It was ripe, but he'd eaten stronger meat than that himself. The King liked his flesh well hung. Cecil could not smell poison, but then it might simply have been inserted into that one haunch. He groaned. This was a disaster.

It had been a tradition for as long as anyone could remember that a lion in the Tower should be named after each new monarch to mark their accession to the throne. A lion was, after all, the king of the beasts, what more fitting tribute could there be? But the commons had come to believe that the King's health was bound inexorably to that of his namesake. If the lion was ailing, they took it as a sign their King would fall sick, and if the lion died, it was certain their Sovereign would follow it to the grave within days. Such omens alone were enough to bring a kingdom to the brink of war, as the heirs began scheming against each other to ensure they secured the succession before the last breath had even left the royal body.

Cecil knew only too well the months of plotting and planning it had taken to install James on the throne. In those last precious weeks, when he'd been desperate to buy the time he'd needed, he had been all too aware that the health of Elizabeth's lion had been studied as anxiously by the populace as the old Queen's piss had been examined by her physicians. Elizabeth had, of course, outlived several lions, each hastily and secretly replaced. Why shouldn't the king of the beasts live for forty-four years, if a queen of England could live for sixty-nine?

But King James was minded to take such omens as seriously as any country crone. As it was, he spent every waking moment worrying about assassination, forever moving from room to room, house to house, for fear of men lurking with daggers or muskets. If he discovered his namesake was not only dead but poisoned, he'd probably have the whole Court decamping to the other end of the country before the day was out. Cecil thumped his fist into his gloved palm.

He was suddenly aware that the steward and his lad were staring at him in alarm, which was hardly surprising since he was pacing back and forth like the King himself in one of his fits of agitation. That only increased his anger, for he prided himself on his control. He rounded on them furiously.

'Have you told anyone of this?'

Both solemnly shook their heads.

'Word must not get out, not to the guards, the servants and, above all, not to the King. No one must learn of it. If I hear even so much as a whisper of a rumour – and I *will* hear of it – I shall make you cut out your own tongues and feed them to the beasts you are supposed to be tending.'

The steward's face twisted in misery. 'But my lord, the King is due here within the hour. He will want to see the lion take exercise in the new yard. If the beast was locked in his cage in the shadows, the King might believe him to be sleeping. But I can't make a dead lion run,' he added with a wail.

'Do I have to do your thinking for you? Release one of the other lions, of course, one that resembles His Majesty's namesake. Tell him that one is King James.'

'But they all look different,' the steward protested.

'To you, perhaps, since you have the care of them, but not to the King. Lower one of the dogs into the yard for the lion to tear apart, a large hound, one that has courage enough to fight and provide the King with good sport. That always quickens His Majesty's blood.' Glancing heavenwards, Cecil murmured, 'God grant, for all our sakes, that in the excitement of watching a hound ripped to pieces, our Sovereign will fail to notice the lion has changed his coat.'

A STIFF BREEZE blew from the river across the wooden platform, rippling the gold and scarlet lions on the royal pendants so that they leaped and ran in the way the mangy beasts in the cages below could never do. Cecil hunched into the shelter of the Tower wall, pulling the fur-lined cape tighter across his crooked back, as he watched his royal master, restlessly pacing up and down the viewing platform, his hand pressing down on the shoulder of a young man to support his weak legs.

Cecil silently cursed. The news he had been steeling himself to deliver to the King this morning had already given him several sleepless nights, and now he had the death of that wretched beast to contend with. He could almost believe himself it really was a dark omen. He had privately instructed the steward to draw up a list of anyone who might have had access to the meat in the Tower. But he held out little hope of discovering the culprit. The poison could have been added to the venison at any time after the stag was killed and a hundred, even a thousand, men might have reason to want to unnerve James, if that was indeed the aim. Some might even believe that by killing the lion, the King himself would weaken and die, like sticking pins in a wax effigy. And that was certainly what James would believe if he got wind of it. All the more reason why the death had to be kept from him.

The King had released his grip on the young man and was now leaning upon the rail for support, peering down into the lions' yard below. The royal visits had grown more frequent since the new enclosure had been built. James had delighted in the remodelling of the Lion Tower. He had ordered that part of the moat around the Tower be filled in and levelled to create an exercise yard, with three trapdoors through which the keepers could release the lions. He was most proud of the high viewing platform, which enabled him, his courtiers and any distinguished foreign guests to watch the fights staged between the beasts, like Roman emperors at the circus. James never tired of his experiments. How many wildcats could a bear fight off at once? Would a lion defeat a tiger? Not all of his guests had the stomach for such bloody spectacles, but they dared not offend their host, who showed off his menagerie with the exuberance of an excited child given a new toy.

But there were no guests or family in the royal party that morning. Cecil had requested an urgent and private meeting. Not that the King had come alone; he went nowhere without his retinue of courtiers, servants, Gentlemen Pensioners and yeoman guards. Most of his courtiers were Scots whose ill-kempt appearance, barbarous speech and oafish manners made Cecil think they'd have been better suited to a life as cattle herders on some savage mountain, rather than the King's Court. The few elegantly and richly clad English favourites of the King stood out among them like damask roses in a field of wild thistles.

The King leaned further over, frowning and shielding his eyes against the low winter sun. A trapdoor was raised and a lion bounded out into the yard below. The beast halted, dazzled by the morning light and the shock of cold air after the dark fug of his cage. He was thinner than his predecessor, older, with an ebony tip to the end of his tail and the fringes of his mane. But the lion was only still for a moment. The steward had had the good sense to lower a dog into the yard before the newly appointed 'James' had been released. The instant the mastiff caught sight of the lion, it hurled itself towards the beast, clamping its jaws on to the lion's face. Both animals tore at each other, the lion trying to fling off his attacker, clawing at it and tossing it, so the mastiff was lifted from the ground still clinging on to the lion's muzzle with its teeth. The roars, snarls and growls must have carried to the deepest dungeons of the Tower. Soon both creatures were covered with blood. The frown on the King's face had vanished. His eyes were gleaming. If there had been any question forming on his lips, it was forgotten. Cecil and the steward let out deep breaths.

As soon as the mastiff lay dead, the new James was prodded and coaxed back through the trapdoor and into his cage. A lioness and her whelps were released and ambled listlessly around the enclosure. The lioness, catching sight of the King leaning over, sprang upwards, clawing and scrambling, but the platform was too high and she fell back snarling.

The King had lost interest and seemed, finally, to remember that his Secretary of State was waiting impatiently – though, of course, both men knew Lord Salisbury was an expert in concealing that, or any other emotion, when he chose. James waved away his servants and guards, who retired to a discreet distance from where they could easily be summoned with a shout or gesture. He sank on to the chair placed ready for him. His fingers, never still, plucked constantly at the furs that had been draped over it to keep out the cold.

'Speak, my little beagle. What's vexing you? You've news for me, else you'd not have come here. I know you've nae stomach for the fight, not between beasts anyway.'

Cecil kept his face impassive, and why should he not? He'd suffered the sobriquets of 'my elf' and 'my little pygmy' from his Queen. 'Beagle' could easily be borne from a King who, in the space of two years, had bestowed upon him the titles of Baron, Viscount and Earl – and all the profitable estates that went with them.

'Sire, I have received a letter from Thomas Brooke. He is, you will recall, Your Majesty's Ambassador in Belgium.'

'I recall it well enough, though *your* Ambassador might be closer to the mark, for it seems it's you he answers to.'

'Brooke does not wish to trouble Your Majesty with trifles. This matter, on the other hand, is something you will wish to know. He is much disquieted that rumours are circulating in Belgium concerning a certain relic of the Jesuit leader, Henry Garnet.'

James's whole body stiffened, and the restless fingers were suddenly stilled. He gripped the arms of his chair as if he intended to snap the wood in two. 'That stinking Jesuit! He was hanged, drawn and quartered back in May, and there was no mention of a relic then. There was talk that his head didn't turn black, nor rot away, when it was spiked on London Bridge. Fools were saying his face stayed as healthy as it had in life, which is why I gave orders it should be taken down. And I had the book detailing Garnet's treachery bound in the priest's own skin. Since Garnet was so fond of his books, I made him into one.' James let out a bark of laughter, slapping Cecil's thigh. 'Is that the relic they worship now? I hope so, for those are the only true words that Jesuit ever embraced.'

'The relic is neither a book nor Garnet's head, Sire. It is . . .' Cecil's tongue probed at an aching tooth. 'It is a piece of straw.'

'Straw! Is this a jest?'

'My sources tell me that, at the time of Garnet's execution, a young Catholic by the name of John Wilkinson was preparing to leave England for the Jesuit training camp in Leuven. Apparently, God told him that if he witnessed the execution in St Paul's Churchyard, he would receive proof of Garnet's innocence. He claims that when Garnet's severed head was tossed into the basket, along with his dismembered body, a piece of blood-stained straw miraculously leaped from the basket into his hand. When the ear of grain was later examined, it seemed to some that the bloodstain upon it resembled a face. Now, it seems, the stain has spread, taking the form of not one but two faces, the larger having grown into the likeness of Father Garnet, with his head encircled by a martyr's crown. The second face, appearing in Garnet's beard, is said to be that of the infant Christ.

'Stories of this miraculous straw are spreading like the plague in summer, thanks to the Catholic printing presses in London. They have produced the entire story in pamphlets which, even now, are being passed through all their networks both here and on the Continent. The latest of these pamphlets declares that this straw has even performed miracles, with a woman cured from fits and another who was like to die in childbirth saved. The names of both are given and witnesses besides—'

James leaned forward as if he was about to spring from his chair. 'I wager these women have invented the tale merely to profit from the credulous who pay to hear their story. I've examined many such in my time, girls who feign they are bewitched and vomit pins for the gawping crowd. And this . . . this face of a traitor appearing in the straw. If it exists at all, it will have been painted by some cunning artist. It is all superstition and trickery!'

'Then it is dangerous mischief, Sire. Thomas Brooke's letter informs me that two Catholic Englishwomen arrived in Brussels demanding to become nuns, saying they were called to offer themselves to the Romish Church, having paid homage to this miraculous straw no less than fourteen times. Furthermore, they report the face now has wings which grow wider each time they see it. And Brooke says they are believed.'

Grasping the rail of the lion enclosure, James hauled himself to his feet and began pacing furiously, pounding the rail as he walked.

'That Jesuit gave his blessing to those who conspired to murder God's anointed King. Garnet would stay silent and see the good Queen, my innocent children and all the lords of England blown to pieces. And they now dare to call him a martyr?' His voice had risen to a bellow of rage, and those courtiers and servants watching from a distance turned their faces towards him in alarm.

Cecil rose hastily and began walking alongside him in the hope that the King might moderate his tone. He hesitated. The last thing he wanted to do was pour oil on the fire of the King's anger, but James had to understand the gravity of this new development. Fakery might well lie behind it, as the King had said, but this could set a whole kingdom ablaze.

'Sire, even a superstition, if it takes hold of the imagination of the people, can be as powerful a weapon as any truth. The pamphlets say this straw is a sign of Garnet's innocence. If the Romish Church, if the Pope himself, declares Garnet an English martyr, then his name will become a rallying cry for all Catholics. It will give them new heart—'

'Aye, it will,' James cut in. 'And the courage and stomach to take up arms. This little piece of bloodstained straw is like to become the banner of war, the standard, which will see a foreign Catholic king upon my throne. I want this poisonous weed found and rooted out, Salisbury, rooted out and burned. I'll not see my kingdom torn apart for a wisp o' straw.'

Cecil bowed respectfully and took three paces back. There was no point in telling James that the straw itself no longer mattered. They could burn it on the highest pyre and it would make no difference. Its seed had already been sown and was starting to sprout. An idea cannot be exiled or hanged, but the men who might act on it could. Jesuits were, after all, merely flesh and blood. And they bled as freely as any other mortal men when their heads were severed.

Somewhere beneath his feet, in the bowels of the Tower, a lion roared in fury. The new James, perhaps. The King is dead; long live the King.

Chapter Nine

DANIEL PURSGLOVE

I BURST FROM a nightmare into wakefulness, unable to move. For a moment I thought myself back in Newgate, then I realised what was pinning me down were not iron fetters but blankets and sheets which had twisted about my limbs as I'd tossed and turned. I lay still in the darkness, my heart thumping and beads of sweat running down my face. It was only as my breathing steadied that I became aware of the noise that must have woken me. The shrieking of gulls? Not in the middle of the night, surely.

I swung my bare feet on to the floor, padded across to the tiny casement which overlooked the street, lifted the latch and pushed it wide. A blast of chill damp air spun into the room, whistling about the rafters. I shivered. As if it had been waiting for admittance, a large black spider crawled over the sill, down the wall and scuttled under my bed. A distant squabble of voices rose from somewhere out of sight – a drunken brawl among men spilling out from an inn? Such disturbances were common in any city, apprentices fighting with foreign seamen, incomers brawling with locals, or bands of rival guildsmen taunting each other. But all the inns in Bristol should have been long closed by now, because of the curfew, their clients snoring in drunken stupors.

I leaned further out, trying to catch what was being shouted. Three men, muffled up against the cold, were hurrying along the street below as fast as the treacherous ground would allow.

'What's afoot?' I called down.

Two of them ignored me and pressed on, but the third paused, craning his neck back to peer up at me, shouted, 'Recusants! Popelings, that's what. But those murdering bastards will not be calling up any more floods, not when we've finished with them.' He lumbered after his companions, who had already vanished into the darkness.

I dragged the casement shut and pulled on my breeches and shirt, fumbling with the laces. I thrust my feet into wet hose and boots that were still caked with mud. But in spite of my haste, I didn't neglect to fasten my belt about my hips, so that the handle of the long knife I always wore hung within easy reach of my fingers.

The street outside the Salt Cat was as dark as a dungeon. Clouds smothered any glimmer of light there might have been from stars or moon, and the candles and lamps in the casements of the houses had long since been extinguished. But the noise ahead of me was guide enough. Pressing my hand to the walls of the buildings, trying to avoid the holes in the road, I followed the sound, vaguely aware that I must be heading towards what was left of the wharf where I had been only that afternoon, but as I rounded the next corner, the din exploded in my ears like a canon on a battlefield.

A large mob had gathered in front of a modest little house which seemed to belong to a craftsman, for the stone-built ground floor was taken up by a small workshop and storeroom, while the wooden overhanging top floor served as the living quarters for the family. Men made up most of the crowd milling around it, but there was also a fair sprinkling of market women and old beldams. The burning links and torches held aloft in the darkness by some of the crowd trailed snakes of smoke in the wind and drove twists of blood-red light and black shadows across their faces, which seemed to be constantly melting and re-forming, as if they were mocking imps risen from hell. Those who were not waving torches carried other weapons – stout sticks, axes, twibills and hammers. The women clutched iron cooking pots, lids and ladles. There was no mistaking trouble was brewing.

There was nothing to mark out the little house they had surrounded, except for one thing. It was the only building that still stood whole and undamaged in the street, while the half-dozen or so others in this short row had been cut down like felled trees. I glanced up at the house, hoping that it was empty, but I caught the glimmer of light from a candle on the ground floor before it was hurriedly extinguished.

A gang of men were dragging an empty cart up the street but were obliged to halt some way off or risk breaking a wheel or axle on the rubble of the ruined houses. It was the kind of cart they made the condemned stand on at the gallows before they whipped up the horse and drove away, leaving the poor wretches to dangle on the ends of their ropes. Two men dressed in the dismal garb of the Puritans clambered up on to it, and one held up his hands for silence. The rumble of the crowd subsided slightly. By the light from the lantern his companion was holding up, he began to read from a piece of crumpled paper, his face as gaunt and grim as a death mask in the lamplight.

Though he bellowed his words over the shuffling mob, I was not close enough to hear them all clearly. But those phrases I did catch sounded vaguely familiar. The crowd whooped and jeered at intervals, as if they were the groundlings at a play. Then I realised what he was reading. It was a copy of the same broadside I'd purchased that morning, which had announced that the papists, hidden among the people like serpents, had called up the flood.

The speaker rolled up the paper and jabbed it towards the house. 'Here is proof set before your very eyes,' he bawled. 'See, all of the houses belonging to this man's good neighbours were destroyed by the waters, helpless women and children swept out to sea and drowned. Those who mercifully survived were driven into penury, their little ones maimed and all that they owned in this world stolen from them by the wave. They've been left to starve in a ditch, without even a byre to shelter them from the winter's cold. But this house, this alone remains untouched. How is that, you may ask? I tell you, because Master Lightbound was one of those papists who called up that flood to take vengeance on his godly neighbours and destroy our fair city.'

A man standing a little in front of me turned, his eyes blazing with excitement in the torchlight. 'Servants of the Devil, every last one of them, isn't that right, brother?'

'You want proof of his guilt? Here it is,' the preacher continued, flourishing the rolled broadside. 'This cordwainer's house is still standing, brazen as a whore, while all its neighbours lie felled. Why? Because this papist was in league with the witches who were flying over our helpless city the night before the flood, setting the church bells ringing. These same witches put charms and spells on this house, so that the wave wouldn't touch it. As the Devil flew over our city, he saw his own mark on this house, and he passed over it and left it untouched. What more evidence do you need? Those who dwell here are the Devil's disciples. And we must drive them out before they destroy us all.'

When FitzAlan had talked of Jesuits, it had been easy to ignore his hostility. Many Catholics would have agreed with him. They, too, resented the fanatical priests who were hell-bent on stirring up trouble for them. But the word *papist* went far beyond priests. It sucked every Catholic into the mire of this mob's hatred. I took a deep breath.

You are not a Catholic. It was forced upon you. It was his faith, not yours, never yours. This is not your fight, brother. This is not your fight.

I glanced back up at the house. At one of the upper casements, pale as a ghost in the darkness, a young child was staring down, wide-eyed, at the preacher. I glimpsed the little face for a brief moment before it vanished, as if someone had pulled the child away.

The man holding up the lantern on the cart began to sing a psalm, something about God delivering the righteous from their enemies, and a handful of sombrely dressed followers clustered in front of the wagon joined in with more vigour than tunefulness.

A man in the crowd yelled out, 'It's not holy music they need, brothers, it's rough music! We've come to give 'em a good old skimmington.'

A roar of laughter and approval went up from the crowd, the women banged their ladles against their pots, and those around joined in the racket, rattling bird scarers, whirling bullroarers, shouting and striking any bit of metal that lay within reach. Those who could get near to the house thumped on its walls, door and shutters with the staves, billhooks and iron bars they carried, till the stones rang and the wood shook. If the Puritans were still singing, not even the angels would have heard them.

The house sat in darkness, and though the din was loud enough to bring the pillars of London Bridge crashing down, no one appeared at the windows or door. That only stoked the crowd's anger. The clanging began to die away as the implements which had been used to make the racket were now wielded as weapons to smash against doors and windows. Men cried warnings to each other to stand back as they hacked at the door with their axes, while others used the billhooks to splinter the wood from the shutters, smashing through the lattice panes of glass and lead on the other side.

Within minutes, a dozen men had tossed the broken wood aside and were scrambling into the darkened interior. The crowd drew back, a sudden silence descending but for the preacher, who lifted his hands devoutly to heaven and began to lead his followers in fervent prayers that the forces of darkness and the demons of Satan would not assail these brave men as they entered this place of sorcery.

A man reappeared in the doorway. 'It's as dark as the Devil's codpiece in here. The popelings are hiding like the rats they are. Give us light, someone!'

Several lanterns and even flaming torches were eagerly thrust towards him. He grabbed a couple of the lanterns and vanished again. He must have used the candles to ignite others inside the house for as we watched, the lights showed first at the smashed lower casements, then glimmers began to appear on the upper floor. Shouts and taunts drifted out through the shattered door. There came the noise of furniture being overturned, pots being broken and wood splintered. The crowd outside added their own jeers, urging the men on, and cheering whenever there was a particularly loud crash from inside.

Somewhere in that house a family was huddled together in the dark, listening to the crashes and yells drawing closer as the men searched for them. A wave of nausea washed over me. When I was a boy, George Fairfax had had secret holes constructed to serve as refuges for Master Waldegrave and any young priests that might be trapped in his house, if and when soldiers came. In so large a manor, half a dozen places of concealment could be made in spaces behind staircases, under false floors or in the walls, but in a house as small as this, no hiding place could remain concealed for long.

I knew I should stay silent. I could not afford to draw attention to myself. But that frightened child's face overwhelmed all my instincts. I pushed my way through the crowd, elbowing people aside, until I reached the cart on which the Puritan stood watching. I tugged at the hem of his cloak. He lashed out with his heel, as if a mouse had jumped on him, and I only just managed to dodge the kick. The preacher spun round and stared down at me, frowning.

'Good brother, there is a child in that house. I saw a face at the window, and likely there are more. They can have done no wrong. Instruct the men to stop what they're doing, until the little ones have been taken to safety. If you gave your pledge that no harm will come to the children, the parents would surely send them out. They might even surrender themselves and spare your men the trouble of searching.'

I'd no conviction that Master Lightbound and his wife would send out the children, much less surrender. Rumours must have reached here of how the children of the men and women suspected of being involved in treason plots had been made to scream piteously in neighbouring cells, within earshot of their parents, to force their confessions. And when I was Secretary to the Gentleman Pensioner Viscount Rowe, I'd even heard one of his guests boast that the King had ordered that a boy be tortured within his parents' sight to break them when they obstinately refused to speak or divulge names. But if this Puritan could just call his dogs off for a few minutes, it might buy the family time to escape.

The preacher stared down at me coldly. 'If you found a nest of vipers, would you spare the young ones, knowing they will grow up to wound and kill according to the nature of their kind?' He turned away from me, as if I was dismissed.

I slammed my full weight against the back of the cart. It jerked forward and he pitched to his knees with a cry of alarm and, I devoutly hoped, pain. I held out a solicitous hand to help him up. 'These are not vipers, good brother. They are children, no different from your own little ones or your nieces or nephews. They could be brought to reason, taught the true faith, and when they understand the mercy that has been granted to them, their gratitude will surely make them devout and faithful servants of the English Church.'

I didn't believe that for one moment, either. Any child who lived through this night in that house would harbour a lifelong hatred for that 'English Church' – if not for all men who claimed they spoke with God's authority – as did I, at this moment.

'You are wasting your breath; I have no control over these people.' The preacher twitched his cloak away from me, as if my touch soiled it. 'I merely—'

His words were drowned out by a great whooping from the men inside the house, like huntsmen cheering the hounds at a kill. Someone inside started hacking at a casement high under the eaves with an axe, and the people standing closest to the house tried to draw back as shards of glass and lead rained down, but they were trapped by the press of the crowd behind them. Several shouted out as the heavy lead fragments struck their heads and shoulders. A razor-sharp piece of glass sliced clean through the tip of one man's nose and another impaled itself in a woman's arm. But no one took any notice of their cries of pain, or the blood which poured from them, for one of the searchers poked his head through the broken casement to yell triumphantly down to those below.

'We've got the bastards, the whole coven of them! Make ready. They're bringing them out!'

Chapter Ten

IN THE FLICKERING red light of the torches, a ripple passed through the crowd as men shifted their grip on their weapons and women bent to gather up stones and rotting fish from the mud. All eyes were fastened on the open door. I wriggled through the crowd and drew back against the ruined wall of the building on the opposite side of the street. I did not want to watch this, but I couldn't tear myself away.

The mob was pressing forward as one, eager to get a first glimpse of the witches' coven, when my attention was suddenly caught by a flicker of movement further down the street. In the ruddy glow from the torches, I could just make out two figures, a stooped man and a boy, standing alone by a tumbled gateway. The old man was bending close and talking earnestly to the lad. He gestured once or twice towards the cordwainer's house. Then, as I watched, he drew a small object from inside his cloak, pressed it into the boy's grasp and flapped his hand urgently, as if he was urging the lad to hurry. The boy took off like a greyhound after a hare and darted past me down towards the wharf. As the light from one of the torches fell full on his face, I saw with surprise that it was young Myles. So, he wasn't quite as friendless as he'd first appeared. I glanced back towards where I'd seen the old man. But there was nothing moving there except the shadows.

A loud jeer rose from the crowd as the cordwainer's wife was shoved out through the open door, a small boy of about three years of age balanced on one hip. She pressed the child's head against her shoulder, her hand shielding his face, though he was struggling to peer around. Two other children followed, a girl on the cusp of womanhood gripping a younger one by her hand. They clung tightly to each other, their heads bowed so low it was as if they made obeisance to the crowd. But that did not appease the mob. A howl of hatred and derision shot up from the townsfolk, who closed around them, those at the back complaining loudly that they couldn't see.

'To the cart with them!'

The preacher had clambered down from his makeshift pulpit, and was trying to make the mob part so that the captors might walk between them. The throng divided, leaving a narrow passage between the house and the cart. I caught a glimpse of the woman staring around, desperately searching for a means of escape, but the crowd were three or four deep on either side and not even a greased pig could have run between them. As the cordwainer's wife and her children stumbled forward, women in the crowd leaned forward to spit at them. Others slashed at their legs with sticks, urging them towards the cart.

Above the roar, a woman's voice shrieked, 'Take the blood above their breath. Make them bleed!'

At once the single cry became the demonic chorus from a hundred throats.

'Bleed them! Bleed them!'

It was an ancient superstition. If a suspected witch was cut on the forehead above her nose, her power to work enchantments and curses would drain from her as her blood flowed out. A scrawny crone standing not far from me began scratching around among the ruins, like a chicken searching for worms. Spying a long iron nail sticking out from a plank of wood. she pounced on it with a squawk of glee, rocking back and forth to loosen it with all the feverish haste of a tooth puller at a fair. She darted forward with her prize, barging into the thick of the mob.

I couldn't see the little family now, though I knew where they had reached by the raised fists of the crowd. Then I glimpsed the two girls again, shrieking as they were raised high in the arms of burly men and tossed to land heavily in the cart. The men tried to tear the small boy from his mother's arms, but she would not relinquish him, and they finally hauled her up still gripping the child. They all clambered to their feet and stood pressed together in the centre of the wagon, trying to keep out of reach of the clawing fingers stretching towards them. Blood, glistening almost black in the red and yellow flames of the torches, trickled down all their faces from a dozen scratches and cuts. The mother's hand, still held across the boy's face, was bloody, but it was hard to tell if it was hers or his, for someone had gashed the child's head and his hair was matted with gore.

Missiles began to fly towards them out of the crowd, handfuls of mud, rotting fish and even a bloated dead rat that exploded as it landed on the elder girl's shoulder, spraying them all with guts and a stench that made those closest to the cart retreat, clamping the hems of their cloaks across their noses. People scattered, searching for more filth, snatching up a lump of tar or an old shoe with a shout of triumph and shrieking as they raced past me towards the cart. I twisted aside as a badly aimed brick shaved my cheek and shattered on the ground. A man backed hard into me, jabbing me in the belly with his elbow as he swung his arm to hurl a handful of shit. He turned a grinning face to me, his wild eyes and drooling mouth glistening wet in the hellish light.

Two members of the city's night watch had entered the street and now stood in the shelter of a wall, surveying the scene. I scrambled towards them over a heap of rubble.

'This mob intends murder! You must stop them.'

'Hear that, Simon, this gentleman reckons we must stop them. No, what we *must* do, my fine fellow, is to make sure we walk home at the end of our night's shift to our wives and children, not be carried home on a bier. You think I'm going to risk my neck for a popeling and his whore, who'll turn round and cut our throats tomorrow?'

His companion shrugged. 'Couldn't save them anyway. That crowd's buzzing like a nest of angry hornets. How do you reckon two of us is going to stop a rabble that size? They're thirsty for blood, and if we get in their way it'll be our blood they'll be supping. I'd not argue with them if you were to offer me a ship full of Spanish gold.'

'Then shift your arses and fetch more men to help you,' I snapped. 'Tell the sheriff to turn out the men-at-arms. You took the oath, didn't you? You've sworn to keep the King's peace. Do your duty.'

'Aye, we took an oath to protect this city, and that's exactly what we are doing, protecting it from traitors like them and saving the good people of Bristol the expense of a trial into the bargain. Way I see it, this city and King James will be a good deal safer when those vermin are rotting in hell.' He laid a great fist on my shoulder. 'You take my advice, sir, either hold your tongue and content yourself by watching the fun, or if you're too lily-livered to stomach it, make yourself scarce. You try defending those traitors and, like as not, you'll find yourself hoisted up on the cart alongside them.'

Another roar went up from the crowd, and I glanced over. Attention had switched to the door from which three men were emerging, a fourth man hanging limp as a wet sack between two of them. It was hard to tell if he was conscious. The two men paused on the step and the one following behind pulled their prisoner's head up by his hair, so that his face was visible in the torchlight. A woman screamed, probably his wife, and little wonder, for his face had been reduced to a bloody pulp and his ears sliced off, leaving two gory wounds.

I'd seen far worse on the battlefield and even at the hands of the King's justice, but this man and his family had not even had the semblance of a trial. I turned in revulsion to the two watchmen. But the street behind me was empty.

'I plead guilty to being a sorcerer and a papist, a traitor to God, the King and the good people of England.' It wasn't the beaten man who was speaking. Indeed, from the strange angle of his lower jaw, it seemed unlikely he could have said anything, even if he had been sensible. The man who stood behind him was shouting the words, as if the cordwainer was a puppet to be given voice.

The speaker released his grip on the cordwainer's hair and his head flopped down. Blood gushed from his mouth and splashed on to the hand of one of the men holding him up, who swore violently and wiped it away on the recusant's shirt, before dragging him towards his sobbing wife and children on the cart.

A man dressed in Puritan black burst out of the house. 'See this, brother. Papist baubles.'

The preacher hurried forward and examined the objects which were thrust into his hand. He turned to the crowd, brandishing each item in turn and shouting out the name for those in the crowd who couldn't see what it was, before hurling the despised object into the mud – a rosary, a crucifix and a book written in Latin, which the Puritan declared to be a book of spells, though even from a distance, it looked to me more like a pocket psalter. Then, taking the final object, he held it aloft in both hands.

'Here,' he declared solemnly, 'is the certain proof that those who dwelt in this abode of Satan were among those who wickedly summoned the monstrous wave to come forth from the bowels of the sea to devour the land. Do you see this? It is a shell that came not from our Christian shores but from heathen lands, where they worship idols they have fashioned with their own hands and pour out the blood of their own children in sacrifice to them.'

He held up a conch shell, but one that was far larger than any I had seen. The fingers of both the preacher's hands had disappeared inside, as if it had eaten them. But the shell itself shone like pearl in the torchlight, strangely ethereal and pure in that place of darkness, as if it had fallen from an ocean far above us in the heavens.

Muttering swelled in the crowd, many shaking their heads, certain it must be the Devil's plaything if it was found in a papist's house. But they were plainly unnerved, for who among them had not played with shells as a child? Indeed, many young women occupied their winter evenings decorating boxes or even their stitchwork with them.

The preacher's voice rose over the babble. 'Those savages who dwell in the land of the damned blow into shells such as this, as if they were trumpets, to call up the wind and waves. See, they have even carved images upon it of the demons who aid them in their sorcery.' He pointed at something carved on the great shell, though not even those standing close could have made out the shapes in the lapping torchlight.

'This is the very shell that was blown to summon the wave. You all heard the sound, heard the great roar before the wave struck us.'

People began to nod and gabble excitedly. The cordwainer's wife on the cart cried out that it was only a plaything her brother had brought for the children when he'd last come ashore from his ship, but several men grabbed the sides of the cart and shook it violently, ordering her to still her tongue.

'What's to be done with them, brother?' someone yelled.

'Take them to the harbour that they destroyed and swim them. Bind them, tie iron weights to their necks and cast them into the sea. If they are innocent then let the saints they worship grant them a miracle. They say St Piran was cast into the sea tied to a millstone and miraculously floated all the way from Ireland to Cornwall on this weighty stone. So, let these papists pray that St Piran will grant them another miracle and help them to float all the way to Spain on a lump of iron!' A bellow of laughter rippled through the crowd. 'And if they do not, why they will perish and drown as they drowned the innocent men, women and children of our city and the villages beyond.' There was no more laughter now, only angry growls.

A Puritan preacher who can name the saints, I muttered to myself. I would wager my horse that you, brother, are a convert. I can always spot them; like St Paul, they're so desperate to prove how loyal they are to their new faith that they're always the first to denounce anyone who still practises their old religion. A pox on priests and Puritans both! If these pious fanatics could murder their way into heaven, I'd sooner stroll into hell with the harlots and highwaymen – at least they'd be honest company.

Six men seized the shafts of the cart and began to drag it down the street. The woman was kneeling down now, her husband's battered head resting in her lap. The three children clung to her, the infant trying to fight his way back into her arms, but she sat with her head bowed, her arms limp, as if she had already gone beyond the place where she could hear her children's sobs or feel their embraces. Many of the crowd fell into step as best they could behind them, clanging pans and waving rattles, making as much of a din as they could, a warning to any recusant or even a poor old crone huddled somewhere in the darkness that the death cart would be calling at their door next.

The preacher and his supporters had vanished, melted back into the darkness. As hell's music was borne away on the vicious winter wind, those who were left in the ruined street rushed to the door of the cordwainer's house, barging and shoving to try to get ahead of their neighbours. Others, who seemed never to have been part of the mob, began emerging from dark corners and ruined buildings in twos and threes, like ravens who always know when a beast has died and mysteriously gather in trees and rocks where before there has been no sign of them. They, too, scurried into the house, emerging a few minutes later clutching armfuls of looted treasure – pewter plates, shoemaker's tools from the workshop, bundles of new leather, blankets, a child's hobby horse, chairs, cooking pots, kegs and sacks. Mattresses and chests were dragged out through the door, pillows, clothes and candlesticks dropped from the windows. Now that the preacher had retreated, no one seemed to fear any object in the house as accursed, so long as it could be spirited away into the dark and stinking alleys.

When the house had been flayed, eviscerated and picked to the bones, someone began the cry, 'Burn it! Burn it to the ground.'

A man ran forward with a flaming torch, tossing it like a spear through the smashed shutters. For a moment or so, a dull ruby glow emanated from the workshop, then with a noise like a rush of wind, scarlet and yellow flames leaped upwards. A dark pall of smoke rolled out, driving the men back. There was a shriek. A tardy looter hurtled down the stairs and out of the door. He was covered with glittering, burning sparks. He twisted and jigged as he tried to beat them out, slapping his back, beard and legs to roars of merriment from the men standing by. Behind him the flames had reached the ceiling of the workshop and were licking outwards towards the men, as if trying to drag them into its fiery mouth.

But the building was not burning quickly enough to please the crowd. More torches were hurled, arching through the dark sky like flaming arrows, striking the thatched roof which, though wet, roared upwards in a blaze of gold and scarlet into the black night. One of the men began to strike two staves together in a hollow, pounding rhythm and a few began to dance in the pool of light cast by the flames. They were blackened by the smoke, only their eyes standing out white and glittering in the firelight, as they stamped their feet in time to the thumping, their cloaks whipped out in the wind. Their shadows danced behind them over the rubble of the neighbouring houses, long and grotesque, clad in the feathers of monstrous demonic birds.

Suddenly, with a great crash, the roof of the cordwainer's home fell inwards and a burst of flame exploded upwards. The house, which had withstood all that the sea could hurl at it, had finally fallen at the hands of men.

Chapter Eleven

I was jerked awake by the rapping at my door. Without even being aware of what I was doing, I was on my feet, my knife gripped in my hand. Then the knocking came again.

'Master Daniel, you awake?'

Rachael. I pushed the knife back beneath the pillow and pulled on a pair of breeches, as I hopped and stumbled across the icy boards to open the door.

She glanced beyond me to the bed, which looked as rumpled as I felt. 'You been fighting the Spanish army in your sleep? Or maybe,' she smirked, 'you weren't sleeping alone.'

'Restless night,' I muttered, which was true. It wasn't until the pale grey light of dawn had crept into my room that I'd finally slept, for the battered faces of the cordwainer and his wife kept rising up in the darkness. I'd tossed and turned, berating myself for not intervening and yet knowing that there was nothing I could have done. They would be dead now, their bodies lying in the mud at the bottom of the harbour.

Rachael nudged me aside and slid into the chamber. 'Old Crugge and the mistress were muttering you might be ill when you didn't appear for your breakfast. Some have had the flux since the flood. They say spoiled food is the cause of it, and Master Crugge wouldn't want it getting round there was sickness in the Salt Cat. He'd have you out of here in less time than it takes to gut a herring. And the mistress is worse. She's made up her mind it's the plague you have, you coming from London. Sent me up to see if you were on your deathbed.' She grunted.

'I knew the only sickness you'd be suffering from is a bone-idle backside, you being a fine lord.'

Setting down a covered basket, she drew out a stoppered flask and wooden trencher on which she laid bread and some chunks of eel. 'I saved you a bite, though I don't know why. I've more than enough to do without fetching food to the chambers. And don't you be telling the mistress. She reckons if a customer doesn't come for his vittles, he doesn't need them, but the master will charge you for them anyway and I'll not see a man cheated.'

I made an elaborate courtly bow and she laughed, though she tried not to.

'There was a commotion outside on the street, long after curfew,' I said, ripping off a corner of the bread. 'That's what kept me awake.'

'Word is a house was burned and the family . . .' A spasm of pain crossed Rachael's face. 'For once, that wasn't down to Skinner and his band of thieves from the castle. There's been a few mob attacks since the flood. They set on an old woman who used to sell knotted ropes that sailors use to call up the wind. She was roughed up badly, poor soul. But they've been mostly hunting down papists. Last night was the first killing, though.'

'Are there many papists in the city, then?' I was careful to repeat the word she had used. 'Do they cause much trouble?'

She shrugged. 'Most lie low if folks will let them, but they say there's a few among Skinner's crew up at the castle, vicious devils they are. But there's all sorts come to this city, and a good number are running from something or someone. I reckon people settle here 'cause they feel safer in a port. Can skip out on a ship at the first sign of trouble, leastways they could before the flood.'

'That easy, is it? I thought any citizen taking passage needed to show the captain their letter of permission to leave these shores. It took my aunt weeks to obtain hers – and if a man's wanted, the only paper he'll receive is a warrant for his arrest.'

'I dare say your aunt was a respectable woman who sought genuine papers. But believe me, more vanishes into that castle of thieves than stolen goods. They say Skinner can arrange for anyone to disappear through there – and in more ways than one, if he's not happy with his fee.'

'Then if my wicked past catches up with me, I'll know who to seek out.'

Rachael snorted. 'Only if you're prepared to risk a knife in your ribs. You need a long spoon to sup with the Devil, but you'd need one as long as a ship's mast to sup with . . .' She trailed off, and I saw that she was staring at my throat.

I raked down my beard to hide it. The day I'd left London, I'd instructed the barber to trim my hair and shape my matted beard, leaving it longer than was fashionable, to conceal my neck. But my restless night had undone his neat work.

'Someone hurt you?' Rachael's voice was kind, but the night's events were too vivid, and I had been tormented too often for that scarlet stain.

'I haven't tried to hang myself, if that's what you imagine,' I snapped. 'It's a firemark, nothing more.'

She flinched, and I softened. 'I'm told it resembles one of those,' I gestured at the slices of bony eel, 'so they say my mother must have been frightened by one when she was with child.' I forced a laugh. 'Or maybe someone tried to throttle her and the bruise came out on me.'

An awkward silence filled the space between us.

Rachael suddenly lifted her head. 'They've found some more corpses. Been digging them out of the rubble since the flood, but they came across a dozen or so yesterday, all huddled together. Laid them out in one of the ruined churches. They'll keep them there a few days to see if their families claim the bodies, that's if they can recognise them after all this time rotting in the mud.' She shivered. 'Tell that lad you brought to the Salt Cat. His family might be among them. Go with him, though. It's not a sight any child should face alone.'

I grunted. 'I haven't the time to go chasing round looking for him.'

Rachael regarded me with the same truculent stare I remembered from the first night I'd met her. 'If *I* were searching for my kin and there was news of bodies being dug out, I'd be just as keen as that lad to find out if my folks were among them.' She threw me a quizzical look, then glided out of the door.

I frowned. The deaths last night had not just grieved me, they had considerably complicated the task that FitzAlan had given me. Any halfwit could see that the cordwainer and his family had neither the knowledge nor the spirit to call up a breeze to dry their washing, much less a monstrous wave to wipe out hundreds of lives. Rumour and suspicion were as dangerous as sparks in a hay barn, but they weren't proof of anything. Although that wouldn't stop the Bristolians lynching any recusant they could lay their hands on, and probably setting the whole city ablaze before they'd finished. Every Catholic in the city would be on their guard against strangers asking questions, and any Jesuits and even the secular priests, who were not bound to any order, would be burrowing even deeper into the mud of the city to escape detection. If Spero Pettingar was here, he certainly wouldn't show himself, though not even a rogue like Skinner could help to get him out of England if there were no ships.

But maybe Rachael was right; I should look for Myles. I'd wager that whoever he'd been talking to near the cordwainer's house had sent him to deliver some small object that would serve as a coded message or a warning. If it was a warning then most likely it was for someone who might be in danger – a recusant family, a priest, even a Jesuit like Pettingar himself? The boy might prove himself useful, after all . . .

I retraced my steps to the ruined church of St Stephen's where I'd found the boy, but the tomb in which he'd been sheltering was deserted. The pieces of stone Myles had used to cover the broken side looked much as they had when he arranged them the previous evening. Trying not to disturb the rest, I moved one fragment carefully aside and peered into the tomb. The little heap of broken and worthless objects were still where Myles had stacked them. I felt inside. My fingers touched a heap of bones and a skull piled in one corner, no doubt belonging to the tomb's previous occupant, but there were no coverings, not even an old sack or heap of straw.

I reached further in. There was something else, pushed right to the back. I drew it out into the weak sunlight. It was a small pewter chalice, decorated simply with two reed bands. It was undamaged and far too fine a piece to have been salvaged from the boy's house. I knew that vicars were once buried with a chalice to offer as proof on the Day of Resurrection that they had faithfully administered the sacraments, but those were usually cheap copies of the ones used in church, nothing valuable which might tempt graverobbers. But this chalice was exactly the kind of thing the priest might have owned in life. It was too large to be the object I'd seen the old man give Myles last night. Had he stolen it, or had someone given it to him for safe keeping? Maybe its owner was whoever Myles had delivered that message to last night? I carefully replaced it and covered the gap with stone, satisfied that the boy's treasure store would appear undisturbed.

I SPENT most of the day searching the city for Myles, and all the while listening out for any snatches of gossip I might pick up, but it seemed the subject of last night's lynching was being studiously avoided. Since James had taken the throne, men had grown increasingly guarded in the marketplace, knowing that a hundred ears were listening for the merest whisper of treason. But there was one place where passion still overcame caution. The thrill of a cockfight heats the blood of many men and when a man's blood is up, his guard is down. I headed for the Salt Cat.

Lamps were already burning in the windows of the cottages and houses when I pushed open the door leading from the street into the parlour of the inn. I expected to find it heaving, but it was almost deserted. For moment, I thought Crugge must have changed his mind about holding the cockfight. But from some-where beyond the door, I heard the excited babble of voices. In the courtyard outside, a dense plume of pungent tobacco smoke, glowing in the light from lamps beneath, billowed up from an open trapdoor set in the cobbles close to the wall of the inn. The broken cart which had covered the door had been dragged aside, and in the darkness of the courtyard the hole looked like the gateway to the fiery depths of hell.

A portly man holding two wicker cages stood in one corner of the yard, bargaining with a bedraggled woman. They seemed to have agreed on some price, for he gave her a coin which she tested with her teeth, before counting out several tiny scraps of paper. I didn't need to ask what they were; I'd seen such things change hands many times. She had sold him some charms, probably verses copied from the Bible, inscribed with magic symbols which she had doubtless sworn to him would protect his gamecocks from injury and bring them victory. He would be instructed to slip them into the leather bracelets that fastened the steel spurs to the cocks' legs. If the charms failed, she'd probably tell him that his opponents must have used counter-charms – and besides, she'd be long gone by then.

I clambered down the narrow wooden steps into the smoke-filled hole, and found myself in a crush of men and boys milling about a dingily lit cellar. It had been hewn from the natural rock and filled in with patches of brickwork to create an oblong cham-ber about the same length as the parlour above. On the opposite side from the stairs, I glimpsed a stout oak door set into a wall of bricks, another storeroom perhaps, but one that remained firmly closed.

In the centre of the floor was a circular raised platform covered with sawdust and surrounded by a low wicker fence, about a foot high, which prevented the birds from falling off. The cockpit itself was empty, but the space all round it was crammed with men of all classes. Those nearest the pit were standing, while those at the back were perched on barrels, trestles and piles of wood, whatever afforded them a good view. As I reached the bottom of the steps, four men clambered up on to the platform, each holding a cockerel, taking care to point the long sharp gaffs attached to the birds' legs well away from them. One kick from a gamecock wearing those razor-sharp steel spikes could rip his owner's wrist to the bone or slash his belly wide open. I'd seen men blinded or even killed by their own gamecocks.

The men held their birds up high above their heads. Jerking the cockerels to make them flap their wings furiously, they strolled around the cockpit so that all the spectators could appraise the combatants' fighting spirit. All the talk around me was about the birds, their condition, the past fights they had won and whether feeding them on live maggots quickened their reactions, or if a mash of raw meat and bull's piss gave them more stamina. The noise rose ever higher as spectators argued and laughed, feverishly making last-minute wagers with their friends, while some sidled up to strangers, offering bets, clearly picking out those men they thought were gudgeons or foreigners.

I noticed a couple of men furtively slip small polished boxes, about the size of walnuts, from their pockets, cupping them to their lips and whispering, or holding them to their ear, before laying their wagers. Someone was evidently doing a good trade here selling dicing flies – familiar spirits that were supposed to tell a man how to bet. You could hardly blame the seller, if men were fool enough to buy them. It was a surer way to make money than gambling, that was certain.

Rachael climbed carefully down the steep wooden stairs, carrying a large pitcher. She was instantly surrounded by a sea of empty tankards all waving to catch her attention. She expertly filled them, pouring with one hand, while pocketing coins with the other. Before her pitcher was empty, Crugge was already halfway down with the next, retreating back up with the coins she had gathered. He was going to do well out of tonight.

But not all those in the cellar were planning to make their profit from gambling or selling wine. I noticed a couple of lads repeatedly glancing across the cockpit towards a hollow-chested man with a heavy black beard and a thin bony nose, who was hunched against the wall. He was not watching the birds or laying wagers, but his eyes would dart sideways towards some unsuspecting man and, at his signal, the two lads would start to close in on their mark. Pickpockets were clearly at work, taking advantage of the distraction.

Someone prodded me in the ribs. I jerked round and, looking down, saw it was old Walter.

'That's the one you want to watch.' He pointed towards the pit. 'The one with the white feathers in its breast and head. He's a good 'un. Seen him fight several times. See the way he's flapping like he'd take them all on, given half a chance? Raring to go, he is. Fancy a small wager on him, do you?'

'I'd have more chance wagering against him,' I laughed. 'It's my bet they've given him brandy to make him savage, and those white feathers will be where he's been ripped in fights. That bird can't keep his head out of the way.'

Walter gave a good-natured chuckle. 'You weren't hatched under a goose.'

'Nor was I born yesterday; there are nips working this crowd, Master Walter. You'd better keep a tight hold of your purse.'

The old man's black-toothed grin turned instantly to a scowl. 'I seen them. That's Skinner with his mumpers and thieves from the castle.'

So, this was the infamous king of thieves. He certainly didn't have the build of a licker, but then men like him don't need to fight. He issues the threats while others inflict the pain. What could be more regal?

'Does Master Crugge know he's down here?'

'Oh, he knows alright, but he daren't say nowt, not unless he wants them to pay a return visit in the dead of night with some muscle, and no man would risk that. Skinner didn't get his name from slicing the pelts off rabbits. But so long as they leave his regulars alone and pluck the gentlemen and foreign sailors, Crugge doesn't make trouble for them and they leave him be.' He nudged me again and rolled his eyes towards the stack of barrels behind me. 'Besides, I reckon Skinner knows Crugge wouldn't be too eager to have the Exchequer's men come ferreting around down here. One hand washes the other, isn't that the way of it?'

As the betting started to slow, the Master of the Mains, sporting several glossy black and red tail feathers in his tall brimless hat, beckoned two of the owners and their birds out of the ring. With a long staff, he drew two lines in the sawdust. The two owners took up their positions behind each line. Leaning in, they held out their birds, pushing them towards each other, jiggling them as the birds flapped and pecked at each other. Then, at a command from the Master, they set the birds down behind the lines and released them.

The gamecocks ran at each other, leaping into the air, their wings spread wide, their necks stretched up as they tried to rake and stab at each other with the steel gaffs fettered to their legs. Again and again, they hurled themselves at each other, screeching. Feathers flew and the sawdust rose up in clouds around them, as the spectators and owners alike howled and yelled encouragement to their favoured bird. As the gaffs tore the cockerels' flesh, drops of blood showered from them, landing on the faces and clothes of those nearest to the pit. The cockerel with the sprinkling of white feathers was lying on its back, the other standing on top of it, pecking at it savagely. The Master shouted and the owners scrambled across, pulling the two birds apart, before the fatal blow could be struck.

The victor held his gamecock aloft, waving him around to the cheers of those who had won their wagers, and the groans and scowls of the others. Blood soaked his breast feathers, staining his owner's hands crimson.

Rachael and Crugge worked feverishly to refill tankards. A lad grabbed a rake to level the red-stained sawdust, and the babble of voices rose again as new wagers were laid. As the next pair climbed into the cockpit with their birds, I sensed the interest among the spectators heighten. Even Walter was shuffling forward to get a better view.

'Is this the new gamecock you were telling me about?' I asked him.

He nodded. 'Aye, Sam Harewell's bird. And that other one is the favourite, Master Ayleward's Prince Harry. Champion gamecock. Won the mains four times in a row, and a Battle Royal, too. Ten birds were set in the pit together in that fight, but Prince Harry came out on top. Ayleward's a vinegar merchant and there's been plenty of vinegar between the two of them ever since they were lads. Harewell's been wanting to best him for years and he's been boasting all over Bristol that he will, this time. Paid a fortune for that new bird of his, so they say.'

The two men paraded their birds around the cockpit, glowering at each other with so much venom, it looked as if they were about to fight instead of the gamecocks. Both men looked to be in their forties. Harewell was a small, stocky man, with sagging jowls and a broad backside, as if all the fat in his body was sliding down towards his boots. His palms and fingers were black, I guessed from the printer's ink. I recognised Ayleward as the man I'd seen up in the courtyard buying paper charms. He was a good head taller than his rival, and stored his fat in his bulging barrel belly. He was evidently the wealthier of the two and wanted you to know it, for he wore several gold rings that glinted in the lantern flames. It was evident by the feverish betting that this grudge fight had been eagerly anticipated. I noticed even Skinner had taken his eyes off the spectators and was keenly appraising the birds.

Minutes after the fight began, it became clear the two cockerels were evenly matched, both in aggression and in strength. They flew at each other, their steel gaffs flashing through the cloud of sawdust and feathers. Men had crowded so close to the ring, I could see only glimpses of the gamecocks as they rose, locked together in the air. The shrieking of the birds and the roars of the men filled the cellar, and even the cockerels in their wicker cages were flapping their wings madly, as if they wanted to join in.

The Master barked an order, and Ayleward and Harewell moved swiftly towards the birds. It appeared their gaffs had become entangled in each other's leather straps and both birds were thrashing helplessly on their backs, unable to free or right themselves. The two owners carefully separated the cockerels, retreating to opposite sides of the pit to retie the cockspurs, while the lad raked the sawdust and the Master redrew the lines. As I watched Ayleward repositioning his gaffs, I wondered if he was taking the chance to fold another of the charm slips into the band.

The fight was restarted, but the battle had barely begun before a huge groan went up from the spectators. The Master snapped out another command and Harewell swooped on his gamecock and held it triumphantly aloft, its wings beating angrily at being snatched away from his kill. A boy came running forward with a wicker cage and Harewell handed him the cockerel, bidding him to grip it firmly, while he removed the gaffs and dropped them into a deep leather satchel, before caging the bird.

Ayleward had already retrieved Prince Harry and was carefully examining the limp creature. A group of supporters crowded around him, commiserating and cursing, for they had evidently lost a good deal of money on the cockerel.

Ayleward suddenly let out a bellow of rage. 'He's poisoned him!' He held out the bird, which gave a feeble flutter, eyes half closed. 'Prince Harry's fought on with a dozen gashes worse than this. Look at him; he's drooping like an old maid with palsy.'

At once it seemed everyone in the cellar was shouting. Those who'd bet on Harewell's gamecock were jeering and insisting Prince Harry was simply getting old, past his prime, like his owner. Those who had wagered on Ayleward's cockerel rounded on Harewell, angrily accusing him of cheating and demanding he repay what they'd lost. The Master of the Mains hastily drained the tankard he was quaffing and, wiping his mouth and beard on the back of his hand, pushed importantly through the throng.

The vinegar merchant pointed a quivering finger at the printer. 'That cheating bastard poisoned his bird's gaffs.'

Howls of outrage rose from all around, some protesting at the accusation, the others at Harewell. The Master sighed, as if he'd heard it a hundred times before.

'Then there's only one way to settle this.' He gestured to Harewell's leather satchel. 'Give me the gaffs.'

The printer shrugged, withdrew them and handed them over, dangling from the leather straps.

'Hold out your arm!'

Harewell pushed up his shirt sleeve, extending his forearm, his ink-stained palm uppermost. Griping his wrist, and carefully holding the razor-sharp spike by the blunt end, the Master dragged the point down the length of Harewell's arm, from wrist to elbow. A thin line of scarlet blood erupted and trickled down the skin. Everyone was watching Harewell's face intently. He didn't flinch, but stared steadily and defiantly at Ayleward. A few beads of sweat burst out on Harewell's forehead, but the cellar was stifling in the heat of all the bodies and oil lamps. Everyone had fallen silent; even the birds in their cages seemed to be holding their breath.

The Master released his grip. 'You all saw that,' he said, raising his voice. 'There was no poison. Master Harewell's bird won fair and square.' He lifted Prince Harry from Ayleward's hands and pinched its flesh. 'You've not been feeding him right, that's the trouble. All the gamecocks in Bristol have been ailing since the flood. It's that mouldy grain and bad meat.' He jerked his head towards Harewell. 'His bird was brought in fresh from outside the city. Stands to reason, it'll be in better shape.'

Still arguing and cursing, those who'd lost the wager reluctantly paid up, their scowls deepening at the grins of the winners. The sawdust was raked once more and the Master, in an effort to put an end to the squabbling, was urging the owners of the next pair of fighting birds into the cockpit. But I'd had enough. I knew from experience the arguments about who had cheated would now be the only thing anyone would talk about for the remainder of the evening. I'd learn nothing useful about Pettingar here tonight.

I began squeezing towards the stairs as the spectators started to regroup around the ring. Rachael had descended once more with another pitcher, and was making her way across to the far side. As the men pushed towards her, waving their tankards, a gap briefly opened up behind them and I saw young Myles at the back of the cellar. Through the thick mustard fug of the smoke from the pipes and whale-oil lamps, I made out his small hand disappearing beneath the short cloak of a young man sporting a lustrous pearl earring in his left ear. As the man stepped forward, Myles snatched his hand back. It was a clumsy attempt.

I started towards him through the throng, but the men were all pushing back the other way. He caught sight of me, alarm in his face, then, like a minnow wriggling through water reeds, he ducked down and vanished. The next moment I saw him on the stairs, scrambling up faster than a squirrel into a tree, and before I could even reach the foot of them, he was out of sight. I clambered up as quickly as I could, but the courtyard above was in darkness and there was no sign of him there or in the street beyond.

Chapter Twelve

THE COCKFIGHT WAS long over, the gamblers had departed and the entrance to the cellar was once more hidden beneath the broken cart, but a light was moving across the dark doorway of the stables. I caught sight of it only briefly, like the corpse lights you sometimes glimpse far out on the marshes on a winter's night.

I had clambered out of bed, half asleep, to use the chamber pot, and heard the horses snorting and squealing in the stable. Stumbling to my chamber door, I'd dragged it open, and that's when I thought I saw the light. The horses were clearly restless and disturbed. Someone was in there. They'd already cut off Diligence's tail. Had they come back to cut his throat, to make certain I understood the warning, or was a prigger trying to steal him? Even without a tail, he was a valuable beast. Skinner or any of his band of thieves from the castle could easily have seen him when they came to the cockfight, and if they could lay their hands on false papers for fugitives, they'd certainly know someone who could fake the proof of ownership needed to sell the horse on.

I dragged on my breeches and boots, drew my knife and edged down the wooden steps, placing my feet carefully to the side where there was less chance of the stairs creaking. Nothing was moving in the courtyard. No lights showed at any of the casements; only a single, feeble torch smoked sullenly on the wall of the Salt Cat, illuminating nothing except the puddle of piss beneath it. I crept to the stable doorway, keeping close to the wall, and listened. The two horses were still pawing and snorting, but at least there were still two, and for now they both seemed to be alive.

Holding my knife ready, I slid through the doorway and into the stable. The reek of dung, piss and horse sweat enveloped me as my boots ploughed into the filthy straw, but there was something else, sweet and nauseating. No one who has ever smelled that stench even once in their life can mistake it. It is the stench of agony and terror, of screams and blazing pyres – it is the smell of burnt human flesh.

But there was not a whiff of smoke in the stable, no sign of a flame in the darkness, only the sallow glow of a lantern hanging on the wall, as there had been the night I'd first arrived. By its light I could just about make out the smudges of the two horses as they pulled against their tethers. But the lantern was hung too far in, and its light was too feeble for me to have seen it from the top of the stairs. And besides, it wasn't moving. And where was that stench coming from? I crept towards the far end of the stables, where Diligence was tethered, walking sideways with my back rubbing along the wall so that I couldn't be ambushed from behind. I was so intent on watching for any sign of movement that when my boot collided with something solid and heavy on the ground, I almost sprawled head first over it.

It took me a moment or two to recognise what I was staring at. Someone was lying in the straw at my feet. Slowly, I crouched down, ready to spring away should they suddenly roll over and grab me. But they didn't move. I prodded the body with the point of my knife, then jabbed it in just far enough for anyone who was faking or asleep in a drunken stupor to stir or at least groan. But they did neither. Snatching the lantern from the wall, I bent down once more, running the yellow light up and down the length of the body.

The man was lying on his back, his eyes open, unmoving, his mouth wide, as if he'd been about to cry out. A froth of dark blood had run from the corner of his lips into his beard. His jerkin and shirt had been pulled open, baring his chest. Blood had soaked into his shirt on either side of his body. He was lying in a pool of it. He had been stabbed in the back, maybe more than once. His hands were raised either side of his head, as if he had thrown them up in shock or pain. The palms and fingers were black. Even if I hadn't recognised his face, that would have left me in no doubt as to who it was – Sam Harewell.

But all of those things only seemed to penetrate my brain later, for as I bent over him, the stench of burnt flesh made my stomach heave. And then I saw it on his breastbone over his heart; a livid burn had been inflicted on Harewell's corpse. And *inflicted* was the right word, for this had been no accident. The lantern light illuminated three scarlet letters seared deep into his flesh – IHS.

I instantly knew what those letters signified, though I'd not seen that symbol displayed openly for many years. It was a sign that could spell sanctuary and life, or seal someone for torture and death, and there was no doubt which of those fates it had brought to this man.

IHS – the mark of the Jesuits!

Stunned, I crouched in the shadows of the stables, staring down at the sign burned into Harewell's chest. As the breeze gusted in through the open door, I was suddenly engulfed by the stench of burnt human flesh again. The knife was still in my hand. Without a second thought, I slashed down into the body, hacking and slicing, trying to obliterate that mark. After what I had witnessed the night before, I knew with absolutely certainty that no one must see this. It would be as dangerous as tossing a burning brand into a store of gunpowder.

I whipped round at the sound of a smothered cry behind me. Rachael was standing feet away, staring at the corpse, her eyes wide with fear and horror, her hands pressed to her mouth, as if she couldn't trust herself not to scream. I clambered to my feet, holding out my hand to steady her, for she was swaying as if she was about to faint. But she backed away from me. Even in the dim lantern light there was no mistaking the terror on her face.

Her eyes were fixed on my right hand and, looking down, I saw I was still clutching the dagger. I hastily dropped the knife into the straw.

'Rachael! I swear on my life, I didn't kill him.'

The Jesuits were now the least of my problems. I could already feel the noose dropping around my neck, the ladder kicked from under my feet. I had just destroyed the one piece of evidence that might have saved me.

Rachael's gaze darted towards the doorway. I moved swiftly to block her.

'What reason could I possibly have to harm him? Tonight, at the cockfight, was the first time I'd laid eyes on him.' I was willing her not to yell for help. 'Rachael, listen to me. I was asleep, but when I woke I could hear the horses were agitated and I glimpsed a light moving in the stable, as if someone was carrying a candle or a lantern. After what they'd done to Diligence, I was afraid they'd returned to do more injury to the horses. I came to try to stop them, if I could, and stumbled over that . . .' I gestured towards the corpse. 'He was already dead when I found him, I swear it.'

That would hardly sound convincing if she'd seen me hacking at his chest, but I had been bending over the body and she'd come in behind me. The light was so feeble, she couldn't have seen exactly what I was doing. Her gaze slid to where I'd dropped my dagger. I snatched it up, wiping the blade swiftly in the straw before she could glimpse the blood.

'I cut open his shirt to check if there was any sign of life, but I think he's been dead for at least two or three hours.'

It was only as I said it that I realised it was true. I had been too intent on obliterating the sign to register it, but I'd felt the first signs of stiffening.

Rachael still hadn't uttered a word.

'It's Sam Harewell,' I said. 'He was probably murdered by someone who was at the cockfight, one of the men who'd lost heavily on Prince Harry. Ayleward swore he'd cheated. Maybe it was even Ayleward himself who killed him.'

'No, not Master Ayleward. I know him,' Rachael said quietly. 'He's a fair passion for his gamecocks. But if he'd a grudge against a man, he'd take them to law, not murder them. He's forever laying charges with the magistrates against merchants or craftsmen he thinks cheated him. Reckon he should have been a lawyer.'

'Then it was one of the men who had lost money on a wager,' I said.

'More likely it was one of Skinner's lads. Some of them were at the fight. Skinner would never have done it himself, but he might have given orders to one of his cut-throats.'

I nodded. 'Harewell would certainly have been worth robbing after his winnings tonight, especially if he wagered heavily on his own bird.'

I did not for one moment believe the motive for Harewell's murder was robbery, but I was more than willing to encourage Rachael to think that. I glanced out at the courtyard. It was still dark, but I knew it wouldn't be too long before people would start stirring. In winter, servants and apprentices were often abroad before dawn. I didn't have much time.

I risked stepping closer to her, and to my relief, this time, she didn't back away.

'If we raise the alarm now, it's likely that you and I will both be accused. They will want to know what we were doing out here in the middle of the night and we will both be questioned before the magistrate. He may even order us held until the next assizes.'

Her eyes flew wide and the fear crept back into her face. I didn't want to threaten her, but I had to make her keep silent.

'You said yourself, Harewell was most likely robbed and murdered by one of the villains from the castle. They will have scuttled back to their lair by now, so there is nothing to be gained by reporting it tonight. Let's leave the body as we found it and return to our beds. When Crugge comes to see to the horses at daybreak, he'll find it and send for the constable. No blame can be attached to him, because Mistress Crugge will swear that he was with her all night.' I grasped her shoulders gently, staring into her troubled eyes. 'If anyone should ask you, you were sleeping soundly. You saw nothing and heard nothing. And I will say the same. They will be able to ask us nothing more. Do you understand?'

She tilted her head in that impudent way she'd done the evening I'd first met her. 'I understand that you'll have a hard time convincing them you were never in here if they see that blood on your nightshirt, Master Daniel. You'd best strip it off and I'll soak it in cold water before it sets.'

She fetched a bucket of water as I peeled my shirt off and handed it to her. As she dunked it, she looked me up and down, the trace of a smile on her lips. ''Tis well you've no hankering to join the rogues up in the castle, you'd be caught and hung within the day.'

I glanced back at the corpse lying in the straw. I could still faintly smell the burnt human flesh, though Rachael, thankfully, hadn't noticed it – or didn't recognise the stench among so many in the stable. I knew that whoever had killed Harewell was no common thief or even a cheated gambler. For a moment, I saw myself lying in the bloody straw, that symbol seared deep into my own chest.

Bristol has become a nest of Jesuits.

Chapter Thirteen

LONDON

THE SUN HAD DIPPED below the horizon and only the pale ghost of daylight still lingered beneath the heavy grey clouds. A chill wind rumpled the surface of the lake, and the trees that screened the stone boathouse on three sides bent over it, as if they were trying to hide it from prying eyes. The boatman gave one final pull on the oars as he guided the little craft through one of the two arches into the dark cavern of the boathouse. The bow grated gently against the stone wall and the oarsman clambered out on to the stone ledge, extending a steadying arm to his single passenger.

Charles FitzAlan stepped unsteadily ashore. As he released his grip, he pressed a silver coin into the man's hand. 'Return in one hour. See you're not late.'

The boatman touched his hat and, by way of an answer, briefly inclined his head. FitzAlan heaved himself up the stone steps and through the oak door at the top into a square room. It was lit by a soft buttery glow from a single lantern burning on the long table. His visitor was already seated close to a glowing brazier. Before he had even closed the door behind him, FitzAlan held up a hand cautioning silence. Tiny windows on the three sides of the boathouse gave warning of any approach from the land, but he crossed to the larger casements that overlooked the darkening lake, watching until he saw the boat glide out from under the archway and the oarsman rowing strongly for the far bank, sending a gaggle of greylag geese flapping and cackling across the water.

FitzAlan turned back to the brazier and, drawing off his fur-lined gloves, spread his long fingers over the glowing charcoal.

'So, you finally have news for me, Cimex. It has been long enough in coming. Or are you going to tell me your wee sparrow's taken wing and flown?'

Cimex smiled. 'He has not. He has arrived in Bristol and found lodgings. It was a long, slow journey, I understand. Took him over ten days, because of the flooding, and as long again for word to get back to me. But he didn't waste time on the journey, except where he was compelled to seek other routes.'

'If he's not fled, that at least shows he has some sense,' FitzAlan conceded grudgingly. 'He might yet prove as useful to me as you assured me he would. But I still don't trust a man who's played as many parts as you say he has. A man who does not put his mind to one profession is a man who'll change his coat whenever the wind blows contrary – all things to all men, and true to none of them.'

'Some men, like Daniel, are forced to seek out a living where they may. When he was obliged to leave Lord Fairfax's house, he'd had a nobleman's education and had been brought up to act the lord. But without money, title or position, what was he fit for? Once word spread, he would not have found work in any of the noble houses, not even as a tutor to their sons.'

FitzAlan gave a sudden bark of laughter. 'I warrant it was not fear of Lord Fairfax's retribution which stopped Master Daniel from seeking employment as a tutor. From our brief meeting, I doubt he'd stomach cramming Latin into brats' heads for more than a day. Serving as a field messenger in Ulster against that traitor O'Neill would set any young lad's blood afire with excitement. It's hardly to be wondered he chose the battlefield rather than the schoolroom. I'd have done the same in his shoes, and I dare say he was skilled at it, too.'

'He was, my lord, but—'

'But the Irish rebels were Catholic,' FitzAlan interrupted impatiently. 'And Daniel was raised in a recusant house. A field messenger is well placed to pass information to the enemy, if his loyalty switches.'

'If he had been even suspected of treachery, he would have been hanged on the field of battle – that's if they hadn't thrown him to the soldiers, to exact revenge in their own way.'

'Or maybe he fled before he was unmasked,' FitzAlan muttered. 'Something brought him back before the end of that campaign.'

'But, my lord, it is the very fact that Daniel was raised in the house of a recusant which makes him so useful to you. Here is a man who understands the enemy as well as they do themselves. He knows how they reason. He knows the subtle signs by which a priest in disguise may betray himself, signs which those outside the faith would not recognise. He knows the ways of the Jesuits, too, where they might hide. And above all, he is able to make such men trust him. If any man can find Spero Pettingar, it is he.'

FitzAlan grunted. 'They may trust him, but can I?'

'Gentleman Pensioner Viscount Rowe trusted him enough to employ him as his Secretary for four years. And as the oft-quoted Viscount Montague writes in his book, such a servant must be "of good and grave discretion and especially very secret".'

'You quote another recusant at me, and think that will serve your argument,' FitzAlan snapped. 'It is his very secrecy that troubles me.'

'All the same, my lord, if Viscount Rowe entrusted him with the letters and documents concerning not only his estates but all of those delicate matters that, as one of the personal royal body-guards, the Viscount was privy to at Court—'

'And then dismissed him without notice or reference,' FitzAlan said. 'Threw him out into the London streets to scrape a living as little more than a crossbiter, a legerdemainist, entertaining the commons with his tricks. Why would an honourable man like Viscount Rowe dismiss a loyal Secretary and put himself to the trouble of training another, unless his trust had been sorely betrayed?'

Cimex shifted uncomfortably. 'I am told certain pressure was brought to bear on the Viscount . . .' The tone, which had become cautious, brightened again. 'But the promise of walking free from prison and keeping his hand will buy Daniel's loyalty, I'm certain of that. He dare not fail you. It is fortuitous for us that he found himself languishing in prison. I would not otherwise have been so certain we could safely use him.'`

FitzAlan sank heavily into the chair close to the brazier. He stared into the heart of the glowing fire for several minutes before speaking. 'Do you know who laid the charges of sorcery against Daniel with the magistrate?'

There was a moment's hesitation. 'It is not recorded, my lord. The document of information the magistrate collected from the witness says only that "God ensured the crimes were discovered."'

FitzAlan grimaced. 'Aye, and we all know that means it was a nobleman who has paid to remain anonymous.'

Cimex nodded. 'It's hard to know who the magistrate was more afraid of offending – a lord who could see him in penury, or a sorcerer who could conjure demons to torment him to the grave. I believe that's why the magistrate claimed he couldn't determine if Daniel should be committed to the assizes for trial and insisted, instead, that someone with expertise in examining witches, such as Sir Henry Molyngton, should question him. That way, the decision was taken out of the magistrate's hands and neither Daniel nor his accuser could blame him for the outcome. The judgement of Pontius Pilate.'

'So, Molyngton will be accursed instead,' FitzAlan said, with what might have been the trace of a smile. 'I saw him but yesterday and he was not writhing in agony, so he may count himself safe from a sorcerer's curse. But will he escape retribution from Daniel's accuser? The man did not dare show himself at the interrogation but sent that young cousin of his to listen and report back to him.' FitzAlan let out a snort of laughter. 'When he heard from his cousin that the charges against Daniel had been reduced to deception and fakery, he roared so loudly the servants thought Auld Hornie had risen up through the earth.'

Cimex looked more than startled. 'You . . . you know who his accuser was, then?' The knuckles of the hand that gripped the arm of the chair were white.

This time there was no mistaking FitzAlan's smile of satisfaction. 'Ye didnae think I'd not do some ferreting of my own, did ye?' His accent had momentarily grown broader, his tone harsher. 'Understand this, I'll not be kept in the dark. I'll not waste my breath asking you whether you whispered the devil in Richard Fairfax's ear, or if he discovered for himself what Daniel was about and brought the charges from spite. I doubt I'd get an honest answer from you, anyway. And if I did, I'd not believe it. But you mark this well, I'll not forget it was you who found Daniel for me. If he does well, I give you my word, you'll be the better for it. But if he proves traitor, you'll smart for it alongside him, that I promise.'

Chapter Fourteen

DANIEL PURSGLOVE

THERE WAS NO MISTAKING the hour when Caleb Crugge found the body, or rather when he told Mistress Crugge he'd discovered a man murdered in the stables, for her shriek outdid even the flocks of gulls and brought half the street running, convinced that it was she who was being murdered. But as soon as they learned who the murdered man was, they quietly slipped away, so that by the time the ward had summoned the constable and the sheriff's men, the parlour of the Salt Cat was deserted, and remained so all day. Most of the regulars had been at the cockfight, and no one wanted to spend the day being questioned about when they'd last seen Harewell.

It seemed I had succeeded in obliterating the sign burned into Harewell's chest, for the knife wounds that I had inflicted were being taken as nothing more significant than evidence of the savagery used by the thieves. But I knew what that mark signified.

In the days when all England was Catholic, IHS had been carved boldly over many doors and fireplaces as an act of piety to protect the house. After King Henry's reforms, those Catholics like my old patrons, the Fairfaxes, who'd stubbornly clung to the old faith had found it wiser to obliterate or disguise the letters by adding elaborate decoration. But over the past twenty years, those three letters had crept back, not to protect the house, but as a covert sign that those within were sympathisers, willing to give shelter to priests in hiding or even to the plotters of treason. A keen eye might spot IHS carved high up on to a wall or over a door, the letters intertwined and all but invisible inside an intricate design of fruit or foliage, except to those who desperately searched for them. They might be stitched into a piece of embroidery left half finished on a woman's worktable for a sharp-eyed visitor. They could appear on an old gravestone or a tree trunk, with a name or a word that would guide a fugitive to a place of refuge. It was a dangerous game, for the hunters as well as the hunted might stumble across them. And the question was, which of these was Harewell?

I pulled a coin out of my purse and, as I often did to help myself concentrate, practised making it vanish in one place and reappear in another. But every coin has two sides, and it occurred to me that the symbol could have been burned into Harewell's chest not to mark him as a Jesuit sympathiser, but to brand him as one who had betrayed the Jesuits, a mark of revenge. FitzAlan had been much concerned by the timing of the flood, exactly a year since the Gunpowder Treason plotters had been hung, drawn and quartered, or at least those conspirators they had managed to round up. The executed had been attainted, their sons and daughters deprived of their titles, houses and lands for the crimes of their fathers, the traitors' wives cast out to beg charity from others. Thirteen men dead. Would not at least one of their relatives try to seek revenge on any who might have informed on their kin or betrayed them?

And there was Spero Pettingar himself, a cold-blooded killer ruthless enough to plot the deaths of hundreds without pity, even to slaughter men of his own faith in the explosion. If Harewell had discovered his whereabouts, a man like Pettingar would make quite sure that, in silencing him, his death served as a warning to any others who might share the secret. If this murder was proof, at last, that Pettingar was here, I needed to tread softly if I was not to end my days like Harewell, lying in a pool of my own blood.

I found Rachael in the courtyard kitchen, plucking and gutting a sack of assorted wild birds. She started as my shadow fell across the open doorway, then relaxed slightly.

'Thought you were that sheriff's man again.' She peered over my shoulder, ensuring the courtyard was empty. 'You needn't fret; I told him I was abed and heard nothing. Reckon the sheriff's heard that tale from everyone he's talked to, not that he'll care much. He'll know that if Sam Harewell's attacker was one of the castle rats, they'll not catch him.'

I was almost relieved to learn that. It meant neither the coroner nor the sheriff would delve deeply into the circumstances of the death.

'Did they say what happened to Harewell's cockerel? Did Skinner's men steal that, too?' It had been niggling at me, for I was sure I hadn't seen a cage in the stables. But if this murder was linked in some way to the Jesuits, I couldn't imagine why they would take a gamecock.

Rachael frowned. 'I think one of Harewell's lads took it away earlier. Most of the owners send their birds back straight after they've fought, so they can have their wounds tended and be fed. They keep them hungry before a fight.'

'Walter said that Harewell was a printer. I don't suppose you know where he worked?' I said, trying to sound as if it was merely an idle question.

She glanced sharply up at me. 'Why would you want to know that?'

'I found this near the body last night.' I pulled out a gold coin from the stock FitzAlan had furnished me with. 'The thieves must have dropped it. I can hardly give it to the sheriff, and Harewell's widow will be in sore need of it now.'

'He had no wife that I know of.'

'All the same, it would weigh heavily on my conscience to profit by his death. I should return it to his kin.'

'You shouldn't be seen there. If the sheriff's men—'

'Even if they do question me, now that the body has been discovered no one will ever learn you were in the stables, I give you my word on that.'

'Perhaps I wasn't worried about me,' she said.

I FOUND THE printer's workshop wedged in a narrow slice of land between a tallow chandler's and a small vegetable plot. As I approached, two men were flinging aside their black-stained leather aprons. One knocked against me as he emerged. 'Whatever business you've come about, it'll have to wait till we've had our vittles,' he growled.

I glanced into the workshop they called the chapel. A crabbed old man and a boy were perched on two stools in the corner of the small room, sharing a wedge of mouldy-looking cheese and some coarse, black rye bread. They glanced at me warily, but quickly returned to the serious business of eating, evidently as hungry as the two printers who had barged past me.

A tall wooden printing press stood in one corner, its long pole handle protruding horizontally from the vertical wooden screw. In the other corner, set beneath a large casement which seemed to have been glazed with an assortment of glass fragments garnered from many different windows, was a table on which cases of lead letters lay waiting to be placed into their frames. Between these was a small table. The wood was stained black with the ink from the two dog-hide dabbers that lay abandoned there like giant mushrooms waiting for the stew pot.

The two printers who'd barged past me had seemed in a dark, surly mood, which I guessed not even full bellies would lift. But I hoped the old man and boy might be more forthcoming. The lad seemed to be a younger version of the old man, with the same flat, broad nose and nut-brown eyes, though the old man's right hand constantly trembled with the palsy.

'I am looking for a man by the name of Sam Harewell.'

The old man looked wary. 'You're too late. He's dead, murdered.'

'God have mercy on his soul. Have they caught the villain?'

'No, and they're not likely to either.' He darted a frightened glance at the open door. 'Happened last night at a cockfight. Sam was putting up one of his birds. Didn't see it myself, but Tobias, our journeyman, he went. He said the rogues from the castle were working the crowd like always. A few got their pockets picked – not Tobias, though, he knows their game. Sam's bird won his mains and he bagged himself a fat purse, but there was trouble. Ayleward, that's the man whose bird he was fighting, accused him of cheating.'

'I saw Tobias—' the boy piped up.

'Hold your tongue, lad!' The old man elbowed him sharply in the ribs. 'Master of the Mains scored Sam with a gaff to settle the matter, but Tobias said Sam was a bit unsteady on his feet after. He reckons the thieves must have noticed and followed him when he went up to the yard to take a piss.'

So, Sam Harewell *had* poisoned that spur to weaken Prince Harry, or maybe the journeyman had done it, if he'd laid a large wager on the fight.

'Did for him proper, they did, poor Sam.' The old man peered anxiously out into the yard again. 'Could have just knocked him out and grabbed what they wanted, but they take pleasure in hurting folk. People are afeared to stand up to them. But the mayor reckons there's nothing he can do about it. Castle belongs to the King, for all that he's never set foot in it, nor the Queen before him. But the constable can't enter without leave from the King, and those murdering bastards know it. Once they're safely back inside, there's no one can touch them.'

'Sam Harewell was employed here as printer?'

'He's . . . was . . . master here. My grandson is apprentice to him.' He jerked his head towards the handle projecting from the press. 'I turn the Devil's Tail, as puller, for him, for the lad's not tall enough to do that yet, but Sam said I may do it till the lad's able to manage it alone. I promised his father, before he put to sea, that I'd take care of the boy. But . . . if there's to be a new master . . .'

It must be no easy task to turn that great wooden screw for hours, and given the man's palsy, even if the new master agreed to the arrangement, I wondered if he'd be able to continue until his grandson was strong enough to take over. The grandfather had clearly offered himself as part of the bargain – two labourers for one wage. I couldn't decide if Sam Harewell had been a kindly man, or a greedy one.

'What do you print?'

The grandfather shrugged. 'Never learned to read, but I hear Sam talking to his customers. All sorts it is he does. Sometimes there's captains and merchants needing to tell folks there's a cargo to be sold off at auction, so they tell Sam where and when and what's to be sold and he prints it. Then there's sheets offering a reward for runaways or murderers, or to tell folks that there's to be a public hanging or other entertainments like dog fighting or a play. The boy can earn himself a few extra pennies from some of the customers after his work's finished here, running about the town, pasting up broadsides for folks who can read, or handing them out in streets and taverns.' He beamed proudly at his grandson. 'And if there's to be an execution there's usually a few men come in with the tales they've written of all the wicked deeds the felon's committed, and the lad can help to sell them to those who go to watch the hanging. But we don't reckon much to the ranters, do we, boy?'

His grandson shook his head vehemently. 'They bring their sermons they want printed. But I can't earn any money from them 'cause they collect the broadsides themselves and sell them to the crowds. Purse strings tight as a cat's arsehole.' He scowled, and his grandfather chuckled, ruffling the boy's hair.

'They always put Tobias in an ill humour, too,' the old man added, 'as he's the one has to set the letters for their sermons, says it is tedious work, and lengthy, too.'

My ears pricked. 'So, Master Harewell was a devout Bible Christian, then.'

The old man hesitated and glanced towards the street, lowering his voice. 'Not him, 'tis well known round here that he is . . . was of the old faith, a Church papist, but he went to the Protestant service whenever the law says he was obliged to. He kept the law in all matters. There's no man who'll tell you any different, and there's none will say a word against him. He was a loyal subject of the King. You'll find none better,' he added hastily, as if he thought one of Cecil's spies might be lurking outside the door.

So, Harewell had been a Catholic. Not a recusant but one who conformed, one who walked with a foot in both worlds. The kind of man the King had promised to allow to live in peace when he'd first come to the throne, though that promise had been short-lived. As both worlds had drawn apart, I knew only too well how hard it was for a man who walked between them to keep his balance. Where had Harewell's true loyalties finally come to lie?

Chapter Fifteen

THE PALACE OF PLACENTIA,
GREENWICH, LONDON

'HE'LL NAE WISH to be bothered with the scrofulas today,' the Scottish lord muttered.

Robert Cecil followed his gaze up to the dais where James was slumped on the throne. The King was fidgeting more impatiently than usual, as if he was wrestling his own fingers in a bid to stop them closing around someone's throat.

'His Majesty must honour the custom, Sir Ian,' Cecil said stiffly. 'He was consecrated with the holy oil of kingship as God's servant on earth, therefore the commons expect that he will heal his subjects as he keeps the health of the nation.'

'It'll be the health of his new deer hound that'll be on his mind, not some scabby puddocks. Any fool can see he's itching to be in the saddle.'

Although he was trying not to show it, Cecil was fast becoming as impatient as his Sovereign by the seemingly endless parade of supplicants and petitioners. It continually pricked him that he was not permitted access to the King's bedchamber. As Secretary of State he should be able to speak with the King alone whenever the necessity arose, particularly when His Majesty had withdrawn for the night. But all the men of the bedchamber were Scots, like Sir Ian, and they took a malicious delight in barring admittance to any Englishman. So, however urgent the matter, Cecil was forced to request a private audience, obliged to cool his heels and wait upon the King's pleasure like a tailor come to fit him for a new doublet.

And Cecil knew only too well that if James was delayed too long by this morning's business, he might well postpone their meeting in his impatience to be out in the deer park. Cecil was almost tempted to give orders that those who were waiting outside seeking the King's Touch should be sent away and told to return another day, but it had been hard enough to persuade James to continue the ancient custom, and given the increasing unrest, it was more vital than ever that James should prove to the commons that God, not man, had placed him upon the throne.

Cecil winced as Sir Ian edged closer, looming over him, as he always contrived to do on public occasions, deliberately accentuating Cecil's lack of height and crooked back.

The Scot's lips twitched into the cold smile that always heralded some barb he found amusing. 'I canna see why James puts up with such nonsense. When England is finally forced to bend the knee to Scotland, the Kirk will put an end to such Romish superstition, as it has put an end to the satanic celebrations of Yule and masques.'

'Pity it cannot also put an end to the cattle raids and blood feuds in your lowlands, Sir Ian,' Cecil said without looking up. 'Or does your Kirk embrace a different set of Ten Commandments to our Church? Perhaps stealing and murder are counted as lesser sins in Scotland than dancing and the singing of carols.'

The Scot opened his mouth to retaliate, but at that moment the door at the far end of the Presence Chamber was flung wide. Courtiers and petitioners parted like the Red Sea, as ten people were ushered in: four men and three women, followed by two little girls, and a wretchedly emaciated boy. Once inside the door, the little band froze, their expressions a mixture of fear and wonder as they gazed up towards the dais at the far end of the chamber.

The Presence Chamber in the Palace at Greenwich had been designed to strike awe into the heart of any supplicant or foreign diplomat. The throne on the raised dais was illuminated by eighty feet of windows, the glass polished until it sparkled like ice in the cold winter sunlight. The bright light haloed James as if he was the risen Christ enthroned in heaven. It glittered from his necklace of diamonds and winked from a huge diamond fastened to his hat, sending spears of light darting around the chamber with the slightest movement of his head, so that it seemed as if God Himself was hurling a shower of lightning bolts from heaven.

The effect of the jewels was so dazzling, the little band of supplicants would scarcely have noticed that their King was more austerely clad than many of his servants. A soft white linen collar rested on the padded shoulders of a dark grey satin doublet, worn beneath a short black cloak which provided the only splash of colour with its blood-red lining.

'Do they expect me to go crawling to them?' James snapped. 'Bring them here.' He beckoned impatiently. 'Come, come. Make haste!'

The small group bunched closer together as they were herded towards him like a flock of geese. The parish authorities who had raised the money to send them to Greenwich had done their best with what funds they had. Most had freshly mended shoes and new, if ill-fitting, clothes. No overseer of the poor wanted it said that his parish neglected their duty. But there was no disguising what had brought these unfortunates to the King's Court, for the shirts and the gowns of the little group had been pulled down, baring their shoulders and the women's naked breasts, so the full extent of their deformities could be clearly seen. The necks of most were covered in swellings and boils, some so large they forced the head into an unnatural angle. Some of the boils had burst into suppurating ulcers, which stank worse than the Thames mud in summer. Not all had the neck swellings, though; one of the men had a great black growth on the side of his face like fungus growing on a dead tree. The faces of the two little girls, who clung to each other, were covered in lumps like those on the skin of a toad, their lips swollen and their eyes squeezed shut by thickened lids. Each of this little band was suffering from what physicians, with a shrug of their shoulders, had pronounced to be the 'King's Evil'. It was a convenient diagnosis, Robert Cecil thought grimly, for no doctor, however skilled, could be expected to heal such a malady, which was inflicted by no less than the Devil himself.

As they approached James, one of the women broke away from the group and ran forward, clambering on to the dais and falling to her knees before the throne. It was hard to tell if she was simply desperate to be cured, or feared that the King's healing power might run out if she was last in the queue. His power wouldn't, Cecil thought, but his patience easily might.

The chaplain came to stand alongside James, and as the King leaned forward and lightly touched the woman on the face, the chaplain recited in a bored tone, 'They shall lay their hand upon the sick and they shall recover.' A page kneeling on the other side of the throne held up a small casket from which James plucked a white silk ribbon on which was strung a gold coin that spun and glinted in the sun. He slipped the ribbon over the woman's head, so that the coin dropped between her ulcerated breasts. She crawled forward on all fours, like a dog, and seemed to be trying to kiss his boots, as if that might secure a greater healing. James recoiled, gesturing furiously for the guards to drag her away.

'DID YE SEE that rabble of beggars? You ken full well they only come for the gold.'

Those who the King had touched were advised to wear the coin for the rest of their lives, to guard against the future assaults of the Devil, but Cecil knew most would sell it eventually, especially if the cure failed to work. Some would part with it before they had even left Greenwich, for there were always rufflers loitering outside waiting to cajole and bully the supplicants into parting with it for a fraction of its value. Those who refused would probably be followed and robbed later.

'They come for your healing touch, Sire,' Cecil said, with as much conviction as he could muster.

'My arse, they do. Next time I should piss on them. If my touch cures them, tell them my piss'll give them eternal youth.'

Cecil did not trouble to reply. He knew James thought the custom mere superstition, as did Sir Ian, but the commons believed that only the legitimate king, the divinely appointed king, could cure the King's Evil, and if he refused then some might say it was because he knew he could not cure it.

'So, Salisbury, what news of Garnet's relic? Has the straw been found?' James was now standing at the window, staring down into the courtyard outside.

Cecil could hear the shouts of men, the clank of iron shoes against the stone flags and the excited yapping of the hounds. They were preparing the horses for the hunt. He did not have long.

'Not yet, Sire. It has been spirited away and could be hidden in any of the Catholic households up and down the country.' The Secretary of State fought to keep the irritation from his voice. If these families could hide men in those priest holes where a dozen pursuivants might search for a week and fail to winkle them out, there was precious little hope of finding a single straw.

'But whether or not it is found, Sire, scarcely matters. It is what it represents that concerns me more – Garnet, the dead traitor resurrected as a Holy Catholic Martyr. Archbishop Bancroft informs me that more Jesuit missionaries have been smuggled into England in this past month. They are urging the recusants to stand firm and refuse to take the Oath of Allegiance to you, persuading them that if they take this oath, it will damn their immortal souls.'

'But their own Archpriest, George Blackwell, took the oath, and he is their Catholic leader in England. Why will the English Catholics not obey him?' James demanded.

If the King had been looking at his Secretary of State, instead of down at the horses, he would have seen the exasperation written on his features. George Blackwell, having first argued against the oath, had finally been persuaded that if Catholics refused, they would be counted as the enemy within, traitors to England and to its Crown. They would be writing their own death warrants. Archpriest Blackwell claimed he was only taking the oath to protect his flock.

But Cecil knew the real reason the old man had capitulated. The penalty for not taking the Oath of Allegiance was praemunire – to be deprived of all rights, all possessions and property and, the most sobering of all, to be permanently deprived of one's liberty. Lord Salisbury had seen the fear in the old priest's face. The thought of spending the rest of his life in prison, without any hope of release or the smallest of material comforts to ease his suffering, was one that terrified him even more than any punishment that might await him beyond the grave. Cecil permitted himself the ghost of a smile. It never failed to surprise him that young men who had many decades of life ahead of them were defiant when faced with the prospect of spending those years in a stinking cell, while frail old men who had only months, or weeks, left to them shrank from it. But then the young are naively convinced they will outlive all things, even their captors. The old know they will not.

James's attention had been caught by a fight between two of his hounds. Cecil coughed, trying to bring him back to the purpose. 'As you know, Sire, many Catholics refused to accept the Archpriest's authority when he was appointed, claiming it was not a title of the Romish Church. They have sought to live quietly and unnoticed, but now the Jesuits are turning even moderate Catholics into recusants and converting godly men to the Catholic faith, including some of the noble families.'

'Aye, they work through weak and addlepated women. That's how they worm their way into households. Even climb into bed with these harlots, so I'm told. They'll use every wile of Satan to seduce them to the Devil's faith. For them it is no sin, like that Jesuit weasel, Garnet, lying and perjuring himself before God and his lawful King and calling it *equivocation*.' He spat out the word with such disgust that a stream of salvia landed on the pane of glass and oozed slug-like down the window.

James ignored it and turned to face Cecil. 'I lay this at your feet, Salisbury. If every priest in the kingdom had been exiled beyond the seas, as I demanded, there would have been no fertile ground in England on which the Jesuits could have sown their pernicious tares. I canna understand why you and Archbishop Bancroft insist on treating the secular priests as if they are a different breed of men to the Jesuits. They both bow the knee to the Pope, and not one of them will be content till they see me overthrown, and England and Scotland a Catholic realm once more.'

'Sire, that would only have led to the commoners, Protestant and Catholic both, pitying these priests. If villagers see a harmless old priest dragged from his cottage and cast on to a ship bound for distant shores, it will arouse nothing but pity in them and a resentment of injustice. The commons must be made to see and feel that these priests are traitors who plot not only against your person but against ordinary Englishmen, and conspire to drag them all back into the bonds of popery.

'That is why this oath is so important. The ordinary Englishman cares little if a stranger, miles away in London, confesses to treason, but when he learns that his own neighbour, who sells him meat or physics his children, refuses to swear the oath and secretly conspires with those who would destroy England, he will hate and revile him.

'But the oath by itself is a dog with no teeth, if you will not enforce the penalty, Sire. If those who refuse to swear it suffer no injury, the Jesuits will find it easy to persuade others to take heart from that and to stand against it. You must act, Sire, before these hornets build a nest so large it cannot be destroyed.'

Chapter Sixteen

DANIEL PURSGLOVE

I'D SPENT THE AFTERNOON in the marketplace and the work-shops making casual inquiries about the printers in Bristol, with the excuse that, as a stranger to the city, I was trying to discover which one to employ who would do the job well, without charging a king's ransom. But I didn't mention the name of Sam Harewell directly again, in case the sheriff's men got to hear that I was taking an uncommon interest in his murder.

If Harewell had simply been knifed, those two surly journey-men of his would have been at the top of my list of likely assassins. Small injustices, harsh words and unfair fines meted out over months or years easily fed a smouldering resentment that could eventually erupt into burning fury. I'd felt that same fury myself long ago and I knew only too well what hot blood could do. But to burn the Jesuit sign into a man's flesh, that was not the action of aggrieved workers, unless one of them had been fanatical about the old faith and resented his master's dealings with what the boy's grandfather had called 'the ranters'.

But ranters were not the only men who sought to have their words printed. Illegal Catholic presses operated throughout London, even inside Newgate prison, the pamphlets and broad-sides smuggled out by bribed guards or visitors. Some presses were hidden in the houses of recusant families, others quite openly displayed in printers' chapels, where they would be employed in their legitimate tasks by day, but by night printed the tracts and news that Archbishop Bancroft would never license. The Jesuits might be forced into hiding, unable to meet with others of their order, or preach to crowds, but they could still instruct, encourage the faithful and plot the downfall of their enemies as long as their words could be printed and spread through the network. A master printer would recognise the work of a rival chapel if he chanced upon an underground broadsheet. He might even realise a fellow guildsman was ordering more materials than he needed for his legitimate work. A Jesuit tract could easily have fallen into Harewell's hands, and if he had recognised its source and threatened to reveal it . . .

As darkness fell, I found a tavern bearing the sign of the Lamb and Flag, not far from another of Bristol's print chapels. Inside, I picked my way towards an elderly man who looked thirsty for drink and company, and seemed willing enough to share both with me since I had a full flagon of wine in my hand. I slid on to a settle opposite, filled his tankard from my flagon and waited until he had taken a deep draught, before launching into the same tale about needing to find a discreet printer.

'Of course, being newly come to Bristol, I don't want to go blundering into trouble. A friend of mine who wanted to hire a horse in Winchester innocently went to a stable he saw in passing. Turns out, though, the inn where he was staying had an arrangement to direct all their customers to a rival one. Their stable lads lay in wait for my friend to ride past them on the street and took their revenge by smearing jading oil on his horse's flank. It drove the poor beast into a frenzy. It bolted to try to escape the smell. Almost killed them both.'

I refrained from mentioning to my drinking companion that I had *persuaded* those stable lads to part with a little of the jading oil myself, which I'd soaked into a dry chicken bone wrapped in some hair and hemp, just as a precaution, you understand, for it had occurred to me that if ever I found myself being pursued by someone on horseback, throwing that chicken bone down between us would turn his horse aside better than any weapon.

My new friend wiped his mouth with the back of his hand and chuckled. 'Aye, I've heard of that trick afore. When I was a lad there was an old besom wanted to get her cart to market ahead of her neighbour so she could sell her crops first, for hers were so wizened and wormy, none would have taken a second glance at them if they'd a choice. She jaded the neighbour's gateway with that oil, she did. Neighbour's horse refused to go past it, neither whip nor carrot could coax it out of the yard.'

I laughed. 'That's just why I don't want to find myself dealing with the wrong chapel. I dare say half the city would know if there was bad blood between any of the master printers. So, I'd be grateful if you'd tip me the wink.'

The man tapped the side of his tankard to remind me how I might best express my gratitude, then he leaned forward. 'I'm not saying it had ought to do with their masters, but a few weeks back there was a good old broil between the men who worked in two of the chapels. Twelfth Night, it was, so every lad in Bristol was as drunk as a parrot, and one of Harewell's men near hacked the arm off one of Upton's lads, all for saying—'

'It's you who talks parrot, you old muckspout!' a voice snapped behind me, and before I could move, two men thumped down on to the settle either side of me.

My arms were pinned down to the table in front of me by two pairs of fists. The man who had spoken wore thick iron rings on his hairy fingers, which, I had no doubt, would considerably increase the damage that might be inflicted if those knuckles were slammed into my face or belly. His long thin nose and protuberant yellow teeth gave him a shrew-like appearance, in contrast to his companion, who resembled a bull, with small bloodshot eyes and shoulders that could probably pull a laden wagon up a hill.

My drinking companion jerked upright at their sudden appearance, then frowned. 'Easy, brothers. This lad's not doing me any mischief. He's newly come to the town, just wants to know the lay of the land. Good sense, I call it.'

'I'd call it ferreting,' the bull snorted, grinding his not inconsiderable weight down on my arm, so that I had to fight hard to keep my expression blank, to avoid flinching.

'Heard him asking about printers in the marketplace earlier,' Shrew-face said. 'Now he's at it again. What's your business here, knave? There's printers aplenty in London, and by that honeyed tongue of yours that's where you're from, I reckon. So why come all the way here in search of one?'

Both pressed their bodies hard against me as if they would squeeze an answer from me. My companion's friendly grin had vanished and he was scowling as if he now suspected he'd been played for a fool and did not like it.

I fell back on the old story. It's always better to stick to the same lie.

'I thought to have some broadsides pasted up about the city, to ask if any had knowledge of my missing kin. My mother's sister and her children set off for Bristol before the flood, to take passage on a ship. I don't know if they managed to set sail before the disaster struck or were caught in it.'

Shrew-face gave a mirthless bark of laughter. 'You'd do better to empty your purse in old Mother Alice's lap. She tells folks' fortunes by breaking eggs into oil. This is a port, slug wit! There's dozens of ships sailing in and out of it, and hundreds of strangers passing through this city who come to board them, or leastways there was before the flood. Your kin got two heads and a tail, have they? 'Cause that's the only way anyone'll recall them.'

'But if they are alive and still in the city, they might see the notice and discover that I'm searching for them.'

Shrew-face ignored this. 'I reckon he's one of Salisbury's spies, come to see who's printing sedition and treason.'

An icy finger stroked down my spine. That was much too close to the mark for comfort.

I forced a laugh. 'Salisbury would be emptying pisspots for the King's scullion, if he'd no more wit than to employ a man like me as a spy. You say you heard me asking questions in the marketplace and again in here. So, you know I didn't trouble to hide what I wanted any more than a babe in clouts bawling for his supper. Speak the truth now, brothers, would I last an hour as an intelligencer without being discovered?' I grinned. 'Wish I was one of his spies, though, I hear with the purses he gives them they can dine nightly on roasted boar's heads and lick custards from the navels of the most buxom whores in the London stews if such takes their fancy. Now that would be the life, wouldn't it!'

I winked at the bull, whose mouth slowly widened into a leery grin.

My drinking companion chuckled. 'If this Salisbury comes here wanting to recruit, you just let me know. I'll be the first in line to make my mark. There's a doxy works out of the Mermaid—'

'And there's your wife works out of your kitchen,' Shrew-face interrupted. 'If that bastard Salisbury wants a spy, I reckon he'd be better off employing her, 'cause she knows exactly which slut you and every man in the city pants after, even before they know themselves.'

'Aye, that's true enough,' my friend said ruefully. 'And her mother's worse. The pair of them can sniff out a man's guilty pleasures better than a brace of bloodhounds. Set them to work and there'd not be a man in England would dare stray from their hearth.'

The banter about whores and harridans continued for some minutes more and gradually the two men released their grip on me and grudgingly allowed me to buy them more wine. By the time I extricated myself, the bull was treating me like a long-lost friend, but several times I caught Shrew-face eyeing me suspiciously with an expression that told me he was by no means convinced.

I had to tread softly. Though the people of the city were well used to all kinds of foreigners and strangers passing through, fear and suspicion were now breeding in its ruined streets like flies in the stinking mud, and I'd no desire to end up in the harbour with a lump of iron tied about my neck.

But it was that broadside which had stirred up the crowd – that and the Puritan who, if he wasn't the anonymous author, had certainly made good use of it. Even if Sam Harewell had not discovered a Catholic press, he was proving to be a man not averse to printing tales of witchcraft and Jesuit conspiracies. He probably wouldn't even have troubled to read what his chapel was printing, leaving it to his typesetter, Tobias, to copy the text he was handed. If Harewell had printed broadsides like the one I'd seen, accusing the Catholics of being behind the flood, that would surely be motive enough for Jesuits to murder him and to mark him, too, especially if other innocent men had suffered like that unfortunate cordwainer and his family. It would be easy enough to discover which printer's chapel was responsible for disseminating those anti-Catholic ravings throughout the city, and make him pay the price. A burning for a burning. A life for a life.

But that was no proof these were the Jesuits who had plotted against the King, much less that Spero Pettingar was one of them. And something else still bothered me. If Harewell had been murdered for printing anti-Catholic broadsides, his killers plainly intended his body should be found as a warning to other printers not to do the same. On the other hand, to mark the corpse and proclaim that the murder was committed by Jesuits would surely inflame the populace far more than even the most scurrilous broadside. So, was that the real intention? Not Jesuits at all, but the work of someone wanting them to be blamed? When I was Rowe's secretary, I often heard him muttering about Cecil's network of spies. He once told me that through their numerous secret drops, Cecil even managed to obtain regular reports about which priests were being smuggled into England from the seaman, Richard Hawkins, while Hawkins was a closely guarded prisoner in Spain. But there were rumours that Cecil went further than simply gathering information about rebellion, some whispered he'd deliberately fermented it though his provocateurs who burrowed away like woodworm in the timbers.

I groaned, causing an elderly goodwife to draw away from me in alarm. The more I thought I had learned, the more questions it seemed to raise. The only thing I was certain of was that the Jesuits were mixed up in this murder somewhere, though whether as conspirators or as victims of conspiracy I had, as yet, no way of knowing.

I pushed out through the door of the Lamb and Flag, into the street beyond. It was as cold as a witch's kiss after the warmth of the inn. I dragged my hood over my head, clutching my cloak tightly to me. The wind had died away and under the cover of darkness a grey, wet mist had come creeping in from the sea, slithering on to the land like some many-tentacled creature, wrapping itself around the buildings and muffling the sounds. I was convinced that I'd not imbibed nearly enough wine to be drunk, but as I stumbled along the street, I felt myself lurching a little, missing my step, and my vision seemed blurred. It was probably the shock of the cold air after the warm fug of the chamber, and the way the fog had of fuddling the senses.

The sea fret hung in dense patches; for a few paces the air seemed to clear and then, in another step, I could barely see a wall inches from my face. Occasionally a light would appear, suspended in the air like a will-o'-the-wisp. I couldn't tell if it glimmered from inside a casement or was in the hand of someone walking towards me. Once I turned towards the beckoning flame, certain it was a lantern hanging in the doorway of a house or inn, only to find myself teetering on the edge of a wide, water-filled hole, one of many that had opened up across the city where the sea had flooded cellars and tunnels. The lantern suspended above it to warn people of the danger had almost lured me to my death.

I groped across to the other side of the street, sliding on the mud and filth, until I reached the solid wall of a house and stood a moment to regain my breath. I tried to picture the route back to the Salt Cat. I must have missed the narrow alley which cut through to the other street. I turned to retrace my steps. Something dark spun away into bone-white mist, making it eddy and swirl. It was gone before my mind could register what it was. A cat? No, too high above the ground for that. A raven? They didn't fly at night. Footsteps running towards me from behind. I whirled round to face the figure, but even as I did, I glimpsed the thing of darkness emerging again from out of the fog.

Chapter Seventeen

A BLOW CAUGHT ME on the side of my head, slamming my skull into the wall. Vomit rose quickly in my throat. Instinctively I lashed out with my fist, but I could sense someone creeping up behind me. I jabbed my elbow violently backwards. The sharp gasp of breath assured me I'd winded the man. But the one who'd struck me had twisted away from my fist. A stave slammed across my wrist, pinning it to the wall. As I tried to kick out, I saw a third dark shape emerge from the mist.

I dragged my arm downwards beneath the stave, skinning it against rough stone. The man was leaning all his weight on it, grinding my bones into the wall. I couldn't free my hand but I managed to grasp the wood and, using it to balance myself, kicked out as high and hard as I could at the newcomer's groin. With a screech, the third man tumbled backwards into mud and rubble, rolling around, clutching his cods, groaning and cursing. But my triumph was short-lived. I felt the thorn-sharp point of a dagger pricking the skin of my throat. I froze, not daring to move my head, my right arm still pinned to wall. As I stood there, another figure emerged through the swirling fog. God's blood, not more of them! But it wasn't a man and, just for moment, I thought I glimpsed a boy's face.

'Myles?'

But the boy, if he had ever been there, was already gone.

'Well now,' the man holding the knife drawled. 'This is a strange hour to be taking a stroll. You not heard about the curfew?'

The night watch! I'd have some explaining to do, but he

wouldn't kill me. The street was too dark to make out the city's badge on his clothes. But as he pressed closer, my belly lurched. Whoever he was, this was not a watchman. He was shrouded beneath a heavy cloak, patched and stinking like rancid milk. A cowl was drawn down over his head and the lower part of his face was masked by a cloth tied around it, so that only his eyes could be seen deep within the cavern of the hood, glittering and steely as the blade.

'Maybe he doesn't know about the curfew?' the man pinioning my numb and throbbing hand answered. 'Foreigner, isn't he?'

'A fuckwit, you mean, wandering around in a fret like this. There are men who stumble straight off the harbour into the icy water when the mist rolls in. Just vanish they do, and no one even knows they've gone. Chances are their carcasses will never be found, save by the gulls and fishes.'

'Ask him!' the other man insisted.

But the man on the ground had struggled to his feet, though he was still stooped over. 'Stop wasting time. Just get rid of him. Stick that knife somewhere it'll really hurt and boot him into that pit.'

The man holding the knife grunted. 'Just 'cause he bruised your plums, there's no need to be hasty. Let's hear what he has to say for himself, afore we baptise him, shall we? I reckon you'd liked to hear him squeal, wouldn't you, after that kick he landed on you?'

My right hand was still pinned to the wall by the stave, but I'd been inching my left behind my back towards the hilt of my dagger, on my right hip. I grasped the hilt and shifted my weight, ready to use both knee and knife together, but as my dagger flashed out, the man nursing his cods yelled a warning. The ruffian holding the knife to my throat jerked sideways. My dagger caught in his heavy cloak and fell to the ground. The sharp point of his knife flashed up from my throat towards my eye. Hot blood spurted from my pierced eyelid. I held my breath; the slightest additional pressure and the blade would skewer my eyeball.

'Now, Master Fuckwit, suppose you tell us what—'

'Back, you dogs, back!' The voice that pierced the fog, though cracked, still held the tone of one accustomed to being obeyed.

The man holding the knife twisted his head round at the shout, and I didn't hesitate. My left hand shot up, dashing the blade away from my face. Blood gushed down my cheek, scalding my eyes. The pressure on the stave slackened and I crumpled to my knees, pressing my hand to my slashed face, scarcely aware of what was happening around me. Blinded by my own stinging blood, I could do nothing except hunker down, covering my head with my arms, and await whatever blows might fall.

I sensed the two men on either side of me drawing back and braced myself for a kicking or for the stave to come smashing down. But moments later, I heard several pairs of feet scrambling away over loose stones. Then silence flowed back, as the chill, clinging mist billowed towards me, muffling all sounds.

I tensed. Someone was still out there. Footsteps were approaching, but not those of the men who had attacked me; these were ponderous, measured. Keeping one hand pressed to my eye, I swept the other across the mud, feeling for my dagger. I heard the rasp of laboured breathing, as someone bent over me. I lifted my head, blinking fiercely, and jabbed the blade upwards. A blurred figure jerked backwards.

'Sheath that dagger, sirrah. Those who threatened you are fled and it is many years since any have considered me spritely enough to be worth drawing a weapon against.'

The figure bent closer, darting out a hand with surprising agility for one who claimed to be old. He lightly touched my face with fingers as cold as the mist.

'You're bleeding.' The voice was sharp with concern, and somehow vaguely familiar.

'My eye . . . that bastard slashed it.'

'My home is close by. Come, hurry. Those dogs are not the only ones that will be hunting under cover of this fret tonight.'

I could be walking straight into a trap, but if someone was planning my death, why bother to rescue me, when that little band had been more than willing to do the job for them? Every thief and cut-throat in the city would be taking advantage of the fog. With blood pouring into my eye, I would be easy prey. I needed shelter at least for an hour or so. I struggled to my feet and allowed myself to be led down the street, stumbling over rubble and slipping in mud. Even in the darkness and fog, my companion seemed to know every obstacle and hole as well as a blind man in his own bedchamber. Using his staff to steady both of us, he dragged me over piles of rubble, tugging me through gaps where once buildings had stood, and down alleyways that stank of rotting fish.

Finally, a stone building loomed out of the mist. From its length and the huge doors set into one side, wide and high enough to admit a laden wagon, I guessed it had once been a tithe barn, but by the looks of the patched and rotting wood, no cart loaded with grain or barrels of pickled pork had passed through those doors for many years. The man's bony fingers fastened on my wrist and drew me through a narrow doorway at the back of the building. I had to fight the urge to pull away, for it felt as if the cold, scaly claws of a hawk were gripping my bare skin.

I found myself inside a passageway so narrow my shoulders bumped against the wood on either side. I guessed we must be close to a privy, for my nose and throat stung with the stench of piss and shit. It was as dark as the Devil's arse. But the man seemed to know his way, turning abruptly and guiding my hand to a rickety rail which wobbled alarmingly as I gripped it.

'Up here. Follow me. Ten steps. But take care, the eighth is almost cracked through. Keep close to the wall.'

I edged up the steep staircase, painfully conscious that the rail would probably come away in my hand if I tried to use it to stop myself falling. The steps to my lodging in the Salt Cat creaked, but at least the wood felt solid underfoot. Each of these treads bowed beneath my weight and some swivelled underfoot as if only a single nail held them in place.

At the top of the stairs was another door, and finally we were inside. I sank to my haunches as the man propped his staff beside the door and crossed to the small brazier which glowed ruby red in the darkness. He lit a taper and held it to a candle impaled on an iron pricket. A yellow light lapped towards the edges of the room as the flame trembled, then began to burn steadily.

The room contained little, but still seemed crowded in the miserly space. A battered hutch table or monk's bench stood in the centre, the top laid flat, covered with several books, quills and paper, and the remains of a meagre supper on a wooden trencher. Since there was no sign of any other sleeping place, I guessed that the chest below served both as a store for bedding and as a bed. The remainder of the room was taken up by shelves, hung on ropes from the roof beams, on which books in various stages of decay were heaped, some without covers, others half chewed away by vermin.

The man motioned me to sit on a box, set on one side of the brazier. Taking a pair of spectacles from among the chaos of papers on the table, and lifting the candle, he bent close to me, peering at my wound. I tried not to flinch as he pressed a rag to it, wiping away the blood and grunting as he leaned closer. His breath was sour. A pungent odour of stale sweat and mould clung to the dark robe and his parchment skin. And the faint bitter-sweet note of something else, a perfume from so long ago that it only faintly stirred a memory, like a tiny creature that flips beneath the surface of the pond and vanishes before you can recognise it.

'You were fortunate, sirrah. You've a cut on your forehead, but the bone of the socket deflected the worst. Your eye is undamaged. The blood running into it is from the gash above. Press this rag to it until the bleeding eases. I've no cloth to spare for bandages, but I am sure you'll find a whore at the Salt Cat willing enough to tear her shift into strips for you, if none else can be found.'

He set the candle down on the hutch table and sank heavily down on to the battered chair on the opposite side of the brazier, massaging his knees.

So, his intervention was not the act of a man who had chanced upon the scene. He knew where I was lodging, maybe a great deal more. And there was something oddly familiar about the ponderous manner of his speech, the way he halted momentarily before the annunciation of each word as if to be certain he had selected the correct one. Had he been in the cellar the night of the cockfight?

'You sup at the Salt Cat?' I asked. 'You will have heard about the murder of one of the gamecock owners?'

The old man grunted. 'Half of Bristol's heard and unless you've a wish to be laid in the grave alongside him, you'd be well advised not to venture from the Salt Cat after dark. The merchants and craftsmen may own the streets by day, but when the sun sets the night creatures come crawling from their holes and the city is their hunting ground. A good number of the watch have been paid to turn their backs and watch the wall. The rest will not venture from their towers for fear of finding themselves floating in the river with a dagger in the ribs.' He gave a grunt of mirthless laughter. The left-hand side of his mouth jerked in a sudden spasm and his eye twitched. He pressed his hand hard against his face to supress it.

I glanced at the staff that lay ready at the door; it was a good aid to walking, but not even the carved eagle head on the top would be heavy enough to stun an assailant in the hands of this frail old man.

'But you are not afraid to go out or . . .' I'd been about to add *or challenge men half your age who run away at the sight of you*. Who can command the rats, except the king rat? I'd been left in no doubt as to the truth of that in Newgate. But the prisoners who wielded power were rarely the physically strongest. There were those who didn't need to use their own fists for they had the cunning and wit to dream up vicious reprisals and persuade other men to carry them out. Some had money enough to buy servitude. And there were the few who simply exuded the aura of those born to rule, as unchallengeable as the divine right bestowed on any king. But if this old man possessed any of these talents, surely he would not be living alone in such squalor.

'Fear is the wise man's shield,' my rescuer said softly. 'And so armed, I go where I am called, no matter what the hour.'

As he turned away from me, the glow of the brazier momentarily illuminated the outline of his hunched stance, just as the burning torches had done on the street when the mob dragged out the cordwainer's family. This was the old man I'd seen talking to Myles that night by the ruined wall.

'It was the boy who fetched you. Why?'

His brows lifted briefly as if he was half amused by the question. 'I understand you showed a kindness to young Myles, fed him. He was repaying the favour.'

'But why you? Why would the boy fetch you?'

'As I have already explained,' he said, his words delivered even more slowly and deliberately, 'it would be useless to alert the watch.'

As I have already explained. The exaggerated patience. I knew that voice. Something in the pit of my belly stirred uneasily.

'You're his kin? He told me he was alone, his family lost in the flood, but I'm sure the brat was lying.'

'He is alone, but his parents were lost long before the flood. Like a feral puppy, he latches on to anyone he thinks might give him a bite to eat or a coin in return for an errand. There are many beggars in Bristol who've discovered that strangers are more inclined to be generous if they claim to have lost family or home in the flood. The boy is merely aping what he's heard others do.'

Was someone paying Myles to keep watch on me?

'Those men who attacked me. They weren't footpads. They made no attempt to search me or demand money. Besides, in that fog, any cutpurse with a peck of skill could have had my purse and vanished before I'd had a chance to cry out.' I thought myself back into that street, trying to recall their exact words 'One said, "Ask him!" Ask me what – what did they want of me?'

The old man shrugged. 'You think I consort with such ruffians?'

'Yet those ruffians fled when you ordered them to go. Why should they obey you?'

'Be grateful they did, whelp. They have been known to gouge a man's eyes out, lead him to the harbour edge and amuse themselves watching him blunder around until he plunges off the edge. If I had not . . .'

He caught sight of the expression on my face as I scrambled to my feet, my fists clenched. The bloody rag that had covered my eye tumbled to the floor. He swiftly rose, turned his back to me, and began poking at the burning wood in the brazier until he was enveloped in the smoke, as grey and dense as the fog outside.

'What did you just call me?'

The old man raised one hand in a half-hearted gesture of apology, but he continued to poke at the embers, without looking round.

'I meant no insult by it. Some days, my temper is so ragged that I scarcely know what I am saying. You wait, one day you'll be wishing you were still young enough for men to call you pup, instead of old fool.'

My whole body had turned colder than a well in winter 'But you did not say *pup*, old man.' I was trying hard to keep my temper. '*Whelp* was the name you used. I've been called that many times before. It is a word I can never forget, nor can I forget the man who uttered it, Master Waldegrave.'

The bent back jerked upright as if a dagger had been plunged between those dry, fragile ribs, and for a sweet moment I felt my own hand pushing the blade, heard the cry of pain, of fear, saw the remorse in those rheumy eyes. But I knew there would never be any remorse in those eyes, no matter how deep the knife was thrust.

'I know no one of that name, sir.' The voice was calm and ice-cold. 'You should leave now, while the mist still covers you. Walk to the left, up the street. There you may find a link boy outside one of the taverns who will light the rest of your way to your lodging.'

'That fog can also conceal any man lying in wait for me. Is that what you hope? But first, isn't it customary when sending a man to his death to give him your blessing? Even felons on the gallows are granted as much.'

The old man didn't move.

I knelt down painfully on the creaking boards. 'Come now. See, I am grovelling at your feet like a true penitent. Surely you haven't forgotten the words. Why don't you look at me? That might jog your memory. You forced me to kneel for your blessing each time after you'd beaten me. Believe me, Father Thomas, I have good cause to remember every word. *Benedicat vos omnipotens Deus, Pater, et Fil –*'

'Stop, how dare you make a mockery of . . . ? Get up, get up!' The old man rounded on me, his face contorted in outrage. He half raised his hand, as if he meant to strike me, but instead he groped for the chair. He sank down on it with such a jolt that the wood groaned, though he could have weighed no more than a sack of chaff.

Maybe it was that sudden realisation that made my fury ebb away. I struggled to my feet and saw the old man raise his hand again, not in anger this time, but in fear, as if he expected a blow. Then, once more, he let it fall, lying limp and almost transparent in his lap as if he was resigned to whatever violence might come his way now, too weak to fight, too weary to resist.

I stared at him, as if I was seeing him for the first time. His eyes, moist in the candlelight, were sunk deep beneath bushy white eyebrows, prickly as thorn bushes, and silver-white stubble frosted his chin and neck. His skull was encased in a stained close-fitting linen cap and his doublet, once black, was turning green with age. Frayed thread hung from the shirt cuffs like torn spiders' webs. His breeches and doublet seemed to have been fashioned for a man twice his girth and I was seized with the notion that if I pulled them open, I would find nothing beneath them but a heap of dry bones.

This was no longer the priest and tutor I had once known and feared as a child; it was a pale wraith of a man long dead. It was like looking at an effigy on a tomb where on the top the nobleman is carved in all his finery and vigour, while the skeletal cadaver carved below reveals the rotting corpse he has become. Waldegrave hunched towards the brazier, massaging his swollen knuckles over its pitiful warmth. I stared around the damp, draughty room, at the water dripping on to rotting boards and the white fungi infesting the beams.

'This is a long way from Lord Fairfax's house, Master Waldegrave.'

'It seems we have both travelled far from there, Master Pursglove. That is what you call yourself now, is it not?'

'How did you learn I was in Bristol?'

'I saw you in the torchlight when you remonstrated with the Puritan the night they attacked Master Lightbound.'

'And you recognised me, after fifteen years?'

'Your frame has filled out, but there is much about you that is still the young man I last saw fifteen years ago. You are still trying to hide the hangman's mark with that high collar and unkempt beard, I see.'

'While you hide your miserable carcass in this rat hole,' I snapped, my anger rising again, made worse as I realised my fingers, unbidden, were raking my beard down over my firemark. I clenched my fist. My hand was sticky with blood.

'So, they finally threw you out, too,' I said. 'But I wager, unlike me, you were not cast out empty-handed. The Fairfax chalice alone would keep a man in food and wine for five years.'

Even as I said it, I caught sight of the remains of his supper on the table, a pottage of dried peas and bacon fat by the smell, with enough left in the bottom of the pot to be warmed again for breakfast. But then food was in scarce supply in the city. Even those who had a few coins could find little to buy.

A bitter smile plucked at Waldegrave's mouth, or perhaps it was another of his spasms. 'Do you really believe I would trade a holy vessel for mere food? After all those years under my tutelage, do you know me so little, Daniel? But since you are so concerned about the chalice, I can assure you it was concealed in a place of safety before I left the house, along with all the other objects so precious to us, until the wind should blow in our favour once more.

'And no, Master Pursglove, I was not dismissed in disgrace, as you were. I left five years ago, shortly before Lord Fairfax met with his accident. You know, of course, that he was killed.'

'A riding accident,' I said. I felt a stab of grief. George Fairfax had been kind to me in his own distant way while I was growing up with his son, Richard. The nearest man to a father I had ever known. Waldegrave's fingers twitched as if they were, from habit, trying to make the sign of the cross.

'Perhaps if I had stayed, I might have prevented . . .' His jaw hardened. 'But I persuaded Lord Fairfax that it would be safest for him and his household if I left. All the houses of any note in England that were suspected of being homes to Catholic sympathisers were being searched from the eves to the cellars. And with each search they made, Robert Cecil's men were learning more about where and how the priests were concealed. They were becoming ever more skilled at finding them and at questioning the servants to discover those priests like myself who hid in plain sight. If I had been arrested then Lord Fairfax and his son, too, would have been dragged to the Tower, caught in the net Cecil was casting. I have no care for my own safety, but I will be not be used to send others to their deaths.'

I studied my old tutor in the flickering light. No one could ever have questioned his devotion to the Fairfax family. I'd often thought the priest would more gladly lay down his life for his patron than for Christ. Even if George Fairfax, or that devious bastard Richard, had been involved in the plots against the Crown, I was convinced Waldegrave would go to the scaffold denying it. I don't even think he would have admitted the truth to his own confessor. The man who had thrashed me repeatedly for lying, when I'd spoken the truth, would not hesitate to lie for them.

And now here he was in Bristol. What had FitzAlan called it? *The nest of Jesuits.* Waldegrave had never shown any love for that Order – not when I'd known him, anyway – but that was fifteen years ago. Could he have changed his allegiance? Many moderate Catholics had turned increasing radical as King James had crushed their hopes of a return to the old faith.

'Bristol is a fair step from Yorkshire,' I said. 'I wonder you travelled so far, if your only concern was to ensure you weren't found on the Fairfax estate?'

'Bristol is many miles from London, too, and from the shadow cast by the King, which is why some men find they sleep sounder here on hard boards than they did in their own feather beds. And if the nets of Cecil's men should float too wide, from here a man might swiftly board one of the vessels bound for Spain, which slip in and out unnoticed from a dozen hidden creeks and moorings on this river.'

The same motive which brought Pettingar here. 'Was that the only reason you came to Bristol?' I watched the old man's face carefully.

Waldegrave made a growling noise deep in his throat. 'Even as a boy you were never content with a simple answer. For every *why* you were given, you always demanded a dozen *wherefores.* I warned you often enough it will be the death of you, whelp.'

He sagged, as if he was too weary to resist any more. 'The missionaries come here and make their converts, then they move on. It is too dangerous for them to remain and they are sorely needed elsewhere. But since the Oath of Allegiance was imposed, many converts, as well as those born to the old faith, have fallen away. It is not just the wealthy recusants who face fines. It wounds them, but they can pay and still survive. But if the poor cannot pay their fines, the King's men seize their goods, the goats that give their children milk, the plough from their fields, the tools from the blacksmith's forge or the cobbler's workshop. I've even heard of them dragging the bed from a cottage in which a woman was giving birth. Many have become terrified and renounced their faith.

'The day of Father Garnet's infamous trial, the day he was found guilty of treason for refusing to break the seal of the confessional, drove fear deep into the heart of every Catholic in England. A consecrated priest condemned to the horrors of a traitor's death for no other crime than keeping a sacred vow made before God! And ever since that foul apostate and traitor to our faith, John Smith, was released from prison, Robert Cecil has been using that renegade to terrify the faithful into giving up their recusancy, and they listen to Smith, because he was once a Catholic like them. His is an evil which must be fought, and I must fight it. It is what I am called to do.'

I studied the old man's face. I could feel his passion, see in his eyes the blaze of anger boiling inside him. Would he be content simply to pray with those whose faith was wavering? Or was he involved in something even more dangerous? He had admitted that, from Bristol, men might escape to Spain and the missionaries just as easily steal in. If Rachael was correct, the castle was one of the conduits through which people were smuggled, but someone had to be helping the Jesuits to find such routes. It could not be pure coincidence that Waldegrave had chosen to minister to the faithful in this particular city.

The old priest darted a pointed glance at me. 'And you, *Master Pursglove*, what exactly brings you here?' He wagged a warning finger. 'Don't try that foolish tale of searching for your aunt and her children. You have no kin. The truth, Daniel. I could always tell when you were lying.'

My jaw clenched. *You could never tell when I was speaking the truth, old man, nor when Richard was lying. Justice is truly blind. But no, that's not quite true, is it? Your eyes were wide open, but you chose not to see.*

I tried to crush my anger. I badly needed answers. If Spero Pettingar was in Bristol, Waldegrave was the one man who might know. I've heard soldiers before a battle, prisoners languishing in chains, and travellers sheltering in barns confide things to each other they would not reveal to their dearest kin. A shared adversity makes blood brothers even of enemies. And if the old man believed I, too, was a fugitive who might be in need of an escape route . . .

'I have been forced to turn my hand to many things since I left Lord Fairfax's household, but of late I have earned a living entertaining, turning sticks into writhing snakes at fairs, or making wine seem to flow out of stone walls in great houses.'

'I remember, when you were a boy, how you pestered the jesters and fools Lord Fairfax employed at Christmas to teach you how to make rings vanish and eggs dance in mid-air. It is a pity you did not attend to your lessons with as much diligence. But that does not answer my question, or did you think there were riches to be earned by a fool in a devastated city?'

My jaw clenched. 'I earned enough in London, but the populace there have become wary of such illusions. They now fear it is more than mere tricks.'

I had always smiled to myself whenever I'd caught old crones surreptitiously crossing their fingers to ward off enchantment as I made birds fly from empty boxes or crosses turn without any hand touching them. But it takes just one person to cry sorcery, for laughter to shatter into fear and coins transform into chains.

'I thought it wise to remove myself to a place where I was not known. As you say, Bristol is far from London, though judging by the attack on me tonight, it may not be far enough.'

'It was not your tricks that made those men follow you, but your questions,' Waldegrave said, studying me carefully. 'If you are here to hide, it is curious that you should be asking about printers – unless, of course, you are thinking of adding that profession to your list of accomplishments?'

'Since you knew a man was murdered at the Salt Cat, you must surely have already learned he was a printer.'

'Did you kill him?' Waldegrave demanded.

Did you break that pot, whelp? Did you tear that book? Did you steal? Did you? DID YOU!

'No!' I took a deep breath. 'But I saw the body,' I added in a quieter tone. 'The man had been stabbed, but there was a sign on his chest. A sign which, after what happened to the cordwainer and his family, I thought wise to obliterate before it was seen.'

I paused, studying the old priest for any reaction, but his features were flowing like melted wax in the flickering candlelight, and I could read nothing. But then that wily hawk had always known how to mask his thoughts.

'The mark took the form of letters,' I said carefully. 'I . . . H . . . S.'

Waldegrave gave a shrug. 'I have heard that pilgrims in Jerusalem have their bodies inscribed with the sign of some shrine or holy place they have visited.'

'I've seen one man so marked,' I said. 'But his emblem was made by pricking ink into the skin. This had been burned into the man's chest.'

Waldegrave flapped his hand impatiently. 'A talisman, then. A mark to keep him safe. Men adorn themselves with all manner of amulets, both holy and profane together. Is it to be wondered at that Christ does not hear their prayers?'

He sighed and drew a deep breath, coughing and wheezing. Painfully, he levered himself from his chair, dragged it closer to the brazier and held his palms over the heat. I saw hands gripping a birch rod, knuckles white with righteousness and rage; hands holding the chalice aloft in that tiny hidden chapel, the neatly trimmed nails gleaming in the candlelight. But these were not the hands I remembered, not these bird's claws, not these broken nails blue with cold, the skin so paper thin I almost begged him to stop rubbing them for fear it would tear away.

Waldegrave stared down into the dying flames. When he spoke again his voice was dull, exhausted. 'I will not press you further to tell me your real business here. I do not wish to carry any more secrets; those I already bear are too heavy. But I beg you to listen to me, as you once did as a boy, as your priest, as your old tutor, as . . . as one who wishes you safe. There are many of the old faith in the city, some who were born here, others newly come who seek refuge here, some good men and some evil, but all are desperate to stay alive.'

The terrified and bloodied faces of the cordwainer and his family, on that cart, rose up in front of me and I found myself squeezing my eyes shut in a futile attempt to banish them, but they would not leave me.

'They know Robert Cecil has spies everywhere,' Waldegrave continued, 'and when a man comes to a devastated port who does no business here, yet has a fine horse and money enough in his purse to pay for lodgings, he is bound to be suspected. You said that those men who attacked you had not done so to rob you. No, they believed you to be one of those spies. And they do not treat such men with any more mercy than the King treats those he suspects of being traitors. I know you would never betray those of your own faith, but others may not be so easily persuaded of that, even by your swift tongue. Take care, I beg you, Daniel. Take great care. Next time I may arrive too late.'

Chapter Eighteen

THE YARD OF THE SALT CAT was in darkness, the inn had long closed, for not even the hardened drinkers and gamblers lingered long at night when a fret was billowing across the city. No one wanted to find themselves walking those streets alone. The fog had even quietened the children in lodgings, silenced, no doubt, as I had been as a small boy, by the tales of the white women who rise from the rivers and the sea cloaked in the mist and glide through the streets, pressing their chill faces against the casements, calling to the living to come and play with them in the cold, black water. A few weeks ago, the children of this city might have laughed at their grandmothers' stories, but they had seen their playmates taken in a heartbeat and they were not laughing now.

I groped my way across the courtyard, breathing more easily now. I slid the dagger I'd been gripping back into its sheath and grasped the wooden rail of the staircase. My head was still pounding from the blow. My cut eyelid had swollen up, almost closing one eye, and my body ached with the tension of holding myself ready to ward off any attack. But in just a few more strides, I'd be safe inside my own chamber, able to bolt the door and breathe easily. Sleep was what my body craved now, that and maybe a beaker or two of wine first, for I wasn't sure that sleep would come without it. Thoughts and memories were clamouring for attention in my head like an angry mob, but I didn't want to confront any of them, not tonight.

I glanced upwards at my door as I wearily mounted the stairs. The door was unlatched and open just a finger's breadth. Yellow light shimmered in the crack. But I had left no lamp burning, for I'd not returned since morning. Once more, I drew my dagger. The hilt was still warm from where I'd last held it. I adjusted my balance. If someone was standing behind the door, waiting to strike as I entered, I wanted to make quite sure they didn't get a chance.

I kicked the door wide, as hard as I could. It slammed back against the wall inside with a crash that immediately brought cries from babies and shouts of alarm from the sleepers below, but all my attention was focused on the muffled cry which came from inside my own room.

Sweeping the dagger in front of me, I slid round the edge of the door frame and stood with my back pressed to the wall. Someone darted across the room, snatched up the candle and whirled round to face me, pulling the candle from the iron pricket as they did. Brandishing the iron candlestick in one hand, they raised the lighted candle in the other. Only as the light fell on her face did I register who it was.

'Rachael!'

'You nearly frightened me out of my skin, crashing in like that, not to mention waking half the street. Are you bousy?'

She set her makeshift weapon down and pushed the candle back on its spike. Somewhere below us, an infant was bawling, while men cursed at it.

I returned the dagger to my belt for the second time. 'Sober as a Puritan. But when a man returns to his chambers at this hour of the night, I think it's natural to be on his guard if he sees someone prowling about his chamber.'

'I was not prowling. Brought you some supper earlier, came back to fetch the dish, but when I saw you still hadn't returned, I was worried. Halfwit like you wandering around in this fret, anything could . . .'

The room was spinning, the floor pitched beneath me. I staggered forward a few paces, reaching for the beam to steady myself.

Rachael's expression changed in an instant as the light from the candle fell on me. 'You're hurt!'

In a flash she was at my side, supporting me to the bed and gently pushing me down on it. 'I warned you not to go sniffing around, now see what's happened. And did you learn anything for your pains?' She held the flame close to my face, examining it as Waldegrave had done, but her breath was a great deal warmer and sweeter.

'Only that men in Bristol mistrust all strangers.'

'I could have told you that and spared your face. You need to stay well away from Skinner's men, else you are liable to end like Master Harewell.' She lightly touched the cut. 'It's stopped bleeding, but it needs tending, else it'll fester. Don't you move.'

I heard her footfalls clattering down the steps and lay back, closing my eyes. If those men were Catholics, it would account for the old priest's command of them, but were they more than that? Ever since the Gunpowder Treason, it seemed that hardly a week had passed without new layers of the conspiracy being unpeeled, leading to new arrests – relatives, friends, servants, each forced to name others, friends of those friends, men and women accused of giving the plotters aid or sheltering them when they fled. And what of those who had escaped, like Spero Pettingar, would they want to show they still had teeth?

Rachael returned carrying a pitcher of water and a basket. She sat beside me on the bed and cleaned away the dried blood with a wetted cloth, then smeared some foul-smelling green ointment over the cut, which stung like salt and made me jerk away. She laughed, calling me a baby, but she was gentle. I could feel the warmth of her thigh against my own. It was a long time since anyone had touched me with such tenderness. I slid my hand round her waist, pulling her closer towards me, and kissed her soft, warm mouth.

She jerked away, springing off the bed, and slapped my cheek so hard it made my head ring again.

'Don't you dare touch me! You think that any woman who

works in an inn is a whore and you can buy her as easily as a flagon of ale or platter of meat.'

'I didn't think that,' I protested. 'I only wanted—'

'I know exactly what you wanted. You bought bed and board here, Master Pursglove, and that is all. If you want more, you take yourself to the Mermaid or Mother Kitty's. I'm sure you'll find girls there willing enough to oblige you.' She stormed from the room, slamming the door behind her, and clattered down the stairs.

I lay stunned, cursing myself for my own idiocy. Did my firemark disgust her so much? Did I? I reached for the jug of wine. I'd no appetite for food, but I drank until the jug was dry and flopped back on the pillow, wanting to think of nothing except sleep. But in spite of the wine, sleep would not come. Waldegrave's withered old face kept rearing up; I had thought the old anger that had almost destroyed me when I first left Fairfax's house had died long ago, but now I knew it had only drawn back into the shadows. I didn't hate him for the many times he had beaten me. It had almost become a game of power, each flogging only strengthening my determination not to let him break me.

No, I hated him because he had fashioned me into a creature that I was never intended to be, like those men who exhibited the dead beasts they have made – a cat with chicken wings, a rabbit with horns, a fish with a monkey's head. I'd come howling into this world in the poorest cottage in the village, but I had been raised in the wealthiest house in the shire. I could pass myself off as a nobleman, but I could never become one, and neither could I return to the life into which I had been born; he had made sure of that.

But Waldegrave was no longer the towering figure who had loomed over my childhood. How could any man have aged so much in fifteen years? It was as if a revenant, risen from the grave, had fed on him each night, sucking the living spirit out of him, returning to its grave bloated with his blood and leaving him a withered husk. As a youth, if I had ever dreamed I would see that power brought so low, made so frail, so feeble, I would have been dancing with glee. But now I felt nothing but hollowness.

As the wine took hold and pulled me down into sleep, a chilling thought seized me. What if FitzAlan had sent a spy to watch me, as he had threatened? Had I unwittingly led them to a priest in hiding? Waldegrave might be an old man now, but that had never yet saved anyone from the gallows.

Chapter Nineteen

LONDON

CHARLES FITZALAN had arrived early, almost an hour before the appointed time, and in consequence had been obliged to wait for so long he had almost begun to doze in the heat of the brazier. But his head jerked up at the dull thud of hooves on grass and, peering out of the tiny casement, he glimpsed movement among the trees in the fading light. He grasped the hilt of his sword, drawing it smoothly from its sheath. A single horse and rider were making their way towards the boathouse. FitzAlan watched them draw closer, saw the rider dismount and tether the beast in the thicket. Twilight gives better cover than darkness, for it leaches away all colour, blurs all forms, tricking the eye into thinking that a bush is a wolf or a man is a rock. In the ghost light, no witness can trust themselves to swear to anything they've seen for certain.

FitzAlan waited, sword in hand, where he would be shielded by the stout wood of the door as it opened, should the rider prove not to be who he was expecting. But the precaution was unnecessary, though it did not temper his foul humour.

'You are late! Am I to be kept kicking my heels waiting on your pleasure?'

This was untrue, but Cimex knew better than to protest the injustice.

'Well, what news?' FitzAlan demanded. Then, noticing for the first time that his guest was breathless and coughing in the damp, chill air, he flapped his hand impatiently to indicate they both should sit. 'Spero Pettingar, has Daniel found him?'

Cimex shifted uncomfortably in the chair. 'We don't know for certain Pettingar is in Bristol. He may not even be in England. Father Tesimond and Father Gerard both managed to evade capture and slip away from these shores, John Gerard on the very day of Father Garnet's execution.'

FitzAlan scowled. 'Aided by the English Catholics and smuggled into the Spanish Ambassador's train, disguised as a footman. Yet more proof of Spanish interference in the affairs of this realm.'

Cimex gave a short laugh. 'They say Father Tesimond did not have such a pleasant crossing to Calais, though. He travelled with a cargo of dead pigs.'

'Would that his own miserable carcass was lying eviscerated among them. It shows how cunning these Jesuit foxes can be, and how our English priests conspire with their foreign brothers.' FitzAlan had gripped the hilt of his sword and was sliding the blade up and down in the scabbard, ramming it home with increasing ferocity.

Cimex swallowed. 'As you say, my lord, but that makes it more likely Spero Pettingar has already been spirited abroad by them.'

'If he had, we would have heard about it. These Jesuits flaunt their escapes to thumb their noses at us from beyond the sea.'

'Then,' Cimex ventured cautiously, 'might it be that Spero Pettingar is not a priest at all? Perhaps he is merely a lowly servant of one of the gunpowder conspirators. If his master is dead, he alone can pose no more threat—'

FitzAlan slammed his fist down on the table that stood between them. 'He is no servant! Though doubtless he'll be hiding in some pauper's garret, trying to pass himself off as one.' He was breathing hard. Sweat glistened on his forehead. He levered himself to his feet and paced restlessly around the room, finally returning to the chair. He stood gripping the back of it, staring down, as if wrestling with his own thoughts.

'A document has lately come into my possession. It is signed by Pettingar, and inscribed with the Devil's letters. It speaks of something only the King and his most trusted adviser could know. This has happened once before, You will recall the circumstances?'

He glanced sharply at the bewildered face before him.

'You had intercepted an earlier letter . . . from Pettingar?' Cimex asked.

'No!' FitzAlan slammed his fist into the wood again. 'My meaning is that *sorcery* was used once before to divine something only the King would know.' He sighed and his tone softened. 'I suppose you cannot be expected to have heard that tale. Doubtless, it was not repeated in London as often as it was in Scotland.' FitzAlan sank back into the chair and stared morosely out at the black waters of the lake.

'It occurred fifteen . . . sixteen years ago. Francis Stewart, the Earl of Bothwell, reckoned to lay claim to the Crown, for his father was the bastard son of James V, our good King's grandfather. Bothwell was a staunch Catholic, and there were those who would have liked nothing more than to see his backside firmly seated upon the Scottish throne. And if our King could not sire an heir, it is likely Bothwell would succeed to the Crown, so he tried by every means to prevent the King's marriage. He was a foul creature. He had made a pact with the Devil and had seventy witches, some say more, at his command. When the King was returning from Denmark with his young bride, the witches conjured a violent storm in a calm sea. One of the fleet of ships was lost, and the King's ship almost floundered. But God protected him and brought them safe ashore.'

'But Pettingar's letter. I don't understand. Did it concern this . . . ?' The question shrivelled away beneath FitzAlan's furious glare.

FitzAlan continued as if he had not been interrupted. 'Bothwell was arrested for high treason, but like those Jesuit foxes, he escaped with the aid of the Devil. But the witches were hunted down. The first woman to be arrested was a servant whose master grew suspicious that she crept from his house at night. She refused to confess at first, but when her master and his friends put her to grievous torture, she admitted she had cast spells to try to kill the King, and she named others. Most were unlettered women, ignorant and of a wanton and brutish nature that made them easily seduced by the Devil. But one, Agnes Sampson, was not of the base kind and her answers were grave and considered. She stubbornly refused to confess, but after she had been stripped and shaved, the witch's teat was found in her intimate place. After she was forced into the witch's bridle and thrawn with a rope about her head, she, too, confessed to many attempts to cause injury to the King by means of wax dolls and the King's garments, which had been stolen for her. She said that she and the other witches raised that terrible storm by baptising a cat and casting it into the sea with dead men's limbs tied to its paws.

'So many things did she confess concerning the witches' sabbats and their spells that the King could not believe she spoke the truth, until she whispered to him something that had passed between him and his bride on their wedding night. He was certain then that she was a witch.'

FitzAlan once more prised himself up and crossed to the casement overlooking the lake. Without turning, he said, 'That is why the King is certain Pettingar, or whatever his true name is, will prove himself to be the most dangerous of all the gunpowder conspirators; the deadly viper that strikes in the darkness and slithers away unseen. If he is not a sorcerer himself then, like Bothwell, he has summoned witches to aid him, and that letter is proof of it. How else could Pettingar have knowledge of what he writes in that message, except by witchcraft? And this priest is

being aided by the Jesuit network. Why else would h
signed it with those Devil's letters of the Jesuits – IHS?'

Cimex hesitated. FitzAlan was already angry, and it was not
wise to annoy a man like him still further. 'My lord, is it not
possible that the writer of the letter merely bribed a palace servant to discover whatever information he has learned? Servants
see and hear more than their masters like to think, and what they
don't witness they can often guess at with disturbing accuracy.'

FitzAlan wasn't listening. 'I fear I have sent the wrong man
to Bristol. The King by his divine anointing is able to withstand
the spells that are cast against him, for he has God's shield for
protection. But Daniel is already weakened in that he was raised
a Catholic. Will he be able to withstand such curses if they are
worked against him?'

'My lord, you know that Daniel is skilled in the art of legerdemain, one of the most skilled in England, from what I have
witnessed. He—'

'Tricks are no protection against witchcraft, and those very
skills he possesses that I have sought to use in defence of the
Crown could equally be used against the King, if Pettingar turns
him to their side. A man like Daniel would be a valuable and
dangerous weapon for his cause. I want him watched every
minute of the day and night, and if there is a shred of doubt as
to his loyalty, I want him dead.'

Chapter Twenty

DANIEL PURSGLOVE

THE SHRIEKS OF THE CHILDREN quarrelling in the courtyard below, and the screaming gulls squabbling on the roof above, told me I'd already slept far later than I'd meant to, but my head was still throbbing from the blow I'd taken the night before. I dashed the dregs of the brackish, brown water in the ewer against my face. Saltwater was seeping into everything, even wells that had at first been spared, as if the city was a floating island cast adrift and sea was lapping beneath every house and alley.

Flinging open the casement, I startled several pigeons fluffed up against the cold. An icy wind had sprung up, but at least it had blown away the fog, though the narrow street outside was so dark that for a moment I thought I must have slept through the day and it was evening again. But the women wandering up and down trying to sell a lump of grey meat, a tawdry brooch or a doll fashioned from scraps of cloth were the morning pedlars; the women who wandered the streets at twilight sold the pleasures of the flesh. Rachael's words came back to me, burning far sharper than any slap.

I dressed quickly and hurried out. But as I stepped out of my chamber at the top of the stairs, I felt something skid away from under my boot. I crouched and retrieved it. It was a small, heavy object wrapped in a scrap of paper, tied with a knotted cord. I slipping the cord off as I stood up. A lump of stone fell out, about the size of a chicken's egg, a fragment of a carving, perhaps, for there were chisel marks on it and flakes of paint still clinging to one side. I turned it over in my hand. It looked as if it had once been the eye of a large statue.

Three children from one of the rooms below mine were attempting to circle the courtyard on the piles of broken furniture, without touching the ground. One of them paused, balancing on the top of a broken table, and stared up at me.

I held out the piece of stone. 'Is this yours?'

The girl solemnly shook her tousled head.

'Did you see who left this up here?'

She stared at me, frowning, then resumed her game. It was hardly surprising my question made no sense to the child, half the city was covered in broken stone. I was about to drop it, when I glanced at the paper it had been wrapped in. Something was written on it. The letters were formed in an educated script, but inscribed with an unsteady hand.

'Come to the High Cross at the lighting of the lamps, when you will see more clearly.'

I turned it over, searching for more, but the note was without signature, nor was it addressed to anyone. If it meant *come at dusk*, then why not say so, or simply name the hour? But the phrase *the lighting of the lamps* seemed carefully selected and it plucked at a half-submerged memory.

I folded the note carefully and pushed it into the small drawstring purse that hung at my belt containing a few small coins I kept ready at hand. I was about to throw the stone away, thinking it had simply been used to weigh down the message. But the fragment of carving also seemed to have been selected for some purpose. I hurried back inside and hid the stone in a dark corner, on one of the low beams. It would do no harm to keep it.

As I crossed the courtyard, I caught sight of someone standing motionless in the shadow of the doorway on the opposite side of the street. One of my attackers from last night? No, those ruffians had been stocky, solid men. I could only see the outline of this figure, but he seemed the very opposite of solid, more like a shadow cast on water. A cart rattled up the street, forcing those on foot to flatten themselves against walls and doorways. As soon as the cart had trundled past, I stared back at the doorway, but it was empty.

I had already decided to search for Myles, convinced that he could tell me something about what Waldegrave was up to. I kept to the streets, where there was a continuous ebb and flow of people, and I avoided the wharf and river, too. A quick shove from behind and I could easily find myself floating in the swift current or drowning in the deep mud. There was no sense in inviting trouble, but I wasn't going to start jumping at every shadow, like the King.

They say he lives in constant fear of assassination – which is hardly surprising, since his own father was murdered. He's not short of enemies, that's for certain, even among his friends. Still, I was beginning to understand what it felt like to see murder in the eyes of every man, and a poisoned dagger beneath every cloak, for I could not shake off the feeling that I was being followed.

Men and lads leaned against the walls in the shadows, in deep conversation or eyeing those who passed by, their hoods drawn low over their faces, and not just against the wind. Some held dogs straining against stout leashes or chains. Their ears were ragged, their muzzles and flanks criss-crossed with white scars and livid swollen bites. They snarled and snapped whenever another dog or man drew close, much to the amusement of their masters. As a matronly woman walked by, one of the brutes lunged at her, causing her to stagger back against a lad lounging on the other side of the street. A cutpurse, I guessed. Another of Skinner's gang?

I drew into the shelter of a doorway, glancing behind me to ensure that no one was closing in. Someone was hurrying up the street. Though little daylight squeezed between the overhanging storeys of the buildings, I had seen that shape, that gliding walk, the urchin tilt of the head often enough since my arrival to recognise them instantly. Rachael was walking towards me, a cloth-covered bundle cradled in her arms, but she hadn't seen me. I was about to step out, when she halted and turned to face a set of narrow wooden stairs that led upwards between two of the buildings. She was talking earnestly to someone hidden from my view. She reached up, handing the bundle to them. One of her arms remained outstretched as if she was being gripped by whoever was standing there. Someone was trying to drag her up those stairs.

I ran towards her, calling her name. She spun round, eyes wide in alarm, but then she seemed to recognise me. She glanced back towards the steps before taking a pace towards me, just as I reached her.

'Why are you here? Are you following me?'

'No!' I said indignantly. 'I came to help you, because I saw someone trying to grab you.'

'The only person who's done that was you, last night.' But her gaze flicked nervously back towards the steps.

I took a pace round her and stared up. The narrow staircase disappeared round the edge of the building. There was no one standing there, though someone had been, I was sure, for I heard the stairs creaking above and the sound of shoes softly striking wood.

'See? All alone,' she said, spreading her arms wide. 'So, there was no cause for you to come charging to my rescue.' She tossed the remark over her shoulder as she swept off, back in the direction of the Salt Cat.

I stared after her. When Rachael had walked down the street, she'd been carrying a bundle. Now her arms were empty. And with all my magician's art, not even I could have made that package vanish into thin air.

Chapter Twenty-one

I'D ALMOST FORGOTTEN about the message, until I was passing an inn late in the afternoon. The smell of stewed pigeon wafted out, making me suddenly hungry. As I dug into my purse, I felt the crinkle of paper and, drawing it out, I read the words again.

'*Come to the High Cross at the lighting of the lamps, when you will see more clearly.*'

The lighting of the lamps, why did that resonate somewhere at the back of my head? It could, of course, be a trap. The men who had attacked me didn't seem the sort to shrug and walk away if their quarry escaped them. On the other hand, neither were they likely to send cryptic notes. But hounds always have their masters, the plotters and the schemers, the creatures of mist and shadow, who quietly whisper the orders to kill, but never risk bruising their own fists on their victims' skulls. But if someone was trying to lure me to my death, they'd choose a less public rendezvous than the High Cross, which stood right at the heart of the city.

The feeble winter light was already draining from the narrow streets, leeching colour from clothes and skin. Almost sunset, not far off the hour when all the goodwives in the city would be lighting their candles and setting them in the windows to guide their sons and husbands home . . . I let out a snort of laughter, startling two whey-faced girls, who drew to the side, then hurried on staring round at me, whispering to each other and giggling as if I was a madman. The hour . . . hora. *Lucernaria hora.* The hour of the lighting of the lamps. I should have recognised that phrase at once; it had been drilled into us often enough as boys.

'What is the most important of the canonical hours, Master Richard?'

'Vespers, sir.'

'Excellent, Master Richard. And you, Daniel, I see you are wool gathering as usual. No? Then you will be able to tell us why vespers should be counted so . . . Come now, you read the passage I set you, did you not? Give me another of its names.'

'Lu . . . lucernaria hora, sir.'

'And what does that mean? Think, whelp, think.'

Waldegrave – the message could only be from him. I could have kicked myself. He'd probably sent Myles to deliver it and I might have nabbed the brat, had I woken sooner. But the old man had seemed reluctant to tell me anything last night. Had the few coins I'd given him been enough to soften that withered old heart, or was he greedy for more? Anger and resentment bubbled up in me again. I would not be summoned as if I was a school-boy, tested to see if I had remembered my lessons. I crumpled the scrap of paper, flinging it into the overflowing sewer where it floated among the rotting fish and turds. Let that old serpent starve in his foul nest. It would do him good; a priest should learn humility.

I strode furiously down the street in the opposite direction of the High Cross. But my pace gradually slowed. If there was a chance of squeezing any drop of information from that bag of dry bones, I could not afford to dismiss it, otherwise I would be back starving in the Hole with the prospect of far worse to follow. I turned and marched up towards Corn Street.

The High Cross stood upon its plinth in the middle of the crossroads, the slender lacy spire jutting into the darkening sky. Statues of the kings of England glowered from its alcoves down each of the four streets, reminding anyone plotting rebellion that the authority of kings was only one tier below that of God. The whole edifice resembled one of the pinnacles on the corners of the square church towers. It looked strangely out of place amid the shops and the bustle of people, handcarts and horses that wove around it, as if a mischievous imp flying past some cathedral tower, had broken off a turret and dropped it in the centre of Bristol. Perhaps the city thought it alien, too, for the stone was sorely in need of repainting. The blue and gold had flaked away in great patches and only the vermillion robes of the kings remained vivid.

Now that the markets had closed and the shops were beginning to fasten their shutters, three beggars had climbed on to the plinth and settled themselves in the space between its pillars. Passing an earthenware jar of some liquid between them, they clattered their staffs against the stone, shrieking at the passers-by to give them coins and insulting those who didn't.

I'd seen that trick played too often to be fooled by it. The mumpers were nowhere near as drunk as they pretended and would have been off like hares at the first sign of the constable's men. I glanced towards the edges of the small square, searching for their accomplices. I spotted a couple of lads lurking in the archway of a shop that had already closed for the night, then I saw one peel off to follow a stout merchant who'd drawn to the far side of street to avoid the beggars; in a flash the lad was back, slipping something inside his shirt. His victim wouldn't even realise his purse was gone till he reached home.

More people were surging through the streets now, some hurrying towards the gates leading out of the city, others heading towards their homes. Carters were trying to force their way through. One, driving down Wine Street, was wildly gesticulating to the carter coming towards him to pull over to the side and give him room to pass. Just as the two drew level, the cart driving up the street lurched sideways in a large hole, titling it towards the other. The two locked together, becoming wedged ever tighter as the horses strained forward and the furious drivers yelled insults and orders at one another, lashing out with their long whips.

I grudgingly conceded that my old tutor had chosen our meeting place well. In all this commotion, no one was even troubling to glance at the faces of those they passed. The streets leading off the square were already dark, and though daylight lingered longer at the crossroads, even here it was becoming hard to distinguish any man's features. I shivered. The day had never been warm, but the night had a new icy edge to it.

It was his stillness that caught my attention. He was standing at the end of High Street, and in the twilight his face was as pale as moonlight against his dark clothes. I could not make out his features, but the way he lowered his head had not changed, like a hawk watching for its prey to break cover. With an imperious flick of his eagle-head staff Master Waldegrave turned and began to thread his way down High Street. I hurried round the High Cross and plunged after him, my mood darkening with every stride.

We wove through the jostle of people, keeping our distance from each other, ducking repeatedly to avoid being brained by labourers and apprentices hefting ladders, planks of wood, kegs and faggots of kindling. When we reached the bank of the Avon, the tide had retreated from the estuary leaving only a narrow ribbon of water in the middle, and the boats had sunk down on to the steep slopes of thick, glutinous mud, their mooring ropes taut as drawn bowstrings. Some of the larger ships had tilted at such an angle that I wondered how the weight of their masts had not dragged them all the way over. The mud must be holding them fast like glue.

Waldegrave picked his way along the bank through the great piles of rotting seaweed and smashed wood that the flood had dumped there. The warehouses that lined the wharf here had taken a heavy beating. Some of the walls had collapsed into the river, the earth below them washed away. Roofs had fallen in or hung perilously from twisted beams, looking as if they might come crashing down if so much as a pigeon alighted on them. Those that still stood had been boarded up, to keep out the looters or the weather or both.

Waldegrave stopped and glanced up and down the length of the wharf. It was deserted but for a few seagulls settling for the night and several cats watching them from beneath upturned boats or the top of broken walls. Without saying a word to me, Waldegrave walked into the narrow space between a ruined warehouse and a disused work yard, and vanished. Slipping over something foul and stinking, I cursed as I hurried after him into the dark alleyway. My foot slid down into nothing and I was forced to throw myself back against the warehouse wall to keep from falling. I was teetering on the edge of a rectangular hole, and for a moment I thought that the old man must have plunged to his death, but a spark flashed in the darkness beneath me, and as a candle flame began to burn steadily, I saw an open trapdoor, with a set of rough stone steps below.

'Lower the door behind you. There is a rope.'

I clambered down the first wet and slippery steps, feeling around for the rope. I tugged, ducking as the wooden door flipped over and fell into place above me with a hollow thud.

Waldegrave was standing at the bottom of the steps, holding a lantern and peering upwards as I descended. Beyond him there appeared to be a tunnel roughly hewn out of the rock, disappearing into the darkness. Patches of poison-green slime glistened in the candlelight.

'What is this place?' I demanded.

'The entrance to one of the cellars. There is a honeycomb of them under Bristol. Further into the city, the shopkeepers and craftsmen use them to store their goods. Along the wharf, the merchants use them to stack wine, skins, barrels of fish, whatever the ships bring in or out. But many of the entrances are well concealed. There are things hidden in some that their owners would not want the King's men to find.'

'Smuggling?'

'So I am told. The Bristol merchants will always avoid paying taxes if they can. It is regarded here as an art as skilful as the craft of the silversmith, and the man who does it well is applauded by all, even by those officials in Bristol who should be upholding the law.'

'Is that all they hide, uncustomed goods?' I demanded sharply.

The populace believed that the gunpowder plotters had spent months digging a tunnel under Parliament – *the Devil of the Vault* – waiting to burst up through the earth. Rowe, my erstwhile master, had chuckled that it was one of Cecil's particularly creative inventions, and the commons certainly relished the thrill of the tale. But the truth was the plotters had no need of a tunnel, the barrels of gunpowder had easily been smuggled into the open cellars below Parliament. And rumour had it that stockpiles of weapons had been hidden in other cellars, too, right across England, ready for the uprising that had been meant to follow. How much more could be hidden beneath Bristol, brought in by those foreign ships – not only guns and gunpowder, but also the men trained to use them.

My old tutor regarded me for a long moment, then turned away without giving an answer. He held up the lantern in front of him. Peering round him, I caught a glimpse of the floor beyond; golden tongues of candle flame were bouncing from the surface and I saw with a jolt that the surface was undulating. Then I realised what I was looking at – water! The tunnel was flooded. Whatever had been stored here, there would be little evidence of it now.

Waldegrave set the lantern down, stretched out his staff and dipped the eagle's head into the water. He swept it back and forth, then gave a grunt of satisfaction. He drew the staff upwards. The sharply curved beak of the carved eagle had hooked a rope, fastened to the wall below the water's surface. Thrusting the staff into my hands, he pulled steadily on the rope until a small, crudely fashioned raft slid out of the darkness and bumped against the step. Taking back the staff, he thrust it down into the water like a punter's pole, stepped unsteadily on to the makeshift craft and unfastened the rope. The raft wobbled violently but steadied as he positioned himself, feet wide, to balance it.

'Put the lantern on first; we shall have need of it. Then you had better lie flat. I fear two of us standing may tip it over.' Seeing me hesitate, he added, 'I assure you it has borne two men before, and the waters were higher then.'

I knelt down on the wet steps and wriggled forward till I was lying face down on the rough, wet wood, and then I rolled over on to my back. The raft rocked perilously. Icy water splashed over my legs and seeped beneath me, soaking the few parts of my clothes that were still dry. Stinking black water gurgled on either side of my head. But at least, on my back, I felt less like a penitent prostrating myself at the feet of a priest.

Using his staff as a pole, Waldegrave pushed us forward. I saw that the floodwater was no more than thigh height. All the same, I'd no wish to find myself wading through it; there was no knowing what might be lying smashed on the bottom to impale or cut. Each time Waldegrave lifted his staff, water sprayed my face and ran on to my lips. It was foul, salty and stinking like a barrel of rotten herring.

The lantern light caught the dark recesses of low archways in the rough walls on either side. I guessed they must be entrances to storerooms or more tunnels, but all I could see inside as we glided past was the oily sheen of dark water. The rock glistened in the yellow candlelight. Fat drops of water clung to tendrils of slime, swelling and engorging until they dropped with a splash. The roof seemed to be getting lower the further in we went, pressing down as if it meant to push us beneath the black water and pin us there.

'Brace yourself!' The warning came as the raft hit the rocky sides.

The tunnel narrowed sharply ahead of us and the raft was too wide to fit through. Did we have to wade from this point? Waldegrave stepped over me and stooped to loop the rope around an outcrop of rock, while I was forced to roll to the other side to balance the raft and prevent it tipping us both in. I was cold, wet and not in any mood to start splashing through this foul sewer. I'd been humiliated enough by that arrogant shit.

'I am not moving until you tell me exactly why you've brought me here.' My fury echoed through the tunnel.

'What I have brought you to see is through that door,' Waldegrave answered, his tone unruffled and calm. 'I suggest you take the lantern.'

I levered myself to my knees, my wet clothes clinging like ice to my back. I lifted the lantern and swept the beam across the rocky wall. A narrow wooden door was set into the stone just above the surface of the water. It scarcely looked big enough to admit a dwarf.

'What are you waiting for?' Waldegrave demanded. 'You were impatient enough a moment ago. There is a small step, just below the water. I'll steady the raft.'

A warning bell began to toll in my head, one I knew should have begun ringing before I ever followed the old priest to this place. Those men that he had ordered away could be waiting behind that door to finish what they started. In truth, there was no need even to have men waiting, if that door led to a closed chamber. All Waldegrave needed to do was lock me in and leave me to die of starvation. But I would not make it easy for him.

'You lead the way. I'll steady the raft until you step off.'

'As you please, Master Pursglove.'

I couldn't see the expression on my old tutor's face, but I heard the amused grunt.

Steadying himself with his staff, Waldegrave stepped off the raft. There was a splash as his foot found the step, and for a moment it looked as if he was walking on water. Then he turned the rusty iron ring and pushed. The heavy door swung open and he stepped into the darkness beyond.

I listened but could hear nothing except for the sounds of dripping water, echoing like hammer blows all around me. I felt for the step beneath the water, thrusting the lantern out ahead of me and bending almost double to squeeze through the tiny door. As I straightened up, there was an explosion of movement. Startled by the light, rats fled in all directions, darting across the floor and scrabbling up walls. One leaped screaming for my face. I lashed out, catching it in mid-air and knocking it away. It fell with a shriek, dived between my legs and plopped into the flooded tunnel behind me. I almost smiled. My time in Newgate hadn't been entirely wasted then.

My breath caught in my throat. We were standing in a vaulted chamber. The floor was higher than the tunnel outside and though puddles still glistened on the flagstones, most of the floodwater had drained away. I was in a crypt. Several stone tombs stood largely untouched on either side, save for the mud and debris littering them. But not so the rest.

Wooden coffins lay smashed and scattered all over the floor, where the floodwater had finally dropped them. The bodies had floated out and lay in grotesque and twisted heaps over the tombs and floor. Bones and skulls had been thrown around as if the Devil had been playing skittles with them. Half-rotted corpses had been torn in two. Others, trailing mud-stained winding sheets, sprawled across one another, their heads twisted, their limbs contorted, resembling those paintings of the damned in hell. One man was lying on his belly, his arms stretched out towards us as if he had crawled from his coffin and had been desperately trying to reach the door. So, this is what the rats were feeding on.

'Where are we?'

'Beneath the church of St Augustine the Less.' Waldegrave took the lantern from my hand. 'Come, this is what I have to show you.'

He picked his way to the back of one of the stone tombs where a small space had been cleared around a corpse that lay in a shallow puddle beneath the filthy sheet. This one seemed to have escaped the worst of the maelstrom, for it lay straighter than the rest. Waldegrave set the lantern down, ignoring the patter of the rats beyond the pool of light. He peeled back the sheet. The face of the man who lay beneath had been gnawed, his lips and nose gone, his eyes, too. But a moustache and the short, neatly clipped beard around the bottom of his chin remained.

The priest levered himself up on his staff, his hand pressed to the small of his back. 'His chest . . . look at it, Daniel.'

Reluctantly, I squatted down. The man was certainly not as long dead as those scattered about – weeks maybe, no more – and I couldn't decide if that made my task better or worse. I pulled the sheet from his torso. The man's doublet, though ruined by mud, water and the fluids of decay, had once been a fine garment. The gold gilt buttons told me that. But it had been cut open and fastened back across his chest with a length of cord tied around the body. I reached for my knife to cut it, but Waldegrave laid a hand on my shoulder. 'No, untie it. You will need to use it to bind the clothes together again.'

I searched for the knot, probing beneath the cadaver, and as I did, my fingers encountered something small and hard, something which had evidently escaped the notice of whoever had laid him to rest here. It vanished up into my own sleeve, without Waldegrave even noticing. The magician's art has its uses. Swiftly, I found the knot wedged beneath the man's armpit. It had swollen tight, but I managed to loosen it. The doublet burst wide and a terrible stench, even more foul than those around us, billowed upwards, making both of us draw back. The shirt beneath the doublet had also been cut open, revealing blue-white skin that had clearly never been exposed to the sun, but that only served to make the marks on it stand out like a burning beacon. The letters had been burned deep into the flesh, raw and livid – IHS.

I stared up at Waldegrave. 'These are the same marks I found on Harewell. How did you . . . ?'

The old priest massaged his knuckles. 'Ever since the flood, the bodies that have been recovered have been laid out in one of the ruined churches. They are left there for a few days in the hope that relatives will claim them for burial. If no one comes forward, they are buried in a common grave. I go there most days to pray for their souls and to offer what comfort I can to those who come looking for their kin. The wave marked each corpse differently, as if it were an artist of death. The faces of some are gashed or staved in, others almost unmarked. Some bodies have been mauled by vermin, others are unmolested. Yet in some ways, the corpses are all alike, the flesh bloated, the skin peeling, and mud oozes continuously from the mouth, noses and eyes. They are weeping mud.

'One evening at dusk, the last half-dozen bodies recovered that day were carried in and dropped by the door. The corpse gatherers were exhausted and anxious to get home to their families before dark, so I told them I would lay out the corpses and cover them, ready for those who might wish to view them in the morning. The light in the church is poor at that hour and, at first glance, this corpse seemed no different from the rest, but when I touched him, I noticed that he appeared fresher than the others, swollen yes, but the skin was not peeling. And there was something else odd. At first, I couldn't think what it was – then I saw there were no dark streaks dribbling from this man's nostrils or mouth. He hadn't been dug from the silt.'

'As I dragged him to lay him straight, his doublet was pulled open and I saw those letters burned on his chest. I found a wound on his back, too . . . a stab wound.' The old priest gave a great sigh. 'He was a man of standing. Someone was bound to claim the body and take him away. They would not suffer him to be laid in the common pit. They'd want a costly funeral, the corpse washed and shrouded. That sign would have been seen at once. Those letters . . .' Waldegrave covered his face with his hand and groaned. 'The mob would have rampaged through the city and dragged out everyone they even suspected of practising the old faith and hung them from the castle walls. No Catholic in the city would have lived to see the dawn.'

'So, you decided to dispose of the corpse before anyone identified it,' I said.

Waldegrave's head jerked up. 'Not dispose. This man had been foully murdered, I would not add to the wrongs that had been done to him. I brought him here to the crypt where he might lie on consecrated ground, beneath the Holy Cross. I knew St Augustine's had been flooded. There is much damage inside the church, much that needs to be cleaned and repaired before it can again be used for worship. It will take weeks, perhaps months, before the debris above is cleared and anyone can open the crypt, much less begin to reinter the corpses. By then the rats and the ravages of decay will have mostly obliterated the marks on his body, and even if some vestiges do remain, I doubt that those men who will be paid to move these poor souls will have the stomach to examine any of them closely.' He took a deep breath. 'Now, if you have seen enough, kindly cover him again. He deserves to be left in peace, if any soul so violently torn from this life may find peace.'

As I dragged at the shirt and doublet, trying to close them across the swollen flesh and bloated belly, something spilled on to the man's breeches, sparkling silver in the candlelight. It looked so out of place amid all that mud and decay that, without thinking, I scooped it up and held it closer to the lantern. Half a dozen tiny fragments of metal lay in my palm, like little drops of frozen rain. Silver? No, it hadn't tarnished in this wet crypt; it must be tin. But this man was no craftsman like the dead printer. His clothes were way beyond the purse of even the most skilful tinsmith, and his beard was cut in the latest London fashion which, as yet, few in Bristol had adopted.

I glanced back up at Waldegrave. 'You said he was a man of wealth and standing. His wealth is evident enough, but standing . . . do you know him?'

'He was a merchant, I believe. I saw him on occasions on the quayside, before the flood. His doublet drew attention; the many gold buttons caught the sun, as no doubt they were intended to do. As to his name—'

He broke off abruptly and suddenly seized me by my arm, shaking me as if I was again an errant pupil, his face contorted with anger.

'No, sirrah, no. You have that same expression you wore as a boy when your curiosity was aroused. I can see the questions forming in your head. I brought you here tonight to make you understand the danger, to show you what I have done to protect our people. Don't you understand, have you not seen that a careless word can ignite a rumour that burns faster and more destructively than a flame in a ship's arsenal? And the cry of *murder* is a spark that will ignite such a fire. You must bury your questions here and leave them to rot among these bones. And you must leave this city tomorrow. Tell whoever sent you that you were able to discover nothing. If you don't, it is not merely your own life you are risking but the lives of all those innocents who will be made to pay for a crime they had no part in.'

Chapter Twenty-two

ANGRY SHOUTS AND LAUGHTER rolled across the courtyard of the Salt Cat as I heaved myself up the stairs. A pool of coppery light spread across the cobbles and glittered on a stream of piss, arcing out from a man too drunk to find his way to the jakes. It sounded as if the regulars in the inn were determined to make up for the gambling and drinking time they'd lost in the fret of the evening before. It was going to be a rowdy night.

As soon as I reached my chamber, I began to peel off my sodden clothes without even taking time to light the lamp. As I stripped off my shirt, something clattered from my sleeve on to the wooden boards. I groped over the floor in the dark, but the object must have rolled away. I rummaged for some dry breeches, then without troubling to find fresh hose, I walked back down into the yard to light my lamp from one of the links burning on the wall. Returning, I knelt and swept the lamplight round the floor, disturbing a couple of mice and sending beetles scurrying into the dark corners. The light gleamed off something metallic. I picked it up and held it close to the lamp.

It was a seal, made to be hung from a belt or around a man's neck. The die was engraved with a merchant's mark such as were used for documents and contracts, but more importantly to identify the ownership of goods being stored or transported. It was simple in design – a small circle with five lines radiating out from its centre, enclosed in the outline of a shield. Here was a man with noble ambitions, someone who wanted not simply a mark but one that, at first glance, resembled a heraldic devise. But it suggested a careful man, too, one who did not want to fall foul of the heralds by claiming to have arms he had no right to bear, for the line that projected vertically up from the circle had been extended beyond the shield's border and was surmounted by something that resembled a pennant flying from a ship's mast.

I took some sealing wax from the small parcel of writing materials that FitzAlan had provided for me and melted the wax on to a scrap of paper, making a careful cast. Then I set it aside to let it harden while I found a safe hiding place for the seal. Being found in possession of a wax impression which might have been torn from any letter could be explained; being discovered with a wealthy man's seal, especially when that man had been murdered, would be enough to send you to the gallows.

I ferreted in my purse for a coin and lay down on the bed, my fingers working it rhythmically, making the coin repeatedly vanish and reappear as I tried to think how best to proceed. I needed to discover the dead man's identity and his allegiance. That might tell me if these murders had been committed by those who supported the Jesuit treason plot, or were revenge against those who did. If I could find the link, that thread would surely lead me to the Jesuit network, and if Pettingar was the spider in the heart of that web, I'd have FitzAlan's arch conspirator. But I could see nothing, except the manner of their deaths and mutilation, to connect a printer and a wealthy tin merchant. The obvious answer was to search the warehouses by the quay where Waldegrave had seen the man walking for any boxes that bore his mark, and simply ask who owned them.

But Waldegrave had told me to leave Bristol. Not that that was an option, unless I wanted to be dragged back to Newgate. And if it had just been a question of a frightened old man's warning, I would simply have ignored it. But I couldn't shake off my unease about those men who had waylaid me. If Waldegrave could order them to back away from me, he could, as easily, order them to attack – and this time, finish what they had threatened. And I was under no illusion that if I was seen poking around on that quayside asking questions, Waldegrave would learn of it within the hour. So, I couldn't go myself, but maybe there was someone who could, if I could catch him this time.

THE SUN HAD not yet inched above the horizon when I crept out of the inn. A faint glow edged along the rim of dark sky. The torches and links in the streets had burned away, but there was just enough light to distinguish any movement in the streets, and so few people abroad that no one could hide among a crowd. Even so, I paused as I turned every corner, drawing back into dark doors or archways, waiting until I was sure no one was behind me before moving on.

When I finally reached St Stephen's graveyard, I was as sure as I could be that I had not been followed. There was no sign of the boy in the tomb, but I hadn't expected there to be. I retreated into the ruined church and waited. It was cold, and my legs were growing stiff from standing still. A beam of milky dawn light was gliding slowly up one of the pillars before I heard the soft grate of stone. Myles was crouched with his back to me. He had removed one of the small slabs he used to block in the side of the tomb. As I watched, he reached inside his shirt and dragged out some small metal object that glinted in the early-morning sun. He thrust it deep into the tomb, then hastily replaced the stone. I waited until he was walking away from his hiding place, then stepped out in front of him, as if I had just rounded the corner.

He looked startled when he saw me. For a moment, I thought he might bolt, but he evidently decided against it.

He wiped his nose on his arm and shivered. 'What you doing here? Lost again?'

I laughed, despite myself. 'Looking for you. I'm told you fetched the old man to drive the men off the other night. I owe you my thanks.' I flipped a coin at him. He caught it deftly and grinned. It vanished almost as quickly as I could have made it disappear.

'Ask you to keep an eye on me, did he?' I was careful not to use Waldegrave's name. I didn't know how much the boy knew about him.

'The Yena said for me to watch out for you, said you might get yourself into trouble.'

'The Yena?'

'That's what them in the castle call him.'

'So, they know him, do they, the men who live at the castle?'

The boy looked wary. 'They know mostly everyone.'

I didn't press him. It was too soon for that. But I was curious to know what dealings the castle thieves had with Waldegrave, or was it simply, as the boy said, that they made it their business to know all that went on in Bristol? So, did they know what he was really up to?

'Do you work for the Yena?'

Myles frowned, plainly offended. 'That old hedge pig's not my master. I work for whoever I please, whoever pays me the most.'

'Then would you do a job for me, without telling the old man or anyone else?'

He frowned suspiciously, lowered his voice and squared his shoulders. 'You tell me what I have to do first, and I'll . . . I'll think on it,' he added gruffly.

Chapter Twenty-three

WINDSOR FOREST

THE HOUNDS BURST OUT between the trees and streamed across the open field. The twenty or so mounted men that followed dug their spurs into the flanks of their sweat-lathered horses, urging them to full and unhindered gallop after the tangle of the woodland. The riders at the back, blinded by the great plumes of dust kicked up by the iron-shod hooves of the horses in front, spread out across the field and pushed their mounts to an even more furious pace. The hart they were chasing was making for the copse on the other side. The fewterers had already released five relays of hounds, and the beast was not in prime condition after the winter privations. He was tiring quickly; the huntsmen could sense that.

The King was leading the field, clad in his favoured grass-green hunting costume. A long, curled white feather decorated his hat and a hunting horn dangled in place of a sword. The King's eyes were afire with exhilaration, spittle foamed at the corners of his mouth and flecked his sparse beard. He repeatedly turned in the saddle to bellow taunts at those who were falling behind. Oliver Fairfax, newly arrived at Court, had been warned about that. His cousin Richard, who had been almost a year in the King's company, had cautioned him that James swore like a drunken pirate in the hunt and constantly goaded his courtiers to gallop ever faster, but there'd be the devil to pay if anyone was foolish enough to outride him.

No one pursuing the hart paid any heed to the man and his two sons who came running to the edge of the field, staring in horror and rage at the mangled remains of their winter wheat, which minutes before had been standing straight and verdant, and now lay trampled into the dirt. Weeks of work, of picking over the seed, of ploughing, sowing, harrowing, of pacing the furrows from dawn to dark to drive off birds, rabbits, hare, deer from the tender shoots – all wasted now. There would be no harvest for their family. No flour. No bread.

Inside the woods, on the edge of the clearing, the hart, exhausted and gasping for breath, had finally turned at bay. The barking of the excited hounds rose to fever pitch as they circled the deer, snapping and snarling as they ran in. The hart lowered his great antlers, spearing one dog in the belly and hurling it backwards. The dog crashed to the ground and tried to crawl away, dragging its two back legs. Blood poured from its wound. The hart would shed his antlers soon, but now they were at their most lethal and could easily kill a man.

The Master of Game could not afford to take chances with his Sovereign's life. As the dogs distracted the deer in front, he signalled for one of the huntsmen to approach the quarry from the rear. With a swift sword slash, the tendon of one of the hind legs was severed and the beast buckled and fell. As a page ran up and took the reins of the King's horse, the Master, with a respectful bow, presented the King with a sword. The King swiftly slid from the saddle.

Everyone was dismounting now. Oliver tethered his horse next to Richard's. As the fewterers held back the hounds with their staves, James waded through the melee, his sword raised.

'Does he mean to kill it or dub it?' Oliver whispered, unable to suppress a snort of laughter.

Richard glanced around to ensure there was no one in earshot. 'He'll wait to hear how it roars. He'll knight any beast if it has a Scots accent.'

James was also approaching the quarry from behind. He thrust his blade into the deer behind the shoulder, ramming it deep into his heart. The creature threw back his head and roared. The scream echoed across the fields until it felt as if even the ancient oaks were trembling. Then it abruptly ceased as the antlered head crashed to the ground. Blood trickled from the open mouth and nostrils.

A great cheer went up from the assembled party. One of the huntsmen came running with the garniture, a broad ebony scabbard, decorated with fine silver inlay and red garnets glowing like burning coals in the watery sunlight. While the hart was rolled over on to its back, James carefully selected a sharp knife from the several inside the scabbard. He laid open the skin of the beast's neck and made several deep cuts down to the bone beneath. At a signal from the Master, the huntsmen blew the death on their horns. The excited hounds renewed their baying. They knew the treat that was in store, and the fewterers could scarcely hold their charges back until the Master gave the word for them to run in and tear at the neck.

At last the dogs were dragged aside and coupled on leashes. As soon as they had been led away, the King castrated the hart, hanging the testicles on a forked stick which one of huntsmen had set ready into the ground. Any dainty morsel placed upon this stick was reserved for the King's own plate.

Thus far, the unmaking of the hart was as familiar to young Oliver as any courtly dance, and he fully expected to watch the King begin the process of delicately dismembering the carcass, carefully slicing and removing muscles, joints and organs, beginning with the tongue, in the painstaking and time-honoured ritual. But instead, James pushed back his sleeves and drew a longer and stouter blade from the garniture. He hacked into the deer's chest, stuck his fist inside and tore out the heart, holding it aloft, as blood dripped from his wrist.

'Behold the heart of the beast who would be King.'

A gale of laughter rippled around the nobles, though some could not mask the flicker of unease that darted across their faces. A forged letter or an old friend arrested, even a careless remark in the hearing of a servant, and any one of them might find themselves waking one morning in a palace and the next in the Tower. Each of the men standing in that clearing had seen the hearts of those accused of treason ripped out and held up for the crowd to 'behold' and mock.

The King's gaze swept across the circle of faces. He was not smiling. He sliced the heart in two and tossed the bloody pieces to the pair of lymers who had led them to their quarry. The hounds who reveal where the quarry is hiding must have their reward. Turning his attention back to the deer, James slit open the belly. He plunged his hand into the cavity, seized the guts, and heaved until the steaming mass of purple entrails slithered on to the ground.

Oliver gaped. He glanced at Richard, who was watching his young cousin with amusement.

'You'll soon learn the King has no patience for French manners. It's the chase and kill that interests him. He leaves the butchering to the butchers. He has his own rituals.' He jabbed Oliver in the ribs with his elbow. 'Come, whelp, there's the blooding to be done. And see that you smile and laugh, else you'll be out of the Court within the hour. But remember, the King's been in the saddle all day, so you might want to breathe through your mouth.'

Oliver frowned, puzzled.

Again, Richard glanced around him to ensure that they were not overheard. 'Have you seen him dismount even once today to piss or shit like the rest of us?'

'I thought he was . . .'

'You thought what? That he was a god, so he doesn't have to? He may claim the divine right of kings, but that doesn't give him a divine arsehole. Though there are some who tell him he has,' he added sourly, glancing pointedly at the particularly handsome and athletic young man who was sharing a private joke with James.

Richard lowered his voice still further. 'He won't dismount during the hunt, so he shits in the saddle, and I'm told more often than a newborn babe. At this end of the day, he's riper than a cesspit in midsummer. So next time you're saying your prayers, give thanks you're not the man who has to clean him up or the girl who has to wash his linens.'

Oliver and Richard joined the group of noblemen who had drawn together in a circle around the King, as if they were preparing to play a children's game. James's hands were scarlet and dripping. He tottered round the circle of nobles, pausing before the handsome young man Richard had earlier indicated, to smear his bloody hands down the man's forehead and cheeks, trailing a fingertip across the man's mouth as if he was a maid painting her mistress's lips with vermillion. The anointed one laughed and made an extravagant bow, like an actor acknowledging applause. It was a public mark of favour to receive the first blooding.

James continued, selecting the next man seemingly at random, but all knew it was not. Although he recoiled at the idea, Oliver found himself anxiously awaiting his turn. He was relieved when the King finally stopped in front of him. Had he imagined it or had James's sticky fingers lingered on his cheek longer than Richard's? When he risked a glimpse at his cousin, Oliver saw from the hard set of his jaw that he had noticed it, too, and was not pleased.

The Sergeant of Hounds and his lad had carried off the guts to be washed, chopped and mixed with bread and blood, to be fed to the hounds, and James, now slumped in a folding chair hastily set out for him, gestured to his boots. One of his pages ran forward and began tugging off the soft leather boots and silk hose. For a moment, Oliver felt a surge of pity; one of James's feet was permanently twisted sideways. Did it pain him? In the saddle, the King had ridden faster and more fearlessly than any man around him. Although Richard had said it mockingly, James was indeed a god on horseback, but as soon as those twisted legs touched the ground, he became all too mortal.

As soon as his feet were freed, James thrust them inside the eviscerated belly of the hart, wriggling them around as if he was an old man soaking his aching toes in a steaming bowl of mustard water. Many of the ladies of the Court would dip their hands inside the beast when it was carried home, for it was said the blood whitened the skin and removed blemishes and sores, but Oliver had never seen anyone bathe their feet in the kill before.

He was about to ask Richard if the King believed it would strengthen his legs. But his cousin's attention had wandered, his gaze darting back to the woods where the shadows were deepest. Was there another hart in there? Or more alarmingly, a boar? They could rise and charge without warning, and at such speeds they could gore a man wide open from knee to chest before he had time to pick up a weapon or even cry out.

Oliver glanced towards the hounds, but they were gorging on the blood-soaked bread and guts of the deer. That was, he supposed, reassuring. If there was a boar close by, the hounds would be agitated. The sun had dropped below the tops of the trees and a cold wind was gathering strength. It would be dark soon, not that the King seemed anxious to move. A servant offered James a goblet of sack, and as he moved away, Richard began edging towards the King. Oliver assumed his cousin was hoping for a private word, perhaps to make some request, seeing that the hunt had put the King in excellent humour.

He saw Richard glance once more towards the thicket. Oliver followed his gaze. Was something moving among the darkening trees? He took a step sideways, trying to get a better view, but before he could take another, there was a warning shout. Richard ran towards the King and, even as James turned in his chair, Richard threw himself forward, striking the King hard in the chest, and hurling him to the ground. Something thwacked into the tree trunk behind them where, just moments before, the King had been sitting.

As if a wasps' nest had fallen, the glade exploded into frantic activity. Men rushed to James's side, dragging Richard off, pinioning his arms and forcing him to kneel. One of the Scottish lords snatched up the sword James had used to deliver the coup de grâce and pressed the point against Richard's back, daring him to move. Others were heaving the still barefoot James upright and trying to brush the twigs and leaves from his green doublet. Two lymers had been released and were bounding into the woods, trying to pick up a scent, with several huntsmen following on foot. Three of the noblemen were already swinging into their saddles and preparing to charge after them.

The Master of Game was examining the tree behind the overturned chair. As Oliver drew closer, he saw the shaft of a crossbow bolt embedded deep in the trunk.

The Master gestured towards Richard kneeling in the grass. 'It would appear you've this man to thank for your life, Sire. If you'd been sitting where you were when the bolt struck . . . It was a miracle he saw the danger in time.'

'On your feet, mon!' James commanded, his accent broader than usual as if he had been frightened back to the land of his birth.

Those holding Richard dragged him upright and released their grip, though the man holding the sword kept the point pressed against his back.

James stared hard into Richard's face, his eyes narrowing in suspicion. 'How did you ken someone would try to murder me? You had warning of it, but you saw fit to keep the intelligence from me. Is that the truth of it?'

Richard sank again to one knee, pressing his right hand to his heart. 'Sire, I swear on my dead father's soul, I did not know that any attempt would be made on Your Majesty's life this day. If I had heard even the faintest whisper, I would have got word to you at once.'

'Then how came you to throw yourself on me? Did you see a fly alight on my head and think to bat it away?'

There was a sprinkling of nervous laughter from some of the men clustered around, but a cold glance from the King swiftly froze it in their throats.

Richard lifted his head, gazing straight into the King's eyes. 'I heard a noise from the trees and thought I saw something move. Whatever I saw, it was too tall for a beast. I was approaching Your Majesty to warn you, when I saw a glint of metal, glimpsed a crossbow being raised. I acted instinctively.' He bowed his head meekly. 'I humbly beg your forgiveness, Sire, for daring to lay hands upon my Sovereign Lord.'

The King frowned at the men gathered about him. 'What say you? Shall mercy be granted for this outrage or should I punish the villain?' There was a moment of silence, no one daring to answer. Then James let out a bark of laughter and, with relief, the men joined in.

The King extended his hand, black with dried blood, grasped Richard by the wrist and hauled him to his feet, pulling him into a hearty embrace. As he released him, he kissed Richard on the lips.

'It seems I do indeed owe you my life, Lord Fairfax. There are some who cautioned me against taking the son of a notorious recusant into my inner court, but you have more than proved your loyalty this day. And it shall not go unrewarded. I—'

He broke off, turning in alarm at the crashing and snapping of twigs and branches behind him. The three noblemen came trotting out between the trees. A man was tied by his wrists between two of the horses, his arms stretched out. He shrieked as the horses pulled away from each other as they entered the clearing. Oliver heard a crack, and saw a spasm of agony cross the man's face as his arm was wrenched from its socket. His face was as pale as bone, and great beads of sweat were popping out on his forehead. Someone cut his bonds and he collapsed on to his knees, his arms dangling uselessly at his sides.

'This is your assassin, Sire.'

One of the men slid down from his saddle, seized a handful of his prisoner's hair and wrenched his head up. 'Who are you, sirrah? Speak!'

'John . . . John Morecote, sir. By our Lady's virtue, I've done nothing . . . nothing.'

'He swears like a Catholic,' someone muttered.

'What were you doing hiding in the trees?'

'I set a few snares, came back to see if I'd caught owt. But when I heard voices, I hid, sir. I feared I might be brought before the magistrate if you thought I was poaching.'

'We found neither snares nor game on him.'

'That's 'cause I hadn't caught anything. Those dogs of yours drove everything off.' He closed his eyes, gasping and bracing himself against the pain from his injured shoulder.

'Did you seize him with the crossbow?' James demanded.

'He will have hidden it in the undergrowth, Sire, or tossed it away as he ran. The hounds are quartering for it now. We've let them get a good sniff of this wretch, so they'll find it. His stench will be all over it.'

The man began to shake and moan, though it was hard to tell if this was from pain, guilt or just plain terror.

'Who instructed you to do this? Who told you the King would be hunting here today?'

'No one, sir, I swear it. I only wanted a little meat for the pot. I've a wife and children to feed. I meant no harm.'

'Take him away,' James snapped. 'Deliver him to those who can wrest the truth from him. But tell them to take care. I don't want him dying before he's revealed who put him up to this, for I'd wager my best hound he was not acting alone.'

But as the man was dragged to his feet, whimpering, Oliver saw his gaze suddenly fasten on the crowd of men near the King. The expression on the prisoner's face was one of abject terror, but there was something else in those eyes, too – utter bewilderment, as if he had somehow been betrayed by one he had trusted, and could not begin to understand how or why.

Chapter Twenty-four

DANIEL PURSGLOVE

I SPENT HALF THE MORNING grooming Diligence, cleaning and oiling the gelding's hooves, so that anyone who was keeping a watch on me might think I was making the beast ready for a long journey. The wound where his tail had been cut off had scabbed over well with no sign of suppuration, thanks to the salve Mistress Crugge had supplied. But the wretched beast looked miserable and listless, though the poor fodder was probably just as much to blame for that as the loss of his tail.

My less than genial host would have sold the feathers back to a plucked chicken if he could, and he was no doubt making a good return on what little hay and oats he provided. But he wasn't stupid – if he'd had better fodder, he would have sold it to his customers and made a greater profit. I'd have to start searching for additional supplies or Diligence wouldn't be able to carry me more than a mile from the city gates. I needed the horse to be rested and fit, if we had to leave quickly.

The remainder of the day I spent in the parlour of the inn, playing primero with the seamen who were hoping to be taken on as soon as the ships were ready to put to sea again. But with the jetties wrecked, ships sunk or damaged and cargoes in the warehouses ruined, they knew they were in for a long wait as their money drained from their purses. I took care to bet only small amounts on the cards and to be seen to lose as often as I won, though it irked me to deliberately throw the game. But I couldn't risk starting a fight or making myself a target for thieves.

Several times, I tried to catch Rachael's eye as she squeezed between the settles with flagons and bowls of stewed mallard, but her expression remained as cold and hard as a frozen puddle. When she pushed past the end of my table, I noticed, with a twinge of dismay, she was wearing a new knife on her belt in place of her old worn one. It was a pretty thing. The smooth bone handle had been inscribed with fine lines depicting flowers and birds, the kind of carving a seaman makes on board a ship to bring back as a gift for his wife or sweetheart. She had a suitor, then, and if he had carved that for her as a love token, she was probably betrothed to him.

It was late in the afternoon, and what feeble light trickled in through the small casements from the narrow street could not penetrate the dense fog of pipe smoke in the inn's parlour. Men were complaining they couldn't see the cards in their hands and were hollering for Crugge to light the candles set in the animal skulls and the jaws of the wicked-toothed conger eel hanging on the walls. He ambled in, wiping his hands on the bloodstained sacking tied over his tunic. He stretched his gangly arms over me to reach the candle impaled on the teeth of a shark.

'There's an urchin waiting for you in the courtyard, Master Pursglove. Seen him hanging around here before. Reckons you'll want to see him. But if he's begging, you let me know and I'll send him packing with his arse on fire from my whip.'

I rose. 'No need, Master Crugge. I sent the boy with a message; he'll be bringing back the answer.'

Crugge grunted, his shiny bald pate winking like polished copper as the candle flame blossomed above his head. 'Aye, well, you know your own business, but if you'll take my advice, you'll use the mercer's boy opposite for your errands. He's a clean, respectable-looking lad. Most would set their dogs on that urchin of yours before he'd even crossed their yard.'

The urchin was nowhere to be seen when I went out into the yard, but I heard a voice coming from the stables. Myles was standing by Diligence stroking his nose and telling the gelding that he looked as handsome as any horse in Bristol. Diligence snuffled the boy's forehead and gently tugged at the tousled hair with his lips as if he appreciated the comfort.

Myles ambled towards me, nodding over his shoulder towards the horse's hindquarters. 'Who did that?'

'Cut the horse's tail? I don't know, but I'll chop something off him if I ever catch him.'

'I'll bet it were a woman who cut it, not a man. There's others in the city had the same done to their horses. The butcher in Marsh Street is in such a fury, he said he'd skin the witch alive.'

'A witch . . . What makes him say that?'

Myles shook his head. 'Everyone knows it was witches. Weave spells out of them, don't they?'

It was dangerous talk; such rumours had taken the lives of women who'd done no harm to anyone except scold a neighbour's child, or brew a few herbs, but I knew from the lad's matter-of-fact tone that there was little point in trying to argue with him, especially when I had no other explanation to offer. All the same, I was relieved it wasn't only my horse that had been targeted.

'So, Myles, did you find another mark down at any of the tin merchants' warehouses like the one I showed you?'

The boy shuffled his feet, hanging his head. 'I searched everywhere, but most of the warehouses down there are closed up 'cause of the flood, and I got chased out of the ones that weren't. Thought I was going to thieve from them.' Myles dragged his bare toe through the soiled straw. 'Suppose that means I'll not get paid.'

I regarded him sternly. 'Swear you searched right along the quay.'

Myles nodded.

'Then take this.' I thrust a few small coins into the lad's grubby palm and he beamed.

'But you'd best not try to buy your supper here. Master Crugge doesn't want you hanging about.'

'Indeed, he doesn't,' Mistress Crugge announced, from the doorway. 'Be off with you.'

Ducking the slap she aimed at his head, Myles sidled past Mistress Crugge's great belly and was gone.

The innkeeper's wife held her lantern higher and waddled inside, peering suspiciously about as if she thought the stable might be infested with a swarm of boys. 'Heard voices,' she said by way of explanation. 'Thought someone might be after the horses. I keep telling Master Crugge we should get a dog, one of those big brutes, and chain him in the yard. He says it'll eat too much, but I says to him, whole point is to keep the beast hungry, that's what keeps them fierce.' She frowned, staring out at the courtyard as if trying to recall what had brought her in here. 'And might I ask what business you had with that lad?'

I hesitated. Why not? She, after all, had no reason to suspect that there had been another murder. 'My mother's sister sent her a parting gift from Bristol. That's the seal that was on the package when it was delivered.' I held out the slip of paper on which I'd stuck the wax cast of the seal. 'If I could find the merchant who sold the gift to my aunt, he might know if she'd secured a ship and was preparing to embark. I thought the boy might be able to find who owns that mark, but he's had no luck.'

'If I'm any judge of lads, he'll not even have bothered searching. You shouldn't pay them, Master Pursglove, if they don't deliver. It only encourages them in their indolent ways.'

Mistress Crugge held the wax seal closer to the light. 'Every merchant in Bristol has a mark, besides all those who come here to trade. You'd be hard put to tell one from the other with most of them.' She peered at it again. 'Though I've seen this one . . . there's something familiar . . .' She waggled her head as if to try to shake the memory loose and another strand of greying hair snaked down from under her cap. 'No, it's gone. I must have seen it on the board outside the Collector's office. You'll not find it there now though. The great wave ripped the board off. Be half-way to the New World, unless some thieving beggar found it and chopped it into firewood.'

'The Collector!' I said, with a sudden surge of excitement. 'He keeps the port record books. The mark's bound to be in one of those.'

Mistress Crugge let out a sequel of high-pitched laughter, her ample bosom wobbling with mirth. 'The gossip in the parlour is the books went the same way as the board in the flood, though most reckon they had a helping hand and found their way to bottom of the estuary after it was all over. Collector's been trying to keep the Exchequer's men from seeing those books for months, 'cause he's in the pay of half the merchants in the city. Gives the Searcher the nod and wink so half the cargoes go in and out uncustomed. My cousin Ned, he's a boatswain and he knows just which palm to grease whenever his ship puts in; they all do. Rest of the town may think the flood was God's curse, the Collector must think it was an answer to his prayer.'

'But you did see this mark on the board at the Collector's office before the flood?' I asked impatiently, trying to bring her back to the point.

She shook her head. 'What would I want to go looking at that thing for? When there's wine and spices and such to be bought for the inn, it's much cheaper to buy them straight from Ned. 'Course, it's all supposed to be sold in markets or shops, but—' She tapped the side of her nose and winked like an aged bawd. 'The captains and officers always keep a little back to sell on the side. And why shouldn't they?' she demanded indignantly as if I'd protested. 'They take all the risks, drowning in shipwrecks and being butchered by pirates and all the while those merchants sit safe ashore by their warm fires, then pay them a pittance for their trouble. And then they bleed poor folks dry by charging twice what it's worth, all for pagging it a few streets into the city.

'Course, since the great wave, there's been nothing coming in, and the merchants have been charging a king's ransom for what they have in their stores. They always find a way to make hay from other men's ill fortune.'

I thought of the casks that I'd seen down in Crugge's cellar and the stout door that lay beyond. I'd wager the merchants were not the only ones profiting from this flood.

Mistress Crugge thrust the wax cast back at me and bustled out, bellowing for Rachael to stir herself and fetch more sack before she'd even reached the inn door.

Having spent the best part of the day in the dark, tobacco-filled parlour, my eyes were stinging and my throat burning. I climbed the stairs to my chamber, drinking in the chill night's breeze, raw and heavy with wood smoke, yet as pure as a mountain top compared to the stench of Newgate's dungeons. And I'd find myself breathing that poison again all too quickly if I couldn't discover something for FitzAlan. I had to discover who this merchant was and what linked his murder to the Jesuits.

The stairs below my casement creaked. I slipped from the bed and crept across the wooden boards, my knife in my hand, listening to the light tread on the stairs outside. I was half expecting someone to try to ease the latch, but instead there was a firm rapping.

'Master Daniel.' It was Rachael.

I smoothed my hair and, from force of habit, raked down my beard to cover my throat, then opened the door.

'Brought you some supper. Wild duck stew, at least that's what Mistress Crugge says it is, but there's more navens in it than meat, and they're as withered and woody as old twigs.' She set down the dish, then fished in her pocket. 'Brought you more of that salve, too, for the cut on your eye. It'll fester else, and that won't improve your looks any.'

She didn't look at me.

'It was good of you,' I said awkwardly.

Her gaze alighted on the wet clothes from the evening before, which I'd draped over the low beam in a futile attempt to dry them. She sniffed, wrinkling her nose.

'Those'll want washing before the stains dry in, else they'll be twice as hard to shift and the smell will linger. There's a woman who comes in to do the linens, day after tomorrow. You'll have to pay her in advance, though.' She was gathering up the clothes as she spoke. 'I'll keep them wet till . . .' She trailed off, her attention caught by something on the rough table.

I took a pace closer and saw she was staring at the scrap of paper on which I'd pressed the wax seal. 'Do you know this seal?' I asked.

'Why would I?' she said with a shrug, dragging my stinking hose from the beam.

'You looked at it as if you recognised it.'

'Just curious, is all. Thought there might be a royal crest on it, what with you being a fine lord.' She bobbed a teasing curtsey.

I repeated the same tale that I had told Mistress Crugge and, taking the damp clothes from Rachael's arm, pushed the seal into her hand, urging her to take a closer look.

'Maybe you don't know the name, but you have seen it before. On a warehouse?'

'What would I be doing at a warehouse? Mistress Crugge only ever sends me to the market, and she's mithering me to be back before I've even set out.'

'Then where?'

She frowned. 'I suppose . . . it must have been the Gaunt's Chapel.'

'Where's that?'

'Opposite the Cathedral. Christmas Eve, it was . . . There was a man fixing up a new escutcheon by lamplight. I noticed him 'cause he was arguing with the Clerk of Works, shouting and cursing. It was late, but the clerk said that the chapel's new patron wanted his friends to see his escutcheon when they came to church on Christmas Day. I *think* that was the one he was fixing . . .' She shrugged.

I sighed. I knew she was mistaken. 'I know this has the outline of a shield, but it's not a nobleman's arms—'

Rachael gave a snort of indignation. 'Why bother asking, if you're not going to believe anything an ignorant serving girl tells you?' She snatched the damp clothes from my arms. 'You'd best find it yourself, then, hadn't you, Master Daniel?' She swept from the room, leaving the door wide open and a cold wind barging in.

Chapter Twenty-five

I STARED UP AT the row of brightly painted wooden escutcheons above the door of the hospital chapel. Rachael had been right, after all, and I would be eating my words for supper. Most of the escutcheons bore the arms of knights or of craft guilds, but among them were a few merchant's marks, some with their initials incorporated into their design, others with the sign of their trade, such as a barrel denoting that they were a vintner, though this was the only merchant's mark with a shield border.

'Hankering to get your badge up there, are you, brother?' a wheezing voice said.

I glanced around to see a hollow-chested man leaning on the handles of the small cart he was pushing.

'I was thinking it strange to see the marks of merchants up there along with the arms of nobles.'

'Some call it the line of honour. I call them the marks of fools. Nobles or knaves, it matters not a jot to the Corporation.'

The man broke off in a fit of phlegmy coughing, spat and then reached under the old sailcloth covering the cart to drag out a stoppered bottle. He took a swig, and proffered it to me. I didn't want it, but I took a gulp of the sour wine, anxious to keeping him talking.

'Marks of fools?' I prompted.

'Wealthy fools, who the Corporation have been fleecing for money ever since they bought that church when the friars were turned out. Any man-jack who gives them a hefty sum for the chapel gets his mark put up as a benefactor alongside the nobles. Flatters them into thinking they're as good as any knight or lord.'

'So which merchants are up there now?' I asked casually.

The man shrugged. 'Like I say, the peacocks and foot lickers, that's who. Why should you care?'

'If they've money to throw around, I thought I might try my luck with a couple of them, see if they'll throw a little my way.'

'You'd be wasting your time if you're thinking of begging men like that for charity. They're the sort that would sooner toss a loaf of bread into the Avon than give it to a starving child, unless there was something in it for them.'

I winked. 'Ah, but if they've fat purses and lean wits, they might be persuaded to invest in a little scheme of mine, if they thought it would make them rich.'

'Now that would be a fine sauce to serve for those crowing cocks.' The man's laughter broke up in a hacking cough, which left him doubled over his cart, struggling for breath. At length he straightened up and grasped the handles of the cart and, straining, pushed it hard to get it rolling. He grinned back over his shoulder. 'Chapel wardens and clerics will know whose marks those are. I wish you luck, brother, but take a long spoon if you're supping with those merchants. They'll not take kindly to being fleeced, and it's money that weights the scales of justice in this city, as it does in most, I dare say.' He trundled away, still chuckling and wheezing.

I found a deacon only too willing to name the owner of each and every escutcheon, his chest swelling with pride as he boasted of the chapel's illustrious benefactors and the fine dinners to which he and his fellow clerics had been invited. He seemed to have convinced himself that being employed as deacon in the only church in the city owned by Bristol's Corporation far outranked even the highest office in the Cathedral opposite, and was keen that I should fully appreciate this. I only escaped the man's relentless prattle when a woman approached who was evidently of some importance and the deacon, dismissing me with barely another word, went scurrying over to greet the newcomer.

I left quietly satisfied. The cleric had been so eager to show that he was a close friend of all the men of wealth and influence in the city that I'd not even had to question him to find out where the merchant I was searching for had conducted his business.

The deacon had shaken his head sadly. 'It was one of the finest and largest warehouses in Bristol, but I regret to say it was badly damaged in the flood. And he hadn't long had one wall of it strengthened. A tragedy, a veritable tragedy! But,' he added, rubbing his doughy white hands together, 'Master Dagworth is a man of some means and quite determined. He will rebuild. He probably already has his men hard at it. You'll see, come summer, his business will be thriving again, probably better than before, for I never knew such a man for turning disaster into triumph.'

Not this time, I thought. Not if Master Dagworth was lying mutilated among the rotting bodies in the crypt. The only ones to triumph from that disaster would be the rats.

I followed the road up to Frog Lane, climbing up the steep slope of Trencher Lane beyond, where the deacon had told me he'd had 'the great honour of partaking of a little supper with Master Dagworth and a select party of guests over Christmas-tide'. It was evidently a wealthy part of the city. The small clusters of houses had three overhanging storeys. Between and behind the dwellings stood orchards and neatly ordered knot gardens with low clipped hedges. The trees were bare and pruned ready for spring, as were the rose bushes. The herbs had been cut back and the ground carefully hoed. The contrast to the muddy, rubble-strewn streets lower down the hill was almost obscene. It reminded me of one of those paintings of the Last Judgement where the righteous gaze down, serene and unmoved, from the tranquil heavens, while below, the damned are churning in a maelstrom of fire.

I spotted what I was looking for on the casement of one of the houses near the top of the street. Like a pissing dog marking its territory, Master Dagworth could not resist displaying his mark. There it was, in a pane of stained glass, looking even more like a knight's arms, with a ship above it, a bale of cloth on one side and a sheaf of grain on the other. He had even stolen a motto to complete the effect. *Faber est suae quisque fortunae. Every man is the architect of his own fortune.* The merchant had certainly built his own fortune, but he was no fortune-teller for that maxim had turned into a sour jest – his fate had not, in the end, been designed by him, but by his murderer.

But as I drew closer, the low winter sun revealed that these ostentations had simply been painted on the pane in imitation of stained glass, and the paint was already scratched and beginning to flake. I stared at the symbols surrounding Dagworth's mark. Cloth and grain, so that's what Dagworth traded in, that's what he proclaimed had made his wealth. He had not, after all, been a tin merchant, in spite of the fragments of metal I'd found in his clothes. Little wonder that Myles had not found his merchant's mark. I'd sent him to look on the wrong wharf.

I could not see inside; the casements were too high. But the plant in the window had withered and died. Wind-blown dirt and brown leaves had accumulated on the doorstep and on the little path that led into the garden at the side. There was no smoke curling from the chimneys.

I paced beyond the house and back the other way, to ensure that I hadn't been followed, before knocking at the door of the neighbouring house. After a few minutes it was answered by a middle-aged woman in a plain brown dress and neat white coif. She ran her gaze over me as if she was well used to appraising the status and trustworthiness of any callers. Behind her a caged songbird began to chirrup, encouraged perhaps by the shaft of light or breeze from the door. I smiled warmly and, though she did not return the smile, her frown of suspicion softened a little. I guessed her to be a maid or housekeeper and calculated I'd learn most by adopting the tone of one accustomed to command.

'I have just called at Master Dagworth's house, goodwife, but there does not appear to be anyone to receive me there. I wonder there is not at least one servant to watch the house.'

She grimaced. 'No one left to watch it, sir, except the young lad who helps the cook, and now I think on it, I haven't seen him about either, these past few days. Morning of the flood, there was only him and the cook at home. Poor Ruth and Tom, the other servants, were both out on errands when the wave struck, God rest their souls. There's been no news of them since. For a few days I hoped . . .' Tears welled in her eyes and she swallowed hard. 'No use hoping after all this time, is there?' She sadly shook her head, as if answering her own question. 'Anyhow, then the cook heard her brother was hurt bad, so she went to tend to him. As for the boy, well, he didn't like being in that house alone. So, it's my betting he's taken off, probably helped himself to a few bits and pieces on the way, seeing as he's not been paid these many weeks.'

'And is Master Dagworth expected to return soon?'

'Not if what my master says is right, sir. Master Dagworth's warehouse was badly damaged. My master says one wall collapsed, as if the sea had punched through it, like a fist through paper. Water surged in and whirled everything round as if it was churning milk for butter – bales, sacks, kegs and the men, too, sir, those working inside and out. Some they found drowned underneath the bales, others they reckon got sucked straight out to sea.' She clenched the door frame, closing her eyes for a moment, as if trying to shut out the sight. 'We heard the noise up here like a great roaring beast, saw the smoke in the sky as if there was a fire racing towards the city, but there were no flames. I never imagined anything could move so fast . . .' She paused, shuddering at the memory.

I pressed her. 'And Master Dagworth? Do they think he was dragged out to sea?'

'When he didn't come home the night of the flood, the kitchen boy ran around telling everyone his master had been drowned. You know what lads are for revelling in death, always at the front of the crowd if there's a hanging. He hoped Master Dagworth was dead, 'cause he's given the lad a few good thrashings in the past for being idle. That man has got a nasty temper when he's riled. Tom had to get between them more than once for fear he'd cripple the lad or worse.

'But as to Master Dagworth not coming home of a night, that wasn't unusual. He was a widower, so he'd no wife to fret over him. Poor Ruth, God rest her soul, said he'd rooms down by the river, where he used to stay sometimes. Told her that if a cargo came in late or a ship was sailing early, he wanted to be on hand. But Tom said Master Dagworth slept there if he was too drunk to ride home – and he didn't sleep alone there, either, if you get my meaning.' She flushed slightly. 'But the flood didn't take him. The sea only takes poor folk, not the rich, that's always the way of it in this world.'

I knew the merchant had not drowned. I raked my beard, trying to decide how to ask the next question.

'Surely if Master Dagworth had escaped the flood, he would have returned to his house. If no one has seen him since—'

'Oh, but they have, sir. That's why my master knows he won't be home anytime soon. He saw Master Dagworth at the Merchant's Tolzey in Corn Street, a few days after the flood. There was a crowd of them gathered there, and some of the merchants who'd lost warehouses and goods were planning to set off to London to petition the King for help to rebuild. Much good may it do them, my master says, for the King's Purveyors still haven't paid the merchants for the fifty-one hogsheads of claret and ten butts of sack they took from Bristol over a year since. But my master reckons Nicholas Dagworth must have gone with the others to London. It'll be weeks before they come back.'

And weeks before anyone realises he's missing, I thought, much less starts searching for him. Meanwhile, the evidence of his murder rots away deep in a crypt beneath our feet –

'*The Devil of the Vault*' – but was Dagworth one of the devils, or one of their victims?

I was thinking hard as I made my way back down the hill. If what the housekeeper had told me was true, then any servant in Dagworth's employ might have had good reason to kill him, and possibly any of the men who worked in the warehouse, too. For if the man did have a vicious temper, it was likely that kitchen boy was not the only one who'd felt the brunt of it. But though even a young lad could easily stab a grown man in the back, if he caught him off guard or in a drunken slumber, I was certain that he wouldn't have burned those letters into him. It seemed unlikely that any of Dagworth's men at the warehouse would, either. Besides, why would any of them have wanted to kill Sam Harewell?

And that was the other thing that made no sense. The murdered printer had been a Catholic, albeit not a very devout one, whereas the merchant had been a benefactor and prominent member of the church owned by the City Corporation. The deacon and other members of the church had dined with him. There could be little doubt that he was regarded as a staunch Protestant in the city. If he was a secret Catholic and rebel, he had concealed it with as much skill as any professional spy.

This had to be the work of the Jesuits. But why kill this merchant? Had he unwittingly stumbled across some rebel plot, seen arms being brought into Bristol from a boat, or one of the gunpowder conspirators – even Pettingar himself – being smuggled on to a ship to escape Cecil's long grasp? The flood could have revealed a stash of arms or a place where priests were being hidden. A merchant with ambitions to nobility would be cock-a-hoop to find himself in possession of information that would gain him admittance to the most illustrious circles of the Royal Court, which even his wealth could not obtain for him. It might even buy him a title. Had this cock started crowing and been silenced for it? If Dagworth had uncovered something important enough to get him killed, I wanted to know exactly what that was.

*

THE RASP OF sharp teeth on wood, and claws on plaster, echoed in the darkness beyond my bed. I knew it was only the inn's resident mice. But tonight I couldn't lie in the darkness listening to them. I'd woken with a single phrase rattling in my brain – *something important enough to get him killed* – and anyone else who tried to learn what that merchant Dagwood had discovered. If I was next to feel the blade in my back, if my own corpse was found with those letters burned into it, would my old tutor set me on the raft and punt me over the black stinking water to lie for ever in that crypt with the rats?

Shivering, I scrambled out of bed and almost fell headlong, tripped by the blankets tangled round my legs. As I dragged myself clear of the bedclothes, something heavy fell from the bed and hit the floorboards with a dull thud. I stumbled forward in the dark, stepping painfully on whatever had fallen. I limped towards the table, fumbled for my tinder box and after several clumsy attempts finally succeeded in getting a spark to catch, and lit the candle.

It was only then that I saw my door was unlatched. A stream of frosty air was pushing through the crack. I hastily closed it. I was certain, though, that I had fastened it before I went to bed. And locked it, too.

I turned to find what had fallen from the bed. It was the large stone eye from a broken statue, the one that the message from Waldegrave had been wrapped around. But I'd hidden that in the far corner of the chamber, up on the roof beam, where it met the wall. The mice running along the beam must have knocked it off. It was weighty, though, so not a mouse then, a rat? But my bed was at the opposite end of the chamber, how could it have fallen on to that? It was too heavy to bounce.

Either I'd left it on the bed and forgotten I'd done so, or someone had come into my room while I was sleeping and had placed the stone there as a message, or was it a warning that they could strike whenever and wherever they chose? I didn't know which of the explanations was worse – that I was losing my wits, or that someone had silently broken into my chamber and had been standing next to me while I lay insensible. This time it had been a stone; next time, a dagger?

Chapter Twenty-six

THE PALACE OF PLACENTIA,
GREENWICH, LONDON

'I TRUST YOU DID NOT grant a licence to print this stinking mess of poison.' James tossed the pamphlet in the direction of Archbishop Bancroft. It fluttered in the air like a shot bird, and drifted down, settling between them on the carpet's scrolling vines and scarlet blossoms.

Richard Bancroft was unsure if the King had cast the paper to the floor in disgust or if he'd been expected to catch it in mid-air like a servant or a dog. Either way, he certainly was not going to rise from his chair to retrieve it.

King and Archbishop glowered at each other until the page, who had clearly been as uncertain as the prelate about what the King had intended, scampered forward and picked it up. After an agony of indecision, and without any clue being offered by either man, he finally laid it on the small table next to the Archbishop's goblet of wine.

Bancroft glanced down at the pamphlet. The contents were only too familiar to him, and he most assuredly had not granted the anonymous author and printer a licence.

'The paper has been brought to my attention, Majesty,' he said cautiously.

At least a dozen times, he thought. It was as if the author was daring them to catch him. This seditious piece of fiction was circulating in half the towns in England, and probably in Europe, too, by now. There were illegal Catholic presses operating all over London. As fast as the Archbishop's men managed to uncover and crush one of these underground publishers, another would spring up from London's filth, like toadstools in a forest.

'Have you read what they are claiming now?' James demanded, jabbing a finger towards the pamphlet. 'According to that, after Garnet's execution a spring of pure oil burst forth at the western end of St Paul's. Most of their martyred saints can only manage a spring of water at the site of their executions. This arrogant Jesuit manages to produce oil. Next they'll claim it was holy chrism for the anointing of a future papist king! And it is not just miracles concerning Garnet. That . . . that *arsewipe* claims that when Oldcorne was executed, his entrails continued burning for sixteen days, exactly the number of years since that devil's disciple was smuggled into England to do his diabolical work. Sixteen days! Not even the entrails of an elephant could burn for so long!'

'Perhaps, the fire was being fed by this miraculous spring of oil.' It was a joke Bancroft had heard one of his own men make, but if he hoped it would lighten the King's mood, he was sadly mistaken. James had delivered his diatribe without once pausing to draw breath, and now slumped back in his well-cushioned chair. He aimed a vicious kick at the footstool, sending it tumbling over on the carpet. The page looked terrified. Should he leave it and be punished for failing in his duties, or right it and risk annoying his master still further? He darted a beseeching glance at the Archbishop, seeking divine intervention, but Bancroft had graver matters on his mind.

James drained his goblet of wine in a single gulp and wiped the drops from his red beard with the back of his hand. He held the cup out to the pageboy, who hurried forward to refill it, looking relieved that on this occasion at least he understood what was expected of him.

The King drained the goblet again as soon as it was filled. 'Do you realise a broadside ballad of Garnet is now circulating in Spain? It is as well Salisbury ensures I am kept informed. Even if others don't,' he added, glaring pointedly at the Archbishop. 'I've told the Spanish Government it must be supressed. Salisbury assures me it will be. The Spanish won't want to risk offending us and endangering the treaty between our realms.'

'I am sure the Spanish will take all necessary steps,' Bancroft said. Or rather, they would claim they had, he thought. That serpent-tongued hunchback might be able to convince the King the ballad could be suppressed, but whatever orders governments and kings issued, they could not prevent a wind from blowing or a fart from stinking. Even if they rounded up every copy of the broadside in Spain, the ballad would still be sung wherever anyone had memorised the words. Banning it would only make it taste sweeter in the mouth, like smuggled wine.

'But I shouldn't have to be clearing up this pile of shit,' James growled. 'You should not have allowed this ballad to be printed in the first place.'

Now Bancroft understood the reason for his summons. James had plainly been deprived of half a day's hunting, or racing his greyhounds, to deal with the Spanish Ambassador, and it had put him in a foul humour.

The King turned his empty goblet restlessly in his fingers. 'My little beagle tells me that in the Queen's reign, it was you who discovered the printing press used by that scurrilous wretch Martin Marprelate and destroyed it. So, it cannot be beyond your wit and skill to discover the pernicious devil who conjured that piece of filth.' He made an obscene gesture at the pamphlet still lying next to Bancroft.

'The printer paid for his crimes on the gallows, Majesty, but few believe he was Marprelate. The name was a mask worn by many different men. In the end the only antidote to their poison was to attack the masquerade through pamphlets written in their own style, make a mockery of them as they had done of the Church, turn the laughter against them, and I still believe that to be the best way.'

'Do you really?' James barked, suddenly leaning forward in his chair as if he was about to spring out of it. 'And is that how you mean to deal with Garnet's straw? Fake another one with my crowned head upon it! Whose face will you have appearing in my beard?'

Bancroft tried to keep his own tone calm and measured. 'Those involved are still being questioned, but my commission is making good progress. By the time we are finished, I intend to ensure the commons believe Garnet's image is nothing more than a fraud, a cockentrice, painted on to the straw to gain money from those gullible enough to pay to see it.'

'How can you prove that, when Salisbury tells me the straw has vanished?' James demanded irritably.

'It is simply a question of discrediting those who discovered it. John Wilkinson, who claims to have caught the straw, is an educated, intelligent and plausible pedlar of lies, but he fled to France within days of Garnet's execution, leaving the straw in the keeping of his landlady, Mistress Griffiths, the wife of a tailor. It was Hugh Griffiths, together with an unnamed "nobleman", who claims to have discovered the image on the straw. Griffiths and his wife can easily be made to look not only fools but knaves, too. And the commons will turn against them in an instant if they think they have been duped by a mere tailor.'

But James was no longer attending to him. Bancroft had been dimly aware of a growing murmur beyond the door, like a swarm of angry wasps, but now the buzzing had exploded into bellows. Before the Archbishop could turn his head, the King was hurrying across the room, drawing his sword. He didn't wait for the page to open the door, but flung it wide. Shouts and yells burst into the chamber. Bancroft glimpsed a knot of courtiers and servants standing either side of two men who were being dragged apart. As the men outside caught sight of their King, silence rolled through their ranks.

The King took a pace into the long gallery, with the Archbishop following. A sword lay on the tiled floor between the two pinioned men. One of those standing close by tried to kick it out of sight, but James's gaze had already alighted upon it.

He gestured impatiently for someone to hand it to him. When they did, he grasped the handle, jabbing the blade towards each of the two men in turn and gesturing to the floor in front of him.

'Here!' he snarled, as if he was calling hounds to heel.

Both men were thrust down to kneel before the King. One looked no more than sixteen, Bancroft thought. His body was already well muscled beneath his powder-blue and dove-grey silk doublet, but his face, framed by dark curls, still bore the angelic beauty of a boy. The other youth was taller and broader, with an unruly rust-coloured beard sprouting from his heavy jowls and chin. His wine-coloured doublet was new but somehow looked ill-fitting on him, as if it had been borrowed.

One of Scots nobles, who had been restraining the older of the two men, stepped forward. 'Sire, it was that lad there who gave insult for nae good cause when my son was about his own business.' He gestured contemptuously towards the youth in the blue doublet. 'That arrogant wee jackanapes drew his blade first. It's the law that any man who starts a fight in the presence of his King must forfeit his hand. I demand you punish him for his insult to my clan.'

'If he is to have his hand cut off, it will be for the insult to me, not your clan,' James retorted.

Bancroft glanced at the lad who was accused, expecting him to beg for mercy, but though he was trembling, he set his jaw and lifted his head defiantly as if he'd go to the gallows before he'd apologise.

A second man stepped forward and bowed with considerable grace and elegance, making the Scottish lord look like a clumsy farmhand. 'I would ask mercy for my cousin, Oliver, Sire. He is young and newly come to Court.'

'Lord Fairfax.' The King turned to the Archbishop. 'This is the man who lately saved me from the crossbow by hurling me to the ground as if I was a skittle to be bowled over.'

'God in His mercy sent you sharp eyes and quick action, Lord Fairfax.' Bancroft had ordered prayers of thanks for the King's deliverance to be said in every church in London on the Sunday following, though there had been as yet no word from Lord Salisbury as to who was behind the attack. Had they not succeeded in wresting it out of the prisoner, or was Robert Cecil keeping the information to himself for his own ends?

'And do you beg mercy for your cousin as reward for saving your king, Lord Fairfax?' Bancroft prompted.

Richard Fairfax inclined his head. 'I ask for justice, nothing more.'

'Justice demands that his hand is severed from his wrist for starting a fight in the King's presence,' James said coldly, 'and I notice you do not deny he began it.'

'It would be wasting your Majesty's time to do so. The Scots would argue that he did and the English, he did not. But that is not the issue, Sire.'

'Is it not? Come, Archbishop, what say you? Is not the question of which man started the fight the crux of this matter?

'It would appear so, Majesty.'

Richard made another bow, this time to the Archbishop, showing due deference, yet Bancroft sensed a trace of mockery in it. 'With respect, Your Grace, it is not. For no fight was begun by either man in the King's presence. When the fight started, His Majesty was in another room.' Richard gestured to the door behind them.

A buzz of voices instantly filled the long gallery, some amused, others angry. All eyes were turning to the King, but his expression was unreadable. He looked from Richard to the two men kneeling in front of him. Then, without warning, he let out a great bark of laughter, though he still did not smile.

'A lawyer's reasoning, Lord Fairfax. It seems you have missed your calling. But you shall have your justice.' He raised his voice so that all in the long gallery could clearly hear. 'Both are pardoned, and let this end the quarrel between them.'

As Oliver rose, James grabbed the shoulder of his doublet and hauled him close. 'Take care you guard your temper, lad. Mercy, like lightning, seldom strikes twice for the same man.' He looked beyond him to Richard. 'A young hound must be kept on a tight leash, Lord Fairfax. See that you keep this one kennelled until he learns which quarry he is permitted to harry.'

James led the Archbishop back into the chamber and stood for a moment, lost in thought. 'It seems Richard Fairfax has both sharp eyes and a sharp wit to match. But does a double-edged blade make for a useful knife or a dangerous weapon?'

Chapter Twenty-seven

DANIEL PURSGLOVE

THE PARLOUR OF THE Salt Cat seemed even darker, damper and colder than usual that Sunday morning. I'd been woken by the church bells clanging in disharmony from a dozen or so towers, the notes whipped around in the bitter wind as if they were engaged in a violent argument with each other. I'd stuffed the pillow over my ears and fallen back into a fitful sleep, only waking when my belly complained it must be near dinner time and it had not yet been fed. But when I marched into the parlour, the fire still smouldered beneath the night's covering of ash. No one had come to rake it out and add fresh wood. The log basket beside it lay empty.

About a dozen men and a couple of women sat grumbling that they were not being served. Three noisy children were jumping from benches and clambering across tables in a boisterous game of mariners and pirates, annoying everyone still further. Spoons and empty beakers thumped on the tables. Urged on by some of his friends, a bow-legged man who stank of fish stomped to the door and bawled, 'Where's our vittles, Crugge? You all asleep back there?'

He was slammed back against the wall as the door was flung wide. Mistress Crugge's bosom sailed into view ahead of her like the figurehead on a ship, a large chopping knife raised in her hand. Her face was scarlet and sweating in spite of the bitter weather, and several locks of her grey hair had already managed to escape from her cap, though the noon bell hadn't yet struck.

'Who was it bellowing for me like a gong farmer?'

Several of the men, smirking, pointed towards the man trapped behind the door, as he tried to squeeze out and sidle away. 'You, was it, Master Holt? I'll have you know I'm doing the work of three in that kitchen.' She jabbed the point of the knife at his belly. 'So, unless you want your own cods served up in a pie, you'll hold your peace.'

'Where's that pretty wench of yours, then? Still romping in bed with some lad, is she?' Holt sniggered.

Mistress Crugge bridled, her many chins wobbling with indignation. 'I only employ respectable girls in this inn, as well you know, Master Holt. Rachael's fetching a keg of vinegar from Master Ayleward. And Master Crugge's gone to Morning Prayers like a good Christian. If you spent your Sundays in church praying like you should, I'd have some peace to get on with cooking your dinner, and you could eat it without fear of the Devil making you choke.' She pushed Holt aside, preparing to return to the kitchen.

'Church? Is that where your Caleb told you he was off to?' Holt grinned slyly round at his companions. 'Services have finished a good hour since. I reckon he's stuffing a goose, and not in your kitchen.'

Mistress Crugge faltered, worry creasing her brow. 'Is it as late as that? Been so busy I hardly . . .' She seemed to realise she was talking in front of a room full of customers and her head jerked up. 'I dare say he got talking,' she said briskly. 'Important man, Master Crugge, there's always someone wanting to consult him about business. It's that idle trull of a girl who should have been back here to help me by now.'

As soon as the door had closed behind Mistress Crugge, several of the customers squeezed out of their seats muttering that they'd try their luck at the Three Cups. But they had only just reached the street door, when it burst open and Caleb Crugge hurried in, his sharp cheekbones and the end of his thin nose scarlet from the cold and his eyes bright with excitement.

'I'd not venture into that kitchen, if I were you, Caleb,' Holt called out. 'Your old besom's got a knife in her hands and a temper twice as sharp. She—'

'There's been another murder! Terrible it was, terrible!' Crugge sank on to the nearest settle.

There was an explosion of questions as benches were hastily pushed back and people scrambled to gather around him.

'Who's been killed?'

'Where?'

'How?'

'Hold your peace!' someone yelled above the din. 'Let the man catch his breath.'

Crugge nodded gratefully and reached for a flagon, but those had long since been drained by the hungry customers.

'Did they cut his head off?' one of the children piped up, unable to contain his fascination. 'Was there lots of blood?'

His mother cuffed him and ordered him to wait in the courtyard. Scowling, the boy stomped to the door, but realising that his mother had already turned back to Crugge, he crawled under a table and settled down to listen.

'Christ Church. Always go to Morning Prayers there of a Sunday. No one can ever say I'm remiss in that.'

'So, who is it you play Watkin's Ale with in there? Pretty, is she?' Holt asked, with a leery wink at the crowd.

'Hush up, let him speak,' a woman called out.

'Church was locked,' Crugge continued. 'The deacon and the lad who carries the cross were outside shivering, complaining they'd never known the church to be locked, and they couldn't get in to make ready for the service. They hadn't seen hide nor hair of the churchwarden or the vicar. Someone sent the lad off to fetch the churchwarden, while we stood outside and waited. It was bitter cold, too. That wind's sharp enough to cut a cow in half, and people started saying that if Reverend Gysbourne didn't appear soon they'd be leaving, as they'd business to attend to and the goodwives had dinner to cook.'

'Aye, we know all about waiting for our dinner, don't we?' one man growled, and several, muttering, joined in.

'So, what about this murder?' someone urged.

'Hold your water, I'm coming to that.' Crugge was clearly relishing being the centre of attention, and wasn't going to rush his story. 'Lad comes back with Symons, the churchwarden, who says he'd come earlier to clear the stray dogs out of the porch and trim the candles. He hadn't brought his key with him; he never needs to, and couldn't understand why the church was locked. But Reverend Gysbourne holds the only other key, so he went to knock on the vicar's door to learn the reason. Symons said he's heard that churches have been locked up on the orders of a bishop, or even the King himself, if there's popery suspected, and if that were the case, he didn't want to fetch his own key and let people in, for fear of being fined or worse.'

I felt my heart starting to quicken.

A ruddy-faced man wearing the badge of the Butchers' Guild gave a huge bellow of laughter. 'That's the last church in England could be accused of popery. My grandfather boasted it was the first church in the land to have the litany sung in English, back in old Henry's time. Grandfather reckons he walked in the procession, half across Bristol, singing that day. 'Course, he was only a little lad then and he mostly remembers the feast after and the strawberry tarts.'

A man who I recognised as owning the nearby cobbler's workshop gave a grunt. 'It's always been a church that's sets its sails to catch a fair wind, not that it's profited from it much lately, a piss-poor place compared to what it used to be. That vicar may have the King's seal stamped on his arse, but loyalty doesn't fill the coffers when he preaches such dung-dull sermons. Miserable as sin they are, I wonder you can stand to go there, Master Crugge.'

The bandy-legged Holt nudged Crugge. 'He doesn't go there to listen to sermons, do you, Caleb?'

The innkeeper glared at him. 'As I was saying, Symons went to the vicar's house, but found no one at home. So when the lad came running up and told him the church was still locked, Symons fetched his own key. Even then, with the whole crowd of us standing freezing, he was in two minds whether or not to unlock the door. "What if Reverend Gysbourne's been arrested?" he says to us. I told him, I said, if the church had been locked on the orders of the King, then they'd have nailed up a paper on the door saying it was forbidden to enter.

'Symons told us to wait outside, said that it was his duty as churchwarden to make sure all was well first. But he'd no sooner stepped inside than he gave a great shriek, as if he'd seen the Devil himself rising up out of hell. We all rushed in behind him. He was standing there, just staring, as if he'd been turned into one of the stone pillars.

'I could see something lying on the floor in front of the communion table, but it was so gloomy inside, I couldn't make out what it was at first. I thought someone had slaughtered a pig. But it wasn't a beast; it was the vicar himself, Gysbourne. He was lying on his back, his shirt torn open and soaked in blood, his arms stretched out on either side like a crucifix. His eyes were staring up at us and his mouth was open as if he was screaming. And . . . and this pool of blood on the flags . . . never thought a man could have so much blood.'

Crugge's earlier bravado crumbled, and the full horror of what he had seen seemed to hit him for the first time. His face turned pale and he swayed alarmingly. One of the women barged the men aside and hurried through the door to the kitchen. Moments later, she was back clutching a tankard, Mistress Crugge hard on her heels. People scattered as she bowled them aside in an effort to reach her husband's side. She seized his hand, pumping it up and down as if she could raise the blood back into his face.

'Did I hear right? The poor vicar's been murdered?'

Crugge gulped down the contents of the tankard, before he opened his eyes again and nodded slowly.

I had to stop myself blurting out the question, but it must have been on everyone's mind, for several people began asking together.

'Who would do it?'

'Is anyone taken?'

'Suspected?'

Crugge shook his head.

'It'll be those murdering thieves up at the castle again,' a pinched-faced woman said. 'No fear of God nor man, they haven't. I dare say they were robbing the church when the vicar surprised them. He must have died trying to drive them off. Poor brave soul.'

'We're none of us safe in our beds,' the butcher's wife added. 'I don't care if that castle is royal property. The sheriff should ride in there and round up the lot of them. Let the King protest all he likes after they're hanging from the gallows tree.'

'If you ask me,' Holt said, 'someone wants to put a few barrels of gunpowder under the castle. Blow them all to hell and what's left of those old ruins, too. Be doing the whole city a favour on both counts.'

There was a murmur of agreement from those standing around.

'I don't reckon it to be thieves this time,' Crugge finally managed to insert. 'As far as Symons can tell, nothing was taken from the church, and they'd not broken into the chest where the church plate is stored. Nor the alms box, either. I think it was Gysbourne himself they were after.'

'He'd not be worth the trouble of robbing, surely, not like Sam Harewell,' the cobbler protested. 'Brought his boots to me to be mended, two or three months back, and they were so cracked and worn down I told him that would be the last time I could patch them.'

Crugge pressed his knuckles against his eyes, as if trying to push out the sight that still haunted them. 'I've not told you the worst of it. When we went into Christ Church, there was such a stench it made you want to vomit.'

'Blood,' the butcher said, nodding sagely. 'No smell quite like it and I dare say there was dung and piss, too. When a man dies suddenly, he—'

'Hush up, husband, there's no call to be saying that,' his wife scolded. 'This is a man of God you're speaking of, not one of your beasts.'

'Vicar or cow or hanged man, it makes no difference,' the butcher retorted.

Crugge raised his head. 'He's right, there was the stink of blood, and shit, too, but something worse, far worse.' He shuddered. 'There was a terrible smell of burnt flesh . . . human flesh. There's nothing else in this world smells like that . . .'

I felt as if a surge of cold water had poured through my body.

'Thought you said the vicar had been stabbed?' Holt said. 'Had they tried to get rid of the body by burning it, then?'

Crugge shook his head. 'Tortured, I reckon. Burn marks on his chest, just here.' He laid a skinny hand across his own breastbone. 'Red raw, bit right into the flesh, like they'd done it slowly.'

'To make him talk, tell them where something was hidden,' the cobbler said, his eyes almost popping from his head.

Crugge nodded. 'I reckon so. Can't think of any other reason.'

'What would he have hidden?' the butcher said scornfully. 'You said yourself, Ben, he'd not money enough to buy himself a new pair of boots, so he'd hardly have had a crock of gold buried in his garden.'

'Well, they must have thought he knew some secret,' Mistress Crugge snapped, gripping her husband's shoulder fiercely, as if she was his mother standing up for her child. 'If you were just robbing a man of his purse, you'd snatch his valuables quick as you could and be off before someone caught you.'

I knew I wouldn't be able to ask to see the body without drawing attention to the wounds or to myself, but I had to know. 'I heard of one man who used to burn a star into his victims' foreheads to torture them.'

'A star? Like the ones that witches draw for their spells?' The butcher said. 'Aye, now that'd make more sense than this talk of secrets. If he stumbled into a coven of these witches, holding one of those sabbats of theirs in the church, they'd not have let him leave alive. Could have been a dozen of them set upon him, and they'd have thought it great sport to desecrate a holy church with the slaying of a vicar and brand him with the Devil's sign, so that Satan could claim the poor man's soul. Remember, that quarter-master on the Bristol ship surprised that nest of witches down in his hold? Never caught the half of them.' He shook his head gravely.

'God preserve us,' someone muttered, and several people surreptitiously crossed themselves, as if they didn't know how else to protect themselves.

'Well, was it the mark of Satan on him?' the butcher's wife demanded.

All eyes turned expectantly to Crugge.

'How should I know what the Devil's mark looks like?' he said defensively. 'They were burns, I could see that much, and I could smell the stench of them. And before you ask, it was burnt flesh I could smell not brimstone. Poor man was lying in a pool of blood and . . .' Crugge wrinkled his long nose. 'And worse, like I said. There was no cause to go paddling about in that mess. We could all see from where we were standing that he was as dead as last week's mutton, without peering and poking at his corpse. Coroner's job, that is.'

'Quite right, too,' Mistress Crugge announced. 'Not respectful to go staring at him, with him being a man of the cloth. Besides, you don't want to go getting his blood all over you—'

She jerked round as the door to the kitchen banged, and Rachael barged through, using her hip to nudge the door wider. She was carrying a tray of steaming bowls. The aroma of stewed pigeon wafted into the parlour and, like fish drawn on hooks, people began to peel away from the innkeeper and slide back into the seats at the tables.

'And where have you been all this time, you idle baggage?' Mistress Crugge yelled, abandoning her husband's side.

Rachael flushed, but continued to place the bowls in front of the grateful customers. 'I had to wait a long time for the vinegar. The whole household was in an uproar. They just found Master Ayleward's mare in her stables with her tail cut off.'

The Crugges glanced nervously at each other and Rachael's gaze darted to me. She gave a grimace and the briefest of nods to my unspoken question. Another horse attacked, just like mine.

'Mistress Ayleward was in a fearful state, knowing someone had been prowling round their yard while they slept. They couldn't understand why the dog hadn't roused them. It's a good watchdog, but then they found it lying dead behind its kennel. It looks as if someone fed it poison to keep it from barking.'

'Did they steal much?' the butcher asked. He turned to those sitting around him. 'Ayleward had taken to storing half his barrels in his yard, said he didn't trust them to the warehouse after the flood. Not that he lost many then, compared to some, but maybe he'll not think it so wise now.'

Rachael set a bowl down in front of me, her expression troubled. She held my gaze for a moment, then turned back to answer the butcher. 'That's the queer thing. Nothing else was taken. He'd got kegs of vinegar stacked in the yard, besides his cart, but nothing had been touched.'

'Who'd go to such trouble to poison a dog,' the pinch-faced woman said, 'and then not even trouble to steal the horse, just its tail?'

'Who?' the butcher echoed. 'I reckon it's as plain as the snout on a pig's face. After what Caleb saw this morning, we all know who's done this. We've witches at work in this city. They're not content with calling up the flood. They're taking the hair of those beasts to weave a net of spells to drag us all to the bottom of the sea.'

Chapter Twenty-eight

NEWS OF THE MURDER spread through the city faster than the plague, and by the time I found my way to Christ Church later that afternoon, a crowd had gathered and were milling around chattering, in spite of the cold. Two members of the ward stood guard in front of the door, which had evidently been relocked. Word had been sent to the coroner, though he was dining out of town and was not expected until the morrow. This might have been an inconvenience to the citizens if the corpse had been found in the street, but the body was safely in a church, and, as one of the wards said with a grin, not likely to complain about being kept waiting.

The two men on guard had at first told everyone to clear off. But when a flagon was proffered and then a little bread and some sausage appeared, they'd grown more affable, and were happily supplying the crowd with all the gossip they could want. It seemed that all of the households in Wine Street had been questioned, but no one had seen or heard anything, save for an ancient beldam who swore she'd been woken by the sound of an unearthly scream, like the wail of a spirit warning of death. She'd peered out of her casement and had seen one of the white women from the sea, all shrouded in mist and glowing in the darkness, glide out through the stone wall of the church.

'Poor old crone's moon-touched,' the ward grinned. He stretched his arms out in front of him and tottered a few paces, groaning and wailing like a madman in chains.

Most in the crowd laughed, but I saw the anxious expressions on the faces of others. It didn't do to go mocking the white women of the sea. In the past few weeks, they and their vengeance had become all too real.

I CONSIDERED waiting until the inn had closed for the night and the streets were quiet, but decided that a lone figure hurrying through deserted streets would attract more attention than if the people were still coming in and out of the taverns, cockpits and whore houses.

Music and gusts of laughter rolled out from the parlour in clouds of smoke each time the door opened. I edged down the stairs and out into the street beyond. I forced myself to walk at a steady pace, drawing into doorways as soon as I rounded a corner to check if I was being followed. It was mostly men abroad at this hour. The solitary ones were hurrying home or weaving unsteadily through the piles of rubbish, as stray dogs bared their teeth or slunk away from their brandished sticks. The younger men in groups swaggered down the centre of the street, talking loudly, kicking stones against doors and shouting lewd comments when anyone leaned out to tell them to hold their noise. Women, their breasts bare in their low-cut gowns, stood about talking in two and threes, puffing on long-stemmed pipes and peeling off whenever a likely customer drew level with them, to twine themselves around them. I gently extricated myself from a couple of these pigeons as they linked arms with me on either side, joking that I'd be back later and I'd take them both on. I heard their mocking laughter behind me as I strode away.

As I drew close to Christ Church, I stepped back into the dark corner of a shop wall that jutted further out into the street than its neighbours. A cat already occupied the space, gnawing on the head of a bird. I accidently trod on her tail and she yowled, sinking her claws painfully into my calf, before shooting across the street. But the noise was so commonplace it didn't attract the attention of the single guard leaning against the church door. He had positioned himself in the centre of the pool of light cast by the torch in the bracket above his head, as if this would protect him from ghosts and murderers alike. He took a swig from a leather flask dangling beneath his short cloak, and blew on his hands. As the wind gusted, pushing the flames sideways, I thought I saw someone standing as motionless as I was in the shadows on the opposite side of the church. It was if I had glimpsed a reflection of myself standing there, though I knew that was impossible.

A prickle of unease ran down the back of my neck. I stepped back swiftly, pressing myself against the wall. Then I heard the crunch of boots on stone. A second guard lumbered towards the church door, cursing as he barked his shin on a tumbled stone. I relaxed a little; that was who I must have glimpsed in the shadows, the relief guard approaching. Who else could it have been?

The two of them muttered together, then the first shouldered his halberd and set off with the haste of a man who can't wait to reach the warmth of a brazier and the shelter of a stout tower room. The second guard strode a few paces along the church wall, as if he was intending to march around it to ensure all was well, but as soon as the other was safely out of sight, he slouched back to the church porch and retreated inside, out of the wind.

I picked my way around the church, keeping to the shadows until I reached the side door. It was much smaller than the main west door, narrow and low, but the oak was just as thick and stout, with a strong iron lock. It would need a battering ram to break it down, which is why the captain of the watch had probably felt no need to set a guard on it. The Devil was supposed to vanish through that door when he was driven out of the bawling infant at baptism. I hoped that the spirit of the murdered man wasn't planning to leave the same way.

I extracted a small metal rod from a pocket sewn inside my shirt, inserted it into the lock and wriggled the spike. I knew from experience that the mechanism inside a centuries-old lock like this one was much simpler to manipulate than any made by the locksmiths of today, but the trouble was that age also made it rusty and stiff. But this door must have been in daily use, for almost at once I felt it yield to my touch. I grinned. My fingers had not lost their skill, even after weeks without practice, but with it came the grim thought that always seemed to follow hard on the heels of any small victory these days – if I didn't succeed in discovering what FitzAlan wanted to know, it was not merely the skill in my hands I might lose.

I paused, listening for any sound of the guard making his rounds, and glanced up at the casements of the houses above the darkened shops, to see if I was observed. Then, turning the iron ring in the door, I slipped inside, swiftly closing it behind me.

If I'd thought the street had been dark, it was nothing to the blackness inside. Outside, it had been possible to see shapes and movement in the faint glow of a candle set in a window, a torch burning on a street corner, or the occasional shaft of bone-white light as the moon briefly emerged from the clouds, but none of those reached me in here. I stood still, hoping that my eyes would adjust, listening to the wind in the tower and the patter of tiny claws as mice scrambled over the wax candles. Even though no wind penetrated, it seemed colder inside than out on the street, as if the stones were sucking the heat from my bones.

Feeling my way along the wall, I came to a spot which, from what I'd observed outside that afternoon, was not beneath or opposite any windows. Using my tinderbox, I lit the candle I'd brought with me. As the flame steadied, I held it up. A strip of sailcloth lay on the floor in front of the communion table. Two arms stretched out from beneath the cloth, the hands smeared with dried blood. The corpse was positioned exactly as Crugge had reported seeing it, and would remain so until after the coroner and jury had inspected it. I mouthed a silent thanks to whoever had detained the coroner this night.

Shielding the candle flame from the casements with my cloak, I edged forward, moving noiselessly. Crugge had been right about the stench and, in spite of the cold, the reek of decay was beginning to mingle with the other smells. I crouched down, pulling the stiff cloth back from the head and chest. The dark pool of blood around the man's body had mostly congealed, except for the deep puddles that lay in the crevices of the worn flagstones. Trying not to kneel in it, I moved the flame close to the face.

Death had not brought peace to the haggard features of Reverend Gysbourne. The eyelids were closed, almost screwed shut as if the man had clenched them in prayer or pain, but the mouth was wide open in a silent shout. A week's growth of grey stubble covered his hollow cheeks and forested the deep dimple in the centre of his chin. The frown lines in his forehead had been so set in life that, even now, they had not softened, as if he was still scowling his disgust at the world. The vicar did not look like a man who had ever taken much pleasure in living, and still less in dying.

I moved the flame down to his chest. It struck me that the vicar was not wearing a cassock; clearly, then, he had not been in the church to conduct a service. He wore a shirt and, in place of a doublet, an old-fashioned, knee-length coat which any of the poorer craftsmen or working men of the city might have worn. Both had been cut open and I could now see why Crugge had been unable to describe the burns. That the chest was burned was unmistakable, but it wasn't until I peeled back the edges of the slashed garments that I could see what I had been both expecting and dreading: the letters IHS had been seared into the flesh at an angle, as if whoever had made them had also been trying to avoid kneeling in the blood and filth.

I felt around for the man's belt. An old leather purse hung from it. I loosened the drawstring without removing it and groped inside. It contained a few small coins, perhaps money Gysbourne carried to give to beggars, or maybe to buy a little food for himself. Crugge was right, whoever had attacked the cleric, robbery had not been the motive. I carefully replaced the coins and adjusted the ripped garments across his chest.

There was no question that the coroner would notice the burn, and I could hardly cut it out as I had done with Harewell's corpse – not now that it had been seen by a church full of witnesses. I only hoped that, like Crugge, the coroner would conclude the burns were nothing more than evidence of torture inflicted in a failed attempt to persuade Gysbourne to surrender the church silver.

I drew the sailcloth back over the corpse, shuffling backwards as I did so, and my boot connected with something that spun away into the darkness, bouncing off the base of a stone pillar with a loud metallic clang which echoed through the empty building. I froze, holding my breath, sure the sound would have carried to the porch outside. I started towards the side door, but curiosity overcame caution and I took a few paces towards the pillar. I bent down and retrieved the object lying at its base. It was an iron key. Heavy and long, similar to the type that would have fitted the side door, except that this was far too large. Too large also to be the key to any man's house. It could only be the key to the great west door of the church.

I heard the rattle of another key, and someone cursing on the other side of that same door. The guard must have heard the noise, after all. Swiftly, I slipped the key beneath the sailcloth. I lifted the candle, trying to memorise exactly where the side door was, before I snuffed out the flame. The great west door shook in its frame as the guard on the other side tried to force the key to turn in the great lock.

I reached the wall and was feeling my way along it, my heart pounding, afraid I'd overshot and was now wandering further down the church. The door at the end of the church crashed open. The guard was clearly unwilling to set foot inside until he knew what he was dealing with. He held the flaming torch in his hand and was jabbing it into the air, as if he was fighting a dual with the darkness.

'Who's there?' His voice trembled. 'Show yourselves in the name of the King.'

The glow of the torch was enough to allow me to see I was only about a yard from the side door, but if I opened it the draught would immediately draw the guard's attention. He was staring at the sailcloth covering the body. Even I could have convinced myself that it was moving, though I knew it was only an illusion caused by the guttering torchlight. I inched forward until I had grasped the iron ring of the door, then I raised my other hand and threw the extinguished candle towards the corpse. It hit the sailcloth, rolling down the side to land with a dull clatter on the stone flags. The momentum sent the candle rumbling across the floor towards the guard. As he gaped at it, I opened the door and dashed out. I heard a shriek of alarm behind me, as the sudden blast of wind rushed into the church. I ducked low and twisted away into the nearest dark alleyway. With luck, the hapless guard would be convinced that the spirit of the dead vicar had just fled through the Devil's door.

Chapter Twenty-nine

THE OLD TITHE BARN where Waldegrave had taken refuge looked even less inviting by day than it did at night. The wisps of grey morning mist, heavy with the acrid smoke of tarry wood and burning bones, drifted through the city, but even this could not veil the broken planks, fragments of sailcloth and split barrels that slouched against the rotting walls of the barn. It was only when a woman crawled out from beneath one of the heaps, and lifted her skirts to piss by the barn wall, that I realised these were makeshift shelters.

Catching sight of me, the woman let her skirts drop and crawled towards me, dragging a leg that was so purple and swollen it looked as if the skin would split wide open if it was pricked. She held out a hand, begging for alms. When I handed her a coin, her face broke into lopsided grin and she cackled like a magpie. There was an explosion of movement as half a dozen men and women emerged from behind the apparently deserted piles of refuse, scuttling towards me with their hands outstretched.

'No,' I said, tersely. 'I must eat, too.'

They persisted, begging and pawing at me, but I pulled the edge of my cloak back, so that they could see my hand grasping the hilt of my dagger. Some shrugged and laughed, others muttered curses, but they retreated.

'You've been here before.'

I jerked round and saw a man sitting astride a beam that poked out from a pile of rubble, threading vertebrae on to a crude wooden handle to make a rattle. The bones looked as if they might have been human, but I tried to dismiss that thought.

'The Yena fetched you. Looked as if you'd been in a fight, you did.'

'Yena?' That was what Myles had called Waldegrave, the name he said the castle thieves had given him. I glanced rapidly behind me, sliding my dagger from its sheath, beneath my cloak.

The man gave a short laugh. 'Old Ambrose . . . he's known as the Yena on account of him having such a fancy for cadavers. There's not many he invites to his lodgings. I thought he'd taken the notion that you weren't long for this world and he'd a mind to collect you while you were still fresh, before anyone else took a liking to your corpse.' He gave another yelp of laughter.

Ambrose, was that what Waldegrave was calling himself now?

The man jerked his head towards the old barn. 'He's inside.'

I picked my way across the rubble to the door, knife in hand. As I shoved it open with the point, two yowling cats tumbled out in a blur of fur and claws, making me stumble back. Behind me, I heard the mad rattle of bones and, above it, the man's laughter. The stench of the overflowing privy was even worse than it had been on the night Waldegrave had brought me here and, though it was daylight, once the door was shut, it seemed just as dark inside. I groped my way down the narrow passage until I found the rickety staircase I remembered from that night.

I edged up the steps, which swayed and moaned beneath me. I was half afraid they might not hold up long enough for me to clamber down again. But there was one consolation, not even those cats would be able to creep up that staircase behind me without me hearing them coming. I knocked. The hollow rap triggered a flurry inside, like shining a lantern on a nest of rats. But rats don't usually scrape back a chair or bang down lids on boxes. Finally, the door opened a crack. Waldegrave peered at me, frowning as if he didn't recognise me.

'Ambrose?' I said loudly, mindful that other ears might be listening.

A hand, cold as a dead chicken's foot, grasped my wrist and pulled me inside.

The room was much as I had last seen it, except that the top of the hutch table was bare. But a trail of sand and a few drops of wet black ink on the boards by the bench suggested that my old tutor had been scratching away with his quill and had hastily thrust papers out of sight before opening the door.

'Young fool, I thought I told you to leave the city,' Waldegrave growled. 'You had no business coming here.'

My hackles rose at the old man's imperious tone, angry that he still expected me to obey him as if I was a quivering boy.

'I can't leave, not yet. There is still something I must do.'

Waldegrave gave a snort of derision. 'So, you have masters who order you to stay. I trust they pay you well for the risks you take. What do they think your life is worth, sirrah?' Waldegrave held up his hand. 'I do not want to know, but it is a question you should ask yourself. What is your value to them? You would do well to remember that no master has to pay the wages of a dead servant.'

I knew the old man was goading me, as he'd often done when I was a boy, hoping that in a flash of temper I'd betray something, however small, that he could tease away at until he'd discovered it all. It had taken me many years to learn how to control my temper and my tongue, so that I didn't fall into his trap.

'I came to ask you about Reverend Gysbourne, vicar of Christ Church. Do you know him?' I kept my gaze fixed on the watery eyes, searching for the slightest reaction.

'Know him?' Waldegrave shrugged. 'I know *of* him. Cranmer's spawn. Gysbourne still spouts that dead heretic's words like a parrot prattling oaths taught it by a mariner.'

'But did you know Gysbourne had been found murdered, his corpse discovered lying in his own chancel?'

The old man's hand shot to the left side of his face to conceal the spasm jerking the corner of his mouth and eye.

'I doubt there is a man or woman in Bristol who does not know that by now. You can hardly expect to close a church and place a guard upon it without the reason becoming common knowledge.'

I leaned closer, lowering my voice. 'But what they do not know yet is what was found upon the body.'

The old man's brows furrowed. 'But plainly you do.'

I studied him, trying to work out whether my old tutor knew more of this murder than mere rumour. But Waldegrave gazed steadily back at me, his face betraying nothing. It was a skill that had kept him from arrest, and worse, for years.

'There were a good number who saw the body,' I said, choosing my words carefully. 'And most couldn't wait to broadcast abroad every detail of what they saw. So, those same rumours that informed you he had been murdered must also have said how.'

Waldegrave paused before answering, as if weighing up how much to say. 'It is said that he was stabbed.'

'And *is it said* there were any other wounds?'

'There is talk of . . . burns,' he grudgingly conceded. 'Some say it was the work of witches, others that thieves tortured the man to make him reveal the whereabouts of treasure hidden in the church.'

'And you, Master Waldegrave,' I said. 'Who do you say killed this vicar?'

For the first time, the old man's gaze flickered away from mine. He sank down on the chair, massaging his temples, as if a great weariness had descended on him.

'I do not know, Daniel, but I fear that you may be about to tell me something I dread to hear. Those letters, they have appeared again on this corpse?'

I nodded. 'I've seen them. They're the same as on the other bodies, except for the angle at which they were made. Those who found him were reluctant to search the corpse thoroughly, and as yet it hasn't been closely examined by anyone in authority. But if the coroner is diligent in his duty . . .'

Waldegrave sighed. 'We must pray that he makes nothing of

it, beyond the fact that the man was deliberately burned. If the letters have little meaning for him, perhaps the coroner will not insist the jury examine the brand.'

'But there *is* a meaning,' I pressed. 'We both know that. And I've discovered the identity of the merchant you laid in the crypt.'

'Pray enlighten me, Daniel, how did you do that without asking questions?' Waldegrave arched his eyebrows. It was the same supercilious expression he'd adopted whenever he thought he had caught me out in a lie as a boy. For once, I didn't rise to the bait.

'It was Nicholas Dagworth, a generous patron of the Gaunt's Chapel. But the man murdered in the Salt Cat was a Catholic, though he certainly wasn't a recusant. And now we have this vicar, Gysbourne, who, as you say, was a follower of Cranmer. I have lain awake half the night and I cannot fathom the connection between these three—'

'There is no link,' Daniel,' Waldegrave said firmly, as if he was announcing that God created the world. 'The robbers in the castle are known to be cruel and vicious. They kill men for sport. No doubt this is their way of reminding the people of Bristol that they may do just as they please, and warning them of the fate that awaits anyone who dares try to impede them.'

And yet they know you, Master Waldegrave, and leave you alone.

'You can't really believe that these letters are the mark of the band of robbers?' I said. 'To use this mark, of all those they might choose! It has to mean more than that.'

Waldegrave looked up me and, for the first time, I saw a desperate pleading in his eyes. Here was a frail old man begging to be spared any more trouble in his life.

'Can't you see, Daniel, it matters not what you or I believe. The townspeople are content to think that it was thieves who took that vicar's life. Let us pray that the coroner and his jury believe the same and let the matter rest. If they do not . . . if any man should even begin to think as you do, there will be another drowning of this city, not in water but in the blood that will run through these streets, and through the streets of every town and city in England, once word spreads. For pity's sake, let the dead take their secrets to the silent grave, else they will drag us all down into that pit of darkness with them.'

Chapter Thirty

I HEARD THE ANGRY BELLOWS of the crowd before I rounded the corner. A small procession of men and women were following a lad who was being dragged along the narrow street. He was thrashing wildly in the grip of two burly men. As they reached an opening that led into a courtyard, the youth stuck his foot against the wall, trying to prise himself free, but someone kicked his leg away and he tipped forward as the men dragged him inside.

God's blood, was this another lynching like the cordwainer's? Was Waldegrave right, had it started already?

I wriggled into the back of the mob who crowded around the gate and I saw the deep fiery glow of a blacksmith's forge. The lad had seen it, too. He was alternately cursing his captors and pleading for mercy, though he was so terrified it was hard to make out his words.

'What are they going to do to him?' I demanded of the woman standing next to me. She barely glanced in my direction. 'What he deserves, I hope.'

'What's he done?'

'Gone fishing, that's what, and been caught at it red-handed. Three houses robbed. All had linens and blankets taken from their bedchambers, and my neighbour's belt and purse were lifted from her table while she slept. He's going to pay for it now.'

I understood at once what the lad had been up to. *Hooking,* some called it. A thief would dangle a hook or barb on the end of a rod and line through the open casement of an upper-storey chamber and simply fish for whatever he could catch that he could sell on – a bedsheet, a jug, a necklace or a shirt. The bolder ones went angling at night as the household lay asleep in bed. Others used their rods in daylight, sneaking to the back of the house, when the master was out working and his wife was occupied downstairs.

The lad's shouts had become shrieks, for the men had tied him by the neck to the blacksmith's anvil, and had pinioned his arms. The blacksmith was holding a long iron in the heart of the furnace, turning it as the end began to glow red-hot. The lad was now deathly pale, and though he couldn't move his head, his eyes swivelled towards the furnace, the whites showing like those of a terrified horse. He scraped his heels frantically in the dirt.

'But he's not been tried or sentenced,' I protested. 'They should deliver him to the constable.'

The woman glanced at me in disbelief, as if she thought I was simple. 'They'd not be able to keep him in gaol long enough to be tried at the assizes. He's one of the castle rats, and they always get their own out. Sometimes they bribe the wardens, but mostly they threaten them or their kin. If he was handed over to the constable's men, that little maggot would be safe back inside the castle walls before dawn, where no one could touch him—'

She was interrupted by a long-drawn-out scream, which was suddenly severed in mid-breath. The mob pressed forward and I could see little until they unfastened the lad and hauled him upright. He hung limply between the two men. His head lolled to one side. He had fainted, but a letter T glowed bright scarlet on his cheek, burned almost down to the white bone beneath.

As I turned away and walked down the street, the stench of burnt human flesh followed me. Something Waldegrave said floated to the surface of my mind. *If the letters have little meaning for him, perhaps the coroner will not insist the jury examine the brand.* And only now did I realise what was wrong with that. Over the years, I had seen many men and women branded – on the face, chest or the base of the thumb, on the battlefield and in the marketplace – the brand seared into the smoking flesh of the writhing victims with a red-hot iron. Three or four felons were often brought to the fire in one session, and each mark was identical to the next. But the burns on the corpses were not like those. They were not clear and uniform, stamped like a printer's letter on a paper, as the T had been pressed on the lad's cheek. The more I tried to picture the marks on the corpses, the more convinced I became that they resembled the way a man would write his letters with quill and ink, except that these had been written in fire.

I raked my beard, watching a cat amble across the street, both of us preoccupied with our own business. What kind of pen had made those marks? A burning stick? Possibly, except that it would have to be held for a long time over each spot to burn so deeply, and that would surely leave little pits rather than a smooth line.

And in any case, where would the fires have been lit? Sam Harewell had been found in the stables of the Salt Cat, but there was no evidence of anyone lighting a fire in there – and with all that straw around, a burning stick or flaming torch would most likely have set the whole stable alight before the work was done. It was impossible now to say where Nicholas Dagworth had been killed, for his corpse had been moved, but judging by the quantity of blood on the floor of Christ Church, Gysbourne had been found where he had been stabbed. But there was no fire or blacksmith's furnace in the church.

So had Gysbourne been tortured in his own house, then afterwards dragged into the church, where he was stabbed? But why would the murderer have taken that risk? Gysbourne had been stabbed in the church, so it was most likely those letters had been burned into him there as well. But how? A candle? A candle flame was no hotter than a burning stick. Could it really have burned the flesh as deeply or precisely enough to draw those letters?

THE PARLOUR OF the Salt Cat was so dense with pipe smoke that the walls of the rooms seemed to be undulating, as if they were about to give way behind the press of people. Most were gathered around Caleb Crugge, who was gesticulating wildly with his own long pipe stem. For once, Mistress Crugge did not seem too irked by the sight of her husband holding court instead of working, but she was making sure Rachael made up for it by bellowing orders at her before she'd even set down the flagons or dishes she was carrying.

I wriggled round the back of the throng and settled myself in the far corner. I could still hear what was being said, for Crugge was addressing the room with all the drama of an actor upon the stage, and even if a word or two were lost, several in the crowd were repeating his words to their neighbours like boys trying to memorise a lesson.

Master Crugge had been summoned that afternoon to give testimony before the coroner about what he had seen in the church. Crugge announced to his audience that the coroner had directed the jury to bring in a verdict of murder. This came as no surprise to anyone in the Salt Cat, but it was what the innkeeper said next that caused the murmurs of the crowd around him to rise sharply like a flock of startled birds.

'But he said that he was certain the poor vicar had *not* been slain by thieves.'

My fingers tightened around the tankard I was holding. Were Waldegrave's worst fears about to be realised? It was not the coroner's role, of course, to determine who had committed the crime, merely to rule on the cause of the victim's untimely death, but according to Crugge, he had ordered an arrest, and an arrest had been made.

The twittering of the crowd rose to fever pitch. Crugge paused, on the pretext of taking a long drag from his own tankard. He was clearly enjoying himself, but even he could not continue to ignore the cries of the crowd for long.

'Who?'

'Who's been arrested?'

'Who did it, Caleb?'

He wiped his thin lips against the back of his hand. 'None other than the churchwarden, Martin Symons.'

There was a collective gasp of shock from the group, which seemed to please Crugge, for he was almost beaming with satisfaction as people stared incredulously at one another. Then another fluster of questions came at him, thick and fast.

He raised his hands, and the group fell quiet. 'Aye, you might well be surprised, but that was nothing to the look on Symons' face when the coroner ordered the constable to arrest him and hold him till the next assizes. First, he turned red as a cockscomb, then all the blood seemed to drain right out through his feet, for his face went white, and when he tried to take a pace forward, he was quivering like a calf's foot jelly and couldn't seem to move his legs. He'd have pitched right on to his face, if the constable and a guard hadn't been holding him on either side. Symons must have thought he'd got away with it and no man would even suspect him.'

'So, you reckon he's guilty, then,' the cobbler said.

Crugge shrugged. 'There's no denying the evidence. They found the key to the main door right next to the body . . .' The innkeeper paused, but it was obvious from the blank expressions of his customers that they had no idea what that signified.

'Well, as I told the coroner myself, the great door was locked when I arrived that morning. So, if the vicar's key was beside his body, the murderer must have used another to let himself out and lock the door behind him,' Crugge said, as if he had reasoned this out for himself.

'But when Symons gave his testimony at the beginning, he told the coroner he had the only other key, and swore he always kept it hidden away at home. Proud of it he was, boasted that as warden he'd never let anyone use it without his being there. And Symons had fetched that very key from his house to open the church when we found the poor vicar's corpse.

'And I told the coroner, I said, Master Symons didn't want to open the door, most reluctant he was, most reluctant, but it was me insisted he did,' Crugge added proudly. 'Symons kept saying we should wait to hear from Reverend Gysbourne first. Of course, now we know why he didn't want to open the church, don't we? 'Cause he already knew exactly what we'd find inside. I reckon he was hoping we'd all grow tired of waiting for the vicar, and go home. Then Symons could move the body after it was dark, and most likely drop it in the river. But I knew something was amiss from the start. I had this feeling in my water, that's why I made him open the door.'

'If Martin hadn't boasted about the care he took of that key, he'd likely have got clean away with it,' the cobbler said, nodding in some satisfaction.

'But I can't see that key proves anything,' said another man, frowning. 'Who's to say it hadn't been stolen? Someone could have taken it from his house, and put it back after the murder. A key won't be enough to convict him.'

'Maybe not, but there's more,' Crugge announced and the crowd, who had been starting to argue among themselves, immediately gave him their full attention again.

'There was that burn on the vicar's chest, remember. Coroner took a long time trying to make out what the mark was. It wasn't easy, because by the time he saw the corpse, the belly was bloating and the mess around it wasn't smelling any sweeter for having been left there two days. He's a strong stomach, that coroner, I'll give him that. None of the jury wanted to get too close, but finally the coroner said it looked to him like the burn made the shape of letters, two of them, M and S. And that's what he said should be recorded.' Crugge looked expectantly at his audience. 'Martin Symons!'

'You mean he burned his own mark into his victim? Why would he do a thing like that? It was as good as signing his own death warrant.'

For the first time, Crugge looked a little uncertain. 'Aye, well, the coroner didn't explain that, but he said it could have been the vicar himself who did it, trying to tell us who the murderer was as he lay there, bleeding to death. They found a candle on the floor, and no sign it had fallen from any of the sconces, so it stands to reason either the murderer or the victim must have used that.'

'To think of burning your own flesh,' a woman shuddered.

'They say when you're bleeding bad, you don't feel pain,' another said, but she, too, was shivering.

'I still reckon it was witchcraft,' the butcher said. 'You said yourself, Caleb, no one could see for certain what that mark was. It could just as likely have been one of their signs or some kind of curse. And I reckon that candle proves it. Casting a spell with it, they were.'

The butcher now leaned forward, his voice lowered, as if he was about to impart something that shouldn't be spoken aloud. 'I heard that one of the watch was in the Three Cups last evening and he was telling all who'd listen that he'd been guarding the church that first night after the murder and heard a noise inside like a damned soul rattling chains. He unlocked the door and, just as he went in, something ghostly pale sprang from the corpse. That very same moment, a terrible wind whipped up out of nowhere, whirling round the church, and the Devil's door flew open wide, though it was locked tight and had not been opened for years. He swears he saw a demon flee through that door and vanish.'

All eyes were now on the butcher, and the Salt Cat's customers seemed even more impressed by this tale than by Crugge's account, a point not lost on the innkeeper.

'That's the rubbish you'll get served if you spend your shillings in the Three Cups. The fools in there would swallow any old tarradiddle, and I don't just mean the ale. Go fishing for the moon in the sea, they would, thinking it was the king of herrings.'

Several of the men laughed. It seemed there was no love lost between regulars of the two inns.

The talk rambled on, people speculating on what the churchwarden's motive might have been for murdering the vicar, though most were agreed that it was a well-known fact that wardens and vicars were always at war with each other over who was master of the church. As one woman said, it was nothing short of a miracle that every congregation in Bristol hadn't arrived some Sunday to find blood on the floor. While the butcher and a few others were still arguing that the warden was innocent and the vicar had disturbed a nest of witches.

I listened for a while, hoping that someone might toss me some small nugget of information or gossip about Gysbourne that might link him to either the printer or the merchant, but it seemed that no one really knew anything. They were simply repeating what had already been said, as if saying it louder might convince others of the truth of it.

I slipped out into the courtyard, breathing deeply in the cold night air. Smoke from the hearths of houses and the beggars' bonfires swirled in the air, but it was at least sweeter and less suffocating than the thick fog of the tobacco smoke that filled the parlour. Somewhere in this city, a man lay shivering on the cold, hard floor of a cell, trying to understand why only that morning he had been a free man, rising from his own warm bed, eating breakfast at his own table, without it ever crossing his mind that he would not be eating his supper at that same table hours later. I felt a pang of guilt but, in truth, nothing I had done that night in the church could have made Martin Symons appear guilty of murder, except in the eyes of a codwit.

I was certain the churchwarden was innocent. But I couldn't convince the sheriff that the letters burned on to the vicar's chest were not the initials of Martin Symons, unless I produced the two other corpses – and even if I did, the letters on their skin would probably not be legible by now, not after the rats and worms had been at work. Master Waldegrave would certainly not bear witness to them. And if there was another murder, another body found with those letters, it might help Symons, but while the churchwarden might be spared the hangman's noose, a great many other innocents would die at the hands of the mob. My best chance, my only chance, was to find the real killer before he struck again.

I LOCKED THE DOOR of my chamber, pushed the small chest in front of it and sank wearily on to the bed. I drew a coin from my purse, repeatedly palming it and revealing it. The death of the vicar proved, beyond doubt, three men had not been murdered because they were secret Catholics. I had learned from the butcher that Christ Church had been the first in the city to embrace Cranmer's Reformation. A Catholic priest, even one trying to conceal his faith, would hardly seek out a post as a vicar in a church that was so blatantly hostile to the old religion. There were many other churches whose congregations and fellow clerics would be far more sympathetic towards such leanings. The three murdered men moved in very different circles. If they even knew each other, it could surely only be by chance. I could see no reason why they should become the target of Jesuit conspirators.

A faint clink made me glance down. The coin I'd been playing with had tumbled to the floor. I heaved myself off the bed and bent to retrieve it. Then I stood staring at the silver disc glinting in my palm. The art of legerdemain is to make the audience look in the wrong place. They swear they have seen you cover a gold ring with cloth, because you tell them that is what you are doing. Then the ring appears in a box they thought empty, a box they were not looking at. But the ring was never under that cloth.

FitzAlan had told me that a Jesuit plot was suspected, told me the city was teeming with their spies, and I had found myself looking for them, because that was what I had been directed to see. But suppose there was nothing to see. Suppose Spero Pettingar had never been in this city. Was the King's loyal adviser nudging me towards reporting a conspiracy that had never existed, simply to create an excuse to finally crush the Catholics and ensure that there would be no uprising, no more threats to put Spain's Infanta on the English throne?

I had no means of knowing who FitzAlan really served. He had declared himself to be the King's most trusted adviser, but then Cecil would claim that same title himself. So, was FitzAlan carrying out the King's orders or obeying the instructions of Cecil, who, it was rumoured, had plotted and schemed behind Queen Elizabeth's back to ensure that King James would take the throne of England on the old woman's death. It was even murmured in some quarters that Cecil had not, as he'd insisted, learned of the Gunpowder Treason in a letter only days before the planned massacre. Some said he had known of it from the beginning, even, it was whispered, used his own agents to foment it, in order to whip up the fury of the people against the Catholics.

My fist tightened around the coin till it bit into my palm. Was this another of Cecil's schemes? *Return with a report that will please the King*, FitzAlan had said. Or should that really be *return with a report that will please the demon who lurks behind the royal throne*?

Chapter Thirty-one

THE TOWER OF LONDON

THE OAK DOOR OF the small chamber thudded shut behind Oliver; the sound echoed through the stone walls as if the porter had slammed the door on purpose to remind him just how solid and impenetrable they were. Oliver's bowels churned. He half expected to hear the key grate in the lock, but clearly the porter had been given no instructions to lock this visitor in. At least, Oliver prayed that was what he still was, just a visitor. He tried to draw comfort from the familiar bump of his sword against his thigh. They had not removed that and, surely, they would have done if they meant to keep him here. All the same, a cold sweat beaded his forehead, and his hastily donned shirt clung damply to his chest. Being shaken awake in the middle of the night to be told he had been summoned to the Tower, then rowed up the oily black water of the Thames in the bitter wind, watching the grim edifice looming menacingly higher and higher in the blood-red torchlight, was enough to send terror coursing through the heart of the most battle-hardened solider. And Oliver, though he'd never admit as much, was scarcely even a man as yet.

But his fear eased just a little at the sight of the small square room. A cheerful fire blazed in the hearth. Several wax candles burned brightly in the sconces on the wall and several more on the prongs of a large iron pricket in the form of stag's head, which stood in the centre of a long table. A stool had been placed at one end of the table and several upright chairs ranged along either side, but these were empty, as was the chair with the high winged back that stood facing the hearth. At least, Oliver thought it was empty. But the chair suddenly creaked and a small hunchbacked man uncoiled from its depths, like a snakelet hatching from its shell.

'Would you care for some sack, Master Oliver, it is from my own *private* cellars, or have you acquired a taste for whisky since you've come to Court?' Lord Salisbury's tongue seemed to linger on the word *private* as if he had invited Oliver to an intimate supper with friends.

Oliver's mouth and throat suddenly felt so dry he wasn't sure he could even croak a reply.

'Sack . . . thank you . . . my lord.'

The river of dark red liquid glinted in the candlelight as it cascaded into the goblet. Oliver had always thought it looked like molten rubies; now it looked like blood.

'Please take your ease, Master Oliver. You look ill. It is the lateness of the hour, no doubt.'

Lord Salisbury's gaze had fastened on Oliver's hand as he took the goblet, and the young man realised his fingers were visibly trembling. He tried to slide into one of the chairs along the table, but his host was blocking his path – was that deliberate? – and he was obliged to perch on the narrow stool. Robert Cecil slowly seated himself in one of the chairs, a goblet of sack in front of him, but he neither drank nor spoke. The crackle and occasional shift of the burning coals in the fire seemed to grow as loud as cannon fire. Oliver, aware that Cecil's large green eyes were drilling into him, found himself studying his goblet with uncommon interest. He forced himself to take only small infrequent sips. He dared not risk gulping it down as he longed to do. An interview with Robert Cecil was not to be undertaken with your thoughts fuddled and your tongue loosened by drink.

'I am told that you witnessed the attempted assassination of the King by John Morecote.'

The silence had stretched on for so long that when Cecil

spoke, Oliver jerked violently. Sack from his goblet splashed on to the table and lay there in glistening red pool.

'John Morecote?' The name seemed vaguely familiar, but his brain had turned to porridge.

'The man who tried to murder the King while he was hunting,' Cecil prompted.

'With the crossbow, yes.' Oliver could have kicked himself. Lord Salisbury would think him a fool – or worse, that he was trying to prevaricate.

'You saw Morecote fire the crossbow?'

'I didn't . . . not really . . . I heard the bolt hit the tree, but I didn't see who fired. Just before Richard started running towards the King, I thought I glimpsed a movement in the bushes, but I didn't actually see anyone. The sun was going down and it was too dark to see much beyond the clearing.'

'Yet you did see movement. How can you see someone move, if you cannot see them?'

'I . . . I think I must have heard it.'

'I am told you and Lord Fairfax were standing close in conversation. The trees are not yet in leaf and he saw the crossbow being raised, but you, a man half his age whose eyesight should be keener, say you did not see the assassin. Curious.'

'I was . . .' Oliver faltered. He'd been going to explain that he'd been watching Richard make his way over to the King, but that made him sound even more of a fool – a boy staring like the village idiot at his cousin instead of watching out for the King's safety.

'Where did you first meet John Morecote?'

Oliver gaped at him. 'I didn't . . . I never laid eyes on him until he was dragged before the King.'

'But he recognised you.'

Aghast, Oliver half rose from the stool, but saw Lord Salisbury stiffen and glance at the door. He'd have men waiting outside. A single cry would bring them rushing in. Oliver forced himself to sit again, gripping his hands together under the table to stop himself shaking. 'That's impossible, my lord, I swear by Christ's blood, I'd never seen Morecote before that day.'

Cecil continued in the same quiet, even tone. 'Then perhaps he saw you when he visited Lord Fairfax's house. George Fairfax was your uncle, was he not? You must have been often to his house. I understand he had many callers at strange hours of the day and night, no doubt Morecote was one of them.'

Oliver shook his head. 'I visited my uncle only a few times with my parents. But I was only eleven years old when he was killed in a riding accident. After my uncle's death, I didn't return to the house at all. I had little contact with my cousin Richard again until I wrote asking him to help me obtain a place at Court. I don't remember any visitors when I was in the house, and I don't remember Morecote.'

'You knew George Fairfax was a recusant.'

Oliver stared at his goblet. 'I knew . . . I suppose my father must have told me at some time, I don't remember. But my parents were not Catholics, and Lord Fairfax never discussed such matters with me.'

'And the Jesuit priests Fairfax hid in his house, did they discuss *such matters* with you? Did you hear them speak of the throne and who should be the Queen's successor?'

'I know nothing about any priests. I was just a boy.'

'But little boys are curious by nature. They hide in corners. They overhear things. They peep through curtains watching who comes and goes by night. They delight in searching for secret places, hidden chambers.' Cecil was leaning forward now, his gaze fixed on Oliver's face, the firelight dancing in his green eyes.

'I didn't see any priests or find any hiding holes.' Oliver knew he was shouting, his voice girlish, shrill and he tried to lower it. He swallowed hard. 'Richard's father was an honourable man, a loyal man, as is his son.'

'A man such as George Fairfax, who gives succour to the King's enemies, cannot be loyal. A lion sires a lion, a fox sires a fox, each according to his kind, as God ordained at the creation of the world. When the lion devours the sheep, his cub learns to kill the lamb, and as the fox steals the chicken, so he will teach his own son how to raid the coop. Sons follow the nature of their fathers.'

Fear and anger blazed up in Oliver. 'My . . . my cousin Richard is no traitor, if that is your meaning, my lord. He is devoted to the King. He proved as much at the hunt. He saved the King's life. All there saw it. His loyalty to the King cannot be in any doubt.'

'Ah, yes, that was most fortuitous. As you say, Master Oliver, his loyalty cannot be in doubt now, can it?'

Oliver did not dare look at him. An image had flashed once more into his head. John Morecote being dragged away, turning to stare at someone standing close by the King, as if he had been betrayed. Oliver knew Morecote had not been looking at him, but what if . . . ? Oliver gazed at the spreading pool of red wine on the table. Somewhere in this city, probably in this Tower, John Morecote was being questioned. If he hadn't already talked, he would soon, no man could hold out for long. And when he did, whose name would he cry out?

Chapter Thirty-two

DANIEL PURSGLOVE

'MISTRESS CRUGGE will charge you more if you take her to your room.'

I jumped at the sound of the voice behind me and the light touch on my arm. Rachael was standing in the darkened courtyard, pulling her cloak tightly around her against the chill air. She was smiling, her eyes shining in the torchlight from the street. She looked happier than I'd seen her in days.

'Take who to my room?'

'The woman you've been hanging around here waiting for. Why else would you be freezing out here?'

'And if the woman I was waiting for was you?'

She laughed and leaned forward, lowering her voice. 'If Mistress Crugge thought it was me, she'd charge you double, because she'd like to be up there in your chamber herself.'

'Her! Don't even joke about it.'

'Don't be fooled,' Rachael wagged a finger at me. 'That one likes everyone to think she's the adoring and dutiful wife, but she flirts like a mermaid with any young man who takes her fancy.' She grinned. 'If I were you, I'd push that chest up against your door at night.'

I looked at her sharply. Did she know I'd done that?

'Thanks for the warning. I won't dare sleep again till I leave Bristol.'

'And will that be soon?' Her expression had suddenly become serious. 'Have you had word of them?'

For a moment, I couldn't think what she was talking about. My head was stuffed full of the murders, and I'd almost forgotten that Rachael still believed I was searching for my aunt and cousins.

'No . . . nothing yet. But I continue to ask and keep hoping I might see them among a crowd in the streets.'

Her face softened in sympathy. 'You're a good man.' She pulled the cloak tighter as a strong gust of wind threatened to snatch it, struggling with the clasp that held it in place at the neck.

'Here, let me.'

She let her arms fall, standing still as I tugged the two sides of the cloak closer about her throat and slipped the hook of the clasp into the eyelet. It was an unusual design, the face of a crowned queen half circled by a new moon with a border of tiny Tudor roses. It glinted bronze in the torchlight from the street, but it had evidently been much used, for in places the pewter beneath the gilding was beginning to show through where her fingers had rubbed against the raised pattern. As I adjusted the folds of her cloak, I brushed the soft skin of her neck. I snatched my hand away, trying to convince myself it was an accidental touch, and took a step back from her.

'A pretty piece,' I said.

Her eyes flashed.

'I was speaking of the clasp.'

She laughed. 'My mother's. It's a likeness of Queen Bess. She came to Bristol once when my mother was but a lass. My mother climbed right up on to the top of a towering pile of kegs to watch the procession, because she couldn't see over the heads of the throng. She never tired of telling me about all the gold and silver, and the fine dresses of the ladies. She swore, to her dying day, that the Queen looked up at her as she passed and smiled to see her balanced up there. My mother was sure she waved just to her. So, my father gave her this when they were wed, knowing what a fondness she had for the Queen. Said she might never have a cloak as fine as the Queen's ladies, but she'd always be clad in the Queen's smile.'

'Your mother died?'

Rachael grimaced. 'Aye, plague took her.' She touched the clasp, rubbing her fingers over the raised features. 'Sometimes I fancy it's her face I wear, not the Queen's. My father always reckoned there was a likeness between them.'

I thought I saw tears in her eyes, but it might have been the smarting of the wind, for the next moment she was smiling.

'Best take myself off. Only a few hours before I have to be back here. Mistress wants me to help press brawn tomorrow and means to make an early start, though what meat we'll use, heaven alone knows, but she says it's coming at daybreak.' Rachael pulled a face. 'As far as I can see, the only beasts we've left since the flood are stray dogs and cats – and rats, of course. So, if you see a row of skinned rats hanging in the yard tomorrow, you might want to buy your supper at the Three Cups.' She giggled.

I laughed, too. But as Rachael turned to go, I called out, 'Let me escort you. It isn't safe for a woman to walk alone at this hour. Harewell was killed here and the vicar was murdered only a few streets away.'

She stopped abruptly and her back stiffened. I took a few steps towards her, stepping around her so that I was facing her. She gave me a brief smile, which carried none of the warmth or humour it had moments before. 'No need to trouble yourself, Master Daniel, I'm used to walking these streets alone.'

'But it isn't safe . . .'

'We've grown used to thieves and murderers in Bristol. If we stayed locked behind doors every time someone was attacked, we'd never venture on to the streets. It's no more dangerous now than it was before you came, nor will be after you leave,' she said firmly. 'Unless you mean to stay here for the rest of your life to escort me round the city.' She threw a mocking glance at me, as if daring me to say I would. 'Besides, someone comes to meet me. He'll be waiting.'

'You have a suitor, then?' I took a step back.

A mischievous grin spread over her face and the hardness in her eyes vanished.

'Suitor? He's my father, you halfwit!' She laughed and, picking up her skirts, darted around me, then ran through the archway out into the street and was gone.

I climbed the stairs to my chamber wishing, not for the first time, that I could erase the last minutes. The worst of it was, I didn't know why it should matter to me. She was right: in days, weeks at the most, I would have to leave for London. What promises could I offer her?

It was only as I flung myself down on the bed that I remembered Rachael's jest about pushing the chest up against my door. Was that her way of warning me to be on my guard? The stone eye was still where I'd left it. I checked my hidden stash of money in the secret drawer of my travelling chest. Nothing missing – everything was in place, including the hidden seal I'd taken from Dagworth. I sank back on to the bed, turning a coin over in my hand and, as I always did from habit, making it vanish and reappear. My mind wandered back to Rachael. I felt again the soft skin of her neck as I fastened that strange little clasp. I smiled. Did she really believe that her mother looked like the Queen?

I saw that face again in my head and shot upright on the bed. Molten metal could be made to form images of queens, beasts . . . even letters. Those beads of tin I'd found in Dagworth's shirt . . . was that what had been used to burn the letters into the skin of those three men – molten tin? But if it had, I would have seen it solidified in the wounds of all three victims.

The image of the silversmith I had watched working on my first day in Bristol surfaced in my mind, drawing the Bristol shield on the brooch. He had sweated the metal into that pattern using nothing more than a candle and a tube. And any man who could control a flame so precisely could easily use the same skill to burn letters deep into a man's chest. He would not need the metal itself, merely the flame used to melt it. That's why there had been no trace of wood ash in the church, and no need for a fire or furnace.

The beads of tin had not been used to cause the burns, but they could well have fallen from the hair or the clothing of the man who had mutilated the merchant, though few men worked in tin. It was too weak and soft to be fashioned into tools, or even a brooch, except when mixed with other metals. But it *was* possible to mix tin with other metals. And Bristol was famous for men with that skill, too – the pewterers who used tin to make everything, from plates to pots and buckles to buttons. My former master, Viscount Rowe, always insisted on Bristol pewter for his table, for it was finer than any made in London.

I leaned back on the lumpy pillow. My head was whirling. How many men in Bristol were engaged in the pewterer's craft – master craftsmen, journeymen and apprentices – all capable of producing those marks? But why would a pewterer want to murder three men who seemed to have as little to do with the pewterer's craft as they had with the Jesuits?

Chapter Thirty-three

THE CLATTER OF A HANDCART in the courtyard below woke me and I wasted no time in scrambling out of bed and dressing. A chill mizzle wetted my face as I marched down the stairs. Mistress Crugge was on the far side of the yard, sheltering under the overhanging thatch. I saw her accost a jug-eared youth and motion to him to lower the sack he was carrying. She peered inside, then gestured imperiously for him to carry it into her cold shed. The lad's hair was plastered to his face by the rain, and his shoulders hunched miserably like an old man's, as he returned to his handcart to fetch another load.

'They're all seals' heads, like you paid for,' he grumbled.

'Then you'll not mind me checking, will you?' Mistress Crugge said firmly.

'But master said he'd use my guts for sausages skins, if I didn't get back double quick. He's expecting me to mind the shop for him.'

'In that case, you had best put your back into it instead of keeping me standing out here getting soaked, while you amble along like a giddy maid picking buttercups.' She glanced at me and her plump face broke into a smile. 'Seals were caught up by the wave and tossed on land. They were trapped and couldn't get back to sea. Starving, they were. It was a mercy to put them out of their misery. The carcasses were snapped up – and the flippers, too, for the making of flipper pie – but I managed to get the heads,' she said triumphantly. 'Make fine brawn, these will.' She must have seen my involuntary grimace, for she added, 'There's no sense wasting good food when it's so hard to come by.'

I gave a brief nod, as if I agreed, though it was certainly not the thought of wasting food which had caused the spasm to cross my face but the rank smell of overripe flesh, spiced with the strong odour of rotten mackerel, that was causing my empty stomach to churn unpleasantly as Mistress Crugge examined another severed head which the boy sulkily held out for her inspection. The large clouded eyes of the dead seal gazed back, unblinking, out of the sacking. She nodded and the boy slung the sack over his shoulder, slouching towards the storeroom.

Mistress Crugge stared after him, compressing her lips as tightly as the drawstring on a miser's purse. 'You have to watch these lads every minute, thieves the lot of them. Neighbour of mine paid good money for meat from the butcher, watched him put it into the sack and heard him tell his lad to pag it to her house. But when she went to fetch the meat from the cellar where the boy had left it, she found her own cat dead in the sack. She nearly dropped dead of shock herself, poor woman. That wicked lad swore her cat must have got into the cellar, gobbled up the meat and died of a surfeit.' She gave a snort. 'Well, they needn't think they can take me for a fool.'

'Nobody would dare, Mistress Crugge,' I said, with a smile.

She glanced sharply at me, evidently suspicious she was being mocked.

'You had some good news, Master Pursglove? I've not seen you look this cheerful since the day you arrived.'

'Not so much good news, Mistress Crugge, but a new idea about where to search, and you gave it to me, for which I offer you my gratitude.'

I bowed and gave her a swift kiss on her plump hand, and she blushed and simpered like a virgin maid.

I walked swiftly out through the archway. The thought had indeed come from Mistress Crugge, at least in part. It was her talk of merchants' marks being displayed on the board outside the Collector's office. It wasn't only the merchants who had their own signs, craftsmen did also. Now that I was certain that the burns had been inflicted by a pewterer, I couldn't ignore the possibility that the letters etched into the victims' skin were never intended to be the sign of the Jesuits, but the mark of a particular craftsman. Every piece of pewter made in England had to bear a touchmark, showing who had made it. Finding the pewterer's workshop in Bristol that used that mark might not instantly give me the identity of the murderer, but it would at least provide a list of likely men.

But as the day wore on, my optimism began to trickle out like sand from an hourglass. There were, or rather there had been, a great number of pewterers working in Bristol, many in the part of the city that lay closest to the river and wharfs. Some of the buildings had collapsed, but even where the walls remained intact, seawater had flooded the furnaces. Striking, as the flood had, without warning, there had been no time to cool them – indeed, most had been at their hottest at that hour, the day's work already underway. Under the sudden deluge of cold water, many had exploded. Burned, maimed and unconscious men and boys had been swept up in the torrent and, unable to climb to safety, had been swept away or trapped and drowned. Those whose furnaces had survived were still trying to dig through mud to rescue precious tools and ingots. I had carefully drawn the letters on a small scrap of paper, as I remembered them from the bodies, but even when I could find men willing to glance at the paper, they shook their heads. It wasn't their touchmark, and it didn't belong to any craftsmen they knew.

I joined the crowd converging on Marsh Gate. Like most city gates, a chaos of people, sledges and carts were trying to squeeze through it in both directions at once, each person convinced his business was more pressing than anyone else's and refusing to give way. As I slipped through the gate, a smell insinuated itself between the smoke of hearth fires and rotting refuse – one that made my stomach sharply remind me it had been deprived of breakfast. I followed the aroma up the street until I came to a small gap between two houses. An old woman had built a fire and was shaping patties of some greenish mixture into balls between her greasy palms, dipping them in a small pot of batter and frying them on a large flat piece of iron which looked as if it might once have been the door for a baker's oven or a furnace.

The old woman nodded at me. 'Fritters, sir? Straight from the fire, good and hot, they are, warm you up a treat.'

I paid for three, which she handed to me on a yellowing cabbage leaf. I ate one leaning against a wall, allowing myself to savour every bite. It was warming and satisfying with its crunchy coating of ale batter. I felt a tug on my sleeve and looked down to see Myles gazing up at me, or rather at the two remaining fritters.

'I suppose there's no point asking if you're hungry?'

Myles nodded without taking his eyes from the balls of batter. I held out the leaf to the lad. He grabbed one of the fritters, then hesitated, his eyes glued to the other.

I gave a short laugh. 'Go on, then.'

His other hand shot out and grabbed the remaining ball. He took such a large bite from one that he almost choked, for the fritter was still steaming inside. Unable to swallow it, he was forced to spit it into his hand and blow on it to cool it. But he gobbled it up again, almost at once.

'Better?' I asked.

He nodded.

'Then I've a job for you.'

'But I've got a job,' he announced gleefully.

'That's excellent news, lad. Where are you working?'

A puzzled frown creased his filthy forehead, as if he had not considered that before. He shrugged. 'But it's on the eve of Lady Day. There's to be a New Year's masque in the city after dark, with costumes and fire and a bone horse, too. They'll parade right through the streets and down to the river.' He drew himself up and with evident pride announced, 'I'm to ride Old Bony.

He's the most important in the whole masque, for he'll make sure the wave won't come again. They'll give me a whole shilling for doing it, and all I can eat, too, that's what the man said.'

'That's a handsome sum for such work.'

With Bristol still in ruins, I couldn't believe the city's Corporation had decided to spend money on a masque, even one to celebrate the New Year, especially when the merchants and city fathers had been forced to go begging for money from the King to rebuild. If word of such extravagance reached London it would not help Bristol's cause. As for the bone horse, the old grey mare, as some called it, the Puritans had long railed against such pagan customs in other towns. I wondered if they knew what was being planned.

'Who's organising the masque? Is it one of the guilds?'

Myles didn't reply.

'Do you know the man who promised you the shilling?'

He shook his head. 'Said he'd come and fetch me at four of the clock on the eve of Lady Day. Said no one's to see their costumes till the masque starts.'

It was common for those taking part in a masque to keep their costumes well hidden until the night of the parade, for fear that rivals would copy or even steal them. Yet I was surprised they'd chosen Myles. If this was being arranged by one of guilds and a boy was needed to take part, wasn't it more likely that one of the guild members' own children would be selected for the honour, rather than a street urchin?

'This man may forget what he promised,' I cautioned.

'He won't. He told me I'm exactly the lad they were looking for.'

I shrugged. 'If you say so, but those fritters won't keep you full until then. So, what about that job for me?'

I showed him the mark I had copied. I had no reason to think he might recognise it, but he told me that a number of the craftsmen had set up temporary workshops outside the city walls, on the Temple side of the bridge, when they had been forced out by the flood. Myles knew the area far better than I did so I sent him off to search, with a fourpence for his dinner and more promised if he could discover the pewterer's workshop.

MYLES DID NOT appear at the Salt Cat that night, and I guessed he'd had no luck, or more likely had simply pocketed the money. I knew better than most how hard it was to survive alone, and I'd done far worse to survive than fleece a few pennies.

But the following day brought me no more success. By mid-afternoon, I had abandoned the search for workshops and had decided to try the shopkeepers and pedlars instead. On the pretext of seeking out a particular pewterer who had in the past made a fine piece for my father, I'd shown the paper with the copied mark to several men who displayed pewter wares for sale among their other pots, lamps or candlesticks. But none recognised it.

'Could be foreign, that touch,' one shopkeeper said, peering at the slip of paper again.

I silently cursed. He was right. It could well be a foreign pewterer working here who had a grudge against those three men – or was that the point, that he was *not* working here? A Dutchman or Frenchman who'd been denied entrance to the guild in England, so that he couldn't work as a master pewterer in Bristol, but had been forced to take a lowly position, even though he was fully skilled. That might account for his hatred of Nicholas Dagworth, if the merchant had cheated him or used his wealth and influence to convince the guild members to refuse him admission. But why should he bear a grudge against a printer or a vicar?

Just as I was leaving, the shopkeeper looked up from the customer he was serving. 'That touchmark of yours – there's a man who might know it. He goes by the name of Hugh. Young Peter Grobbam took him on in his works in Baldwin Street to do the patching and repairs of old pieces, after Hugh lost some of his fingers in an accident. Hugh used to be a master craftsman, had his own works once. He can't do the fine work now, like he did, but he was reckoned to be one of the best pewterers in Bristol in his day. Head of the guild at one time, so he'd know the old touches, if anyone would.'

Chapter Thirty-four

EVENING CREPT IN, trailing a cloak of thin grey fog that curled through the archways and slithered round the casements. The street had emptied of goodwives and pedlars, and the pace of the men delivering their last loads of wood or water had quickened. A few lanterns had been lit in Peter Grobbam's workshop and in the whittawer's yard next door, all determined to squeeze the last few drops of working light from the husk of the day. But finally, it grew too dark even for men desperate to catch up, and the clanging of hammers ceased. The furnace was banked down, and weary men and boys began to emerge, scattering towards their homes or their favourite tavern. But none had missing fingers, nor appeared old enough to be Hugh, for I reckoned if he had owned a works some years back – and been master of a guild, too – he must by now be in his fifties at least, and probably older.

I turned and hurried after the last man, who was plodding wearily up Baldwin Street. He was a head shorter than me, his skinny legs bowed as a tar barrel. As if to mirror his legs, his chest stuck out, round as a pouter pigeon, not from the padding in his doublet, as was fashionable in London, but from years spent blowing through the sweating pipes to fuse the metals.

As he reached the old city gate, at the top of the street, straddled by St Leonard's Church, he half turned his head as if he could sense he was being followed. He quickened his pace until he was under the archway beneath the church whose shadowy corners were lit by the flames of several burning torches. Wisps of mist swirled red in the torchlight, like blood in water. I hoped he was making for a tavern, where I knew it would be easier to strike up a conversation, but as soon as I entered the archway he rounded on me, yelling for the guards.

Two men hurtled towards me, charging at me like knights in the joust, the lethal points of their halberds aimed straight at my guts. I leaped aside, swivelling as I did. One of the halberds hit the wall with a clang, the rebound knocking the watchman flat on his arse. The blade of the other sliced across my chest and would have opened me up like a smoked herring, if my doublet had not been leather and padded. He prodded me towards the corner with repeated jabs of the weapon, as if he was driving an unruly pig into a pen. Not wishing to give him any excuse to run me through, I raised my hands and obligingly shuffled backwards until I was wedged against the wall.

The scowling watchman who had fallen looked barely old enough to be entrusted with a wooden sword, much less anything as dangerous as a halberd. The other, moon-faced and gorbellied, appeared a decade or so older but scarcely more at home with the weapon. Not that that was any comfort, since the point of his blade was now pushing between my ribs, and a swift thrust would require no skill to pierce a lung at the very least.

The pewterer had backed well away while the watchmen cornered the dangerous felon, but seeing that I'd been captured, his courage flowed back and he jiggled from side to side in his excitement, though taking care to keep well behind the guards.

'You arrest him, take him straight to the sheriff. He's a robber, he is. Been watching Master Peter's works, he has. I reckon he means to break in and murder poor Peter and his wife and young 'uns while they sleep. Followed me all the way here.'

'Why would I have followed you if I intended to break into Master Peter's house?'

The journeyman hesitated, then addressed himself to the two watchmen. 'Maybe . . . he thought to force me to tell him how to get in.'

The older of the two watchmen nodded sagely. 'It happens. Two of the castle rats got hold of a maidservant, threatened to cut her nose off until she told them about a broken catch on a casement in her master's house.'

'And there was that vicar,' the journeymen cried out. 'Tortured to death in his own church to force him to tell where the valuables were.'

The watchman pressed the spike of his halberd harder into my chest.

'I'm not from the castle,' I said, trying not to move an inch as I spoke. 'Lodging at the Salt Cat . . . Ask the innkeeper, Caleb Crugge, he'll . . . vouch for me.'

'He doesn't look like one of the castle rats,' the watchman said. 'Unless he stole this.' He flicked the edge of my ruined doublet with the point of his weapon. 'Looks far too clean for any of them.'

'So why was he watching the pewter works and why was he following me?' the journeyman demanded indignantly.

'I wanted to speak to a pewterer named Hugh. A shopkeeper told me he worked for Peter Grobbam.'

'Oh, aye,' the journeyman said suspiciously, 'and what would you be wanting with Hugh?'

I saw no reason not to tell him. 'I was told that he used to be a master of the Pewterers' Guild once, and so he might recognise an old touchmark.'

The two watchmen exchanged nods, as if that explanation seemed reasonable enough to them, but the journeyman was still glowering at me. 'So, why didn't you come in as an honest man and ask for Hugh?'

'Anyone interrupting a man's work with questions that bring him no profit is apt to get short shrift, and your Master Grobbam did not look to be in a sanguine humour.'

The journeyman's frown lifted a little. 'You're right there, he doesn't have time for idle chatter. We lost a good deal of stock. He's a lot vexing him just now, as have we all.'

'When you came out as the last man to leave, I hurried after you, in the hope that I could buy you a flagon of ale and you might point Master Hugh out to me.'

'Ale?' The man licked his cracked lips, as if he had just remembered how thirsty he was.

'Now see here!' the older watchmen said indignantly. 'Did this man try to rob you, or not?'

The journeyman hesitated, clearly not wanting to be hauled before the constable for wasting their time, or worse, making false accusations.

'I'm to blame, brothers,' I said. 'I should have made myself known to this man sooner. He was right to be alarmed if he thought his master's works were threatened. He was just doing his duty as a law-abiding man in summoning you.' I dug into my purse and pulled out a couple of coins which I held out to the watchman. 'For your trouble, brother.'

His chin jerked up as if I'd insulted him.

'For the city's alms chest,' I suggested.

He gave a grunt and both coins vanished inside his tunic. I was certain they would not be dropping into the poor box any time soon.

The journeyman and I were soon settled in the Goose and Goat, sharing a flagon of weak ale and two bowls of stewed eel. When I thought that the food and ale had mellowed my companion sufficiently, I asked if he knew where I might find Hugh.

The journeyman leaned back and regarded me with a frown. 'Master Peter would like to know that, an' all. Folks have been digging out their pewter from the wreckage of their houses, so they want it mended. There's any amount of work piling up for him. Master Peter's threatening to hang him higher than any black-hearted pirate – and he's been venting his spleen on the lads, so I reckon they'd help him tie the noose.'

'Hugh is missing? Was he taken in the flood?'

'Not him, nor any from our works, the Lord be praised. We were all on our feet, before the wave struck, see. Master Peter's wife started calling out for us to come quick and look from the casement on the other side of the house. She said there was a cloud of sparks and lights in the sky, looked like a host of angels were flying towards us. Well, we couldn't make head nor tail of it. But then we heard this roaring, like a thousand stags in rut. It felt as if the breath was being sucked from your chest. Master Peter hurried up the stairs and we all started to follow. Then there was the biggest thunderclap you ever heard and the wall of water came racing along the street.

'I scrambled up those stairs as if the hounds of hell were snapping at my heels. A couple of men – Hugh was one of them – were behind me. The water hit before they could get up, and they hung on for dear life. The force of it washed them clean over the railings, but we managed to haul them back. That current was so strong, I was sure we'd lose our grip on them, it was like trying to drag a wagon uphill with your bare hands, while a team of horses were pulling it downhill at full gallop.' He shook his head in wonder, then sighed and took a long draught of ale.

'So, Hugh survived the flood? And you saved him?'

'Shouldn't have bothered . . . ungrateful bastard,' the journeyman said sourly, and spat on to the mouldering rushes covering the floor. 'After the wave had come and gone, we waded back to our cottages. 'Course it was a foolhardy thing to do. Couldn't see what was beneath the water. There's a fair few who survived the wave but drowned after, when they got sucked down into holes and cellars they couldn't see, or ended up in the river. But every man was desperate to get home, see if he'd still a house left standing and, more important, find his wife and young 'uns. A good many didn't,' he added sadly.

'And Hugh, did he lose—'

'No, and that's what not a man-jack of us can understand,' the journeyman said grimly. 'It was more than a week before the water went down far enough for us to come back and start shifting the muck out of the works. Besides, we were all too busy trying to get the water out of our own homes and salvage what we could. But Hugh didn't turn up that first day, nor the next. Master Peter went himself to his house to see if he needed help or had fallen sick. But he couldn't find him, and he's not been seen since.'

This was sounding all too familiar. Was this man Hugh another victim of the killer? 'You said men had been drowned trying to reach home that first day. Could he have met with an accident?'

The journeyman popped a chunk of eel into his mouth, working it with his tongue until he could spit out the bones. 'His landlord said he went home that night and was living there as well as any man could, after what had hit the city. A few days later, as the waters went down, they said he'd joined in the search with them for a neighbour's husband and son who were still missing.' He sucked the meat from the bones of another slice of eel before adding sourly, 'If he walked into this tavern right now, I'd punch him straight back out that door again. Arse wipe! After Master Peter took him on and gave him work, even though he was that clumsy, at first, a babe in clouts would have been more use to us. I'd have let the sea take him, if I'd known how he'd use us.'

A man who needed work as badly as Hugh evidently had wouldn't simply walk away from it. We talked on a little longer. I showed him the drawing of the touchmark, but he stared at it blankly, not the smallest twitch betraying that he'd seen it before. He grudgingly conceded that Hugh might recognise it, but that only set him off again, and even as I slid off the bench he was thinking of more choice words that I could deliver to Hugh, if I did find the 'churlish, dog-hearted old ingrate'.

But I was just praying the old ingrate wasn't lying dead somewhere with that touchmark burned on his chest.

Chapter Thirty-five

OUTSIDE THE GOOSE AND GOAT the darkened streets had emptied of most women, except for a few poor souls desperately trying to sell a fistful of tallow lights to buy their supper and, of course, the mermaids, who were trying to coax their customers into churchyards or up rickety staircases to attic rooms with their siren promises of paradise on earth. But the night mostly belonged to the men, roaring into and out of the taverns and gaming houses. The curfew had become even more lax since I'd first come to the city, not that the watch had ever seemed diligent about enforcing it.

From the tail of my eye, I saw a figure emerge from the side of a church and begin to walk down the street behind me. There was nothing odd in that, yet something about the way he kept pace with me made me uneasy. At the first turning I came to, I swerved abruptly into the narrow alley and speeded up. The man was still behind me.

He was spindly and leaned forward as he walked. Bobbing slightly, his shoulders hunched, he looked like a carrion crow searching for flesh. But he wasn't looking at the ground, he was staring at me. He seemed to be carrying something, too, though I couldn't see the shape of it clearly. My back prickled, as if a knife was already tickling my skin. Always trust your instincts, not your brain, to protect you from danger.

I wheeled round and ran at him. For a moment, he stood frozen in the darkening street, as if he couldn't believe his prey had turned. Then he stumbled backwards, trying to turn and run at the same time, but he had left it too late. I hurtled into him, using my shoulder and arm to send him crashing against the wall. The sack he was holding flew from his hand and hit the ground with a muffled clang. He slithered down the wall, coming to rest on one knee, raising his arms to shield his face. He tried to scramble to his feet as I took another pace towards him. I grabbed him by the throat with both hands, and dug my thumbs into his windpipe. His small eyes bulged. He fought to push me away, but he was struggling to breathe. His grip slackened, his fingers flapping helplessly. I hauled him to his feet and spun him round, pushing his arm up his back and pulling him in front of me like a shield.

'Now, Skinner,' I growled into his ear. 'Suppose you tell me why you're following me?'

The man was still gasping for air like a fish hauled from water. He swallowed hard, several times. 'No harm . . . Trying to do you . . . a favour . . . brother.'

'What favour? Oh, let me guess. Someone sent you to warn me to leave Bristol before I end up in the sea as food for the crabs. Is that it?' I jerked his arm higher up his back and he yelped in pain. 'Who sent you?'

'No one, brother . . . I swear it,' Skinner protested, rising on his toes in an effort to ease the pressure on his shoulder socket. 'Heard you were looking . . .'

'Looking for who?' I asked suspiciously. I was certain he'd been sent to scare me off and I wasn't going to let go of him until I knew who was behind this, even if I had to drown the little weasel in the nearest horse trough.

I must have jerked his arm again, for he gasped. 'Not who, w . . . what.'

Puzzled, I stopped trying to wrench his arm from its socket, though I still held him, ready to tighten my grip at the first sign of a threat.

'Young friend of mine, Myles, said you were looking for something. Might have what you want.' He pointed with the toe of his patched shoe towards the sack that lay close to the wall. 'Rumour is you're looking for quality pewter to buy, and I have just the thing that might interest a man of discernment such as yourself.'

Myles had told the castle thieves I was looking for that touchmark? For a moment, I almost wanted to strangle the boy. But no, Skinner hadn't mentioned the mark, only that I was looking for pewter. The same tale that I'd given out. Myles had been careful, maybe even clever.

'If you'll let me go, I can show you,' Skinner said, twisting his head round with what I assumed he'd meant to be a reassuring smile, though at that angle it gave him more the expression of a snarling ferret.

I released him, but took a step back and drew my knife as he bent to retrieve the sack, wary in case it contained a weapon. I half expected him to snatch it up and run, but he ambled towards me, holding open the sack.

'Now I heard that you were looking for a very particular piece of pewter . . . for your father, was it? Hoping to get him to write his will in your favour? Trust me, I know all about these old gentlemen, petulant and contrary as spoiled children they are. But if you were to give him this . . .'

He was cradling the bottom of the sack, pushing the object upwards till it lay partly exposed in a nest of cloth. The faint light from a casement above glinted off dark metal that glistened like oil. I could just make out the shape of a lidded flagon, with a fine handle. I reached to take it from him, but he quickly let it drop down to the bottom of the sack, his gaze darting anxiously up and down the street.

'Not out here, brother. There's more thieves than cats that prowl these streets at night.'

Aye, and you're one of them, I thought. But thief or not, I had to examine that flagon, though I knew he wouldn't allow me to look at it in the street. Besides, even if he did, it was far too dark to make out any marks on it.

He leaned against the wall, as if suddenly too weak to stand, massaging his throat. 'Shaking like an old biddy with the palsy,

I am. It's the shock of you leaping on me like that in the middle of the street and near throttling me.' He broke off in a spasm of coughing, clutching his chest as if in pain. 'My throat's afire,' he complained, massaging it again to make sure I got the point.

'Would a mug of ale soothe it?' I suggested, guessing what he was fishing for.

'Best be making it something stronger,' he countered, 'for the shock. There's a place not far from here.'

'An inn?'

He batted the question away with a flap of his fingers. 'Nice and private, it is, nice and quiet. The lady who runs it is a good friend of mine. She'll see you served with only the best, if I vouch for you.'

I guessed it was a stew, and though I had nothing against them, I knew that the kind who welcomed customers like this man were likely to fleece their customers of far more than the price of a girl or a flagon of wine. I'd known men to wake up naked in an alley with a large bump on their heads after visiting such places, that's if they woke up at all. All the same, I didn't want to take him back to the Salt Cat. So, much to his disappointment, I eventually ushered him into the Pelican, where I hoped I would be unknown to any of the customers. But my companion evidently wasn't. Had I been manipulated into coming here, after all?

The innkeeper nodded at him from behind an iron grille. 'Not seen you for a while, Skinner.' His gaze flicked to me, evidently expecting that I would be paying for anything my companion drank.

I ordered two measures of sack, pushing the coins towards him through the grille. He held out his hand for another, which I grudgingly parted with, knowing full well I was being overcharged, but this was not the place to argue.

The innkeeper pointed to the far corner, on the other side of a miserable fire that sulked and spat on the hearth. 'You'll not be disturbed over there.'

The long narrow room, smelling of burnt bones and mouldy straw, was largely deserted, except for six men seated around a long table, engaged in an illicit game of dice. They paused, watching us, until we had squeezed past them, then leaned towards each other, their voices low, but I had little doubt we were the objects of their muttering. I sat with my back to them; my new companion took the bench opposite me, from where his gaze darted restlessly about the room, as if he was memorising the position of every table, bench and man.

'Let's see it, then,' I said as soon as we were seated.

But he held up a hand, as if he was telling a dog to sit and wait for its bone, while he gulped the sack. In the light from the candles, Skinner looked even more like a ragged crow. The skin was stretched tight over a thin, bony nose which had a dark blue tinge. The lower half of his face was masked by an untrimmed black beard. The nails of the hand that gripped the leather beaker were black-rimmed, yellow and thickened like claws.

Finally, he laid down the beaker and with a glance at the men, who had resumed their noisy game of dice, he pushed the sack towards me, gesturing that I should open it on my lap where it wouldn't be seen. I could feel my pulse quickening as I pushed the edges of the cloth down. The flagon was an elegant piece, with that silky texture of good pewter, almost like fingering a fresh rose petal. It was slender, tapering up from a broad skirt base, with a gracefully curved handle, thumbpiece and hinged, heart-shaped lid. It was hard to see any details in the mustard light of the inn, and even harder since I was holding it beneath the table. I ran my fingers over the surface until I found a touchmark close to the top. I lifted the candle on the table, holding the flagon as close to the flame as I dared without raising it above the table. Although I couldn't see the touch clearly, I could see enough to know that it wasn't the letters I sought.

But I'd examined enough pewter by then to realise this might not be the only mark on it. In addition to the touch showing in which workshop it had been made, some pewterers added their own initials to pieces they were proud of, and any craftsman would have been proud to lay claim to this. I searched inside the lid with my fingertips, then turned it upside down to feel the bottom. Part of a broken buckle decorated with fleur-de-lis, a bone button and another of twisted metal, a small length of cord, along with a few scraps of paper, slithered out and fell on to the sack in my lap. I glanced at one of the pieces of paper. It was a bill of sale, the ink faded and almost unreadable. The flagon had evidently been used to store such scraps, which, for one reason or another, the owner thought might be wanted one day. I guessed many homes had a box or old pot which served that purpose. Skinner snatched the flagon back from me and dragged the sack from my lap, scattering the rubbish that had fallen from the pot on to the bench beside me.

'Fine piece, you'll agree, brother. You'll not find better in the whole of Bristol and beyond.' He leaned forward, his breath as foul as an old dog's. 'So, how much you willing to pay?'

'Nothing for stolen goods,' I snapped.

'Stolen?' He kept his voice to a whisper but still managed to infuse it with as much outrage as a Puritan accused of worshiping a saint's relic.

'Any shopkeeper putting this on sale would have emptied it first, as would whoever sold it to him. So, if it's not stolen, where did you *buy* it?'

'It was payment,' he said carefully. 'Man owed me for food and lodgings.'

'Would these lodgings be in the old castle, by any chance?'

His gaze flickered across to someone behind me. Now that I was no longer trying to shield the flagon from inquisitive glances, I was becoming increasingly uneasy that I had my back to the room and the door. I slid on to a stool at the side of the table, from where I could keep a better eye on those behind me.

'If you didn't steal it, then I'd wager the man who paid you with this did. And either way, if you want money for it, you'll have to try some other squab. A piece like this could be easily recognised, and I don't want to find myself accused of theft.'

I began to lever myself to my feet, but his hand shot out, grabbing my wrist. 'I can tell you've seen a bit of the world, know how to take care of yourself, too,' he added, pointedly rubbing his shoulder. 'So, I'll not try to gull you. I'll admit that owing to Dame Fortune having turned her pretty little back on me, I have taken up residence in the castle. There's nowhere else a wretch like me can lay his head, these days, without being whipped from the city simply for falling on hard times through no fault of his own. But I swear, as St Peter will be my witness on the Day of Judgement, I didn't steal that flagon. Nor did the fellow that gave it to me.'

I snorted.

Skinner shook his head. 'No, I'd stake my life on it. He's not the sort – and I've been around plenty that are, to know. Get all sorts of rogues and villains up in the castle, but this man's different. Not the kind that we normally get seeking lodging with us.'

'Did he say where he worked before?'

Skinner gave a small chuckle. 'No one asks what a man did before he came to the castle. There's some that'll spin you a tale. It whiles away a dark hour, but there's as much truth in any of those stories as there is silver in a forged shilling.'

'But could he have been a craftsman? I persisted. 'Maybe he fashioned that?' I nodded towards the sack.

'A fine piece like this?' He managed to look as if I'd deeply wounded him. 'Any man who could make this wouldn't have the need to seek his lodging with us. Besides, he's a clumsy oaf. Couldn't scratch his own back without hitting himself in the eye. I dare say that's why his master let him go. That's why I'm trying to do him a favour, see, selling this for him. But I can't sit here all night, I've other business to attend to, so let's talk money. I can see how much you admire this. You'll not find better for your father.'

I shook my head firmly. 'It's not the piece I'm looking for. My father is very particular in what he wants.'

Skinner tried to cajole me for several more minutes, but seeing that I wasn't going to budge, he angrily scooped up the sack, muttering furiously about the amount of his valuable time I'd wasted if I wasn't intending to buy. My annoyance matched his own. He had conveniently forgotten that he had sought me, and I had bought him a large measure of overpriced wine.

'OVER HERE, Master Daniel!' The voice came out of nowhere, as I was crossing the courtyard of the Salt Cat, and it took several moments before I saw Rachael standing in the open doorway of the stables, beckoning urgently.

For a moment I feared there had been another attack on Diligence – or worse still, another murder – but as I hurried over, Rachael laid her hand on my arm and pulled me gently inside.

'Where have you been?' she whispered fiercely. 'Poor lad's been waiting for you half the evening. She nodded to the far corner. 'I've given him a bite. He was starving. But he's fallen asleep waiting for you. If you send a lad on an errand you ought to be here when he gets back,' she scolded. 'And you'd best get him out of here before the master goes to bed. He's taken to checking in here last thing, ever since Harewell was found.' So saying, she brushed past me and out the door.

Myles was lying half covered by a heap of straw. Asleep and in the soft light from the lantern, he looked even more vulnerable than usual, but I had a few questions to ask him. I prodded him with the toe of my foot and he scrambled to his feet, poised to run, relaxing only when he saw who it was.

I was too tired and irritable to waste time in subtleties. 'You told that thief Skinner, up at the castle, what I was looking for.' I grabbed him by the front of his ragged shirt. 'Have you been spying on me for him? How much did he pay you?'

Myles looked sullen, but he didn't try to wriggle from my grasp, as if he'd been roughly handled so many times before, he knew it was useless to resist.

'I don't spy for him. I don't spy for nobody. And he paid me nothing. Two of his men was bat-fowling, only you went into the shop and ruined it, so Skinner wanted to know what you were up to. Threatened to cut me if I didn't tell. So, I told him the same tale as you was spinning. Didn't tell him about the touch, though. I reckoned it was your business.'

I must have inadvertently thwarted an attempt by Skinner's men to steal from the shop. 'You did well, lad.' I had already released my grip on him. 'I take it you didn't find who owned that touch, though?' Myles shook his head.

I fished out a coin and handed it to him. He regarded me warily.

'For keeping your wits about you,' I said. 'If you've a mind to earn another, there's something I need your help with tomorrow morning.'

I heard a door open and footfalls across the yard. 'Out of here, lad. That's probably Crugge. Meet me on the corner of Duck Lane when the clock strikes ten of the hour,' I whispered.

Myles grinned, snatched the coin from my hand, dodged through the doorway and disappeared into the darkness.

Chapter Thirty-six

THE CHURCH CLOCK had barely begun striking ten as I hurried passed Christ Church, where Gysbourne had been murdered, and along The Pithay. At the end of the street, I glimpsed Myles waiting on the corner, rocking impatiently from side to side, as if he'd been standing there for some time.

'Have you told anyone I asked to meet you here?' I asked sharply.

He regarded me reproachfully. ''Course not, and I made sure I wasn't followed neither,' he added with a note of pride.

I'd been checking the same thing, and I continued to watch as I made my way down Duck Lane. I kept a wary eye on the boy too, looking for any signs of tension or lingering glances that would warn me he'd seen one of Skinner's band.

We halted in front of a tall, narrow house of three storeys. I had already discovered that each was occupied by a different family – even the ground floor, which had the appearance of once having been a baker's shop. The remains of a sign, in the form of a sheaf of grain, still hung drunkenly above it. I'd learned from the journeyman that Hugh occupied the middle floor. Myles followed me down a narrow passageway, which emerged in a courtyard.

Smoke rose from the chimney of a low brick building, which once must have been the bakehouse for the shop, but was probably now used as the kitchen for all three families. Set into the main building behind me was an open doorway, with a flight of stairs leading up to a small landing on which there was a door.

The staircase narrowed still further as it spiralled on upwards to the top floor above.

We climbed up and I knocked. Hearing nothing, I twisted the handle. It was locked, as I had guessed it would be, but using the tiny spike I always carried, it yielded almost at once.

Myles gave a low whistle, and gazed at me with undisguised admiration. 'I don't reckon even Castle Joan could pick a lock as quick as that.'

God's bones, I missed performing, hearing the gasps and seeing those awestruck faces. 'In my profession we call it lock charming,' I said. 'Now, this is where I need your help. I'm told that the landlord and his wife live below, and the man who lives here has not been seen for days, so if the goodwife hears someone walking about up here, she might come up to investigate. You go down and knock on the door. Keep her talking out in the street till I'm finished here.'

Myles looked uncertain. 'What'll I say? Better if I go in. She'd not hear me moving about. I'm lighter.'

That was certainly true, but if Hugh was lying dead inside with those letters burned into his chest, I didn't want the lad stumbling over his corpse.

'You'll think of something to tell her. You were quick enough to come up with a good tale when we first met.'

He opened his mouth, as if he was going to deny it, but saw the expression on my face and grinned instead.

'See if you can find out anything about a pewterer called Hugh. These are his lodgings. Ask her when she last saw him and if he has any family. A wife?'

I waited until I thought Myles would have reached the front of the house, then I eased the door open a crack and stood, listening for the slightest creak of movement. The distant shrieks of children, the trundle of handcarts and the rasp of a saw filtered through the fastened windows from the street in front of the building, but from the rooms beyond there was nothing but a deathly silence pressing down like earth over a grave. I slipped inside, pulling the door shut behind me.

I was standing in what must have served as the parlour, but it was in chaos, as if a violent wind had swept through it, though the casement was closed and there was no sign it had been flooded. A stool lay on its side where it had rolled against the leg of a plain table. A large pot was cracked open on the wooden floorboards, and several others were tipped over, their lids scattered as if the contents had been emptied in great haste. A square of cloth, knotted at the four corners to form a makeshift bag, lay abandoned on one of three wooden chairs, into which someone had thrust several wooden spoons and a horsehair sieve.

The ashes in the small hearth fire were cold and unraked. A few crumpled balls of paper had been dropped on top, perhaps tossed there to serve as kindling when the fire was relit, though by the state of disarray in the room, it seemed unlikely anyone was intending to return.

A small oak cupboard stood in one corner, set on a frame to raise it to waist height, the two carved doors flung wide. There was something carved on the top – H and two other letters. Could it be . . . ? I edged across, keeping to the wall where the boards would be less likely to creak. There was barely any light filtering in through the tiny circles of dirty glass in the casement opposite. I traced the letters with my finger. There was an H, but it wasn't IHS. It was a rough carving of the letters H&P, with a date beneath – 1585. It was the kind of cupboard that would be presented as a wedding gift, Hugh and his wife's probably, but like all the shelves in the room, the chest was empty.

This was the home of a man who had once been a master pewterer, but there were no pewter candlesticks or prickets, no pewter plates or jugs. Glancing up, I noticed a row of rusty hooks. The whitewashed walls were brown with years of smoke from lamps and the hearth fire, but here and there I glimpsed the ghosts of shapes on the wall marking where spoons, ladles, pans and knives had recently hung. The place had been stripped, ransacked. Everything of value had been taken.

And what of the man who had once owned them; had he been robbed of more than his possessions? I glanced down at the floor. The boards were old and worn, scuffed by many boots, and pitted here and there with small black scorch marks made by sparks from the hearth fire or dropped candles. I was relieved to see there was no pool of congealed blood, as there had been on the floor of the church, but the door which evidently led to rooms beyond was shut. Was Hugh lying dead behind that?

I nudged it open and found myself in a smaller room, furnished with a bed topped by a wooden tester, from which hung worn and faded drapes. The only other furniture was a small table and a battered chest. It looked just large enough to contain a crumpled body. Steeling myself against the sight and stench, I eased up the lid. But the chest was empty, and the only smell was the faint whisper of lavender, cloves and dried orange peel. I spotted a small muslin bag of herbs tucked into one corner, put there to discourage the moths. A woman's touch – Hugh's wife, I guessed.

Two narrow beds were squeezed into the third room, though it was even smaller than the first bedchamber, leaving no more than a foot of space between them. All the beds had been stripped of blankets and linens, but thankfully there was no trace of blood or of a body in this room either.

I returned to the first bedroom and I stared about me, searching for anything which might link this vanished pewterer to those three murdered men. As I studied the bed, it suddenly occurred to me there was one place I hadn't searched. I ducked under the threadbare curtains that hung from the tester and clambered up on to the lumpy mattress, running my hands over the wooden panel above. Towards the back, directly above the place where a man's head would have rested, I found it, a slim wooden box fixed beneath the tester. It was the place where old Rowe used to concealed his rings and watch, when he was serving the King in London, for no one breaking into any house at night could reach it without waking the person sleeping in the bed, not even one of Skinner's fishermen with his rod and hook.

For the second time that day, I charmed a lock, lifted the panel and fumbled until I found the hidden catch that released the little drawer. I pulled it out and emptied the contents on to the mattress. There wasn't much – a tiny leather drawstring purse, a pewter ring, some locks of hair bound with thread, and a snippet of stained blue cloth. The purse might contain some clue, or even the ring if it was engraved, but it was too dark to examine them properly in there, and I could not risk being caught in rooms that had obviously been plundered. I swept the contents of the box into the pocket beneath my doublet, slid the drawer back into place and made my way back towards the stairs.

But as I edged through the parlour, my eyes were once again drawn to the pieces of paper, discarded on the remains of the fire, for they stood out white against the blackened hearth. Had whoever thrown them there thought the embers were still hot enough to burn them? Curious, I picked up one of them, smoothed it out, and tilted it towards the dim light from the casement, but before I had a chance to read it, I heard a bellow from the street outside. Myles! Hastily, I snatched up the rest, stuffed the crumpled sheets into my pocket and hurried outside.

In the street I saw at once what was causing the commotion. Myles had inveigled two small boys into joining him in a reckless game of football using a wooden pail. They were kicking it vigorously against the street doors, hollering and yelling. Several women had emerged from their houses to shout at the boys, their bawling infants on their hips or clinging to their skirts. I could have been dancing the galliard up there and no one would have heard me. Myles must have been keeping an eye out for me, for moments after I emerged on to the street he ran off, leaving the two boys to face their mothers' wrath.

I caught up with Myles, who was waiting for me around the corner.

'Couldn't keep her talking any longer.' He grinned.

I cuffed him playfully around the ear. 'And I suppose you expect to be paid now for causing mischief.'

He nodded cheerfully.

'Did she tell you anything about Master Hugh?' I asked, as I delved into my purse for the promised coin.

'Said she'd not clapped eyes on him for three weeks, maybe more. But it's as well you asked me along. She'd have heard you. She's like a cat, that one, been listening out for him. Said there's been a couple of nights she heard him moving about up there. Prodded her husband to get up and talk to him, but he'd not stir himself. Said he wasn't going to go disturbing folks in the dead of the night, and by morning, the door was locked again.'

'She was sure it was Master Hugh she heard?' I remembered the carved initials on the cupboard and the little bag of lavender. 'Could it have been his wife?'

'Not unless it was her ghost up there throwing things about. He's a widower. That's what he told her, when he first took those rooms.'

'Did she say if he owed her rent?'

Myles nodded happily. 'She reckons that's why he's been sneaking back at nights and leaving before sun's up, 'cause he can't pay them. She said if I was to see him, I was to tell him from her that she'll give him another week, that's all. If he's not paid up by then, she'll be up there to clear out his belongings and move others in. She says she'll have to sell his bits and pieces to get back the money he owes.'

I was afraid she'd be in for a grave disappointment if she was relying on that to get what was owed to her. She'd find precious little left up there to sell, for I guessed most of the furniture was already hers, except that marriage chest. Was that the simple explanation for why Hugh had vanished? He was just a man who couldn't pay his rent and had crept out in the night with his belongings, before they could be seized for debt? It was a common enough game and one I was ashamed to admit I'd been forced to play myself more than once in my days on the road.

I parted company with Myles, who reminded me excitedly that the following evening would be New Year's Eve and the night of the masque when he was to ride Old Bony. Although I had no desire to go, I found myself promising I would be there to watch him. The lad had no one else to cheer him on, and after his performance today, I suppose I owed him that much.

But I forgot about it the moment he went running off, for something else was nagging at me. Hugh was more fortunate than many in Bristol whose livelihoods had been stolen by the great wave. The workshop where he was employed had survived, and though the men may have gone a week or so without wages, it was surely not long enough to have built up a huge sum owing in rent. If he did owe money, it was all the more reason for him to return to work as soon as he could. And why had he left in such evident haste and panic? His disappearance simply didn't make sense, unless he *was* lying dead somewhere, after all, and it was his murderer who had returned in the night to remove all traces of the victim.

I was still puzzling over this when I reached my chamber and pulled out the assortment of objects I had removed from Hugh's lodging. There was nothing of any great value among the contents of the hidden drawer. It seemed to have been used as a hiding place for mementoes. And in any case, they may not even have been put there by Hugh. If the bed belonged to the landlord, any of the previous tenants might have left the things there, especially if they had died.

The bag contained a few coins amounting to about five shillings. The ring was a simple pewter band, with no touchmark or inscription, and decorated with a pattern of interlocking hearts – a wedding band perhaps? The three locks of hair were of different shades of brown, keepsakes from parents, children or sweethearts? It was impossible to say, and the fragment of blue silk could have been snipped from any garment. I could learn little from these, except that whoever had placed them in the tester box was a sentimental soul, or maybe someone who'd known great loss.

I drew the candle closer and turned my attention to the pieces of crumpled paper I'd retrieved from the hearth. One immediately caught my eye, for it had a rough engraving printed among the words. It was another of those wretched broadsides about the monstrous fish-child born to some woman in Bristol. I glanced briefly at it, thinking it must be a copy of the one I'd read when I'd first arrived. But this account had plainly been printed before the flood, for its author did not have the benefit of hindsight. The writer didn't interpret the wondrous birth as warning of an impending disaster from the sea. Instead, he was certain it was divine judgement on the mother herself.

'*Such monstrous creatures do proceed from the judgement, justice, chastisement and curse of God which suffereth that the mother bring forth such an abomination as a horror of her sin.*'

A fire was the best place for it, and I tossed it aside in disgust. The next piece of paper had only a single sentence on it.

'*And will not God avenge His elect who cry to Him day and night?*'

The line stirred a deep memory in me. It was from St Luke's gospel, though I knew the passage better in Latin. I'd been forced to copy it from memory often enough as a boy. How did it go?

'*Deus autem . . . non faciet vindictam electus—*'

'No, no! Have you learned nothing, whelp? Not electus – electorum, ELECTORUM.'

'*Electorum suorum clamantium ad se die ac nocte . . .*'

It was probably from the same source as that broadside. It was a typical passage you heard shouted by the preachers on street corners. Perhaps Hugh attended Reverend Gysbourne's church, for it was a theme a devotee of Cranmer might take for a sermon. I set it aside and examined the rest.

The other papers proved to be a series of sketches of small objects: spoons with knobbed figures or animals on the handles, salts, a buckle with a fleur-de-lis design and a brooch in the form of a swan. They were the kind of drawings a craftsman might make for the approval of a customer, or even that a customer might produce to show a metalworker what he wanted.

My stomach was growling and Mistress Crugge's supper awaited, though I hoped it wasn't to be the seal's head brawn. I gathered up the pieces of paper and slid them into my chest, beneath my clothes, together with the little money bag and keepsakes. I was on my way out of the door when to my irritation I noticed I'd left one of the papers on the bed. It was the dog-eared copy of the broadside – that I certainly did not need to save – and I was on the point of ripping it into tiny pieces when my attention was caught by something written on the back.

It was a list of five names, but I didn't register who these were at first, for what leaped out at me were the letters IHS, written twice. The writing of the names was shaky – in some places I couldn't be sure of some of the letters – but the IHS beside two of them had been written in a different hand, and those initials were clear and unmistakable. The letters appeared beside two names – Hugh Leynham and Edward Brystowe, or was that Bristame? The second name meant nothing to me, but the first – *Hugh!*

I turned the broadside over, carefully scanning the list of witnesses who claimed to be able to testify they had seen the fish-child. But even allowing for my misreading one or two of the letters, no similar names appeared in the printed account. I guessed the broadside had only been a convenient scrap of paper on which to make a list, like you might use the back of a bill or letter.

It was only then that I looked at the other three names and my pulse quickened. These I knew only too well, I had been thinking about little else for days – Nicholas Dagworth, Sam Harewell, Luke Gysbourne. Each had a cross marked next to it. Three dead men, three crosses. Then I noticed one more thing written across the corner of the broadside, not a name, but a date – twenty-eighth day of March. But if that date connected these names, was it one that lay in the past, or was it still to come?

Feverishly, I pulled out the other papers, shuffling through them until I found the only other one with writing – the verse from Luke. '*And will not God avenge His elect . . .*' Three men murdered and branded in the name of God's elect. Those weren't words of comfort, that was a threat, a threat that would make any man named on that list flee in terror for his life.

Chapter Thirty-seven

MYLES WAS SITTING on the steps of St Stephen's Church, leaping to his feet every few minutes to stare up and down the street. I wondered if he had been waiting there since dawn. He looked puzzled, then grinned as he caught sight of me.

'Come to watch me ride Old Bony? I knew you'd not forget.'

''Course I wouldn't.' Actually, I'd been so preoccupied since last night I had forgotten, but it was as well now that I'd come as promised, for it might make him more willing to do what I asked.

'Myles, you know Skinner and the men at the castle?'

His expression grew wary. 'What if I do?'

'I need to get into the castle. There's someone living in there I must speak with. There are town guards posted on the gates, but Skinner and the others still seem to get in and out without being challenged, so they must use other routes. Maybe tunnels?' I suggested, remembering the passage that Waldegrave had used to reach the crypt.

Myles wasn't looking at me. He sat, his shoulders becoming ever more hunched as if he was a snail trying to retreat back into its shell.

'How do you get in, Myles?'

'No one gets in unless Skinner says so. And any that try don't never get out.' He darted a glance up at me and drew a grubby finger across his throat.

He looked scared and I realised, to my shame, how much danger I was putting him in. If what the townspeople said about the castle rats was true, I had no doubt that they were capable of murdering anyone who they suspected of betraying their secrets, even a boy.

'Find Skinner for me and tell him I need to speak with him. Don't mention anything about the castle. Just tell him I've changed my mind about the flagon. Tell him I'm interested, after all.'

But I wasn't sure if Myles was even listening to me, because his gaze had wandered to somewhere behind me. He leaped to his feet and rushed past me. I turned to see a man striding towards us.

'Ready, lad?' he called out

Myles grinned, his eyes blazing with excitement.

The newcomer's face and stance were familiar, but it took a few moments before I was able to place where I'd seen him before.

'You're one of Sam Harewell's men, aren't you?'

The man frowned. 'And who might you be?'

'Master Pursglove, of course,' Myles piped up, before I could answer. 'I told you about him, Tobias, remember? The man at the Salt Cat.'

So, this was the typesetter who hated printing sermons, not that I blamed him. I'd had my fill of them as a boy, being forced to copy them out as penance for whatever crime old Waldegrave deemed me guilty of that day.

'Salt Cat, is it?' A grimace briefly contorted his face. It looked suspiciously like a spasm of guilt, but for what?

'Myles tells me you're paying him to take part in the masque tonight?'

'What of it?'

'I thought there was an apprentice at your chapel, I wonder you didn't ask him, instead of some street urchin.'

'A lad all alone, like Myles, needs the money and a good meal in his belly. Charity, isn't it, to help the poor? Besides, we need someone who's small and light, for he's to be carried till the New Year's in. We feed our 'prentice too well. He's grown as fat as a hog's belly and we don't want Old Bony collapsing under his weight.'

Unless the little lad I'd seen in the printer's workshop with his grandfather had suddenly put on a remarkable amount of weight, he had seemed to me to be even lighter and smaller than Myles.

'I wonder the city is holding a masque while it's still half in ruins from the flood.'

Tobias's eyes narrowed. 'We'd have our masque even if the whole city had been flattened, just to show those Scottish barbarians we can't be pushed around. The Kirk banned the masque up in Scotland, well, just let them try to do it here! They think to force us to mark January as the start of the year, instead of Lady Day as its always been. Well, we're Englishmen is what we are, and we'll never suffer ourselves to be called Britains, no matter who sits on our throne.' His voice had risen angrily and he seemed to realise that he was attracting attention. He glanced round uneasily, then clapped his hand on Myles's shoulder. 'Come on, lad, best get you into your costume. Don't want to miss the parade.'

'You'll come?' Myles called back to me as they hurried off.

I would – if only because, without him, it might take me days to find Skinner, and I had the uneasy feeling that by then it might be too late.

I had spent half the night staring at the papers I'd found in Hugh's lodgings, and could find no more clues in any of them except for one. The more I looked at that sketch of the buckle, the more certain I had been that I'd seen it before. And then it came to me as I stared at the heap of paper and locks of hair on the bed. I pictured another assortment of oddments and paper. This one slithering out from the flagon Skinner had tried to sell me and, among lengths of cord and buttons, a piece of broken buckle with the fleur-de-lis pattern. I couldn't swear to it unless I compared the two, but I was as sure as I could be that the sketch I held in my hand was the design for that buckle, or for one very like it. I had suspected, the night Skinner had shown it to me, that the flagon had been purloined and now I was sure it had been stolen from Hugh's lodgings, either by his killer or by someone who knew that Hugh had fled and would not dare to return. Whoever Skinner was sheltering in the castle held the key to these murders, I was certain of that.

I fingered the crumpled broadside in my jerkin. I had not been able to put it out of my mind all day. Dagworth, Harewell and Gysbourne were dead, those little crosses, standing like gravestones beside their names, a cruel and sinister reminder of their grim fate. But what of the last two names? Hugh Leynham and Edward Brystowe might still be alive, but for how long? Had the names and that verse been delivered to Hugh to tell him that he would be the next to die? Was the twenty-eighth day of March the day revenge was to be meted out to Edward and Hugh, as it had already been to the first three? But revenge for what?

I knew that date – every Catholic in England did, and even the renegades like me. It was day the head of the Jesuit order in England, Henry Garnet, was found guilty of treason, for refusing to divulge what had been told to him in confession concerning the Gunpowder Treason. As Waldegrave had said, it was the day that had driven fear deep into the heart of every Catholic in England. They said King James had secretly watched the trial, hidden behind a screen, and it was the King himself along with his spymaster, Robert Cecil, who had ordered the torture of Henry Garnet. So, was it possible these murders *were* connected to the failed Gunpowder Plot, after all? Had these men all somehow had a hand in bringing Garnet or his fellow Jesuits to the quartering block? I could not escape the chilling thought that the twenty-eighth day of March might well be an anniversary that the compiler of that list intended to mark in blood. And if that was so, I had only three more days to stop him.

As soon as the sun began to set, people started emerging from houses and workshops, making their way towards the High

Cross. They were in fine spirits, laughing and chattering loudly, well wrapped up against the chill wind as if they expected to be out on the streets for some hours. I followed and found myself on the edge of a great crowd of people. Those whose casements overlooked the streets were already hanging out of the open windows, yelling at the children and youths below who were clambering up on to their yard walls, and even low roofs, to try to get a better view, much to the annoyance of the households.

A small knot of fur-clad dignitaries and their wives had occupied the exulted platform inside the High Cross, and the watch was fighting a losing battle trying to prevent a gang of ragged boys clambering up there, too, brazenly swinging from the delicate stone tracery and kicking the statues of the kings in the teeth. But the guards no sooner made a grab for one boy than another clambered up on the other side, shrieking insults, delighting in the game of cat and mouse.

It was dark now and the crowd was growing restless, craning their necks to get a first glimpse of the procession. Finally, we saw the flames approaching, the gold and ruby glow of links and torches held high in the air, and with them came the first notes of music. Four waits, clad in scarlet robes, marched past the High Cross, blowing on cornet, sackbut and serpent, their silver collars and brass instruments glinting blood red in the torch flames.

Following the waits came an elderly man in long robes seated astride a donkey and carrying a large hourglass on a long pole. His knee-length white beard and wig fashioned from sheep's wool lifted in the wind and kept blowing across his face, so several times he blindly steered his beast towards the crowd and, with shouts and laughter, they were obliged to push the beast back into the procession again. The old year was passing.

Then, flanked by more link boys, the masque proper hove into view. The players, all masked and clad in flamboyant costumes, pranced and cavorted down the street. They were a strange assemblage of characters. Several men were dressed as fishing boats, the frame of the hulls circling their waists, suspended from broad straps slung across their shoulders, sails hoisted over their heads and nets trailing behind them. They were chivvied back and forth by four men representing the four winds of the oceans who belaboured them with pieces of wood fashioned into the shape of lightning bolts, the blazing sun, jagged rocks and water spouts, causing the little fleet to crash into each other to the crowd's jeers and delight. Horse-drawn sledges and carts rolled by, decorated to resemble galleons under sail or huge fish with men sitting inside their open jaws, trapped by the fishes' teeth, feigning to wail that they had been swallowed alive.

Men ran in and out between the carts, clad in barrels or stuffed sacks, with their legs sticking through the bottom, and great tall brimless hats perched on their heads, exaggerating the fashion of the wealthy gentlemen. Their faces were concealed behind grotesque masks of goats, hogs, donkeys and other beasts, in mockery of the merchants. They made mischief wherever they could, goosing matrons, twisting the noses of men and trying to drag struggling girls away with them into the procession.

A rabble of young apprentices followed. Some were playing pipes or small drums, others rattling dry bones threaded on cords, whirling bullroarers or beating on any scrap of metal they'd found to make as great a din as possible. I felt a shiver of unease, for the noise, though this time made in merriment, reminded me of the mob that had descended on that poor cordwainer's family. I prayed that the mood of this crowd would not turn.

A hand grasped my arm and I whirled round to find Rachael laughing behind me.

'I thought you'd be hard at work in the Salt Cat at this hour,' I bellowed close to her ear.

'Master barred and bolted the door till the procession is over,' she shouted, her face so close to mine I could feel her warm breath on my cheek. 'Afraid of thieves.'

A horse-drawn wagon was approaching, forcing those at the front of the crowd to squeeze themselves back to avoid the wheels, while those behind them yelled in protest at being trodden on and squashed against the walls. The wagon carried King Neptune seated on a shell-shaped throne. It was lit by fish-shaped lanterns that swayed from long poles, sending giant shadows of the king racing up the walls of the houses as he passed. Neptune jabbed his great long trident at some of the spectators who, in their efforts to avoid being pricked, tried to twist away, several slipping on their backsides in the mud, to gleeful shouts from the others.

A shoal of half-naked women surrounded the king on the wagon, clad in nothing more than crude fish tails They jiggled their bare breasts at the crowd. Young lads ran after the wagon, daring each other to clamber on board and fondle those mounds of flesh. A few succeeded before being slung roughly to the ground by the attendants marching alongside. The crowd shrieked with laughter and the lads, far from being abashed, clapped each other on the back.

I recognised some of those on the wagon as the women who plied their trade in the streets near the Salt Cat, and so apparently did some of the men, for the girls called out to their regulars in the crowd, shouting their names and making lewd comments. A few of their customers yelled back, joining in the jest, but many tried to melt away, pretending they were not the ones being addressed, though that was evidently not convincing the wives and sweethearts standing with them. I could tell there were going to be a few broken heads and blistered ears in some homes that night.

Rachael tugged at my sleeve again. 'Something troubling you?'

'Young Myles is supposed to be taking part in the procession, but I haven't seen him.'

She squeezed my arm. 'It's not over yet, look.'

Behind Neptune's wagon, all heads were turning to whatever was next approaching. There was no raucous rattle of bones or high-pitched piping accompanying this part of the masque, but the tolling of a single bell and the muffled slow beat of a drum.

A few minutes earlier neither bell nor drum would have been heard over the shrieks and laughter of the crowd, but an uneasy silence was washing up the street ahead of them.

A hooded figure approached, dressed in black robes, ringing the doleful death knell as he paced with measured steps. He was flanked on either side by more hooded figures bearing burning torches, smoke streaming behind them like the pennants of ships risen from hell. The figures that followed came in single file, performing a strange slow dance to the rhythm of the drummer, who beat time as if he was leading the condemned to the scaffold. Two figures clad as skeletons twisted in their macabre dance, displaying their grinning skull faces to the crowd; one bore a scythe, the other a gravedigger's spade.

A man followed in a black ship which hung around him, suspended from a shoulder harness. Black tattered sails flapped in the wind, and a single lamp glowed in the bow. The ship trailed three ropes behind it, bound to the wrists of three men as if it was dragging them through the waves in its wake. One had a noose about his neck. The second, naked to the waist, had livid fake boils stuck to his whitened skin, and the third was covered in gory wounds which made the crowd gasp and several women almost faint at the sight. I glanced down at Rachael, but she was watching with fascination.

A murmur went up from the crowds and they started to laugh, the nervous laughter that erupts when tension is broken. Two teams of six men were each leading a figure dressed as a horse. The black horse had a wooden head held up on a pole. The horse's head had hinged jaws that banged together with a loud crack whenever it was jiggled. The man beneath was draped in a long cloth, stitched with layers of feathery black rags that fanned out in the breeze as the beast twisted and turned. A girl sat astride him. She was dressed in scarlet, her brown hair hanging loose to her waist. A chaplet woven from red, blue and yellow ribbons crowned her head and rippled down her back. She clung on, giggling madly as her mount lumbered back and forth, pretending to attack the crowd, while the men who held it were feigning a struggle to rein it in.

Then I saw him. Myles was sitting astride a white horse. But its head was a real horse's skull, the bone glowing pale as the wolf moon. Its teeth snapped together as the jaw flapped up and down, and yellow candlelight glowed out of the empty eye sockets. Like the black horse, the white cloth was sewn with layers formed of long strands, with more dangling from the base of the skull. They flew out around the horse as it ran towards the crowd. Some of the strands were dun-coloured, others dark, even black. I couldn't make out what they were made from, but they were not rags or ribbons and they moved too fluidly for straw.

Myles was evidently enjoying himself as much as the girl. He was dressed in a loose white robe. A chaplet of ivy crowned his curls which looked, for once, as if they had been combed. He'd been given a dry bone to carry as a sceptre, about as long as a man's forearm, which he was gleefully using to belabour his mount and urge him on.

'He looks like a princeling,' Rachael said. 'Acts like one, too. He'll be lording it over the other street lads for days after this.'

At the High Cross, the two horses separated, the black horse trotting round it clockwise, while Myles's horse careered round in the opposite direction. The dignitaries inside the cross tossed handfuls of pennies at the two horses, which the waiting urchins scrambled for, trying to grab them from the dirt before the horses' attendants could retrieve them. When the horses met on the other side, they charged at one other, their jaws snapping wildly, each team trying to push the other back with such force, I feared Myles and the girl would be knocked to the ground, but they clung on. Finally, they both lumbered off down Corn Street towards St Leonard's Gate. The crowd seemed to realise this was the end of the procession and surged forward, some following behind the horses, most peeling off and wandering away in small groups, taking children home to bed or seeking out the nearby inns.

Rachael wrapped her cloak tighter about her, evidently preparing to leave, too.

'Where will the procession end?' I asked.

'Last time, they finished up on the pasture they call the marsh, near the bowling green, where the two rivers meet. Roasted a great ox on the common land there, and some hogs besides. There was such a tower of barrels of wine, and another of ale, lads were flying up and down ladders like a squabble of squirrels all night to keep the flagons filled.' She nodded towards the backs of the crowds. 'Looks like that's where they're headed again tonight. Come on, I've not had a bite of good meat since the flood, and if there's an ox or even a sheep roasting . . .' She licked her lips as if she could already taste it.

'Won't Mistress Crugge be yelling for you?'

'She will, but she'll be yelling in an empty parlour. I don't reckon there'll be anyone eating or drinking in the Cat tonight, not if there's decent meat and ale to be had elsewhere. Even if the beast died of old age and it's as tough as saddle leather, it has to be better than seal's head brawn.' She laughed. 'And I reckon old Crugge himself will be down there, too. If he can slip the leash.'

She slipped an arm through mine and we joined the stragglers trailing behind the procession.

A raw wind hit us as we emerged from the shelter of the last of the houses in Marsh Street and out on to the common pasture, as if the night was sucking up the chill breath from the two rivers surging beneath it. Furthest away from the water's edge, where the land was slightly less boggy, a heap of rubble had been dumped and flattened into a rough platform, in the centre of which was a shallow pit of stones in which a fire had been set. The land was still far too wet to dig a fire pit, without it immediately filling up with water. As Rachael had hoped, there was a skinned beast roasting on a spit, though it looked more like a small milk cow than an ox, and there were only half a dozen kegs set on some broken beams. But though it appeared that this feast would be little more than a meagre supper, a fair crowd had gathered close to the fire, trying to find a warm spot upwind from the stinging smoke.

The waits were playing 'Go bring me a lass', clearly a popular choice, for many voices were singing along. The masqueraders had discarded the more cumbersome parts of their costumes and were gulping down mugs of wine or ale, while the mermaids had been forced by the cold to wrap themselves in blankets or were snuggling beneath the cloaks of their admirers, giggling as they allowed the men to hold tankards to their lips or rub them on the pretext of warming them. No one was dancing; most were finding it hard enough to pick their way to and from the trestle tables and the fire on the makeshift paths that had been laid through the mud.

The night seemed even blacker than it had inside the city. The only light came from the glow of the fire in the pit and the flames from the torches used in the procession, which their bearers had stuck into the soggy ground. The flames, whirling madly in the breeze, sent light and shadow racing across faces, distorting them into ever-changing masks more grotesque than any worn in the procession.

Rachael, holding her skirts high, squelched her way closer to the fire, while I went to fetch us both beakers of wine. Although the smell of the roasting beast was making my stomach gurgle in anticipation, it was not yet ready to be attacked with the great long knives that lay gleaming close by. There was no sign of Myles, though I was sure that as soon as they began to serve the beef, he'd pop up like a mushroom after rain. I couldn't see either of the masque horses but I assumed that, like the others, they'd taken off their disguise and were now mingling with the rest.

The songs of the waits became bawdier and the crowd more lusty in their singing of them. I tried not to sing, though I found myself tapping and humming, for Rachael seemed suddenly to have grown pensive and was staring into the flames. Eventually, the cry went up that the beast was ready, and the platters of fragrant beef, still dripping with fat, were set out on the tables.

People jostled forward to spear themselves a slice. The meat was every bit as tough and stringy as I had expected. The poor creature had evidently been old and half starved, but then no one was likely to send a good cow for slaughter at this time of year. But the moans of satisfaction, and the grease glistening on lips, chins and in beards, proclaimed how much pleasure each and every mouthful gave to those who had tasted no fresh meat since the flood struck. It was only as I swallowed the last morsel of my portion that it occurred to me I still had not seen Myles – or, for that matter, Tobias.

I turned to Rachael, who was still savouring her last bite. 'Have you seen the lad anywhere?'

Her mouth full, she shook her head. A couple of the men brushed past me, heading back towards the barrels of wine, the bright rags of their costumes flapping around their legs, visible under their half-cloaks. I caught up with them and asked where I could find those who had been with the bone horse. The two men exchanged glances, but didn't answer. Ignoring me, one hurried off towards the kegs.

The second began to follow, then turned back. 'They've taken Old Bony to the water. They'll be back here quick enough when they're done, wanting their share of the meat.'

'Done what?'

He glanced in the direction of his companion, who was standing a little way off, watching us. 'They mean to calm the sea, that's all, keep her in her bed. It's an old custom, though it's not been done for years. Some say that's why the sea came roaring on to the land. She's a spiteful mistress when she's neglected. Aren't they all?' He gave a wan smile. 'But they'll put it right this year, soothe her feelings.'

I looked behind me, staring over the dark marshy ground towards the river. It was too dark to see the water, but I thought I could just make out the faint glimmer of light moving in the far distance, roughly where I remembered the confluence of the rivers Frome and Avon to be.

I started towards it, but had not taken more than a pace when a hand clamped down on my shoulder.

'You're best not going down there this night. Death's horsemen don't take kindly to being spied on. Liable to kick up rough, and some of them are sturdy lads, handy with their fists – and knives, too. There's some in this town would have them arrested, claiming it sorcery or some such. But it's nothing of the sort, just a bit of fun you might say, but they know the law won't see it like that. So, if they catch any stranger poking his nose into their affairs they'll cut it off. You'll leave them be if you know what's good for you.' He wrapped an arm around my shoulder. 'Come and have another drink, before it all goes. It's rare enough to get anything in this world you don't have to pay for, so you'd be a fool not to take all you can while it's there.'

I thanked him for his advice and extricated myself from his grip, saying I'd a girl waiting and I'd better not neglect her, for her temper was worse than any storm.

The man craned his neck to look at Rachael, then winked and gave me a friendly punch on the arm. 'Lucky dog!'

I hurried back to Rachael and led her away from the lights of the fire and torches. 'I need to find Myles. I think he's still with the masqueraders down by the water. They're taking part in some ancient ritual which could bring down trouble from the law, and I want to get him away.'

'I'll come,' she said at once.

'No, I've been warned they could get violent if they discover outsiders watching.'

It was the last thing I should have said to a woman as spirited as her. I couldn't read her expression but, silhouetted against the flames, I saw her chin lift and knew she was about to blaze as fiercely as any torch.

'They will have posted lookouts, and two people moving in the darkness are twice as lightly to be spotted as one,' I said hastily. 'You keep watch here, make sure those men I was talking to don't follow me or try to give warning that I was asking questions. I need you to distract them if you see them making for the water's edge.'

There was a moment's silence, before she finally agreed that she could see the sense in that. But there was an edge to her voice, which told me she was still annoyed.

I circled around until I saw the glint of the river. The tide was in and water was surging between the banks as sea and river wrestled with each other. The pasture was sodden, and several times I sank to my knees in mud, alarmed that I might get stuck fast. The wind was gathering strength, and though it was bitterly cold, I was glad of it, for the rush of water and the roar of the wind through the trees covered the sound of my approach. But even above the wind and water I heard the slow death beat of the drum.

Keeping low, I ran towards the smashed remains of a small boat that was wedged on its side, trapped in some reeds. I crouched down and crept inside the hull, ignoring the splintered planks snagging my clothing, too intent on trying to see what was happening on the other side. On my hands and knees now, in several inches of mud and water, I squinted through a hole in the broken hull. They were standing just a few yards away from me, in a circle, on a crude landing stage for small boats that jutted out into the river.

Unlike the other masqueraders, these men still wore their costumes and masks. The hooded figures with their burning torches stood close to the edge, the churning black water stained blood red in the gusting flames. The two skeletons, with the scythe and the gravedigger's spade, flanked the black-robed man who had carried the bell, their ghastly skull heads turned towards him as if waiting for him to give an order. The men dressed as the black ship, the hanged man, the plague victim and the man covered in blood all stood with their backs to the marsh. In the centre of their circle was the bone horse, Myles astride it. The yellow flames still flickered through the empty sockets in its white shining skull, but the jaws were no longer snapping. There was no sign of the teams of men who had led it through the streets or of the black horse and the girl.

Myles clung on, but he seemed exhausted and half asleep. His head was bent forward, almost touching the back of the horse's skull, and the hand which held the long bone hung at his side, his fingers so limp I guessed the bone must be fastened to the sleeve of his white robe.

The black-robed man raised his arms in the red torchlight. One of the skeletons handed him a small bowl, and like a priest blessing a man with holy water, he flung drops of it towards the bone horse. The liquid was dark, almost black in the torchlight, splattering over the white cloth. The drops must have fallen on to Myles's face, too, but he barely stirred and made no attempt to wipe them away. Perhaps he was too cold to feel them.

A gust of wind snatched at the long strands sewn to the body of the horse and beneath the skull, and as I watched them move, I suddenly realised what they were – horse tails. The one dangling from the base of the skull was the same colour and length as Diligence's, severed the night I had arrived. It was for this that horses all over the city had been mutilated. The death horse was dressed in the hair cut from the living beasts.

But I had scarcely had time to register this when the two skeletal figures dropped their scythe and spade as they took up positions on either side of the horse. They lifted the drooping boy from the horse's back and laid him across the outstretched arms of the black-robed man. His robe swirled about him in the wind as he turned to face the churning river. Before I even understood what was happening, all the men in the circle had turned as one towards the river, raising their arms, the drumbeat quickened, pulsing faster and faster, then abruptly it stopped. The black-robed man hurled Myles up and out. For a moment, he seemed to hang suspended between sable sky and black earth, before he splashed, screaming, into the maelstrom of water.

The pole to which the glowing horse's skull and severed horses' tails were attached arced like a great white bird through the dark sky and hit the river with such force that the skull snapped off. The pole bobbed up again and, still trailing the white cloth, it spun away in the racing current. Then I saw Myles, his face as white as the skull, and terrified, as he was swept past the edge of the pool of light, out, out in the black, churning water.

He was gone.

To this day, I don't know where she came from, but even as I struggled on cold-stiffened legs to free myself from the wreckage of the boat, she shot past me. Dragging off her cloak in one fluid movement, Rachael was racing towards the wooden jetty. The men were still gazing into the river but suddenly sensed or heard the movement behind them. The man covered in fake gore seized her arm, but she twisted away from him, cannoning into the black-robed man. She sent him reeling, and dived headlong into the water.

I saw her surface briefly in the red light, then the strong current caught her, too, and dragged her away, as helpless as a fallen leaf in the river's grip.

Chapter Thirty-eight

I SPRINTED TO THE BANK and was on the very brink of plunging in after them before reason took hold and I jerked back. The river was bearing them both away too swiftly for the strongest swimmer to reach them. If they had been pulled beneath the water, even in daylight, finding them in the churning silt and filth would be almost impossible; at night there was no chance at all.

The men were crowded at the water's edge, stretching out their torches over the water, but I didn't care whether or not I was seen now. I ran up the side of the river until I reached the quayside. The current had swept Rachael and Myles out into the channel where the two rivers merged. It would push them to the far side of that, before dragging them downstream towards the rocky gorge and the open sea beyond. Sense told me they had already been swept way beyond the city by the ebbing tide and a river still swollen from the water draining back off the land. But I had to do something.

I was forced to slow, for the buildings were badly damaged along the quay. In places, walls still lay where the sea had tumbled them, right across my path, and several times I had to clamber over them, with only the torches on the bridge ahead casting a distant flicker of light. The moving shadows deceived me more than once into thinking a hole was a solid stone and a great beam was a gap.

The stone bridge still stood, though much battered. I'd feared I would be challenged by the watch at the gate on the far side, but no one was on guard, though raucous laughter spilled from the room above the gate, where the men were plainly celebrating the New Year. Keeping close to the wall, I slipped through.

There were more people than usual abroad at this hour. A tangle of drunken revellers came towards me. One, sweeping off his hat as if he was taking applause on the stage, bowed so low his fellows had to rush to right him before he fell on his arse. They urged me to join them, and cursed me for a Puritan and a crab when I rushed on. Several times, I glanced behind me, wondering if Death's horsemen were in pursuit, but there was no sign of any of the macabre figures, though it occurred to me that if they had taken off their costumes, I wouldn't recognise any of them, except Tobias. I was sure he must have been one of them.

I was running down the opposite bank of the river now. A faint glow of light shone through one of the high windows of the Cathedral, though the rest were in darkness and silent. The Church was not welcoming in the coming year. All the same, I offered a silent prayer. But what could I ask for – that I could, by some miracle, stop the river taking them? I was praying for that with every beat of my thumping heart, though I knew it was already too late.

I was squelching through marshland again, almost opposite the spot where Myles had been thrown in. In the far distance, across the water, the cooking fire on which the cow had been roasted still burned, sending a plume of warm golden light into the chill black sky, and tiny figures flitted in and out of the torch-light like drunken bats. But the landing stage by the water was dark and cold. The men were not looking for Myles or Rachael. They knew that the river had taken its human tribute and would never surrender them.

It was pointless carrying on and yet I couldn't stop. I fought my way through the reeds and boggy grass. But the more desperate I became, the deeper my feet plunged into icy mud as I tripped over half-buried timber and ensnared myself in tangles of weed and old nets. Birds flew up from under my feet as I blundered into their roosts. A pair of ducks shot squawking and flapping into the river. Other creatures stirred in the grasses around me, with small scurryings, shrill screams and menacing hisses, as if the imps of hell had gathered in the sucking marshes to watch the old year die.

My eyeballs ached from peering into the seething river, desperately searching for any glimpse of them, though I knew, deep down, that by now their lifeless bodies were being battered and pulped on the savage rocks of the gorge. Sections had fallen from the bank and I was forced to step away from the river to avoid plunging in myself.

Here the mud was just as deep. I slipped and fell, twisting my knee. I dragged myself out of the glutinous sludge and sat up, trying to massage away the nerve-jangling pain. My hand brushed across a piece of what felt like cloth jutting out of the slime. I dragged it out. There was something solid inside. I bent closer. The stench, and the realisation of what I was clutching, struck me at the same time. It was a sleeve. The hand that dangled from it was putrid, half chewed away by rats and crabs. The body had been buried by weed and mud, dropped there by the retreating wave. I guessed that even if this area had been searched by daylight, cloth, hair and skin would have been indistinguishable from the silt that covered it.

I scrambled up and staggered away. How many more corpses lay scattered on this marsh? Would their bones ever be found, their names returned to them? How soon before Myles and Rachael, too, became nothing but pieces of rotting flotsam? I stumbled on down the bank of the river, not even knowing why I was walking any more.

A faint mewing sound carried towards me on the wind, another wretched bird complaining I had disturbed its night's rest. The sound came again, but there was no startled flapping of wings. A stray cat, perhaps, out stalking for its supper. Another faint wail that sounded almost human, as the cries of gulls often do. Then I saw something pale in the black mass of reeds and mud. God's bones, not another corpse. I turned aside, intending to give it a wide berth. But the cry came again, and this time I was certain it *was* human.

But just as I called out in answer, an explosion of noise erupted from the city behind me. Bells tolled, horns were blown, drums were being beaten hard enough to split their skins, and men were bellowing at the top of their lungs. I whirled round, expecting to see flames leaping skyward and the town under attack, but then I remembered it was the eve of the New Year and it seemed every man, woman and child was determined to send the wicked spirits of the old year fleeing, taking with them every misfortune and disaster that had plagued the city.

The cacophony was so distracting that I'd half forgotten what had caught my attention moments before. I edged cautiously towards the white shape ahead. I was almost upon it before I could make sense of it. Two figures lay intertwined. The boy lay face down, his hands locked around a long pole half tangled in a sodden white cloth. Beneath him and the pole lay a woman. Neither was moving. It was too dark to see their faces, but I didn't need to.

Chapter Thirty-nine

I CALLED OUT THEIR NAMES as I dragged my legs through the knee-deep mud, but I could hardly hear my own cry above the thundering river and the noise from the city, much less any answer. Then I was kneeling beside them. I touched Myles's hand. It was as cold as the grave. My fingers found Rachael's cheek . . . even colder.

'No, no! Rachael! Wake up! Wake up!'

I dragged the boy off her and pressed my hand to her mouth. Nothing . . . Then I felt her lips tremble. Had I imagined it? She gave a jerking gasp and rolled over, coughing and vomiting.

Next to her, Myles, too, was stirring, though it took some time for me to warm his fingers in my fists sufficiently to be able to prise the pole loose from his grip. The men who had thrown their horse's head into the sea had unwittingly saved his life, probably the lives of both of them, and they had ridden what remained of that bone horse to the safety of the reeds.

Later, I was to learn that Rachael had been swept towards the boy, who was clinging desperately to the pole, which had wedged itself between the timbers of one of the many wrecks lying just below the surface. She reached him just as the force of the current dragged the pole loose, and clung to him as they were both hurled downriver till they spun into a slower current, close to the far bank, where she managed to drag herself and the lad out. Exhausted and half drowned, she remembered nothing more after she collapsed on the reed bank, until she found me crouching over them.

Both of them were chilled and numb beyond shivering, and with their clothes soaked and the icy wind cutting into them, I knew that even if they were alive now, I had to get them off the marsh and into the warmth, if they were going to survive the night. Myles was already drowsy. I know Rachael thought me cruel, but I forced him to walk, for I'd seen strapping men die of the cold on the road simply by falling asleep. Even with me supporting them both, it seemed to take us hours to cross the marsh. I tried to steer us away from the river, but the ground was still treacherous and they had not the strength to battle through the mud. In the distance, the noise had died away as people retreated to their beds, for though it was New Year's Day, it was no holiday.

The streets were deserted by the time we reached the city, save for those sleeping in doorways or graveyards, and I hoped they would remain so. I would have a hard time defending the three of us, if I should run into any of Death's horsemen – and I couldn't expect any help from the watch, who would most likely be snoring in their guardrooms after the night's excesses.

But much to my relief, we reached the Salt Cat without encountering anyone. By this time, I was carrying Myles and Rachael was hanging on my arm. I could feel her shivering violently now, which was a good sign, her teeth chattering as loudly as the snapping jaws of the bone horse. But the boy was limp under my wet cloak, his body seeming to suck the heat from my flesh as I pressed him to my chest for warmth.

'He needs a fire, and there's none in my chamber,' I said.

'Kitchen.' Rachael forced the word out between clenched teeth.

The fire had been banked down for the night, but a basket of kindling stood ready for the morning. I lit the lamp and coaxed the embers into a blaze. Rachael was trying to drag the wet robe from Myles's thin little body, but her own hands were so numb they were as useless as if they had been severed. As she went to warm her hands over the fire, I pulled her back. I knew from experience, she'd be in an agony of pain, and unbearable itching, if she thawed her fingers too quickly.

'Take your own gown off,' I ordered.

I stripped the boy and wrapped him again in my cloak. But Rachael was still struggling to untie the laces of her gown, and I was obliged to help her, dragging the sodden skirts over her head. Something clanged to the floor.

She quickly bent to retrieve it, but her swollen fingers couldn't grasp it. I picked it up. It was a key, heavy, rusty and old. 'You were lucky the weight of this didn't drag you to the bottom.'

She pulled it from me, using her two palms like pincers. 'The key to my father's house,' she said.

'Shall I fetch him—'

But before she could answer, the kitchen door burst open. Master and Mistress Crugge both stood in the doorway in large voluminous nightgowns, caps on their heads. Master Crugge was slightly in front, an axe in his hand, looking as if he might have been pushed there by his wife, who held a lantern in one hand and an iron candlestick brandished like a cudgel in the other.

'It's you, you little trull,' Mistress Crugge exploded. She pushed her husband aside and barged through the door. 'I thought it was robbers from the castle. Not a wink of sleep have I had all night for the commotion in the streets, and when I do finally manage to close my eyes, I'm dragged awake by you, whoring in *my* clean kitchen. Look at you, you brazen hussy, standing there in your shift. It's clinging to you so close you might as well be naked.' She raised the candlestick and for a moment I thought she was going to strike Rachael. I stepped between them.

'As for you, Master Pursglove . . .' She suddenly gaped at us as if, in her fury, she had only just noticed the wretched state we were all in. 'You're as wet as a cat that's been drowned in a well, girl!' And you look as if you've been dragged through a midden by your heels, Master Pursglove.' Her gaze fell on Myles, wrapped in my cloak, his eyes closed and his lips blue. 'Heavens above, whatever's happened?' She turned from the boy to me, her face suddenly full of fear. 'The great wave, it's not come again?'

I hastily reassured her. 'The boy was . . . knocked into the river in the revels. Rachael, with exceeding courage, jumped in to rescue him. They were swept away and washed up on the marsh. But they're chilled to the bone. We need to get them dry and warm, before –'

'Before they take a fever or worse,' Mistress Crugge finished. For all her bluster, she was a practical soul and a kindly one at heart. Within minutes, she had set me and her husband to work, mulling ale and rubbing both Myles and Rachael's limbs briskly with lard to restore the blood, while she fetched blankets, a nightgown for Rachael, and one of her husband's shirts for the boy. Caleb mildly protested at this commandeering of his property, but was naturally overruled.

Rachael was dispatched to her own bed, with a brick that had been heated in the bread oven, while we worked on the boy. Mistress Crugge repeatedly waved sharp vinegar beneath his nose, and eventually colour began to seep back into his face, though he cried piteously from the pains in his hands and feet. But Mistress Crugge kept rubbing them with grease till finally, swaddled in several blankets, he sank into a natural sleep. She sat back on a stool watching him, with a tender expression in her eyes which I had only ever seen once before when she looked at her husband.

Suddenly, I felt as empty as a punctured bladder, as if every drop of energy had been leached out of me. Relief that they were both alive had given way to another thought entirely. Myles was safe now, but if he returned to the streets, how long would it be before Tobias or one of his fellow masqueraders saw him? Would they accept that the sea had spared him, or make certain this time he died? Even if the hour for offering the tribute was past, they might kill him anyway, fearing that he could identify them as the men who had taken part in this witchcraft. One thing was certain, Myles could not be sent back out there alone.

'Mistress Crugge, the lad must stay here tonight in the warmth of the fire. As you say, I fear that he will take a fever if he goes back out to the streets tonight.'

She glanced out of the small window. The sky was beginning to lighten. 'I can't be doing with him underfoot in here. There'll be customers wanting their breakfast within the hour, and it's me that'll have to do it all myself. I'll be like a dog chasing its tail. I told that foolish girl to keep to her bed today. Sleep's the best physic. But there's a truckle bed in her room. I suppose the lad could sleep in there, but only for today, mind, then I want him out of my inn. Master Crugge won't have street urchins running about, thieving and making mischief.'

I nodded gratefully and bent to scoop the lad up, but she bustled me aside.

'You get yourself to your own bed, Master Pursglove, I reckon you're in no better shape than them. Master Crugge and I'll see to the boy. Besides,' she added with a disapproving look, 'I think you've seen quite enough of young Rachael's charms for one day.'

Chapter Forty

'I DID NOT EXPECT to see you here at this late hour, Archbishop,' Robert Cecil said stiffly as he entered the small antechamber. It would have been more truthful to say that Archbishop Bancroft was the last person he *wanted* to see, but truth and diplomacy seldom make good bedfellows.

Bancroft was around twenty years Cecil's senior, and his face was deeply lined, giving him a permanently melancholic expression as if he despaired at the state of the world and his fellow men. Cecil often reflected that his countenance would have sat better on a Puritan, which was ironic considering the Archbishop railed against those would-be reformers with as much fervour as he did against the Papists.

Cecil seated himself on the opposite side of the fire. He drew off his long leather gloves and warmed his hands over the blaze. A fine rain was falling outside and a spiteful wind had blown against them all the way up the river. In spite of his fur-lined cloak, the damp and cold had burrowed into his bones. He glanced up at Bancroft, tying to gauge how long the Archbishop had been kicking his heels in here. His black robe was steaming at the knees, and the dark curls of hair snaking from beneath his hat clung damply to his forehead. Not long enough to get dry, then. Was James planning to entertain them both together? Cecil tried to mask his annoyance. Bancroft would side with the King against him on this matter and make his task twice as difficult.

'The King has summoned you?' Cecil asked.

He was quietly satisfied to see a look of indignation cross Bancroft's face. The prelate was bridling like a ruffled hen. The Archbishop of Canterbury never bothered to conceal his belief that the divine right of his own office outranked even the divine right of kings, and was plainly affronted at the idea of being summoned by anyone.

'I bring news of my latest inquiries into the matter of Garnet's straw. His Majesty is most anxious lest the commons should start to believe in this foolish superstition.'

Cecil's eyes flicked up at the oak beams above their heads. The antechamber in which they were seated was directly below James's bedchamber. The Archbishop followed his gaze and seemed, for the first time, to register the marks carved into the wood beneath the room where the King slept. There were criss-cross carvings of the kind inscribed over the doors or fireplaces of cottages to trap demons and evil spirits, and between these were a series of scorch marks and daisy marks to ward off witches. But more curious were the interlocking VV signs, *Virgo Virginum*, which had been carved on some of the beams, a symbol invoking the protection of the Virgin Mary. A strange prayer for a Protestant King. Had James ordered these witch marks to be inscribed beneath his bed to protect his sleeping chamber, or was someone else responsible? The Archbishop swiftly dropped his gaze and began to pick at a loose thread on the lace trim of his cuff.

'Have the tailor and his wife been persuaded to confess the straw is a forgery?' Cecil inquired.

Bancroft looked annoyed. 'Naturally, they have been questioned in great detail about when and how they made this alleged discovery, but we have no intention of *persuading* them, as you put it, to any confession. We certainly don't need to create any more martyrs for their cause. Once the commons learn that Master Griffiths and his wife thought the straw of so little consequence that they did not even bother to examine it for five months after Garnet's execution, and furthermore the "nobleman" who claims he first saw the image of the face on the grain is, in fact, nothing more than a lowly footman, that will be enough to convince the populace that this straw is a crude hoax.'

'And are those really the facts, Archbishop?' Cecil asked with feigned innocence.

Bancroft scowled at him. 'And what news do you bring the King of the crossbow assassin, Lord Salisbury? Have you *persuaded* this marksman to confess the names of his co-conspirators yet?'

Unlike Bancroft, Cecil was well skilled at masking his irritation. 'The prisoner is dead,' he said, keeping his tone as dispassionate as if he was merely remarking on the weather. 'He died before he could tell us anything beyond the feeble story he had invented, that he had gone hunting to feed his family, and when he stumbled across the King's party, he panicked, fearing he would be arrested for poaching. In his haste to get away, he tripped and, the bow already being primed, fired. He ran, without even realising where the bolt had struck.'

Cecil had no intention of sharing with the Archbishop the intriguing details young Oliver Fairfax had unwittingly revealed. That the boy might yet prove a useful pair of eyes at Court, now that they had been opened by his visit to the Tower.

'So, the wretch was allowed to die before you could discover the identity of his co-conspirators. That is unfortunate, some might even say careless. I take it your interrogators were too eager to extract the truth. Did the King specifically give orders that he was to be tortured? Or the Privy Council? For unless you received such authority, Lord Salisbury, it is my duty to remind you that the law of this land, and of God, says a man may be induced to talk by infliction of pain only if it does not lead to visible maiming or death. Anything else, except when one is examining a witch' – Bancroft's gaze darted to the marks on the beam – 'is unlawful and may even be counted as murder.'

'Even against traitors, Archbishop, those who would kill a King appointed by God?' Cecil asked, managing in the raising of an eyebrow to suggest that such an idea might in itself be treason. 'But your tender conscience need not be troubled. Although the King of Scotland may have sanctioned the tearing-out of finger-nails or crushing a man's feet to pulp in the iron boot – and perhaps that is the only way to deal with the savages up there – you may rest assured, such barbarism was left north of the border.'

'Except for the rack,' Bancroft snapped.

'The *fear* of the rack is usually enough, Archbishop, and it produces more reliable testimony than its use. But in any case, Morecote's interrogators didn't even get as far as showing him the instruments of persuasion. John Morecote was poisoned. A basket of food was delivered to him by a woman claiming to be his wife. The choicest portions did, as usual, find their way on to his gaolers' plates, but the poison must have been cunningly concealed elsewhere, for the next morning Moreton was found in a pool of vomit and bloody excrement.'

The Archbishop leaned forward, his eyes alive with interest. 'His wife, you say? Such things are not uncommon, prisoners asking for some means of escaping justice at the executioner's hands to be smuggled into them by their families. But he will not escape the justice of God so easily.' Bancroft spread his hands. 'It will see them both in hell.'

'I said *claiming* to be his wife, Archbishop, but she was not. Morecote's wife is confined to her bed, paralysed by an accident over a year ago. A dozen worthy men will swear to it that she cannot even walk to her own hearth, much less to the Tower.'

'Then it is plain someone wanted him silenced, Lord Salisbury.'

Cecil briefly closed his eyes, giving way to a rare moment of visible exasperation. *Has that point only just occurred to this half-witted cleric? Give me a Jesuit any day instead of a bishop, at least you can sharpen your wits on them.* But he knew his irritation stemmed more from anger at himself than at the Archbishop. He was responsible for having Morecote moved from the Gatehouse in Westminster to the Tower, where Cecil had men skilled enough to question Morecote. He had been convinced that the mere sight of the infamous stronghold would induce such fear in the man that he would readily name all those who were behind this latest attempt on the King's life.

'Yes, indeed, Morecote was silenced, Archbishop, and that proves beyond any doubt he was not acting alone. Whoever lies behind this knew that the King would be in that part of Windsor Park at that hour, which means the traitor is a member of the King's inner Court, or someone outside who is wealthy enough to pay for such intelligence. That is why we have not yet released the news of Morecote's death and have threatened the gaolers that, if they do not hold their tongues, they will find themselves on trial for aiding the King's enemies by poisoning the prisoner. As long as the other conspirators believe Morecote is still alive and might yet talk, their nerve may fail and they may betray themselves.'

Bancroft nodded gravely. He rested his elbows on the arms of the wooden chair, pressed his fingertips together and studied Robert Cecil thoughtfully. 'And, pray tell me, how is the Secretary of State planning to use this latest attempt on the King's life?'

'Use it?' Cecil repeated. His face remained expressionless.

The Archbishop continued to study him, then wagged a beringed hand at him. A large amethyst stone flashed purple in the candlelight. 'The Oath of Allegiance, Lord Salisbury. That is what you intend to press with the King tonight. You mean to convince him that this attack is the work of the recusant nobles, encouraged by the secular priests, so he will enforce the Penalty of Praemunire.'

'And why are you so reluctant to see the oath enforced, Archbishop?' Cecil countered. 'You know that James does not recognise any difference between the secular priests and the Jesuits.'

'Then we must convince him otherwise, Lord Salisbury. I

have always believed that we should foment division between the secular priests in England and the Jesuits abroad. We must take care that we do not drive the seculars into the Jesuit camp by too zealously enforcing the laws of recusancy. If we do, with the Pope and his foreign princes to ready provide the army, it will be as if the legions of hell are marching against us, besieging us both from without and within. Lord Salisbury, you worked hard to make it known the Gunpowder Conspiracy was the work of the Jesuits, so that the secular priests and lay Catholics would turn against them, appalled at the murder of innocents they proposed. Why do you not support me in the matter of the oath?'

'I no more want to see this country torn apart by civil war than you do. But it was you, Archbishop, who drafted the Oath of Allegiance. What is the use of a law if it is allowed to be flouted with impunity? It simply makes a mockery of both law and lawmaker. The Oath must now be enforced, with the full Penalty of Praemunire for those who will not take it.'

'Must it, Lord Salisbury? Already it hangs like the torturer's chains within the sight of recusants. And as you have just pointed out, the threat is oftentimes more persuasive than the deed.' Bancroft glanced shrewdly at Cecil. 'But I suspect your interest lies not in persuading them to loyalty, but ensuring they refuse. It is no secret that the King is now spending more than one hundred thousand pounds a year on his household, twice what he used to spend as King of Scotland. At this rate, the treasury will soon see the bare boards at the bottom of their coffers. The recusant families, on the other hand, are some of the wealthiest in the realm, if not in coin, then in estates and possessions. If they refuse to swear the oath then all they possess – lands, property, goods – becomes forfeit, and that golden rain would certainly fill the empty wells of the Treasury. And you believe this latest attempt on the King's life will finally force him to act.' A mirthless chuckle escaped the Archbishop. 'A less charitable man than me might even begin to suspect that you yourself had arranged for this would-be assassin to be poisoned, Lord Salisbury.'

Chapter Forty-one

DANIEL PURSGLOVE

'MOTHER KITTY'S HOUSE is in that short-arsed street near St Peter's Church, close by the castle walls. There's a rose painted above the door.' That was all young Myles had told me, but at least it was a start.

After what had happened on New Year's Eve, I could not send Myles out on the streets and risk him being seen by Tobias or another of Death's horsemen. But I had eventually coaxed out of him that the one place I might find Skinner, outside of the castle, was at Mother Kitty's, where, I'd been told, the girls were willing enough to oblige any man. I didn't want a girl, but I did want Skinner.

The house, when I eventually found it, was squashed among an assortment of ill-favoured dwellings that seemed to have sprung up like toadstools however they pleased, with extra rooms or whole storeys being jammed in where even the smallest gap presented itself. Mother Kitty's establishment had a tall, narrow frontage, though I suspected, like its neighbours, it probably extended far back, nudging against the houses at its rear, as if trying to shove them out. The door looked far more substantial than any of those surrounding it, and a red rose of sorts was indeed painted over it, beneath a swinging lantern, though it was certainly not the chaste flower of Lancaster. But I was not there to pluck rosebuds.

In answer to my knock, a wizened old face peered out of the grille in the door. I couldn't tell if it was a man or a woman, and the voice was so cracked it gave me no clue.

'You must have a fierce itch to come at this hour. Girls are still preening themselves. Come back at sunset, you'll have the pick of them then.'

'It's Mother Kitty I've come to see.'

'So, the cockerel has a hankering for ripe meat.' A cackle of laughter broke off in a bout of coughing. 'But you're wasting your time. She'll not oblige. Never has, never will. As she always says, old Queen Bess didn't put herself to the trouble of sailing the seas to get her treasure when she'd a hundred coxcombs falling over themselves to fetch it for her.'

'I've not come seeking *company* tonight,' I said, trying not to give offence. 'Someone told me that she might be able to tell me where to find an acquaintance of mine. I'll pay her, of course.'

'Aye, you'll pay alright. They all pay.' Grimy fingers slithered through the grille, and I pressed a coin into them. 'Wait there.' The shutter behind the grille slammed.

She left me standing there so long, I began to think she had no intention of returning. Three lads shambled along, nudging and smirking at one another when they caught sight of me, calling out the names of the girls I should ask for and what they would be prepared to do.

But just as I was walking away, the door opened behind me. 'You're lucky; she's in a fair humour.'

The doorkeeper was a short, wizened creature, clad in a plain servant's gown, but with long heavy earrings that dragged on her lobes and a dozen necklaces, dangling to her hips, made from a gawdy assortment of glass beads and bone. She clanked her way along a passage lined with doors, behind which I heard the chatter of women's voices. Then she clambered up a small circular staircase and flung open the door at the top. I followed and found myself standing on a small landing in a dimly lit, wedge-shaped room, with a single window tucked high up under the ceiling. Two more steps led up to the main part of the room, where a bed stood, hung with heavy drapes which were pulled closed around it. Several banded chests lined the walls, but the only occupant of the room sat before a table on which stood a lighted candle and a small French mirror in a carved frame.

A man sat at the table, with his back to me, clad in a red doublet, slashed with green and yellow. His legs were encased in tightly fitting hose and breeches and his attire was crowned by a voluptuous wig of long scarlet hair.

The door closed behind me with a soft thud, and for a moment I feared this might be a trap. The figure slowly swivelled around to face me. Standing as I was below the level of the room itself, I felt as if I was seeking an audience with a king seated on a dais, except that now that I could see the face, I saw it wasn't a man, but a woman. Her skin was plastered in a thick layer of white make-up, with a vivid circle of vermillion on each cheek. She had arched black eyebrows and a cupid's bow mouth that had been painted on in almost the same shade of flaming red as her wig. It was a style that had been fashionable among older noblewomen in London when the aged Queen had been on the throne.

Mother Kitty laughed at my startled expression, but her face remained stiff beneath the ceruse that covered it. 'I see Magpie is right, as always. You've not visited my girls before.'

I made a courtly bow. 'I regret I have not, Mistress Kitty, but charming as I am sure they are, on this occasion I have come to you on a more pressing matter. I was told you might be able to help me contact Skinner. I have urgent business to discuss with him.'

'After they are introduced to my girls, my gentlemen find their urgent business will wait an hour or so and not suffer for it.' Mother Kitty rose and took a few paces towards me, forcing me to look up at her. Her eyes glittered in that dead white mask. She reached out and softly caressed my cheek and beard.

'My girls will scratch each other's eyes out over you,' she murmured. 'But I have a special one for you. Young, innocent, unblemished as new snow. I wouldn't waste her on any of those ham-fisted seamen, but I can see you know how to handle a rare treasure.'

I twisted my head away from her hand. 'I will pay you, Mistress Kitty, but not for a girl. Tell me how to find Skinner.'

She laughed and teasingly slapped my cheek. 'Pity, but you'll be back, they all come back.' Her tone brisk now, she added, 'It's ten shillings for a girl, the use of a bed and a flagon of best wine. But since you won't be having the girl, I'll be generous; five shillings to answer your question.'

I handed her two shillings. 'And another two after you tell me.'

She went back to her table and rang a small handbell. As if she had been hovering just outside the door, the gatekeeper entered, her beads clattering.

'Is Skinner in his usual place?'

'He is, Mother. Just settled him there myself. Says he'll see the fine gentleman. Knows him, recognised his firemark.'

My hand went unbidden to my throat, and the old woman chuckled.

'Don't you go thinking my eyes aren't as sharp as a ship's spike, just 'cause my back's crooked. Isn't that right, Mother?'

'Enough prattling, Magpie. Take our new friend to Skinner, and see you bring me back the *three* shillings he'll give you. And be quick. The regulars will be hammering at the door soon and they won't want to be kept waiting.'

I followed the Magpie, rattling and chinking, back along the passage. She paused in front of a narrow door and pulled it open. In the small space behind, a staircase led upwards, the angle so steep it was almost vertical.

'He's up there, dirty little ferret that he is. Doesn't go with the girls. He pleasures himself watching them with others. Pity you didn't fancy it, 'cause he'd have enjoyed watching you. Pays for it, of course, they all pay.' She held out her hand.

I dropped two shillings into the grimy paw.

'Mother Kitty said three. And three she'll have, or it's my hide that'll smart for it.'

Once the door was closed behind me, the staircase was plunged into darkness and I was obliged to grip the sides of the ladder-like stairs to feel my way up. I climbed carefully, stopping a couple of times to reach up above me to ensure I didn't suddenly brain myself on what I knew must be a trapdoor above. When I finally felt the wood, I rapped on it. If Skinner was indeed pleasuring himself, I had no wish to emerge through the floor and find myself at eye level with that spectacle.

Light edged down the stairs as the trapdoor slowly lifted and I scrambled up the last few steps to emerge into a tiny chamber. Hard against the wall on one side was a pallet, on which two or three stained blankets lay in a crumpled heap. On the other side were a narrow table and chair, on which Skinner was seated, pouring wine from a flagon with one hand and spearing a small piece of meat from a dish with the point of a wicked-looking flesher's knife. He popped the morsel into his mouth and chewed, open-mouthed, half closing his eyes as if in ecstasy. Brown saliva trickled into the moth-eaten black beard. I glanced around, trying to see where the spyhole might be, and spotted four round holes at intervals in the floor, each plugged with a lid of wood and a little iron ring to lift it out.

He followed my gaze, gesturing at the holes with the point of his knife. 'Too early for the entertainment, but you're welcome to join me when it starts, brother.' He laughed, and the blueish skin across his beak of a nose shone in the candlelight as if he'd been polishing it. 'Changed your mind about that lovely bit of pewter, have you? I thought you might.' He grinned.

'I'm willing to buy it, but I want to meet the man you had it from.'

'Any why might you be wanting to do that?'

It was a question I knew he'd be bound to ask. 'I want to trace the man who made a certain piece of pewter. The craftsmanship of the flagon you showed me is so like it, I'm certain it comes from the same workshop.'

His small eyes narrowed. 'But you said it wasn't what you were looking for, and now it is? Discovered it's worth more than you thought, that it?'

'I'd wager there's not a man in Bristol who's a better judge of what an object is worth than you, Skinner. The piece itself is still of no interest to me. But I'll pay you the price you wanted for it, if you take me to its owner. Think about it; you'd get the same sum and keep the flagon to sell to another pigeon. Only a fool would refuse that bargain, and you're no fool.'

I knew I was taking a huge risk going into that castle; both Rachael and Myles had warned me of that. And if the man who had stolen that flagon from Hugh was not merely a thief but the compiler of that list, maybe even the man who had murdered Dagworth, Gysbourne and Harewell, then I was walking straight into the lair of a ruthless killer. But time was running out. I had only three days left. I had to discover what he knew. If FitzAlan learned, as he surely would, that the Jesuits had murdered five men loyal to the Crown, and I had done nothing to stop them, then my life would end in agony on the quartering block and I had no wish to a die a martyr to any cause.

Skinner studied his platter in silence, before stabbing his blade into another morsel. When he'd finished chewing, he raised his eyes to me again. 'I *could* get you in, but see I'd be sticking my head in a noose. You might be peaching for the sheriff or spying for the King's men and looking for a way to put us all on the gallows. And if my brothers thought I'd let one of those in, why they'd cut me into pieces while I was still talking and feed me to the hounds, and you along with me.'

'The sheriff could ride in there with a posse of men and arrest you all without my help, or save himself the trouble and blow the place to hell with you all inside it. But you and I both know he won't, because the castle belongs to the King and he can't set foot in it, much less destroy it. So, what could I learn and pass on to him that he doesn't already know?'

Skinner shrugged. 'True enough, but then my brothers are not as reasonable as me. Take offence if a cat looks at them sideways, and they don't like strangers who ask questions. I'd have to stand surety for you, and it would be my blood they'd be wanting payment in, if you annoy them. My blood's worth a good deal more to me than any flagon.'

'How much?'

Skinner held his knife, point down, on the table and spun it faster and faster until the glint of steel in the candlelight seemed to be a ball of silver hanging in mid-air.

'Fifty pounds,' he finally announced.

I snorted. 'I could buy that ruin of a castle from the King for less, and all of you in it.'

''Course, it won't do you much good if you get in but my friend refuses to talk to you,' Skinner said, still staring at the knife. 'And he doesn't speak to anyone except me. I'm the only one he trusts. I'd have to persuade him, coax him to talk, as a personal favour to me.'

'I don't have anything like that sum,' I protested.

'Maybe you do, maybe you don't.' Skinner skewered another piece of meat. 'But it seems you've a desperate need to talk to my friend, else you'd not have taken so much trouble to track him down. So, I'm thinking it's more than a piece of pewter you're after. And when a man's desperate, he can always find a way to pay. Sell, borrow . . . steal even, if he has to. You'd be surprised how resourceful a man can be if he wants something badly enough.'

He was a shrewd man and I'd been a fool for revealing how important this was to me, but I hoped Skinner might prove the bigger fool yet. A man's vice can always be twisted against him, and Skinner's was greed. I made him wait, trying to give the impression I was wrestling with myself. He filled his glass and took a deep draught of wine, watching me intently over the rim.

I sighed and moved closer, lowering my voice. 'I am desperate,' I admitted. 'If I wasn't, there is no way you would persuade me to do this. The question is, are you a man willing to forego a little to win a prize that could bring you far greater riches?'

He gave a crooked smile and flicked his dirt-encrusted fingers at me. 'If you've a map showing where some pirate has buried his treasure, then you can use it to wipe your arse. There's a man draws a dozen of them a week and sells them to any pigeon egg who comes to take passage on the ships in the hopes of making his fortune.'

I raked my beard and studied him carefully. 'No maps, I'm not fool enough to try to gull a man like you. In fact, it's only because I can tell you know every flimflam that's practised on the streets that I thought what I have to offer might suit a man of your talents. But then again, it might prove too dangerous a temptation for one of your calling.' I stepped away from him as if I was preparing to leave. 'I can see that a little money in the hand is worth more to you, now that you're getting on in years. Taking risks is for the young.'

'I'm not ready for the bone grubbers yet!' Skinner said indignantly. He stretched out a hand with its long, thickened yellow nails. 'You show me what you've got.'

I reached inside my purse, then let my hand fall away as if I was having doubts. 'How do I know you won't talk? This could see me dancing on the gallows.'

Skinner sniggered unpleasantly. 'Oh aye, next time the sheriff invites me to partake of a dainty mess of larks at one of his feasts I'll be sure to tell him.' He was leaning forward eagerly now, his eyes fixed on the purse hanging from my belt, almost drooling.

I fumbled around and pulled out the dry chicken bone, around which was twisted a few strands of hemp and human hair. It was the bone I'd soaked in jading oil, which would make any horse turn aside. I was rather sorry to sacrifice it, but if I could use it to tempt a weasel . . .

I held it up. Skinner squinted at it suspiciously. 'What's that, then, a love charm? A curse?'

'A key,' I told him. 'A key that, if used right, will open any lock. A gift beyond price for a man who might want to enter a house silently, open a locked chest perhaps, but leave no trace that the lock has been broken. It might be hours, days, weeks even, before the owner of that chest discovered anything missing and raised the alarm. And should such a man find himself locked up, why he could open every door that stands between him and freedom, and melt away like a phantom into the night.'

'It looks like nothing more than a bone and a bit of rope.'

'That's the beauty of it,' I said. 'Even if a man was searched, who would bother to take that from him. You see this rope, this strand of hair?'

He peered, frowning.

'That is the lock of hair of the highwayman and thief Gamaliel Ratsey, and a piece of the very noose that hanged him. The name is known to you?'

Skinner's eyes gleamed in the candlelight. His mouth grew slack as if he was watching one of the girls perform in the chamber below. 'The Hobgoblin – the most famous thief and highwayman that ever was. They say the first time he was taken, he walked right through the door of the prison under the very nose of his gaolers. Two hundred pounds he took from some men in a single night.' Skinner spoke in the kind of awed tones that old Waldegrave employed when reciting the miracles of the Catholic martyrs. We all have our heroes.

Some thieves believe the hangman's rope used to execute a successful robber would open doors and keep them from getting caught. I was gambling that Skinner was one of them. He reached out eagerly to snatch the talisman, but I held it out of reach.

'It's yours after I have entered the castle and you have persuaded the owner of the flagon to talk to me.'

Skinner's face twisted, so that in the candlelight he looked as if he, too, was wearing Ratsey's hobgoblin mask. 'How do I know it'll even work? Could be any old bit of rope and hair.' He pulled a key from inside his shirt and jerked his chin towards something behind me. 'Behind that curtain is a door. I locked it myself when I came in here. You unlock it without touching this key and I'll take you into the castle.'

A heavy curtain hung on the far wall directly behind the trapdoor through which I'd entered. I walked over to it, pushing aside the hanging whose original colour was lost under a pall of dust and mildew. The door behind it was low and heavy. I turned the iron ring and tugged. I knew it would be locked, but I wanted to be sure that Skinner wouldn't convince himself that he had neglected to lock it or that it had been unlocked from the other side.

Behind me, I heard his cackle of malicious delight, like an old crone at an execution.

'Thought as much, that bit of rope of yours couldn't open a dead oyster.'

I made a show of letting him see me cup the bone with its rope and hair close to my mouth while I murmured to it. Then I touched it to the door, using my shoulder to block his sightline just long enough to insert the metal rod I had drawn from my shirt into the lock. Before he could shift to get a better view, I turned back to him, my hands clearly empty except for the little bone. I could have opened the door myself, but I was suddenly uneasy about what might be behind it. With a flourish, I held the curtain aside and bowed. 'Would you care to try the door now, Master Skinner?'

With that odd carrion crow gait of his, he sidled across to where I stood, and turned the ring. The door opened with a groan of wood and hinges. He stared at me, surprise and suspicion fighting for control of his features. But I was used to that. I'd seen it often as I made eggs float in mid-air or a roasted pigeon turn into a live one and fly away.

I slipped the bone back into my leather purse and patted it. 'After I have spoken to the man . . . By the way, you never told me his name.'

'The Wraith. That's what they call him in the castle. Tries to make himself invisible, never smiles, rarely talks, but he can't rest either. It's like he's dead, but doesn't know it.' He gestured towards the open door. 'You were eager enough to get into the castle. What's keeping you?'

'Through there?'

He chuckled. 'Think we can just stroll up to the gates, do you, like we were guests of the King? They keep a watch on those gates day and night, for all the good it does them. May as well plant a hedge around a tree to keep a cuckoo from flying away.'

He gestured again to the door. I peered in. A smell of rotting wood and the ordure from cesspits slithered out on the cold damp air. I leaned over, trying to see a passageway or steps, but there was nothing. It was like peering down into a black, bottomless well. I swiftly drew back, pressing myself hard against the safe, solid wall.

'Not quite so bold now, are we?' he jeered.

'Not so bold that I am reckless. I prefer to have the man with the knife pointing it ahead of me, not at my back. So, after you, Master Skinner,' I said, with a mock bow.

'There's some at the castle could learn a thing or two from you,' Skinner said, with a tinge of respect in his tone. He turned back into the room and picked up a lantern which he lit from one of the candles. He bolted the trapdoor to Mother Kitty's, so that it couldn't be raised from below, then thrust the lantern into my hand and backed through the door I had opened and began to descend. Holding the lantern out, I could see he was in a small square shaft. The metal rungs set into the wall below the door descended into the blackness below, though how far down they went I couldn't see.

I turned, as he had done, and scrambled over the edge, feeling for the narrow bars of metal beneath my boots. It was a perilous descent, holding the rungs with one hand and the lantern with the other. Suddenly, the door above me slammed shut. Skinner must have pulled on a cord or some mechanism below me. It echoed down the shaft like the fall of a coffin lid.

Chapter Forty-two

I DON'T KNOW HOW LONG it took to make the perilous descent down that shaft, but it was so deep, I thought I must have reached the roof of hell. Finally, my foot searching for the next rung sank into something soft, then connected with solid ground. I was standing on the floor of the passage, which extended in two directions on either side of the shaft. A rushing sound filled the tunnel as if a great wind was blowing down it, but the icy air was still and stagnant.

'I'd best take that,' Skinner growled, and pulled the lantern from my hand. 'It's as slippery as a greased pig underfoot. You'll be flailing around like a cow on ice, and we don't want you dropping it. Step lively!'

The tunnel was carved out of the rock, wide enough for two men to pass each other, but so low in places I was forced to stoop to pass through. Skinner held the light high as he led the way, which at least warned me of the sharp lumps of stone ahead, jutting out of the top and sides, threatening to brain anyone who didn't duck smartly. But I could see nothing of the floor. I found myself squelching through mud and splashing through deep, cold puddles where water had collected in the hollows.

The passage seemed to be sloping downwards, but the castle was on a mound, higher than the surrounding houses. Surely, we should be climbing up. Was this a trap? As that unpleasant thought struck me, I realised the rushing sound I'd heard from the beginning was a surge of water, and the noise was growing louder.

Skinner stopped so abruptly, I almost cannoned into him.

Beyond him, just visible in the dim yellow lantern light, was something grey and viscous, glistening like a giant slug.

'Always a drop of water collects here, where there's a dip, but since the flood it's been a bloody lake. Half the jakes in Bristol have washed in here, too. Stinks worse than a beggar's crotch,' he added, as if I couldn't smell it. 'There's a corpse or two, and worse, floating in that.'

After finding that rotting body on the marsh, I wasn't sure what he thought could be worse than a corpse, but there are some questions it's better not to ask. He lifted the lantern, shining the light ahead. A long narrow beam of wood had been wedged across the pool. The water was so high in places that the top of the beam was barely visible above the thick malodorous soup. A rope strung above it provided some kind of hand hold. Skinner grabbed the rope above his head with one hand and edged rapidly along the sodden wood, shuffling sideways. Swaying dangerously, he stood for a moment to regain his balance, but reached the other side without mishap, and stepped off. In the dim light from the lantern flickering about him, I could see that the passage sloped upwards on the other side. Slowly, he swung the lantern until the light glistened on the oily water and I could just make out the beam, above the surface.

I reached for the rope and hauled myself on to the wood. It was as slimy as an eel and the rope was not much better. I clung on with both hands, buckling forward then back, and trying all the while not to look into the foul water lapping over the soles of my boots, much less think about what might be bobbing in it. It was not helped by the low roof; I was forced almost to crouch in order to pass beneath sections. A foul miasma rose from the festering water. I was finding it hard to breathe. My head swam and I was sweating in spite of the cold. I knew I had to move faster, get across before the fumes made me pass out.

Suddenly, and without warning, the feeble light was extinguished and I found myself in darkness so intense, I feared I'd been struck blind. I wobbled violently and tipped forward, the toes of my boots barely touching the wood, my whole weight hanging from the rope. I was suffocating in the foul mist. Every gasp of air I took only served to make me more dizzy, my limbs more numb and heavy. I held my breath, though my lungs were bursting, and fought to swing myself back upright again. As soon as I did, I moved with a reckless speed along the plank towards where I had last seen the light. It was probably only a few steps, but it felt like a mile. The lantern swivelled back towards me, as Skinner opened his cloak and turned. The candle lit his face from beneath, enlarging the bony beak of a nose till it looked as if he had really turned into a giant crow.

'Thought I heard someone behind us,' he announced casually. 'Don't want to reveal our secrets to any Tom, Dick or Harry now, do we?'

He'd covered that lantern on purpose, I was sure of that, just to remind me that the castle might be without cannon, but it still had its own defences against any who might be planning to double-cross its residents.

Once more I trudged behind Skinner, ducking and slipping, but the passage was sloping up now and at an increasingly steep angle. He halted in front of a wooden ladder. Water dripped down from somewhere above and splashed into a puddle below. He gave the ladder a slight tug, and it rocked, falling back against the wall with a dull clatter. It was not attached. But at least I'd been warned.

He passed me the lantern and, using both hands to grip the sodden sides, climbed up. As I angled the beam upwards to light his path, I saw that the rungs of the ladder were far from evenly spaced, designed to make the climb even more hazardous. Skinner, though, was plainly used to the uneven spacing and hauled himself over the gaps with the agility of a man half his age. He paused near the top and, pulling a key from around his neck, inserted it into a lock in a narrow door set into the rock wall, pushed it open and heaved himself up over the threshold. If there was any light in the chamber above, it did not penetrate the shaft.

'What you waiting for?'

I was still holding the lantern. If I set it down to grip both sides of the ladder, as Skinner had done, I would be making most of the climb in darkness. It was hard to decide which was the more hazardous, but the candle in the lantern was burning low. I climbed as rapidly as possible, convinced Skinner would slam the door before I got there, leaving me trapped below with a light that would go out before I could get back to the shaft leading to the brothel. As I scrabbled over a large gap in the rungs, the ladder tilted alarmingly, but I used my weight to swivel it back. Above me, I could hear Skinner's cackle of laughter. He was enjoying this.

Finally, I reached the top and leaned forward, wedging my shoulders through the open door and pushing the lantern ahead of me. When I finally stood on solid ground, I saw that we were in a small underground chamber. A feeble shaft of light on the opposite side filtered down through a mass of dead weeds from a grille set into the ground above.

Skinner locked the door behind me and rolled a great rusty iron disc across it, which would crash down on to the stone floor with an echo loud enough to wake the dead, should any man attempt to force the door from the other side. As he led the way towards the archway and the staircase behind it, I guessed that we were in the dungeon of the castle's keep.

The spiral stone steps were only wide enough for one man to pass. I wondered how many prisoners over the centuries had been thrust down those steps ahead of their gaolers, pushed so hard that they tumbled, smashing their skulls on the walls. Skinner and his light were already out of sight around the corner, before I'd mounted the first two steps. Ahead of me, I heard the hollow echo of wood on stone. Skinner must have opened a trapdoor at the top of the stairs and then let it fall back into place, for there was not even the faint glow of light above me. I quickened my pace, fearing he would bolt the door behind him.

Then sense took over. If he had bolted it, I would smash my head on the wood as I came up. I slowed and took each step carefully, one arm raised above my head, to feel for the trapdoor above. Sharp stabbing pains shot through my upraised arm. I tried to jerk away, but it was caught fast. I wrenched it free and heard the cloth of my sleeve rip and tear. For a moment I thought a viper had sunk its fangs into me, but I knew it couldn't be that. Something warm was trickling down my hand. I didn't need light to tell it was blood.

Chapter Forty-three

'SKINNER! Remember I still have Ratsey's rope,' I bellowed. 'So, if you don't open that trapdoor, I will – and I'll drag you down through it by your throat.'

A sliver of light appeared above me, gradually widening into a square.

'Door fell shut. Has a nasty habit of doing that.'

I scrambled through and turned to look at it, blood dripping from my fingertips. I guessed there must once have been a locked iron grille over the entrance to the dungeon, but it had been replaced with a thick wooden hatch. As it lay open, I saw what had bitten me. A set of sharp metal spikes had been driven through the wood, so that when the door was closed, the points projected vertically downwards a good four inches. Any assailant storming up those stairs in the dark would impale his own skull on those spikes.

I knew Skinner was armed, but at that moment I was too angry to care. I grabbed him by the front of his ragged shirt and threw him back against the wall. He hit it hard with his back, which seemed to knock the breath from his body, and slid down the wall. But before I could move, a brawny arm was locked around my neck from behind, and a blow from a huge fist hit me in the side, felling me to my knees. White lights exploded in my head. I fought down the numbing pain, trying to reach my dagger tangled in the folds of my cloak, but just as my fingers touched the hilt, a huge hand seized it and wrenched it from its sheath. The man crushing my neck loosened his grip only to seize a fistful of my hair and yank my head back. I felt the freshly sharpened edge of my own dagger pressing against my throat.

'You want Runt to finish him, Skinner?' a woman's voice sang out.

Skinner levered himself to his feet, staring down at me, and for a moment I thought he was going to say yes. But he grunted and flicked his fingers.

'Let him go . . . for now.'

My knife vanished and I was released. I was hauled to my feet by several pairs of hands and found myself surrounded by three young lads, a middle-aged woman and a snub-nosed girl who looked like a younger version of the woman, except for a broad raised scar that ran from the corner of her mouth to her ear. The man who had grabbed me was not much taller than I was, but with his thick, corded neck and the muscles of a plough ox, he looked as if he could have single-handedly pulled a laden galleon into port on the end of a rope.

They pushed me out into a dismal square hall. I guessed we were on the ground floor of the keep, for there was a heavy door on one side, sagging open on its hinges, and arrow slits high up in the thick walls. The stones were beginning to crumble away around the slits, as if a giant rat had been nibbling them. Mouldy straw, bracken and rubbish of every kind littered the floor, and several dogs, infants and chickens were scrabbling about in it. A great iron pot steamed over the fire in the hearth, and three women sat close by, plucking geese. I wondered where they had found them, for I'd seen none for sale in the market since I'd come to Bristol.

A group of lads had scraped the stinking straw back to expose the flat bare flags and were spinning coins across some crudely painted lines, yelling and squabbling over who had won. Among them was the youth I'd seen branded by the crowd. A filthy bandage covered the wound on his cheek. Behind them, a cord was strung between two beams with a score of purses and pockets of various shapes dangling from it. Each purse was hung with bells. So, this was how Skinner trained his young nips.

A handful of men squatted nearby on kegs and boxes, drinking smoke from their pipes or sharpening knives. It was a common enough sight in any port to see men who'd lost legs or hands, but nearly every adult in the room, and some of the younger lads, too, were maimed or marked, though not, I guessed, from accidents at sea.

'Brought us a nice, plump coney, have you, Skinner?' a man called out. 'Where did you find him?'

'He's business with the Wraith,' Skinner replied.

Several of the men exchanged knowing glances, but I could not interpret them.

As I followed Skinner across the hall, I became aware of an angry buzzing. A girl was sitting on the floor, scratching magical symbols on to dark brown nutshells with a sharp knife. Each of the shells had been cut in two and hinged with a scrap of cloth. Beside her was an earthenware jar plugged with a wad of rags, which was clearly the source of the buzzing. Then it dawned on me what she was doing – creating boxes for dicing flies, the same ones I'd seen men whispering to at the cockfight. You had to admire them; the castle rats could find a way to shave the beard off a herring if some fool could be gulled into buying it.

Skinner prodded me in the back, gesturing towards the door. 'He's made his bed in one of the old towers outside. Could have been warm and cosy in here and dipped into the common pot with the rest of us, but he prefers his own company, that one.'

We squeezed out through the sagging door, which was permanently wedged half open. It seemed even more gloomy outside than in, for night was approaching swiftly and twilight was already imprisoned within the high walls of the courtyard. Although the mighty walls had not collapsed, as so many had under the onslaught of the wave, they were cracked and battered as if they had been pounded by cannon, though they still stood defiant. Weeds and scrubby bushes had taken root in the yard and in the crevices in the walls. Pigs, horses and more dogs wandered among piles of rubbish, broken timbers and stacks of kegs.

Sensing movement behind me, I turned and saw the man who had held my dagger to my throat lumbering in our wake. My kidney still throbbed from where he had punched me.

Skinner followed my gaze. 'Don't mind him, he'll not be whispering your secrets to any. Lost his tongue, but not to a cat. Fed it to the dogs when they cut it out, that's right, isn't it, Runt?' he called cheerfully. 'Over yonder, that's the Wraith's haunt.' He gestured towards a ruined tower in the corner of the courtyard which formed part of the outer wall of the castle. The top had fallen away to the level of the wall, though it appeared to have surrendered to time and neglect, rather than the flood.

We picked our way around the heap of rubble and scrub. In front of the wooden door at the base, two dogs were fighting and snarling over a shrieking rat they had clamped in their jaws, as if it was a juicy bone. A stone hurtled past me, hitting one of them, but Runt had to strike them with two more before they ran off with the rat still gripped between them.

Skinner opened the door to the tower and marched in. I paused in the doorway, waiting for my eyes to adjust. It was dark outside in the yard, but even darker inside the tower, for there were no arrow slits on this level. I took a step backwards and found Runt so close behind me that I stumbled against his massive chest.

'Going to stand there catching flies all night?' Skinner called out. 'Drags me away from the few pleasures a poor man like me has, then keeps me waiting,' he grumbled to himself. I couldn't hear the rest, for his voice faded as he mounted what I guessed to be a set of stairs to the upper room.

Unable to back out, I took a pace or two in, and Runt followed. Now that he was no longer blocking the little twilight from the courtyard, I could just make out the dim outline of some stone steps. I headed for them, but before I could reach them Runt's arm shot out, catching me on the shoulder and sending me crashing into the wall.

I whirled to face him, reaching for my dagger, remembering too late that it was gone. But his fist wasn't raised. He pointed down at the floor. I had almost fallen into a deep open shaft, probably an old well. Runt had saved my life.

I mounted the stair warily, expecting at any moment to feel a step slide away and drop me into oblivion, or an iron ball to crash down on my head, but I reached the top without mishap. I was greeted by the roar of the river beyond the castle wall and the icy blast of air from the arrow slits. A small fire glowed in the brazier in the centre of the room and the mustard glow of a tallow candle was spreading through the room as Skinner impaled it on a sconce on the wall. The chamber was furnished with a straw pallet, heaped with blankets, together with a box and keg that served as table and stool. A small chest, the kind that a man might carry on his back, stood behind the bed, with a pewter candlestick set upon it, glinting dully in the flickering light. There were other pieces of pewter, too, a plate, bowl and tankard, and a ladle dangling from a small iron cooking pot. All had probably once been fine pieces, but now they were badly stained, and pocked with dents and patches. Of their owner there was no sign.

I picked up the candlestick and examined it, still half expecting to find that touch, but if there had ever been a maker's mark on it, whoever had mended the stick had obliterated it. Anger and frustration boiled up in me. Time was running out, and Skinner had had me playing games, passing his little tests all evening just for his own amusement. I wanted to take him by the neck and shake the truth out of him, but I was only too aware of his human guard dog standing behind me.

'Where is he?' I demanded. 'Where is this Wraith?'

Skinner spread his hands, his lips drawn back in a malicious grin. 'Who knows? Every man's business is his own here. He may come and go as he pleases, so long as he pays for the privilege.

Only castle in England where no man is a prisoner save of his own choosing.'

'You told me he never went out.' My jaws were clenched so hard I could barely force out the words.

'I said he never talks to anyone except me.'

'And if I wait?'

'Gone all night he is, sometimes. He's a living to earn, same as the rest of us, and the night's when we earn it, when respectable folk are tucked up all snug in their beds. 'Course you're welcome to wait, if you've a mind to, but I wouldn't advise it.' He gestured back in the direction of the keep. 'Seems you've riled some of my brothers. I warned you, they don't like strangers who come into their city asking questions. So, I'd start running, if I were you. They'll leave you be so long as I'm here, but soon as you're alone, they'll come hunting, and if they catch you, they'll skin you alive and feed your carcass to the pigs.'

'Aye, that they will,' someone said from the doorway. 'And the pigs'll make short work of him, too. Been at least a week since we fed that last snitch to them.'

The woman who had suggested that Runt finish me off was leaning on the archway, her arms folded, grinning as if she was a cook and I was a plucked goose hanging in a butcher's shop.

Then her gaze darted to Skinner 'Thought you'd best see these. Worth nowt, but . . .' She stepped into the room and held something out to him. As he took it, I saw at once what it was, the chicken bone bound with the rope and hair, and a slip of paper. My hand flew to the leather purse that always hung from my belt. It was gone.

All three of them were chuckling now. She'd cut my purse when her daughter and the lads crowded around me and helped me to my feet after the Runt had released me. It was the oldest trick in the marketplace. I couldn't believe I'd fallen for it after all my months on the road.

The jading bone vanished instantly inside Skinner's clothing. He clearly wasn't going to share that secret with the woman.

Then he turned his attention to the slip of paper. I knew, before he unfolded it, what she'd found. It was the copy I'd made of the mark burned on the murdered men.

Skinner's eyes narrowed. 'What's this?' His face showed no sign of recognition.

'A touchmark. I wanted to ask the Wraith if he recognised it. If he knew the man who'd made it.'

'That's what you were looking for on the flagon.' Skinner took a step closer, peering up into my face. 'See now, that's what makes no sense to me. Why would you go to all that trouble to find the man who made some bit of pewter? And don't go repeating that tale of looking for a gift for your father. I know a mare's nest when I hear it.'

Runt moved closer behind me, and I found myself squeezed between the two of them, like an apple in a cider press. If the Wraith had sent that death threat to Hugh, then either he was a Jesuit in hiding or he was working for them, but one thing I knew for certain, if I had even the faintest hope of getting out of this place alive, I could not reveal what I suspected to Skinner.

'Revenge,' I said, as coldly as I could. 'You read me right, Skinner. I don't want a gift for my father. I want my father's murderer. My father was found hanging by a belt. The coroner said he'd taken his own life, but no one in the household recognised the belt that he'd used as a noose or the fine pewter buckle on it. I am sure it belonged to his murderer.' I gestured at the paper. 'I think the man who crafted that buckle might remember making such a piece, or maybe he has a record in his ledgers of who he made it for or who bought it.'

Skinner plucked at his beard. 'Coroners!' He spat a glob of yellow phlegm on the floor. 'Cry murder fast enough when they can pin it on some poor bastard who just happens to be passing, but if the killer is one of their cronies, they'll swear on their children's lives that a man with a bloody dagger sticking out of his chest died from a surfeit of lampreys.' He thrust the scrap of paper into his shirt. 'Save yourself the shoe leather, brother.

If the owner of that belt is a wealthy man, you'll get no justice from the law. More likely you'll find yourself in chains for accusing him.'

'That's always been the way of it,' the woman said. 'The poor hang and the rich make a profit on the rope.'

'Aye and there'll be no profit to be made standing here,' Skinner said, moving towards the doorway.

The woman tried to slip past him, but Skinner's arm shot out like an arrow fired from a bow. He seized her by the wrist. 'Forget something, did we, Joan?' He held out his other hand.

She looked as if she was about to argue, then laughed. 'Would I forget you, Skinner?' She reached inside her gown and dropped a few coins into his palm.

He waggled his fingers, grinning. 'And the rest.'

More coins landed in his palm, *my* coins. He juggled them up and down as if judging the weight of them.

'That's all, Skinner, I swear it, save for my wages.'

He made a deep growling noise in his throat. 'One of these days, your greed will find you down that well with your throat cut.'

Joan grinned, as if she didn't believe a word of it.

Skinner snuffed out the candle flame between his finger and thumb, leaving only the dull bloody glow of the embers in the brazier. In the doorway, he made a crooked bow. 'Pleasure doing business with you, Brother Pursglove. Runt, you take him out. Quick way, mind, seeing as he's our guest.'

'Won't the Yena have something to say about that?' Joan said. 'Stopped our lads cutting his throat and pitching him in the harbour a while back. Seems to have an uncommon interest in this one. We can't afford to lose the old man's services. There's none of us can do what he can, and we need those papers.'

'Why do you think I brought the peacher here? Those dungwits go attacking him in the street, word gets round, questions get asked. But if he just disappears, the old man thinks he's seen sense and left Bristol like he was told.'

Joan chuckled and made for the stairs. 'Treat him gentle, then, Runt, remember he's an orphan.'

Runt laughed, opening his mouth wide and revealing the splintered teeth and empty cavern where his tongue should have been. Skinner vanished in a swirl of his black rags. I heard the slither of his footfalls descending the steps until the sound was swallowed by the rush of the river outside. I lunged for the candlestick, but Runt's knife was across my throat before I could turn and wield it. He pressed harder, forcing me to drop my makeshift weapon with a clang of metal on stone that seemed to echo to hell and back. Then his massive paw seized my shoulder and he began to steer me towards the stairs and the darkness beyond.

Chapter Forty-four

RUNT, STILL GRIPPING my shoulder with fingers of steel, propelled me down the uneven steps. The staircase was in darkness and the windowless room at the bottom of the tower gaped beneath me like an open grave. All I could see was a thin wedge of ghost light from the partly opened door that led into the tower. Somewhere between me and that door was the well shaft. I didn't know which I feared more, drowning in the black water below, or falling into an empty hole and lying there in agony with a broken leg or back until I died of hunger and thirst. One thing I knew for certain, Runt wasn't about to show me out of the gate with a wave and a smile.

As I took the next step down my foot sank into the layer of loose stones and dirt, and I knew we had reached the floor at the bottom of the tower. Where was the well? How many paces across the room? I reached out, trying to feel my way round by pressing close to the wall, but the great hand on my shoulder was dragging me towards the centre of the room, hauling me relentlessly forward. Each time I took a step, I expected my foot to fall into empty space. I was naked and helpless without my dagger, made worse by the thought that it was in the possession of the man who was walking behind me.

Runt stumbled. He pressed down hard on my shoulder to steady himself. I instantly dropped into a crouch, directly in front of him, snatching up a handful of dirt, and as he pitched forward over me, I hurled it into what I hoped was his face. He blindly flung out an arm, trying to grab hold of me again, but I twisted sideways, slamming my fist hard into his body, and threw myself towards the wall. I could hear stones clattering as he tried to right himself, but I didn't wait. Groping along the wall towards the faint grey triangle of light, I reached the door and slipped through it. Behind me, I heard a long-drawn-out scream and then, from somewhere deep below, the echo of a splash.

I ran, following the line of the castle wall, until I reached the remains of a small roofless building. I clambered behind it and sank on to a pile of rotting weeds, gasping for breath. Was Runt still alive down there, still struggling? How long did it take for a man to drown, a man who couldn't call for help? And how long before anyone in the keep realised that he hadn't returned and began searching for him? If I was still here then, I'd discover for myself exactly how long it took to drown down there, that's if they didn't cut me into joints for the pigs' supper, as Skinner had threatened. One thing was certain, I couldn't get out of the castle the way I'd come in. I might be able to find a way up on to the walls, but if I jumped down from that height, I'd break my legs at the very least, or impale myself on a broken spar in the rubble below. I was trapped.

I crept along the back of the ruined building and peered out into the courtyard. The only lights came from the keep. Skinner had said none of them could get in or out of the main gate, but I was equally sure that the rest of the castle's residents were not using Skinner's route. Mother Kitty wouldn't tolerate them traipsing in and out of her establishment half the night in their hunt for prey. There had to be other entrances. If I could just find one of them, or if someone could show me . . . It was a risk, and it could be the most stupid gamble I had ever taken in my life. If it was, then it would certainly prove to be my last.

It was hard to see anything now that it was so dark, but I was pretty sure I remembered seeing what I needed by one of the old wooden huts. I ran back towards them, keeping in the shadows. I could just make out the outline in the faint light spilling from the keep. I crept closer. A large dog suddenly ran out from behind the hut, barking furiously. I glanced anxiously at the keep, but no one came running. I guessed most had already gone out into the city, and the others were too accustomed to dogs snarling and barking to investigate. I groped for a piece of wood and threw it as hard as I could away from me. The hound, distracted, chased after it. I grabbed up a length of rope, praying it was long enough, and set off back to the tower. The dog came bounding after me, snapping and growling at my legs. I flailed the rope end at it, trying to hold it back, as I raced to the tower with the hound lumbering after me. I slipped inside and slammed the door shut in its face. Its claws scrabbled at the wood.

With the door closed it was as dark as the Devil's crotch inside. I stood still and listened, then to my relief heard the sound of splashing and faint moans.

'Hold on!' I called. I looped the rope over my neck and, pressing myself to the wall, began to work my way round it. If I was right, somewhere, like in the Hole, there would be iron rings or brackets embedded in the stones, for the tethering of animals if not people. After what seemed like an age, my hand brushed against a ring. It felt rusty, eroded with damp and age. I tugged it, though I dared not pull hard in case it suddenly broke and sent me crashing down into the well. I couldn't be sure it would hold, but there was no time to look for another. I tied the rope around it and, dropping to my hands and knees, edged forward in the dirt. I felt the chill, wet air on my face before I felt the edge of the well, and lay flat.

'Runt, I have rope, I'll let it down to you, but only if you swear to help me get safely out of the castle. I know you can't speak, but I'll drop the rope down to you. If you're willing to swear on your life you'll help me, tug the rope twice. If you don't, I'll untie this end and the rope will fall in. Do you understand?'

I heard a sound somewhere between a roar and a grunt, which I took to mean he could hear me. I pushed the end of the rope forward and heard it slithering across the ground as it dropped. There was no splash. It hadn't reached the water. Would he be able to stretch up and grab it?

I could hear him thrashing around in the water, trying to find the rope, but without being able to see it, he could exhaust himself long before he found it. I suddenly remembered Skinner's candle. I called out again that I was fetching a light, and groped up the stairs. The dull red glow from the brazier was feeble, but it was sunlight after the utter darkness below. I lifted the candle and lit it in the embers. Shielding the flame as best I could, I stumbled back down the stairs. Kneeling, I held the light over the well. I caught a glimpse of a pale face turned upwards, and the glint of water. I held the light down as far as I dared. There was another frantic splash and then I saw the rope go taut. He'd caught it.

'Will you help me get out? Give me the signal or I let the rope fall.'

The rope gave two feeble shakes. If he was stretching upwards, that much had probably cost him a huge effort.

'Climb up, then!'

The rope creaked against the side as he put his full weight on it. I raised the candle, looking back anxiously at the ring in the wall. It was rusted into the stone, but I prayed the metal would hold. The rope groaned and strained, as he shinned slowly up, grunting with the effort. I moved back and stood ready to flee if he should turn on me.

The bolt embedded in the wall lurched forward; the edge of the stone was splintering beneath his weight. He must have felt the jolt, for he paused and then began climbing again. I could see his hands a few inches below the edge. The bolt jerked forward again. Only the angle at which he was pulling down was keeping it in the wall, but for how much longer?

I dropped full length in the dirt and reached down, grabbing one of the meaty wrists. I heaved as he groped for the top. The bolt shot from the wall. The iron ring clanged to the stone floor. For a moment, Runt seemed to hang in mid-air, suspended by the wrist I was grasping. I felt myself slithering forward, dragged through the stones and grit. We were both going to plunge down.

Then he swung his other great arm over the edge and slowly, between us, we hauled his body out. We both lay in the dirt, panting. Every drop of my strength had drained away. Sweat trickled down my face, and it was several moments before I could move. But as I sat up, he scrambled to his feet and seized me in both arms. I struggled in his grip, sure that he was trying to hurl me down into that well, until I suddenly understood that he was hugging me.

Chapter Forty-five

SOMETHING TICKLED MY FACE. I batted at it, my eyes still closed. It tickled again. I slapped my skin, turning over to bury my face in the pillow with a groan, then felt something wet trickling across the back of my neck. I jerked upright and heard a shriek of laughter. Prising my eyes open, I saw Myles standing by the bed holding a beaker poised to drench me with more.

'Get out of here, you little bastard.' I hurled the pillow at him as he darted towards the door. It missed and he flashed me an impudent grin.

'Said you wanted waking when you came home last night. Tried calling you, but you were snoring like a hog.'

'What's the clock?'

'I came up when the bells rang eight, like you said.'

I grunted. I knew I should be grateful he'd remembered to wake me, but I was too testy from lack of sleep to bother thanking him. When he'd gone, I splashed cold water on my face, and finally tipped half of it over my head in an effort to wake myself up.

Runt had kept his promise. He'd led to me to the old church in the outer courtyard of the castle and to the steps concealed on the other side that led down to a locked iron gate, which opened out inches above the moat. A rope bridge had been lowered beneath the water, so that it was not visible unless you knew it was there. He hooked it up, winding the ropes tightly around two ship's cleats until the swaying bridge was just clear of the moat, and prodded me on to it. The moment I stepped off on the bank on the other side, he let it sink again. As I turned to look at him, he drew his hand across his throat and pointed at me.

I was left in no doubt that if our paths ever crossed again, he would kill me. But I was running out of fingers to count the number of people who wanted to see me dead.

I had just two days left to find the murderer before he struck again, and I was no closer to doing so. And now I couldn't risk venturing on to the streets after dark. I'd no desire to run into Skinner or any of his cut-throats on a lonely street, or even in a crowd where they could easily slip a dagger between my ribs.

Having checked to ensure that Mistress Crugge was occupied elsewhere, I unlocked my small travelling chest, slid out the bar of wood and fumbled for the hidden catch that would allow me to lift the false bottom. I pulled out the remaining money that FitzAlan had given me. It was dwindling fast. I'd told Skinner the truth when I said I didn't have anything like the sum he'd demanded, and being robbed last night had not helped

But no one gave away information for nothing in this city, and I'd have to replace my purse, though it had better be a second-hand one from a pawn shop. But I told myself that was all to the good, for a purse that looked old and worn would be less of a temptation to thieves. My most urgent need, though, was for a new dagger, and a sturdy one, which fitted my hand and was well balanced. I couldn't scrimp on that, not when my life might depend on it.

I suppose it was that thought that made me glance to the beam where I'd placed the stone eye. It wasn't there. I felt along the wood, then dropped to my knees, searching the floor. It wasn't anywhere. I had taken to checking its position last thing each evening and, exhausted though I was, I was sure it had been there before I crawled into bed last night. Someone had stolen in here while I slept. Not Myles, he was too short to reach it. Skinner? I'd already be dead if it was him. Waldegrave? The stone had originally come from him, but he was an old man, he could never have entered my chamber without waking me.

Then who?

*

I FELT SLIGHTLY more at ease when I was finally walking down the street, feeling the weight of a dagger pressed against my hip. I was pleased enough with my purchase, for though it was plain, it was sturdy, with a good clean edge to the blade, and better still, it was cheaper than I'd dared to hope; the bladesmith had been anxious to sell, for he'd evidently suffered much damage in the flood.

In spite of Skinner's attempt to send me to my own watery grave, I had to find the two remaining men on that list. I had been unable to find any connection between the three murdered men, but there might be a link between the missing pewterer, Hugh Leynham, and the dead vicar, Luke Gysbourne.

Hugh's lodgings had been only a couple of streets away from Christ Church. It was likely, then, that this was the church Hugh had attended. I knew Gysbourne to have been a fervent Protestant who would, most likely, have been only too eager to inform on the Jesuits or any other Catholic conspirators. If Hugh had been of the same persuasion, he might easily have confided something he had discovered to his vicar, who would in turn have passed it on to the authorities. Finding the murdered Gysbourne's name on that list, along with his own, would certainly have terrified Hugh into fleeing.

If Hugh was a congregant at Christ Church, then the one person who would be able to tell me would be Gysbourne's unfortunate churchwarden, Martin Symons, who was still languishing under lock and key for the vicar's murder. He might even have some idea where Hugh had gone.

SYMONS HAD fared better than those who were cast into the London prisons. Many of the underground chambers where prisoners had formerly been housed in Bristol had flooded and remained so. The corpses of the unfortunate souls who'd been lying in chains or trapped behind locked doors when the sea had surged in still drifted in the filthy water. So, they'd had to house anyone arrested after the flood, mostly for looting, up in the old guardrooms in the many gatehouses of the city.

The turnkey led me upstairs to the small circular room where about ten men and boys were confined. Several of the prisoners had visitors, mostly wives or daughters, who squatted on the floor in front of them, passing them food and muttering in low voices. But the man the turnkey gestured towards was alone. I couldn't see much of him, for he was sitting propped against the wall, a heap of mouldy straw stuffed beneath his legs and a blanket pulled low over his head and tucked tightly beneath his crossed arms. Wind whistled through the arrow slits, and the icy stone flagstones were leaching the heat from my body even through the soles of my boots.

I threaded my way through the women and crouched down beside him. 'Master Symons?'

He flinched, squinting up at me, with apprehension in his gaunt face, drawing his legs up as if he feared a kick or a blow. I'd not seen the man before he'd been arrested, but I could tell that, even in the short time he'd been here, his health had suffered. His eyes were sunk into dark pits and his skin hung loose like a deflated bladder. He scratched furiously at the scaly skin on his hand, which was already rubbed raw and bleeding.

'Do I know you? From Christ Church? I can't always recall . . .' He shivered, as if even his memories were slipping away from him in this place.

'I've not been to the church, but I have heard of what you stand accused. I want to help.' I thrust a parcel into his hand.

He stared at it uncomprehendingly until I peeled back the wrapping and he saw a small pie. His gaze darted anxiously around the room, then he bent low, using the wall and my body to shield himself from view, as he gobbled the pie so voraciously, he almost choked.

'Thank you . . . thank you, sir.' He grasped my sleeve. 'I swear on the Holy Bible I did not kill the vicar. I swear it,' he repeated earnestly. 'But they say my initials were burned on to his chest, and the key . . . the key will see me hanged.' He began coughing as if he could already feel the noose tightening about his throat, and leaned wheezing against the wall, beads of sweat popping out on his brow.

It wasn't just Hugh and Edward who were in danger, but Symons' life, too, depended on me finding the murderer. How else could I prove that what had been burned into Gysbourne's chest had not been poor Martin Symons' initials?

A shriek pierced the whispered conversations. Most of the prisoners had a heavy weight attached to one of their legs to prevent escape, but other than that, they were free to move around. Only one young lad was fettered to the wall by his neck. He repeatedly banged his head against the stone, moaning and occasionally letting out a sudden screech like a wounded gull. Blood trickled from his bruised face and from his neck where the edge of the metal ring bit as he rocked.

'Shut up, you little shit,' one man growled.

Symons flinched. 'The lad does that all day and half the night. His mother brought him to the vicar once. She reckoned a witch was sending her imps out to torment the boy, sticking him with pins to make him cry out. She said he shrieked like the very Devil when they baptised him as a babe, and after went as stiff as a ship's mast whenever water splashed on his face. She blamed her sister-in-law, said she'd cursed the lad because she was barren and twisted up with jealousy.'

'Did parishioners often consult Reverend Gysbourne on the matter of witchcraft?'

Symons scratched at his raw skin. 'A few maybe . . . when he first came here, but he'd a sharp tongue on him. Had a way of making folks feel it was them who were to blame. Like the lad's mother.' He nodded towards the whimpering boy. 'Said if her son was cursed, then she must have been neglectful of her prayers, which would have protected him. Evil couldn't enter a house, he said, unless a woman let it in, like Eve let the snake beguile her into tempting Adam. The vicar was a powerful preacher against sin and temptation.'

'Did he preach much against Jesuits?'

Symons' head jerked up and he stared at me. 'He rightly warned us against all the wiles of the Pope and his spies.'

'And the Gunpowder Treason – the traitor, Henry Garnet, did he ever mention him?'

The eyes of the churchwarden widened in fear. 'On the fifth day of November last, he read out the Thanksgiving Act, every letter of it, just as the law commands, and he preached a powerful sermon against Fawkes and those other traitors, upon my soul he did. There's none can accuse us of not keeping the law.' He was gabbling now, his fingers working compulsively.

I squeezed his shoulder gently, trying to calm him. 'Take heart, Master Symons, I know that as churchwarden you would never have allowed the law to be broken. But there is one more thing I must ask you. There is a member of your congregation, one Hugh Leynham. Do you know him?'

There was a long pause. Symons scratched at the raw skin on his hands.

'A pewterer,' I prompted. 'Has fingers missing on one hand. Worked for Peter Grobbam before the flood.'

'I . . . not Leynham . . .' He frowned hard, as if he was struggling to remember. Then he gave a heart-rending sigh. 'I can't recall. It's all . . . my head's full of sea fret. Can't recall . . . I can't . . .'

I tried one last question, though I knew I was wasting my breath – did the name Edward Brystowe mean anything to him? There was no flicker of recognition in his haggard face, though I wondered if he'd even heard the question, for he'd withdrawn deep into himself again, pulling the threadbare blanket tightly around him as if he could shut out all the misery of the place, and wake to find it had only been a terrible nightmare.

As I rose to leave, his hand shot out and grasped my ankle. His anguished face peered up at me from the folds of cloth.

'They'll not hang me, will they? Our Saviour wouldn't let an innocent man hang?'

'The murderer will be discovered before you come to trial,' I assured him. But I knew, even as I said it, that I was the only man still looking for the real killer. And if I didn't find him soon . . . Just how many innocent men had died at the hands of the executioners in all those centuries since Christ himself had been condemned?

Chapter Forty-six

'I WARNED YOU not to come here again,' Waldegrave growled. 'Why can you not leave me in peace?'

The old man scraped the bottom of the wooden bowl with his spoon, then ran his fingers around the surface to capture the last few drops of the grey pottage, licking them from his grimy fingers. I'd done it myself when times were hard and food scarce, but somehow the sight of the old priest licking his bowl clean appalled me. I remembered the last time I'd watched him eat, in Fairfax's house. Delicately spearing only the tenderest portions of sliced veal that glistened beneath the rich fruit and butter sauce, and slipping them into his mouth without spilling a drop of buttery verjuice on the snowy cloth. Washing his soft hands, though they had not touched the food, in the silver laver scented with rose water and drying them on a pressed white linen towel held out for him by a servant.

I moved closer to the old man, tense for any creak on the rickety staircase outside. I had taken a huge risk in coming here. If any of Skinner's watchers had seen me, his men could already be on the way here.

'Answer me one question swiftly, then I will leave you and I swear I shall not return. The three men who were murdered—'

'You never listen, whelp. I have told you already it was the castle rats looking for what they could steal. They hurt and kill for sport.'

'And yet you work for these killers.'

His gaze didn't falter. 'Unlike that foul renegade John Smith, I work for no man.'

I almost smiled. It was an equivocation worthy of any Jesuit.

'Why do you ask me about those murders again?' His tone had changed from one of annoyance to anxiety. 'Has there been another?'

'I fear that there will be. I have discovered a list. It has five names on it. Three are those of the murdered men, each with a cross beside it. But there are two other names on that list, and both are marked with the same letters we found burned on the corpses.'

'Is one of those names mine? Is that why you've come here?'

There was no trace of fear in his voice or eyes. He had learned how to control that, but I saw the clawed hands momentarily tighten, gripping the edge of the hutch table.

'Hugh Leyburn . . . Edward Brystowe.'

'I do not know them,' he said, his tone level.

'But if you did, you should warn them.'

'I have told you,' he growled, 'those names are unknown to me.'

I found my gaze drawn to the ink-stained hutch table, the papers and quills he had bundled out of sight last time I was here. Rachael had told me that Skinner could arrange for anyone to vanish through the castle, and she hadn't only meant into the grave. But if a man wanted to leave England, he had to seek royal permission. Anyone attempting to obtain passage on a boat would have to show a paper granting him that permission. That's what the castle rats couldn't produce themselves. And a priest escaping Cecil's clutches would need forged documents, too. I glanced back at the pitiful bowl of pottage Waldegrave had scraped clean. Was the old man so desperate he'd be prepared to forge papers for others, too – even for members of that holy order he had once despised? I'd played his game long enough. I had to know. This was my last chance. I was running out of time.

'If a man was hiding in Bristol under a false name and others got to learn of his real identity and were likely to expose him, that would be reason enough to murder those men.'

'Aah!' He smiled faintly. 'And does this man in hiding, this *Jesuit*, have a name?'

'There must be many who travel though this port, many names . . . Spero Pettingar, perhaps?'

I watched his face intently. For a fleeting moment I thought I detected the beginning of a spasm, but it passed.

'So, that is why you are in Bristol, Daniel. I knew you would confess it in the end. But you have been sent on a fool's errand.' Waldegrave massaged his swollen knuckles. 'I have read that when a witch is arrested, she is put into a chamber which has a hole in the bottom of the door, just large enough for a toad or a cat to creep through. The witch is bound in a position that makes it impossible for her to sleep, and her interrogators watch her night and day. They believe that her familiar, her imp, will come to her through that hole during the hours of darkness to suckle from her, for without that nourishment it will die. So convinced are they the imp will appear that a spider running across the floor, or a shadow darting across the wall, is enough to convince them that they have seen what was never there and does not exist. So it is with Spero Pettingar.'

'He was present at the last meeting of the gunpowder conspirators.'

'Was he? What does Spero mean, Daniel? Remember the proverb?'

I shook my head in irritation. I refused to be tested as if I was an errant child.

'*Dum Spiro Spero.* "While I live, I hope." Have you not asked yourself if this Spero is not a man at all, but an idea that unites men?'

'And is that not just the kind of clever name a Jesuit might choose as his mask?' I retorted furiously. 'I may not have proof that Spero exists, but I do have proof that a murderer does. I have seen three corpses, and the Jesuit sign burned deep into the flesh of each, almost into their hearts. Are you trying to convince me, or yourself, that this is nothing more than the shadow in the cell of a foolish old woman?'

Waldegrave sighed, closing his eyes. I could see he was failing, like a deer brought to bay, exhausted by the chase. 'Think, Daniel! Why did the J. . . J. . .' He paused and took a deep breath. 'Why did the Jesuits adopt that sign?'

I stared at him, hearing not his question, but the way he had spoken it. Suddenly, I understood why my old tutor had always used that strange halting delivery, pausing between the words. I had always believed that he was carefully selecting each one like an executioner selecting a knife. Now I realised that, all these years, it had been his way of fighting his stammer. Was it courage or stubbornness for a man to choose a profession that would force him to battle, word by word, for a lifetime against such a foe?

'Those letters,' the old man continued, as if nothing had occurred, 'are an ancient symbol of piety that existed centuries before the Spaniard Ignatius of Loyola founded the Jesuit order. They are as old as the sign of the cross itself, and nothing more than the abbreviation of the name of our Lord Jesus. That is all they mean – *Jesus*. There is no mystery. Half the graves in England bore them, before that Boleyn whore bewitched King Henry's mind and soul. Most likely, these two men on your list are already in the grave and the letters are a prayer for their souls that they might rest in peace. Where did you find this list, anyway?'

I ignored the question. 'There was something more on the list, a date. The twenty-eighth—'

We both heard it, the stair creaking somewhere below us. We froze. The sound came again. Someone was climbing the stairs, moving stealthily, but the boards were so loose it was impossible to tread even lightly without them betraying the movement. Had the cunning old priest deliberately removed those nails?

I slid my new dagger from its sheath and spun to face Waldegrave.

'You must leave now.' His voice was barely above a whisper, but there was no mistaking the alarm and urgency in the tone. 'This way quickly!'

He moved swiftly to a dark corner of the attic chamber where the roof slanted down to its lowest point. Hooking his finger into a tiny hole in the wooden boards that covered the wall, he pulled the panel into the room and stood aside. A sharp gust of wind blew into the room from a small aperture. 'Keep low. To your left there is a wheelhouse standing proud of the roof. It will hide you from below until it gets dark.'

'How I do get down?'

'The rope on the wheel, of course,' he snapped, as if this was obvious. 'Hurry!' he urged, as the perilous stairs emitted another groan, closer this time.

Almost before I had crawled through the hole and dragged myself clear, I heard the wood panel behind me grating back into place. I was crouching near the bottom of a steeply pitched roof, which was dizzyingly high. On one corner was a small hut-like structure, which blocked my view of the ground, but beyond that was nothing except the edge of the roof. I could glimpse the marsh and, in the far distance, a glint of water. I'm sure it would have been a view I might have admired, had I not been trying to keep my balance on clay tiles, slippery with moss and seagull droppings, with many that had already been broken or dislodged.

Behind me, through the wooden panel, I heard a door bang open and Waldegrave's voice raised in anger. I dropped to my belly to spread my weight and slithered the few feet down towards the wooden shelter on the edge of the roof. It resembled a large dog kennel, and peering through the slats at the back, I saw a large wooden pulley wheel, with a cranking handle, bolted to a massive beam. It must once have been the mechanism for raising and lowering sacks and kegs when the building was a barn. The hut was probably built for the man turning the wheel, though I suspected it had been erected to keep the wheel from seizing in wet weather, rather than for his comfort. It was open at the front and the wooden platform inside, on which the man must have stood, was now sodden and warped. There was no way of telling how rotten it was, or if it would bear my weight. For now, I had no choice but to do what Waldegrave had instructed and crouch behind it until nightfall.

The grey sky was already darkening, tarnishing like old pewter, as dusk gathered. The wind, as always at this hour, was growing sharper, making my eyes water. Gulls swooped, diving lower and lower, their wings slapping my face and their razor beaks passing inches from my eyes. From the large quantity of their fishy shit and feathers I was sitting in, I guessed that my spot behind the wheelhouse was their accustomed roost and they were trying to drive me off. I resisted the temptation to hurl bits of tile at them for fear the noise would draw the attention of anyone below. Eventually, they settled, squabbling and screeching, on the roof ridge, glowering at me with their pale eyes as if they really were the drowned souls of mariners come back to accuse the living.

There was a crash somewhere behind the wood panel, as if something heavy had been kicked over. I clawed halfway back towards it. I heard Waldegrave's voice raised again, but there was no fear in his tone. I slithered back down the roof and wedged myself behind the shelter, trying not to imagine how far I'd fall, if the wood gave way.

I was wasting precious time, risking my neck, and for what? I should have known that the old devil would tell me nothing. If he knew for certain that Spero Pettingar did not exist, Waldegrave must know more about the Gunpowder Treason than mere broadside gossip. And if he had just spun me a tale to dissuade me from searching for the man, was that proof he knew Pettingar's real identity? Had the old priest forged the papers that had helped him to escape?

Yet, I supposed I had learned something, or rather been reminded of something I should have remembered. It wasn't only the Jesuits who used that abbreviation for the name of Jesus.

Once again, I'd fallen into the trap of misdirection, simply because of what FitzAlan had set me up to expect.

Forget the Jesuits, just think about the name – *Jesus*. Could it refer to a church or chapel? I'd already ruled out Gysbourne's church – neither the printer nor the merchant had any links to that place, as far as I could discover. All of the other churches in Bristol I'd so far come across were named for saints, not for Jesus. So, not a place of worship. Something else, then, the name of a street or an inn perhaps? I tried to recall the names of those I knew, but none seemed to fit.

The last of the daylight had seeped away over the edge of the horizon. Except for the lights of fires in the distance, all was dark. I was so numbed, I could hardly feel my feet, but still I could hear Waldegrave's voice and another's behind the panel, though nothing of what they said. But I was sure now that whoever was with the old priest was not one of the castle rats. I hadn't told Waldegrave about my visit to the castle, so whoever he'd believed had been creeping up those stairs, it wasn't Skinner. But it was someone he was extremely anxious I shouldn't meet.

I pulled myself around the shelter, until I could reach the platform, but the stink of rotting wood convinced me that it would never bear my weight. The beam above, on the other hand, had evidently been salvaged from a ship, and was well seasoned with tar and brine. But if the rope was as old as the platform, it was likely to snap like a thread. I leaned in, hooking it towards me. It was pale in the moonlight, reassuringly thick, and it smelled new. It had obviously been replaced very recently, but why? Was this Waldegrave's planned escape route, if the authorities closed in on him? I couldn't imagine the old man being agile enough to use it, even if his life depended on it. This had been installed for someone else. But for now, all that mattered was that I got to the ground safely, without breaking a leg or worse. Muttering a silent prayer to whichever saint might be on duty that night, I grabbed the rope with both hands and jumped.

Chapter Forty-seven

I WOKE WITH THE same feeling of dread as I used to each day as a boy in the Fairfax house, that nameless fear which paralyses your mind and freezes your soul, until you are awake enough to remember what you are afraid of. As I listened to the squalling of a fretful child in the chamber below and the rumble of a hand-cart in the yard outside, the realisation seeped into my mind. Today was the twenty-eighth day of March, the date on which I was certain two men were to die, and I was still no nearer to finding the killer.

I had spent all the previous day tramping the streets searching for taverns, brothels, streets or any place that might have some connection to the name Jesus – the Mitre, the Lion and Lamb, the Salutation. I visited the Chapel of the Three Kings of Cologne and made inquiries among the old men living in the alms house nearby. I even returned to the High Cross, talking to the merchants trading close by and the street urchins. I'd walked around the cross, examining the statues of the kings and queens, looking for . . . I know not what.

I had been so intent on my search that I almost forgot about Skinner, and it was by chance I glanced up and saw Castle Joan standing on the corner of Wine Street. She was half turned towards the counter of a chandler's shop, as though intending to buy candles or soap. But her gaze kept darting to the crowds passing her. She might, of course, have been looking for another purse she could cut, or she could have been looking for me. And if she was there, the chances were her family were nearby, ready to close in on me, as they had done that night in the castle. Trying not to draw attention to myself by moving too quickly, I used the cover of a passing wagon to slip away.

Now I heard footsteps mounting the stairs outside my chamber, and leaped from my bed, dragging my breeches on over my nightshirt. The latch rattled up and down, but I had bolted the door and pushed the chest in front of it.

Myles's voice called cheerfully and somewhat impatiently to be let in. I opened the door and he rushed through, a small flagon clutched to his chest, slopping cider on to the boards. I hastily grabbed it before he spilled the lot. His eyes were shining with excitement and I could tell he was bursting to tell me something, but before he could, a heavier and slower tread heralded the arrival of Mistress Crugge, bearing a platter of bread and slabs of the glistening grey seal's brawn, which smelled even more like whale oil than it had before.

She surveyed my half-dressed state with a slight sniff. 'You'll pardon me rousing you so early, Master Pursglove, but I must get ahead with my chores this morning.'

The grin broadened on Myles's face. 'There's a monkey coming from a ship,' he announced, unable to contain himself.

'Now, what have I said to you about gossiping, boy?' Mistress Crugge scolded, but I thought I detected the hint of a smile on her plump face. 'Off you go now and get that table scrubbed, like I told you. You'll not be seeing any monkey unless that table smells as sweet as a bunch of violets.'

The lad skipped out of the door, and Mistress Crugge stood shaking her head with the indulgence of a grandmother. 'Boys, nothing but trouble until they're grown into men and then they're worse.'

'It's good of you to let him stay here.'

She snorted. 'It's only till he's well again, mind, then he'll be out. I'll not have brats under my feet.'

I didn't like to point out that Myles seemed fitter than I'd ever seen him. The sores on his face were healing and I swear he looked to have a little flesh on his skinny carcass.

'He said something about a ship?' An uneasy thought seized me. 'Mistress Crugge, do not let Myles go down to the wharf.'

'He knows better than to set foot outside the yard, I've seen to that.' She laid a hand on my arm. 'Now don't you go fretting. I keep my eye on him, as does the girl. Between us we keep him busy. That's why I told him my cousin Ned was coming here with his monkey, so the lad isn't tempted to go skipping out once news spreads. Ned always comes to tip me the wink, slips away while the Searcher's men are inspecting the cargo, and I make sure there's a handsome plate of vittles and a flagon waiting for him. After weeks of ship's biscuit and salt beef, he can scarcely wait for me to set a good dinner in front of him before he's shovelling it down.'

She beamed. 'Not been a single ship put into port here since the flood. But if this one makes it up the channel without mishap, and they can unload, they'll carry the news back and there'll be more ships to follow. You'll see, every merchant in Bristol will be outbidding each other for whatever cargoes they land today. Prices will go higher than a church steeple. There'll be a handsome profit for the ship's master on this voyage, I can tell you. But the quartermaster always keeps a bit back for his own customers, and seeing as how my cousin Ned is the boatswain . . .' She winked. 'One hand washes the other, isn't that the way of the world, Master Pursglove?'

I seemed to recall that was just what old Walter had said.

A clattering below in the yard made her start and she bustled towards the door like a hen which has spied a juicy worm, calling out, 'Much to do, Master Pursglove, much to do.'

I finished getting dressed, forced myself to gulp down the slices of brawn, and hurried out into the street. As Mistress Crugge had predicted, news of a ship was already spreading. There was a hum in the air like bees about to swarm. Men and boys were scurrying down towards the quay with more alacrity than I'd seen anyone display since I arrived in the city. I followed, expecting the ship to already be within sight, but the stretch of the Frome leading down to the River Avon was empty. The tide was out and the steep-sided banks of silt and slime bristled with shattered spars, jagged pieces of metal and the remains of smashed boats and buildings. It resembled a battlefield in which pikes, spears and sharpened stakes had been embedded in the earth to impale the charging cavalry.

An old man, bent almost double by a twisted spine, sidled up next to me, staring down into the narrow channel of water.

'I heard a rumour that a ship was due in,' I said. 'But they'll never be able to sail a laden ship up here without smashing her hull.'

He slowly twisted his head sideways, so that he could look up at me, a frown creasing his brow, as if he was trying to decide if I was a jester or a simpleton. Finally, he lowered his head again. 'They'll not try to tow her this far up into the city. Anchor her out in the deep channel of the Avon, they will, beyond the marshes. Ferry her cargoes in.'

He gestured further down the quay, where several groups of men were already carrying newly patched and mended boats towards the bank in readiness to float them as soon as the water began to rise. The wherries had shallow-enough draughts to skim over the wreckage when the river was high. But it would take many journeys to empty the ship, though there was no shortage of men willing to help.

Carts and the sledges the locals called 'gee-hoes' were also drawing up alongside the wharf, and heated arguments were breaking out as the drivers urged their horses through impossible gaps in an effort to get as close as possible to the quayside. With the warehouses nearest to the quay in ruins and the cellars half flooded, anything that was unloaded would have to be transported away from the river to be stored. More carts were arriving all the time. Newcomers, trying to force their way ahead of those already waiting, were being beaten back with whips and poles, and found themselves unable to dodge the blows as their carts locked wheels with their rivals. My new companion shuffled around, painfully raising his head to watch, as the shouting and cursing rose above the shrieking of the gulls and the neighing of the trapped horses.

'They'll end up in the mud before the tide comes in,' he said stolidly. 'It's happened many a time. Sledges and carts clip each other as they pass too close to the edge, whole lot goes over. Seen them crash down on the wherries below, men and horses all drowned.'

'They all seem very certain the ship will arrive today,' I said.

'Already had word she was guided safe up the channel as far as Pill. She's been under tow on the river these past days. She'll reach us now on the next high tide. Besides, the *Jesus* is never a day late. Master prides himself on it. If he's said he'll reach Bristol today, you can wager your fortune down to your last farthing that he will, even if every man on board has to help the hobblers drag her in.'

Two of the drivers, unable to get between the carts to prise them apart, had clambered up on top and were swinging wildly at each other, much to the amusement of the crowd. I was watching them and only half listening to the man beside me. So, it was a moment or two before that single word shouted loud enough in my head to make itself heard.

'*Jesus*. Did you say the Master's name is Jesus?'

The man raised his head in that slow way he had. This time, there was no mistaking his expression. He was certain now that I was a halfwit.

'What kind of name is that for a good Christian? Master goes by the name of Francis Estney. He's been sailing the *Jesus of Bristol* these past ten years and never been a day late. You ask anyone.'

IT COULDN'T BE a coincidence: the date, the symbol. And then it struck me with all the force of a cannonball. *Not Leynham.* That was what the churchwarden had meant: Hugh the pewterer was *not* Hugh Leynham. Leynham and Bristow were on that ship, and as soon as they set foot ashore, I was certain they would be in mortal danger. I could not stand by and watch them murdered. And, if someone saw those marks and cried witchcraft or popery, those two men would not be the only ones to die. Many innocents would perish if the mob ran riot.

The *Jesus of Bristol*, the old man had called her. If the ship came from this city, then it was more than likely many of the crew did, too. And even if this was not their home, the *Jesus* plainly plied this trade route often enough to suggest that most of the men aboard would have regular lodgings here, or lovers they visited in the city while the ship was being repaired and restocked. Would the murderer know where the two men would make for? Would he know the streets they would walk, the taverns they frequented, and lie in wait for them? Or was he already here, somewhere among the throng, watching for the men to come ashore, ready to follow them and ambush them in some dark corner?

I began to watch the people arriving at the quayside more carefully. It wasn't just the drivers and their lads, or the men preparing to go out in the wherries, but merchants and goodwives were gathering, too. It seemed everyone who was not employed about his own business had drifted down to welcome in the crew of the first ship of the New Year and, more importantly, the first ship since the flood, for the *Jesus* seemed to carry the hope that the worst was over and life in the city might once again return to normal.

The trouble was, I had no idea what the man I was searching for looked like. If he was the Wraith, he would not be well dressed, not if he'd been living in the castle, and that brought another uneasy thought. Cutpurses and thieves are drawn to crowds and chaos, like rats to a corpse. Skinner and his men would already be on their way here. I hastily moved away from the water's edge, clambered over a heap of twisted metal and ducked into the corner of what remained of a hut, from where I could watch without being seen.

The tide slowly crept in and little boats began to rise from mud until, finally, a lad riding bareback astride a scrawny mule came clattering over the bridge, yelling, 'She's here. She's dropping anchor.'

A cheer went up from those on the quay and the men who had been drinking and sucking on their pipes now came alive and raced towards their crafts, hauling on the mooring ropes and dragging the wherries close to the edge so they could scramble in. Muscles bulging with the effort, they began to row, each trying to push their boat ahead of the others, as the drivers had done with their carts. Insults were exchanged as wherries bumped against each other. The rowers bellowed for others to give way and jeered at those who fell behind. The men on the sledges and carts added to the cheering and jeering as their favoured wherrymen passed, but they did not stir from their lofty positions, knowing it would be a while before the flotilla returned with any goods for them to carry.

Dusk was settling before the first of the little boats hove into view, and at once the drivers crowded round, seizing the mooring ropes and clamouring that the cargoes should be assigned to their carts or sledges. I scanned the quay, looking for a man who was watching the returning boats but not joining in the scramble for the cargoes. But I could see no one. Even the merchants were pressing forward around the wherry, anxious to keep track of any kegs or boxes that had already been assigned to them and see them safely loaded on their own carts.

More boats returned. The paggers rolled barrels or ran with a bale on their backs to deliver it to the carts and return for the next. As the drivers of the carts and sledges finished loading, they tried to lead their horses out of the throng, and more arguments ensued. None of the wherries could carry more than a few boxes or barrels, not daring to take a full load for fear of sinking too low in the water and holing themselves on the wrecks that lay beneath. As soon as the last of their cargo was heaved on to the wharf, the men took a few swigs from their jars to quench their thirst, mopped their sweating brows and prepared to row back down to the Avon.

The wherrymen now sculling up to the quay had lit the lamps in their bows. Lanterns swung from the carts, their glow transfiguring the faces of the drivers into skulls, as if they were the collectors of dead souls. A few link boys had strolled down to the waterside, their torches streaming like battle pennants in the strengthening wind, the reflections of the flames darting like scarlet fish across the glassy water. But still everyone worked on; there were only two or three hours more before the tide would retreat too far for even the wherries to float safely, and they couldn't afford to waste a minute of it.

No one seemed yet to have disembarked from the *Jesus*. I guessed all hands were needed on board for the unloading before the tide went out and the ship sank down into the mud. If the murderer was lying in wait for Brystowe or Leynham, then he could be anywhere in the city and I still had no way to warn his next victims, unless I could speak to someone on board that ship.

Now that it was dark, it was becoming harder to see anyone clearly unless they chanced to step into the light cast by the links or one of the lanterns. I clambered back out of my shelter, edged along the jagged wreckage of the warehouses and slipped down towards the water. Across the river, candles flickered in the upper storeys of houses, and where there were gaps between them, like missing teeth, small fires blazed – the homeless trying to keep warm or cook what supper they'd managed to find. In the far distance, across the marshes, there was another cluster of lights bobbing and darting back and forth, which I took to be the lights of the *Jesus of Bristol* and all those working around her to relieve her of her cargo.

Along the wharf, the women had mostly departed, leaving the men who were still loading the carts or trying to persuade the wherrymen to give them the next load. Then I spotted Rachael threading her way towards the quayside; the hood of her cloak was pulled low over her head, but I knew her walk by now. She hadn't seen me, and when I grabbed her arm she turned sharply, a look of alarm on her face.

'Forgive me, I didn't mean to startle you.'

'I didn't expect to find you here, Master Daniel.'

'Nor I you. I thought Mistress Crugge would have you hard at work at this hour. Is it Myles? Has he run off?'

Rachael shook her head, though her gaze had been darting around all the time I'd been talking. 'Myles was cleaning the stables, last time I saw him, and was promised a bite of bread and cheese if he did it right. He'll not pass that up. Lad's got a stomach like a bottomless well. Besides, he won't want to miss the monkey. He's talked about nothing else all day.'

She paused, her attention caught by another boat ploughing its way towards us through the black water, the men straining at the oars. The tide had turned and they were having to push against the current. It would be that much harder now to bring the rest of the cargo upriver.

'So, what brings you down here?' I asked.

'Oh, it's the mistress's cousin. She was expecting him earlier. Sent me to find out when he'd be along and remind him there's a supper waiting for him.'

'I think the crew are all still on board. I haven't seen any come ashore yet. I suppose it's possible they won't be able to leave until high tide tomorrow.'

Rachael stared back along the row of moored boats, as if wanting to be sure. She seemed agitated. I guessed she was impatient to be back at the Salt Cat. The news that her cousin was still aboard would no doubt put Mistress Crugge in a foul mood and she'd vent her spleen on Rachael if the girl was away too long.

'If you need to return to the Cat, I'll bring word if any man does come ashore from the ship. I'll ask him if he knows when the boatswain is likely to be released from his duties.'

'I'd best . . .' She bit her lip. Then she looked at me as if she'd only just remembered who she was talking to. 'Anyway, what are you loitering here for? Thought you'd have better things to do than stand around watching men break their backs pagging loads. Hoping for news of your kin, were you? You'll not get it here. The ship's not put into Bristol for months, and you said your aunt only arrived just before flood. Or was that another lie?'

The chill in her voice stung like a slap. The torch flames glittered in her eyes. I couldn't tell if they were full of anger or hurt, but suddenly I was desperate to redeem myself, and, as anyone will tell you, that is when even the wisest of men become the most codwitted of all fools.

I took her hand and gazed earnestly into her face, wanting to ensure that this time she believed me. 'I'm here because the lives of two men aboard that ship are in danger. Three others have been killed, and I have good reason to think that these two men will be next. I mean to warn them. The murderer may be here already among the crowd, or he may be waiting in the city for them. If any man comes off that ship tonight, I must speak with him and find those men.'

She frowned. 'Do you know who they are?'

'Their names, yes. Hugh Leynham and Edward Brystowe.'

'And the person who wants to kill them?' she asked.

'That's all I know—'

A sudden bellow of 'Hold her steady, you fools!' made us both glance back along the row of boats. A man was attempting to clamber aboard one of the wherries that was on the point of departing again, for the plank that had been used as a bridge to unload the kegs had been pulled in. The boat, like several others, had been caught in the strong ebbing current and been dragged away from the quayside. It strained and bucked against its mooring ropes. The wherrymen were paying little heed to this gap, men and boys springing down into the boats, as if they were salmon leaping over a weir. In contrast, the would-be passenger was as awkward as a seal on land, making ineffectual attempts to step across the impossible gap, evidently too nervous to risk jumping across the stretch of black water.

One of the wherrymen clambered over towards him, pulling on the mooring rope to swing the bow into the wharf while reaching up to steady the man. As he stretched out his arm to take the boatman's hand, the light from one of the torches fell on him, and in that instant I realised who I was staring at. There was no time to explain to Rachael; I had to get a closer look. I darted forward and tripped over the taut mooring line of one of the boats. I only avoided plunging head first into the water because Rachael grabbed the neck of my doublet and jerked me back. I crashed against a mooring post, a roar of laughter rolling up from all those around.

'Fancied a swim, did you, master?'

'Maybe he thinks he can walk on water.'

'There's some'll try anything to keep from paying the ferry-men.'

I mumbled my thanks to Rachael, my gaze still riveted on the man standing by the boat. Like everyone else, he'd turned to stare at me, and I knew instantly that I'd seen his face before, just a glimpse, in the courtyard of the Salt Cat. He must have recognised me, too, for he hastily stepped back from the edge, slipped between two wagons and ran up one of the little streets.

I started after him and then turned back to Rachael. 'That man who was standing by the boat, he's the assassin. I know it.'

She clutched my arm. 'Follow him . . . quickly. There are other boats moored at St Nicholas Back. He may be headed there to get one. I'll go to the ship, find the men and warn them to be on their guard.'

I dug into my purse and thrust a handful of coins into her hands. 'Here, you'll need this to pay the wherrymen.'

She nodded. 'Now go! Hurry, Daniel! You must stop him.' She pressed her lips swiftly to my cheek, and began running towards the wherry the murderer had fled from.

Chapter Forty-eight

I WOVE BETWEEN the wagons, only narrowly avoiding cannon-ing into a man hefting a bale, who cursed me roundly. I darted up the street I thought the Wraith had taken. After the crowd and the lights at the quayside, it was dark and deserted. Many of the buildings were still in ruins, black caverns, which could conceal anything or anyone. Occasionally I saw the flicker of a fire in the depths, or a light moving on an upper floor behind a broken wall, as if the spirits of the dead still walked there.

I stopped and listened. Timber creaked. Stones rattled. But those sounds could be made by scavenging rats or stray dogs . . . or by a man. The killer could be crouching within a yard of me and I wouldn't know it. A dozen guards could search these ruins at once, and their quarry would simply melt away, before they got close. But a man so bent on murder wouldn't simply hide, not if he was determined to kill this night. Rachael was right, the Wraith would be looking for another way to get out to the ship.

That was when the stupidity of what I had done hit me. Rachael! I had sent her straight into the arms of a murderer. If the Wraith succeeded in boarding the *Jesus* and found Brystowe and Leynham while she was still with them, he'd kill her, too. He'd have to; he couldn't risk leaving her alive as a witness. I took a few steps back towards the quay, but Rachael would already be halfway down the river. The only way to protect her now was to stop the Wraith reaching that ship.

I started running. I could barely see the jagged outline of the buildings on either side of me, and the street was pitted with holes and heaps of stones, but I dodged most of them, until I saw the flickering torchlight in the archway beneath St Leonard's Church, which straddled the road. Two watchmen were leaning either side of the gate, propped up by their halberds. One was whittling a piece of bone into some kind of toy animal.

'You come from the quay? Still unloading, are they?'

'And will be until the water level sinks too far.'

The watchman spat on the ground. 'Never known so many carts and sledges come through of an evening. By rights they shouldn't be bringing them in after nightfall. But sheriff says we've to let them pass.'

'That's only because he wants his own shipment of wine safe in his cellars before it gets thieved.' The other grinned, then drew himself upright as there was a rumble from the street behind me. 'Look lively, here comes another one.'

They stepped forward to stop the cart, and I slipped away, running down towards St Nicholas Back and the old wharf.

The Back was as deserted as it had been the night old Waldegrave had taken me there to see Dagworth's corpse. I was standing a few yards from the entrance to the honeycomb of tunnels. Behind the derelict warehouse I could just distinguish the dark smudge of the church roof beneath which the corpse of the merchant lay rotting in its crypt. Did the killer realise one of his victims was now concealed down there?

Lights shone from the upper storeys of the buildings that lined the bridge, but they couldn't reach down as far as the black snake of water twisting through the muddy banks and slithering beneath the keels of the boats moored there. Some of the larger vessels still dangled from their mooring ropes, their backs broken and half submerged. A few of the smaller ones, which had evidently been repaired, bobbed against the current.

I peered up and down the wharf. Had the Wraith gone to ground in the tunnel? No, if he was here, he was searching for a boat. I edged along the bank of the river, trying to move as quietly as I could and hoping that the rush of water and the whistle of the wind through broken rigging would cover my footfall. I was walking in the direction of the castle, thinking that he might instinctively head in that direction, where he could take refugee or even call for the castle rats to help him. Then again, if he knew I was following, he might be deliberately leading me into a trap. I turned and headed back towards the bridge.

Then I saw it. At first I thought it was the black hump of a mooring post or a pile of nets close to the edge, but it moved. Someone was bending over the side of the wharf, trying to unfasten a mooring rope from a wooden post sunk in the mud below. Something about the clumsy movement and hunched form told me it had to be him.

I ran, hurling myself towards him. I saw his head turn at the last minute, his arm raised to defend himself, but before it even occurred to me he must have a knife, I sprang at him. He collapsed, pitching sideways, with me on top, pinning him down. We were hanging half out over the surging water. I glimpsed the silver gleam of the river twisting beneath me, felt the cold draught of air on my face as we struggled. It seemed we were both about to plunge headlong between the boat and the wharf, but I thrust my knee into his belly and heaved him over me. The momentum of his body dragged me back on to the bank, both of us rolling over and over until we slammed into a wall. He tried to fight free, but I clamped him to the ground, having the advantage of weight and strength. I gripped his right wrist, raising his hand against the light trickling from the casements on the bridge. Though faint, it was enough to show me that only a swollen stump of hand and part of a thumb remained.

'Master Hugh, is it?' I gasped, trying to get my breath. 'You have an unusually solid body for a wraith.'

He struggled again and I sensed he was trying to reach his knife. I jammed my elbow against his windpipe, pressing his neck into the stony ground. I released the pressure on his throat only after I had dragged his knife from its sheath, and dug the point up under his chin.

'Is this the knife you used to stab Harewell, Dagworth and Gysbourne? Is it?' I demanded, pressing the blade harder against his throat. 'Speak.'

He coughed and choked, throwing his head back as he gasped for air. 'You think I would deny it? Yes . . . yes, I killed them, Master Pursglove. Does that satisfy you?'

'But why? Why single out these men? Why mark them with those three letters?'

'Why does an executioner hang a man, Master Pursglove? Because he is guilty of a crime. But the law would not execute these men, so it fell to me to bring them to justice.'

'But what crime—'

'Drop that knife, sirrah!' A voice barked behind me, as I felt the sharp pressure of steel pierce my doublet and press into my back.

The knife clanged on to the stones and was at once kicked away. Then the same voice ordered me to get to my knees, slowly. As I obeyed, a watchman stepped round me, hauling Hugh to his feet and gripping him tightly. The man standing behind me eased the point of his halberd away from my spine, and locked an arm about my neck.

'Now suppose you tell me what this quarrel is about,' he growled in my ear. 'One of the good citizens who lives on the bridge reported he saw someone trying to steal his boat. He thought it was that vermin from the castle. Then we come and find you trying to rob this man at knifepoint. So, what's your name, sirrah?'

'It's this man you should be arresting. He was trying to get aboard the *Jesus of Bristol* where he plans to kill two men. He's already killed others with that knife, which I took from him.'

'And you've proof of this, have you?' the watchman asked, in a tone that suggested he didn't believe a word of it.

'I can name the men and show you the list he drew up that includes the two men he planned to kill tonight. He murdered the printer Sam Harewell and the Reverend Gysbourne, who was stabbed in Christ Church, and a—'

I stopped myself. I could never reveal that I knew Nicholas Dagworth was dead without involving Waldegrave.

The two watchmen exchanged glances. 'Whole city's talking about that vicar who was tortured and done to death.'

'Aye,' said the man holding Hugh, 'but I heard there was a man already locked up for it and like to hang after the next court sitting.'

'I'll not let any innocent man hang for me,' Hugh said quietly. 'I killed Gysbourne and Harewell, and Dagworth, too.'

I felt as if the breath had been knocked from me. What man wouldn't deny everything when the noose dangles before him? I could barely comprehend it.

The two watchmen seemed equally taken aback at this ready confession. 'His wits are wandering. Senile, I should think, like my old father.'

The watchman holding Hugh gave him a slight shake. 'You don't want to go around saying things like that unless it's true. You'll end up on the gallows, or chained up for a madman.'

'Have to take him in, though,' the other said. 'If it proves true and we've let a murderer go . . .'

'Aye, well, we'll see what the constable makes of it.'

The man holding me released his grip and attempted to brush the filth from my doublet by way of an apology.

'You'd best get yourself home now, master. Tomorrow, you'll need to come and tell the constable what you told us, and bring that list of yours. He'll want to see it.' He gave me a final pat down. 'If what you say be proved, there might be a reward in it for you, for catching a dangerous murderer, that's if the Corporation is feeling generous.' He stepped towards Hugh, preparing to seize his other arm.

The pewterer stared behind him towards the bridge, then turned back to me, his chin lifted. All trace of the docile man had vanished. 'You're too late to save them, Master Pursglove, far too late. Brystowe and Leynham will never see another dawn.' With a howl of triumph, he shouted into the black night, 'The *Jesus* is already damned!'

Chapter Forty-nine

HUGH DID NOT RESIST or turn to look at me again as the watch marched him off, shaking their heads and muttering that he was indeed raving. As their footfall died away, the silent shadows crept towards me. The only sound was the singing of the wind in the rigging and the rush and gurgle of the water. I thought of the rats gnawing on the corpses lying somewhere beneath us in that stinking crypt, and suddenly the castle seemed far too close.

I needed to get to the quay. Rachael would be returning, perhaps with Brystowe and Leynham, and I wanted to assure them the danger was over. Hugh was on his way to a prison cell. Now I could finally discover what all of this had been about.

I turned in the direction of the wharf and for the first time wondered what Hugh had been staring at. There was a faint glow in the sky behind the bridge. It couldn't be dawn breaking already, that was still hours away. I glanced up again. The red glow wasn't steady but shimmering, like the candle flames in the windows of the houses. Fire! It seemed to be blazing on the far side of the marsh. Were Death's horsemen holding another bonfire? Could they have taken Myles again?

Once more, I found myself running through the streets back towards the quay. But as soon as I burst through on to the waterside, I could see at once that something had changed. There were no bales or crates being loaded on to the carts, and most of these were gone, but people were running to and from the boats in great agitation. Wherries were casting off and rowing feverishly down the river. On the opposite bank, torchlights were moving across the marsh, and for a moment I thought that my fears were realised and Death's horsemen were out there again. But the flames lighting up the sky were not burning on the marshlands but beyond them, out on the Avon.

A wherry was pulling in and people rushed forward to catch the ropes. The two men rowing were glistening with sweat, which ran in rivulets down faces and arms black with soot. Three shivering seamen crouched in the bottom of the boat. They were soaking wet. Two clambered up, helped by outstretched arms, but the third had to be lifted up on to the wharf. He lay there, jerking and moaning, his left arm and leg burned and blistered. Fragments of scorched cloth clung to the red-raw skin. It was only then I realised where those flames were springing from – the *Jesus* was afire.

I raked the crowd frantically for any glimpse of Rachael. I was sure she wouldn't have returned to the Salt Cat without me. Then I spotted the boatman that Rachael had been hurrying towards when I'd last seen her. He was clambering up from his wherry.

'Did you row a woman out to the *Jesus* this evening?' I bellowed over the din. 'Did she return with you?'

'Took her out, but she didn't come back with me,' he shouted up. 'Last glimpse I had of her was on the ship's deck. But that was before the blaze broke out.'

'Take me out there. Now.' Seeing his hesitation, I thrust all the coins I had left in my purse at him, not even looking at what I'd given him. 'If she's still on board or in the water, I have to help her.'

He looked at the coins I held, then shrugged. 'I'm not lingering there, mind. If the fire reaches the powder store the whole ship will explode, and anything close to it will be blown to pieces, boats, men and all.'

Between the ebbing tide and the river's strong current, any boat caught in it was dragged rapidly downstream, so the exhausted wherrymen had to put little effort into the rowing, except to keep their craft to the middle of the channel. The water level was dropping fast and the steep banks of glutinous mud now loomed over our heads. The lethal arsenal of broken spars and jagged metal trapped in the mud threatened any boat or man who came too close.

The men rowed with their backs to the fire, but the sky behind them glowed a ruddy orange. The stench of burning wood, tar and fish oil wafted towards us on the chill wind. At a shout from ahead, the wherrymen drew their boat to the side, digging their oars into the mud to hold us steady as another boat passed us, struggling upstream, the oarsmen straining and groaning against the current. Two men, their wet clothes clinging to them, sat hunched inside it. One clutched an arm snapped in two, the bloody bone sticking out of the mangled flesh. But I couldn't drag my eyes from the other; his face was burned, the right side a swollen mass of raw and charred flesh. A few wisps of singed hair still clung to a scalp that was bald and blistered. A bulging eye peered from the wreckage of his face, but the eyelid was gone. I couldn't tell if he could still see. He kept trying to press a cloth to his face, but his hands were so burned they couldn't grip it.

I shuddered. God's blood, what had happened to Rachael? Was she burned like this man, or screaming in terror, trapped by the fire? Had she jumped and was desperately trying to stay afloat in the chill black water? It was my fault she was out there. I should never have told her about the men in danger on board the ship.

As we neared the confluence of the Frome and Avon, the burning ship loomed into view. A roaring fire was leaping up from the stern, black smoke billowing from the tar-soaked timbers and caulking. The mizzen mast was ablaze; scarlet flames clawed into the dark sky from the furled sails. The stiff wind was blowing the flames sideways over the river, away from the rest of the ship. But judging by the dense smoke oozing up from beneath decks, the fire was probably spreading below. Some of the men on board were running back and forth, hauling buckets of water and pouring it through hatches, others were trying to chop through the base of the mast to topple it into the river, but even as I watched they were beaten back by the flames. A burning rope fell on one man's shoulder and in moments his shirt was ablaze. He ran, shrieking, to the side and threw himself in. The water gleamed with the hell-red light from the burning ship, and I could see several heads bobbing in the river. Some were thrashing about, trying to swim, though I knew that not many mariners could, but even those who had made it to the muddy banks were unable to climb up the steep slippery sides, each attempt only making them sink deeper and deeper into sucking mud.

'Take me closer. I have to get on board.'

The two wherrymen eyed each other.

'I've seen some fool things done for a woman, but this. . .' one said, and waggled his head, mystified. 'Can you swim?'

I nodded.

'Then I'll take you a little closer, but you'll have to swim from there. And I'll not hang around. Sooner or later that ship will blow, and I've no mind to be trapped alongside her when she does.'

The wherrymen allowed their boat to be carried a few yards closer to the ship, then both men jammed their oars into the muddy bank to stop it drifting.

'If you've a mind to go, do it now. And God have mercy on you, body and soul.'

I stood up unsteadily, and edged to the side of the boat furthest from the mud.

Bizarrely, all I could think of was the voice of the elderly sewing maid from my childhood. *That firemark on your throat, that's lucky, that is, means you'll never drown.* I only hoped it didn't mean I was destined to burn, because right at that moment, drowning seemed the better of the two deaths on offer. I took a deep breath and plunged into the water.

Chapter Fifty

GASPING, FROM THE icy shock, I fought to the surface, knowing that I had to keep my feet clear of the bottom or risk being caught in the mud, or tangled in wreckage. I struck out for the ship. The current did most of the work, bearing me towards it. All I had to do was keep my head above the water and make ready to grab hold. As the tide threw us together, a man floundering in the river seized my neck, clinging to me and nearly choking me. I had to hit him hard to prise him loose, knowing that he would drag us both down.

A cargo net hung low over the side of the ship, a large wooden crate still swaying and banging inside, but the boat that should have been waiting beneath to receive it had long since departed. I wasn't sure I could even reach up to it from the river. I was in danger of being swept past, but as I tried to break free from the current, the ship juddered. One of the mooring ropes on the other side must have burned through and snapped under the force of the water. The stern swung out and I only saved my head from slamming into the salt-hardened timber by twisting so that my shoulder took the impact. A bolt of pain shot through it, but there was some blessing in the numbing cold.

I reached up, sweeping my arm along the side of the ship as the river dragged me along, and my fingers caught the sodden rope. For a long moment, I hung there by one hand, my arm almost wrenched from its socket by the pull of the water. My fingers were slipping and I knew that if I didn't move, I would lose my grip. I reached up with the other hand and, finally, a wave lifted me just enough to grasp the bottom of the net.

I dragged myself up, hand over hand, until I got a foot on it, too. I clung on, like the boatswain's monkey that young Myles had been so desperate to meet, trying to summon the strength to scramble higher. Finally, I heaved myself up until, by standing on the wooden crate still suspended in the net, I managed to pitch myself over the gunwale.

Once on deck, I found myself enveloped in the thick acrid smoke of burning pitch and tar. Men loomed in and out of it, appearing and vanishing like demons silhouetted in the red glow. No one paid any heed to me as they ran with buckets, screaming orders to everyone and no one. Heat rolled up in waves from the stern and the blazing mast. A line of fire was running along between two of the planks, only a few inches high, but it threatened at any moment to burst up into great jets of flame. I skirted around towards the bow, where the heat was less intense. The wind was still pushing smoke and fire towards the stern, but if it gusted or veered . . .

My eyes were stinging, but I had to find Rachael. In spite of the heat, I was beginning to shiver as the raw wind cut through my sodden hair and clothes. I could barely distinguish the faces that briefly appeared, but the fleeting glimpses of their forms told me that none was a woman.

I squelched over to the nearest hatch. I hated the thought of going down below, where I could find myself trapped by the flames. But I had sent Rachael here; I could not abandon her now. I clambered down the steep ladder and found myself in a low passageway with coils of rope, sailcloth and boxes stacked beneath hammocks. It was deserted, all hands up on deck or fled. Lanterns had been lit and were swaying with the motion of the ship. Below deck, the smoke was mercifully less dense, reduced to a misty grey haze hanging in the air. It was easier to breathe and thick timbers were, for the moment, holding back the heat and flames. But for how long?

Above me, feet pounded on the deck. Shouts and bellows mingled with the distant crackle of fire.

'Rachael!' I yelled. 'It's Daniel. Are you here? Are you hurt?'

There was no answer, but further along I noticed a door, and thought I heard movement on the other side. Was it the sound of something falling as the flames reached it? I pressed my hand to the wood. It didn't feel hot. Cautiously, I pushed it open, ready to slam it shut if flames leaped out, but the compartment beyond lay in darkness. Yet, on the far side, I thought I saw a light, and it was moving.

'Is someone there? Rachael?'

Now that I was further away from the hatch and the shouts of the men on deck, I could hear something else, the pitiful whimper of someone in great pain. I crept closer to where I thought I'd seen the small flame of a candle or lantern. The light had vanished, but there was a yellow glow beyond the bulkheads. I hesitated. I had no idea how close to the stern I had come and to the fire that raged beneath the deck there, nor where the powder kegs in this ship were stored. If the flames were beginning to burn through into this section, the whole compartment could burst into a fireball at any moment. But if someone was trapped down here, I couldn't simply leave them. And what I had heard sounded like a woman in agony.

Still calling out, I groped through the dark space towards the glow, my muscles so rigid I had to will them to move. I tried to remind myself that at least my clothes were wet enough to protect me from sparks. But that wouldn't be much defence if the ship exploded.

That high-pitched whimper came again, and then a sudden piercing shriek that seemed to last a lifetime.

'Rachael! Rachael, is that you?'

Something was lying on the floor ahead of me. I couldn't make out what it was at first. I edged closer. A leg, encased in filthy white hose, was sticking out from behind one of the bulwarks. And the leg was not moving.

Chapter Fifty-one

I ducked through the low doorway and found myself in a small cabin, evidently the sleeping quarters for two of the higher-ranking men on board. It contained little except for two bunk beds suspended by chains from the sides, a small table and stacks of wooden boxes. But I barely registered that at the time.

The man whose leg I'd glimpsed lay sprawled on his back on the floor, his eyes wide, staring sightlessly up at the low beams above, his face as pale as a skull in the lamplight, his shirt soaked in scarlet blood. A second man lay face down across the lower bunk, his leg and arm dangling as if he had struggled to rise. Blood soaked the bedroll beneath him, flowing from two wounds on his back. It ran down his arm, dripping steadily from the limp fingers of the dangling hand, like rain from the twigs of a tree. A small dark-furred monkey with a white face and front was running agitatedly up and down the bed above him, peering down and stretching out a paw towards the man, whimpering and shrieking, as it sniffed the blood.

I could see, without touching them, that both were dead. I had little doubt that I was looking at the corpses of Edward Brystowe and Hugh Leynham. Rachael had arrived too late. I stared at the rapid drip, drip, drip of the blood as it ran down the lifeless fingers. The wounds were still bleeding. But that didn't make sense. If Hugh had killed the men before I'd seen him at the quayside, then the blood should not still be flowing freely. Unless it had taken the victim this long to die, and that hardly seemed—

The monkey raised its head, staring at something behind me, its cries rising to shrieks of fury. I turned and caught a glimpse of movement, as someone darted out from behind the pile of boxes and ran into the dark compartment from which I'd entered. Hampered by having to duck beneath the low beams, I hared after them, slipping and sliding in my drenched boots. I emerged into the space lit by the lanterns, but it was empty, though the smoke from the open hatch was getting thicker. But I was sure I'd been only moments behind them. No one could have climbed that vertical ladder so swiftly. I'd have at least seen their legs as they clambered up the last few rungs.

A shrieking behind me made me whirl round. The monkey was on the floor in the dark passageway, standing on its hind legs, flailing its arms and screaming at something behind the bulkhead. I crept towards the little creature, hoping, in its fury, it wouldn't bury those long teeth in my leg. Someone rushed out of the darkness, cannoning into my shoulder and sending me spinning. They ran towards the stairs and had already mounted three rungs before I managed to cover the gap and grab their leg. They kicked out, but I held on and with a jerk brought them crashing down on to the deck below. A knife spun away from their hand and clattered against the wall. The person was sprawled face down but raised their head to look at me, and I found myself staring down into Rachael's face, contorted in pain.

For a moment I was too startled to do anything, then I hauled her to her feet, dragging her into a fierce embrace. 'Rachael! Thank God! Are you hurt?'

She struggled in my grasp, her eyes wide with fear. 'Let me go! Get away from me!'

I could feel her whole body shaking. 'But I didn't kill them, Rachael, I swear. When I heard the ship was ablaze and you hadn't returned, I feared you were trapped, or worse. So I—'

A gust of smoke billowed down the hatchway, making us both cough and gasp.

I caught her arm. 'I'll explain, I promise, but we have to get off this ship before she blows. Can you climb up? Let me help—'

As I looked at my hand on her arm, I saw it was stained with blood. For a moment I stared at it blankly. Rachael had half turned away and only then, as the smoke cleared a little, did I see that the front of her gown was scarlet, as were her hands. I caught her about the waist to support her. 'God's bones, you're hurt! Did he stab . . . ?'

But she wasn't leaning weakly on me. Her gaze had darted to the knife that lay against the bulkhead, and for the first time I looked at it, too. It lay in the pool of light from the lantern, its bone handle carved with delicate patterns of birds and flowers. Then two things hit me like a shock of cold water.

The knife was Rachael's.

And the blade was glistening with fresh blood.

She yanked herself from my grip and bolted again for the ladder, but I stepped in front of her.

'Let me go!'

'Not until you tell me who killed those men.'

'How should I know?' She coughed as a gust of smoke swirled around her. 'Came here to warn them, like you said, but by the time I'd found them they were already dead.'

'Then why did you run?'

'Thought you were one of the crew, and if they'd found me with the bodies, they'd have accused me.'

'And with good reason, since you're covered in their blood, as is your knife.'

She darted towards it, trying to snatch it up, but I grabbed her wrist and held her bloody hand up, forcing her to look at it.

'*Their* blood, Rachael.'

There was a great crash on deck above us. A shower of sparks fell through the hatchway and a great billow of black smoke rolled in. The terrified monkey suddenly bolted past us, screaming. It scampered up the ladder and vanished into the red glow above. Only then did I realise what I should have seen at once.

Ned's monkey . . . Edward.

'God's arse, Edward Brystowe is . . . *was* the boatswain. That's Mistress Crugge's cousin lying dead in there!'

'The ship,' Rachael gasped, as the crackle of flames grew into a roar. 'We have to get off.'

I shook her, trying not to choke in the smoke. 'I swear I'll shut you down here and leave you to burn alongside the corpses of those men unless you tell me the truth. Did you kill them? Did you kill the others, too – Dagworth, Harewell, Gysbourne? Did you?' I shook her.

'Yes,' she hissed. 'Yes, I killed them and I'd do it again if I could . . . Does that satisfy you, Master Daniel?'

'But the pewterer, Hugh, confessed he had killed them. He boasted of it. Why would he do that?'

'Because Hugh is my father.'

Chapter Fifty-two

WE CLAMBERED UP the ladder on to the deck. The black smoke was so dense now that we could barely see the leaping flames. The roar and crackle of the fire was louder even than the screams and shouts of the men. I pulled Rachael down, yelling at her to keep low and crawl. I shoved her roughly ahead of me and kept pushing until we collided with the side of the ship. We were in the bow. We had to jump, but I knew that if we landed in the mud, we'd be trapped, unable to move as the ship blew apart next to us. Our best hope was to leap into the narrow stretch of water that still remained in the channel. Choking and gasping, I peered over the gunwale, but my eyes were streaming and even when the wind lifted the curtain of smoke for a moment, I could see little. We would have to risk it. I pulled Rachael up until she was standing.

'Jump!' I yelled.

She struggled in my grip. 'No, I will die here. I want to die here. Leave me.'

She tried to push me over the side and almost succeeded, but I was heavier. I tore free and before she could dash back into the smoke, I grabbed her, lifted her in my arms and threw her over the side. If there was a splash, I couldn't hear it above the fire. I clambered over, lowering myself as far as I could, then let go.

The icy water enveloped me, closing over my head, and I kicked, coughing and spluttering, to the surface. The current was pushing me back against the ship and I steadied myself there for a moment, staring around for Rachael. The smoke was rolling a foot or so above the river. In the darkness I could see little except the red glow on the water. Then I spotted her, a yard or so in front of me. She was swimming towards the muddy bank.

'No,' I yelled, 'stay in the channel! The mud will trap you.'

She glanced around and I knew she'd heard me. She hesitated, then turned and began to swim up the river. I followed. It took all my strength to push against the flow of icy water. I could just make out Rachael ahead of me. She was tiring, and as she rested for a moment the current caught her, pushing her back towards me. I seized her and gripped the back of her gown, hauling her forward.

Glancing up, I could see the wherry bobbing on the river ahead of us. Someone was leaning over the side, an oar extended towards us, mouthing something I couldn't hear over the roar of the flames, but I knew he was urging us to hurry. My limbs were growing numb and I was swimming with only one arm, the other still gripping Rachael, though she, too, was pulling with all her strength. But the gap between us and the safety of the wherry seemed wider than ever.

The ship exploded behind us. Shards of flaming timber and red-hot metal were hurled into the black sky and began to crash all around us, sizzling as they hit wet mud, making the water boil and bubble where they struck. Bodies arched through the air, twisted and torn, tumbling like birds shot from the sky. I dived beneath the surface, dragging Rachael with me. We stayed down as long as our bursting lungs would allow, but the smaller fragments of blazing sail, rope and wood were still falling towards the river as we rose. The ship blazed like a great bonfire behind us, but every sound had grown strangely muffled – the roar of the flames, the screams – as if my head was still deep beneath the water.

For a moment, I floated there, stunned, in the water. Then I felt a hand grip my belt. Rachael was dragging me forward, as the current pushed us back towards the flaming ship. She was swimming with a strength I had not thought possible, and finally I summoned what little energy I could muster to strike out with her. The wherry was still there and miraculously undamaged, though the two boatmen were splashing water on the burning fragments as they continued to drift down from the blackened sky, falling on them and the boat. They heaved us on board like monstrous fish, and before we were even able to summon the strength to sit upright, the two men were rowing back up the river away from the ship as fast as any man could.

We lay, half propped up in the bottom of the boat, in several inches of bilge water, retching and coughing, as the ruby sparks fell like snow. Rachael was staring back at the flames churning and writhing in the billows of smoke. Her hair had been dragged loose and lay in wet strands about her corpse-pale face. The sleeve of her gown had been ripped away, exposing a deep, livid burn on her upper arm, but she neither attempted to protect it nor did her face register any pain, as if she wasn't even aware of it. The river had washed her hands clean of blood, and much had leached from her gown, but not all, and only the sight of that stain convinced me I had really heard her say those words. *I killed them and I'd do it again if I could.*

How could I not have seen what was right in front of me? Was it possible, could Rachael really be these two people, the woman who had almost given her life to save a street boy, and the woman who had killed in cold blood? I would have understood if she had stabbed a man in anger. My temper had got the better of me many times, and I'd come dangerously close to killing in a blind rage. I *had* done once. But to plan the murder like an executioner, to draw up a list of who must die, showed a ruthless malice that, even looking at her now with their blood on her gown, I did not want to believe. How could I have so misread her?

God's bones, I had actually paid the wherrymen to row the murderer out to that ship. She had played me for a fool and, like a bull with a ring through its nose, I'd let her lead me to the slaughter.

Chapter Fifty-three

I WAS AWAKE the next morning long before Myles's impatient knocking came at my door. He marched in and set down a platter of bread and salted herring. He glanced up, mildly surprised to see me dressed. Then his face fell into a scowl.

'I waited and waited, but Ned never came with the monkey. Master says the ship caught ablaze last night. Exploded into a thousand pieces. I heard the bang, but I never saw nothing. Didn't even see the flames. Had to work in the kitchens all night, 'cause Rachael didn't come back. Mistress was blazing like a rat with its arse on fire. Banging pots and pans like my ma did whenever she was mad.' He frowned. 'Hope she doesn't send Rachael away, 'cause I liked her.'

So did I, Myles, so did I.

I'd gone straight to my lodgings in the Salt Cat after I'd handed Rachael to the watch. It almost tore me in two to do it, but what else could I have done? If she could murder five men in such a manner, she was either mad or one of the most ruthless and cold-hearted villains I had ever met. I daren't risk turning her loose, knowing she might well kill again. She did not resist when I delivered her to her gaolers, only asking that she might be locked up with her father. As she was led away, she glanced back at me with a soft sad smile, as if she pitied me.

As I emerged from the Salt Cat in the morning light, I found a city in uproar. The hopes and dreams that the *Jesus* had carried had been turned to ashes in every sense. The hulk would have to be removed from the Avon before craft of any size could enter or leave the port. She was too badly damaged even to tow at high tide, which meant sawing her apart, piece by piece. Walkways would have to be laid across the sodden marsh so that horses could be brought in to drag out the remains of the heavy beams, wooden scaffolding erected in the muddy banks, else more men would become trapped in the mire, slowly drowning as the tide flowed in.

Search parties were already being assembled to comb the banks, rocks and reedbeds downstream for the mariners who'd jumped into the river and been carried away, in case by some miracle they'd managed to crawl out somewhere and were still clinging to life. Then there were the cargoes to be accounted for. It would be all too easy for those kegs and bales already brought ashore before disaster struck to be spirited away by those who would swear the goods had been burned with the ship.

I quickly discovered that no one had time to bother taking sworn statements or hearing testimonies about two corpses on a sunken ship, when so many were injured or missing, and so it was that I found myself making my way to the place they told me Hugh and Rachael had been taken. They had been locked in the bottom of an old bell tower. The top was in ruins, the bells long since removed, but the small circular room at the base still stood solidly enough.

As I arrived, an old man who had evidently just delivered the daily ration of bread and water was locking the heavy iron grille that served as the door, with a key that hung from the ring chained to his waist. 'You want to make that last,' he warned Rachael. 'I'll not be back with more till morning.'

He nodded amicably enough to me. 'Keep them company, if you will, master, but see you don't bait them. Constable gave me orders they was not to be damaged till they've been questioned.'

He shuffled past me, his pail cranking. Evidently no one would bother with the prisoners again that day, and there was no need to waste a guard on them when every man was needed elsewhere. Not even a half-starved cat could have squeezed in or out through the bars on that door.

On the other side of the iron grille, three steps led down to a tiny circular chamber. It was bare of any furniture and I guessed it had been flooded when the great wave had struck, for water still festered in stinking puddles on the floor, and gravel, seaweed and silt lay where the sea had washed them. Rachael sat with her back to the wall, on a heap of sodden straw, cradling a grey-haired man who rested his head in her lap to keep it from the cold, wet flags.

Hugh had looked dishevelled and gaunt when the watchmen had led him away, but his face was now ashen and his breathing laboured, his chest heaving in small shallow breaths like a wounded bird. I had seen men suffer like that in Newgate. They seldom survived long enough to die on the gallows.

Rachael looked up at me as I drew closer to the grille. She had wrapped a rag torn from her gown around the burn on her arm, and her hair hung tangled and loose. But the turnkey had evidently obeyed orders, for she had no fresh bruises or marks that I could see.

'Your father looks ill.'

'He frets that I was caught. He hoped—'

'He hoped that by acing as decoy to lure me away, you could murder those two and return to the Salt Cat as if nothing had happened. He hoped that by admitting to me he had murdered the first three men, no one would ever think of looking for his daughter. You have a fond but foolish father, Rachael.'

'I love both my daughters, Master Pursglove.' Hugh opened his eyes and pushed himself upright, shuffling round so that he was sitting next to Rachael. 'I spoke the truth when I said I'd killed those men.' His voice was cracked and wheezing, but a fierce light blazed in his eyes.

'Hush, Father.' Rachael grasped his fingerless hand, lifting it to her lips. She kissed it, then continued to hold it tenderly. 'He is only confessing to protect me. But you can't save me now, Father, don't you see? What does it matter if I am hung for one man or for five? I can only die once.'

'I can't lose you, too. I can't watch you die.' He lifted his chin. 'Master Pursglove, tell them. . . please tell them it was me, just me. And that she is innocent. What will they care, so long as someone is punished?'

'And if she kills again?' I demanded.

'She'll not. Have no fear about that. It's over, finished. Justice has been done. My sweet child is avenged.'

I stared at Rachael who was gazing sadly at her father. 'Justice? What did those men do to you that made them deserving of death?'

'Not to me,' she whispered. 'To my sister. If the law was just, then they would have hanged for her as I will for them.' Rachael's voice had lost the bitterness and anger I'd heard in it the night before; now it was flat, cold, as if she had exhausted all emotion.

'Tell him,' Hugh urged. 'The man's a right to know the truth now. He's earned it.'

Rachael hesitated, her gaze flicking between me and her father as if she was trying to make up her mind. Then she sighed. 'We didn't know what they had done to Anne,' she murmured, staring dully at a slime-filled puddle. 'She was ashamed. She wouldn't even confide in me.' Rachael swallowed and glanced up at me. She must have seen my baffled expression, for she took a deep breath in an effort to assemble her thoughts into an explanation.

'Anne was my younger sister. My mother died a few years ago from the plague. After that we kept house for Father, and tended him, for he was sick with fever for many weeks after his accident. Once he was well again, he worked harder than ever, harder than any man should, but he wasn't able to earn as much as before, not enough to keep the three of us.'

Hugh flinched, passing a hand over his eyes as if he was weeping.

'I found work in the Salt Cat, for though I'd learned the pewterer's skills from my father, no workshop would employ a woman in that craft. But Nicholas Dagworth took Anne on to keep his books in his house. She'd kept Father's accounts for him and written his letters when he had his own works. Anne could write and reckon as well as any clerk, but Dagworth only had to pay her half as much as any lad. He'd have skinned a flea for its hide.'

'My Anne was a clever girl, sharp as vinegar,' Hugh said with pride. 'I told Master Dagworth so, many a time, when he came to buy pewter from my workshop. My wife always grieved that she never bore me a son to carry on the business, but I said to Master Dagworth what need have I for sons when I've been blessed with two daughters? The elder who's as skilled with her hands as any apprentice or journeyman in my employ, and my youngest who can reckon a column of figures in her head to the last farthing quicker than the best clerk in the royal treasury.' His face crumpled. 'I told him that. I boasted of her skills to him, like the father who bragged his daughter could spin straw into gold, and this is my punishment.'

'It was not your fault, Father, none of it,' Rachael said wearily, squeezing his hand again, as if she had assured him of this a thousand times. She looked up at me and resumed her tale in a dull voice.

'Anne was always a merry little creature, not like me.' She gave a rueful smile. 'Trusting, ready with a kind word for anyone, for she'd only ever worked for Father and that mostly at home. Being the elder, I'd always watched out for her, so she'd never known hurt from anyone. But those last few weeks she changed. She'd barely looked at us. Sat for hours staring into the fire, face as wooden as a painted doll, not eating enough to keep a sparrow alive. I was afraid she was suffering from the green sickness. I nagged her worse than any scold to go to the physician, and in the end she did.

'That night when I came home from the Salt Cat, I found her in the room we shared, sobbing as if her heart would break, and mine nearly did, too, at the sight of her, for I thought the physician had told her she was mortally sick. She said it was worse than that, though I couldn't imagine how it could be, but finally she told me she was with child.'

Hugh groaned as if he was hearing the news for the first time all over again.

Rachael's hands clenched. 'I thought she'd been making merry with a young lad from one of the ships and he'd gone back to sea and abandoned her, and that was why she was weeping. But she swore she hadn't. Finally, I managed to drag the story from her. When the *Jesus* last sailed into Bristol, Dagworth had taken Anne on board with him, telling her he needed her there to draw up the bills of sale and keep a reckoning, while he negotiated with the quartermaster for a cargo of grain. The boatswain was there, too, Mistress Crugge's cousin, for he had business of his own with Dagworth. He regularly smuggles in wine and other things on the *Jesus* that the Exchequer's men never get to hear about. The three men drank a good deal as they bargained, and Leynham, the quartermaster, began to joke that he fancied Anne as part of his payment. Anne thought he was teasing. She'd heard me talk about the foolish things men say in the Salt Cat when they've had a bellyful, but it went far beyond that. Dagworth, Brystowe and Leynham took her by force and held her down while each of them had his way with her. She tried to fight them off, but she couldn't stop them. How could she? She was only a young lass, and they were three strong men.'

'You mustn't think that I ever blamed her, Master Pursglove,' Hugh said, his face twisted in misery. 'I told her, over and over, she was the one who'd been wronged. I said her and her babe would always have a home with me. I tried to make her believe that I'd be glad to have a grandson or granddaughter, however it had been brought into this world, and I swore to her that I'd let no man or woman cry shame on her.'

'You didn't go to the sheriff and report it?' I asked.

Hugh hung his head. 'The *Jesus* had sailed and wasn't due back for months. It would have been her word against that of a wealthy merchant. He'd deny everything, and she'd be the one branded a whore for having a child out of wedlock. I couldn't do that to her, not force her to stand up in public before all the city and tell what had been done to her to the judges. Master Dagworth was one of the grand patrons of the Gaunt's Chapel. Had his mark up there alongside half the nobles and guilds of Bristol. Even if she could have got the words out, no man would take her part against a merchant like him.'

'We kept her at home. No one knew of her condition,' Rachael said softly. 'And when the pains came upon her, I delivered the child.' She suddenly pressed her fingers to her eyes as if trying to blot out the image that had risen up in her memory. 'If proof were needed of the wickedness that was done to my sister, it was written in that poor, innocent little babe. It had a sweet face, like a little angel, but what there was of its legs were welded together, as if the two had been melded into one. I couldn't rightly tell if the baby were a boy or a girl. But it fought for life, wailing as if it was born raging against the world.' She drew a deep breath, trying not to cry.

'But it couldn't live, for though it cried for milk, there was no hole to shit with. Anne knew it was going to die, but she couldn't bear the thought of an innocent babe going to hell. She said in heaven her babe would be made whole as any child. I said we might christen it ourselves, but she got it into her head that only water blessed by a vicar would save its soul. She wrapped the babe up and crept out after dark to the vicar at Christ Church, that being nearest to us, and begged him to baptise the infant. She was sure he'd look kindly on a child that wasn't long for this world, for he often railed in the pulpit against parents who delayed bringing their newborns to be christened and said that their slothfulness put their child's soul in peril of damnation.

'Gysbourne knew Anne was not wed, and when he unwrapped the babe he raged at her, saying that God had allowed her sin to be marked on the child, so that what she had tried to hide would be laid bare for all the world to see. She tried to tell him what had happened but he wouldn't believe she had not willingly given herself to the men. He said it was she who had led them into sin, like Eve tempted Adam.

'He told her that she must bring the child to the service on Sunday for all to see and publicly confess her sins before the whole congregation. If the child was to be christened, Anne must stand before all and renounce the Devil and all his works. Even though the little mite was dying, Gysbourne refused to baptise the babe in private. He told her that if the babe perished before Sunday, that was a sign that God had marked it for damnation to punish her.

'Anne crept home and just sat there, rocking and rocking the babe in her arms, long after it died. It was as stiff and cold as iron before I could take it from her, and then only because she'd fallen asleep from exhaustion.'

Rachael and her father gazed at each other, reliving the misery of that dark night. I felt their anger boiling up in me. If Rachael had told me this before she'd gone to the ship, I would have stopped her killing those men, but only so that I could have had the satisfaction of doing it myself.

Rachael took a deep breath. 'But even though Gysbourne had turned my sister away and condemned her babe to hell, he didn't let it rest. He wrote an account of the birth, making the child out to be far more maimed than it was, as if she'd given birth to a demon, and saying that its mother was a whore who, by her wiles, had tempted three God-fearing men and seduced them into committing all manner of abominations with her, which was proved by the deformities of the child—'

'And he had that account printed as a broadside for all of Bristol to read,' I finished, the last piece suddenly falling into place. 'How on earth did your sister bear it?'

Tears welled in Hugh's eyes. 'She didn't leave the house for days after her babe died, and we thought we'd kept that foul paper from her. But one day, about a week later, I came home and found her gone and the broadside lying on the table. Someone must have pushed it beneath our door. We feared the worst. We searched everywhere for her, asked everyone. Then one of the wards said on the day she went missing he'd seen a woman who he thought to be Anne riding out of the city gate on the back of a wagon with some other folk. They'd taken the road to Bath, he reckoned. So, we thought she'd run away to start afresh, though it hurt me sorely that she'd not said goodbye.'

'But I told Father that she'd most likely done it on the spur of the moment,' Rachael said. 'After the birth, she'd hardly known what she was doing, even before she'd read that broadside. I told him we should take comfort that Anne had not harmed herself, or maybe she'd tried to, but someone had stopped her and persuaded her to go away with them instead. I said, it was all to the good. Away from Bristol, she could begin again where no one knew her, maybe even marry. And one day, when she was settled, she'd surely send word to us to let us know she was well and happy.'

Hugh grimaced. 'I let myself believe that, because I wanted to. The thought that she might be dead was so terrible, I knew that if I even looked at it, it would devour me, so I pretended it couldn't be.' His voice had shrunk to a whisper, as if he dared not even speak the name of death. 'And that's how it was, until the day of the flood. The wave swept away many buildings, brought down walls that seemed as solid as rocks. People said Master Dagworth was lucky, only the corner of his warehouse was damaged. The wall was weaker there, they said, because it had recently been patched. I don't know what made me look inside, but now I know I was meant to see what lay there.

'Once I heard a man preaching in the streets about the end of the world when the sea shall give up her dead. She did that when the wave came. Cast her corpses up on the land, their flesh all lacey and white, half eaten away. But it wasn't exactly like the preacher had said, for though the sea gave up her dead, it took

402

the dead from the land in exchange. It raked open graves and smashed coffins wide; some of the corpses it took back to its bed, but not all.'

I thought Hugh was rambling now and the events of the last few weeks had finally robbed him of his wits.

He pressed the stump of his hand hard against his eyes. 'The sea dragged her out of her grave in the warehouse wall, when the corner caved in. She washed up against the loft ladder and caught in the rungs. The land wouldn't let the sea take her, but the sea wanted to show me what they'd done to her. That's where I found her, her poor body caught in the ladder, dangling like a broken doll. I'd not have known her face, that was all but gone. But I knew her beautiful long hair, for I'd caressed it every evening when I'd kissed her goodnight. I knew her mother's pewter brooch, for I'd made it with my own hands, and I knew the bright blue scarf that her sister had given her for her birthday, knew it even though they had knotted it so tight around her throat it had nearly severed her head. And I knew it was Anne, my own little Anne.'

He bent forward, sobbing like a child. Rachael gathered him in her arms, stroking his hair, rocking and crooning to him as if he was her babe.

I knew what lay ahead for the two of them. Too late, I realised that the key which had fallen from Rachael's gown the night she saved Myles must have been the one they had used to enter and leave Christ Church by the Devil's door. Had they murdered the first three men together, or was one trying to take the blame for the other? As Rachael had said, it scarcely mattered now. I knew they would both plead guilty. Dagworth had taken for his motto *Faber est suae quisque fortunae*. But there was a more fitting translation. *Every man is the architect of his own fate.* Those five men received the justice they deserved, but the law would make no allowances for that.

I had resolved to leave Bristol at once. I didn't want to be forced to give testimony against them. But my absence wouldn't spare them. The watchmen would surely report Hugh's confession and his cry that the *Jesus* was already damned. When it was discovered that Rachael had been aboard, she would likely be accused of setting fire to the ship.

She had sworn to me the night before that she had had no part in starting the blaze, and I believed her now. She would not have wanted to see innocent lives lost. Most likely, in their haste to unload the cargo in the dark on a pitching ship, with no cranes to aid them, a lantern had been smashed down in one of the holds. But if no one came forward as witness to the cause of the fire, the whole of Bristol would be howling for Rachael's blood. Her execution would be prolonged and agonising. I wished with all my heart that I had left well alone, but it was too late now.

Chapter Fifty-four

LONDON

THE MESSAGE CAME late in the evening, less than four hours after Daniel had arrived back in London and found lodgings in a piss-poor inn, which was all he could afford. He knew he'd not enough money remaining in his purse to pay for more than two nights, but he'd inveigled his way into lodgings before when he couldn't pay for even one night, and right now, that was the least of his concerns. He devoured a bowl of stew that was supposed to be mutton, though he could only find gristle lurking beneath the oats, then staggered to a bed whose mattress was even lumpier than the oatmeal he'd just chewed. He hadn't even managed to drag his boots off before he fell asleep, only to be awoken minutes later by persistent knocking.

'I want no company tonight,' he groaned into his pillow. 'I've neither the strength nor the money for a whore.'

'Open the door, Master Pursglove.' The voice was soft, but it had a tone of authority which could not be ignored.

He was fully awake now and, sliding his dagger from its sheath, he edged towards the door. He positioned the toe of his boot so that the door could not be pushed wide, and opened it a few inches. His visitor was clearly not someone who would normally frequent such an insalubrious part of the city, though he did not seem ill at ease, quite the contrary. He inclined his head in a manner that contrived to be both courteous and condescending. He was beardless, though not by any means a youth, clad in closely fitting black silk breeches and a padded doublet trimmed with silver thread. His auburn hair was voluptuously curled beneath a tall-crowned capotain hat, and a long lovelock snaked over his shoulder. He made no attempt to push the door wider, but stood regarding Daniel with thinly disguised amusement.

'Lord FitzAlan bids you attend him tomorrow at two of the clock at Newgate prison. He trusts you are acquainted with the address.'

'Newgate!' The single chilling word penetrated Daniel's exhausted brain like the bolt from a crossbow. 'But I haven't yet delivered my report.'

'You will tomorrow, in person. He feels it . . .' The man frowned, considering the selection of the word. '*Imprudent* to have your report committed to paper.'

That ball of oatmeal had suddenly become as heavy as a cannonball in the pit of Daniel's stomach. He'd intended to compose a report, draft and redraft it several times, carefully selecting his arguments. Had he already been condemned before he'd even uttered a word? He was unnerved that FitzAlan should have discovered so quickly that he was back in London and where he had taken refuge. What else did he already know – that his emissary had singularly failed to discover anything about Spero Pettingar? Had FitzAlan arranged the meeting in Newgate so that he could be dragged straight back down into the Hole?

Daniel jerked back out of arm's reach as the man slid his hand beneath his short cloak, fearing he was drawing a weapon. But he held out a small purse.

'Lord FitzAlan believes you may require this.' The man's gaze travelled pointedly over Daniel's stained clothes, tousled hair and unkempt beard. What he saw seemed to amuse him. There was something unnervingly familiar about that smile and those dark blue eyes. Daniel was sure he had seen him before, but he was too unnerved by the summons his visitor had brought to remember where.

The visitor dangled the purse in his gloved fingers, inviting Daniel to reach out for it like a rich man teasing a beggar's brat with a coin. 'I suggest you buy yourself some soap and a pair of breeches that don't look as if you've used them to wipe your backside. Otherwise, the turnkey might take you for an escaped prisoner and clap you in irons.'

Daniel didn't move. He was damned if he was going to reach for that bag. The man laughed softly and tossed the bag over his shoulder into the room, where it fell with a muffled clunk to the boards.

'Remember the hour tomorrow, and I advise you not to be late.' His gaze locked with Daniel's for a long moment before he briefly inclined his head and turned away.

As soon as Daniel had closed the door, he kicked the money bag across the room and sank on to the bed. He was exhausted, but sleep had fled.

He had left Bristol the same day as he'd visited Rachael, delaying only to hurry back to the Salt Cat, pack his few belongings and saddle up Diligence. By then, Mistress Crugge had learned that her cousin was missing, like so many others aboard the *Jesus* – missing, presumed killed in the explosion, or drowned. Although, she seemed to be grieving more over losing her supplier of smuggled booty than the death of her cousin, for as she said, 'When a man makes his living from the sea, it stands to reason that sooner or later the sea will take its dues.'

Daniel had reminded himself sternly, several times, that Myles was not his responsibility. He was a street urchin who had latched on to him like a stray cat, as orphaned children did the world over, cadging coins or a bite of food from anyone they thought wouldn't kick them away. He needn't give him another thought. But . . . but if he went back to the streets, he'd be seen by that bastard Tobias or another of Death's horsemen, and this time no one would be there to save him from the sea. The question was, who would take in a boy like that?

'. . . if you had a quick-witted lad to run errands for you, Mistress Crugge, make himself useful in the kitchen, especially now that you're so short-handed. And Caleb isn't getting any younger. Once the travellers and merchants start returning to Bristol, your husband will need someone to help with the heavy work, shifting barrels and mucking out the stables. Much cheaper to take on a boy and train him up in the work than employ a cellarman.'

Mistress Crugge had frowned as she considered the matter. 'I suppose we could make use of the lad now that idle trull has been locked up, as well she ought to be. I always said she'd end as meat for the ravens. I told Master Crugge not to offer her work, but he wouldn't be told. Too soft-hearted, that's his trouble, but I can always smell a bad fish.' She closed her eyes. 'It's a mercy she didn't cut all our throats while we slept. When I think of what that wicked girl did to poor Reverend Gysbourne . . .'

Daniel had been sorely tempted to tell her what Rachael had done to her cousin Ned, and why, but he forced himself to stay silent.

'Myles will have to work hard for his bed and board, mind. I'll not stand for idlers.' She had folded her arms under her massive breasts. 'Can't abide lads, myself, as well you know, Master Pursglove, but a man hankers for a son to teach him what he's learned.'

Master and Mistress Crugge had come into the courtyard to bid Daniel farewell as he led Diligence out under the archway. Myles was standing between them and Daniel noticed that Mistress Crugge's arm had crept around his shoulder and she was giving him a motherly squeeze, for all that she couldn't abide boys.

The journey back to London had been wretched. Although the floodwaters had drained, and villagers had cleared the roads of fallen trees and made temporary repairs to the bridges for horses and those on foot to pass over, no serious attempts had been made to replace roads and tracks that had been washed away, or to build bridges for wagons or carts. No work of that kind could begin until the sun had dried out the land, and there was precious little sign of that. Even if homes were rebuilt, farmland

and pasture would remain poisoned by the sea salt for months, perhaps years, to come, and many had been forced to abandon their land or starve.

Even when he was beyond the reaches of the flood, he was reminded that the land was still in the grip of the hungry months before the first harvest, for food was scarce and costly. What little money remained to him was dwindling fast and he knew he must save enough for lodgings in London, for he'd no wish to find himself sleeping with the beggars there. So, for several nights of the journey he'd bedded down wet, cold and hungry in barns or woods.

Several times he had been sorely tempted to run, had even turned aside once or twice, but he'd forced himself back to the London road. FitzAlan would find him, and he could not spend the rest of his life fearing that every footfall behind him, or shadow on the stairs, was one of FitzAlan's men waiting to drag him to the agony of a traitor's death.

Each grey dawn, in that sweet world between sleeping and waking, he thought he heard Rachael's knock, or her voice, only to find it was a falling twig or a blackbird's call. He knew he should have been planning what he was going to tell FitzAlan, but he couldn't force his mind to it. And now his time had finally run out.

Chapter Fifty-five

THE HEAVY DOOR closed with a thud that echoed through the massive stones. The stout iron key grated in the lock. The turnkey waited until he was sure Daniel was following, then shambled along a dark passage, squeezed up a narrow staircase and flung open the door at the top. The man barred Daniel's way, hovering expectantly, then finally extended a paw. Remembering that the gaoler might soon have the power to make his life more unpleasant than the deepest pit of hell, Daniel grudgingly dropped a coin into it, though he'd have sooner shoved it down the man's throat. The turnkey stepped aside, and Daniel had barely taken a pace into the room before the door slammed shut behind him.

FitzAlan was seated behind a table on the single chair in the chamber, warming his hands over the small brazier, his face half in the shadow cast by the red glow. But the heat could not banish the icy, damp air of the room. A flagon stood on the table, a goblet of dark purple wine already poured, beside a platter of dainty pastries and another of chicken legs glazed in red-gold honey and spices.

Charles FitzAlan was plainly clad in a brown doublet, with a serpent-green stripe and a flowing white lace collar. He reached out a grubby hand towards one of the chicken legs, lifted it, then seemed to change his mind, setting it down.

'You've returned to London, Master Pursglove.' His accent was as thick as porridge. 'At least you didnae try to flee to France. You've that much good sense.' He took a gulp of wine, some of which dribbled from the corner of his mouth. He smoothed his beard, sending the drops of wine showering down on the table. 'Don't keep me waiting, sirrah, what report am I to make to His Majesty?'

Daniel told him what little he had rehearsed: the lynching of the cordwainer and his family, and how the mob had been whipped up by the broadside; discovering the corpse of the printer and the vicar, the letters burned into them, and how he had wasted time believing them to be a symbol of the Jesuits.

He told FitzAlan of a grieving sister and father, of a cold and judgemental man of God, a printer who peddled lies for money, a merchant who thought he was entitled to take the virtue of any woman who crossed his path. He wanted the King's 'most trusted adviser' to understand how easily a man may be led into seeing conspiracies of witchcraft or popery, where there was nothing more than human lust, cruelty and revenge. Sins that were as ancient as Sodom itself.

Daniel did not tell him he'd seen the merchant's corpse. He could not do that without mentioning Waldegrave, and if he was to be returned to prison, or worse, he would not add to his guilt by dragging an old man down with him. It was the one thing he could still do, the one shred of power left to him: protect Waldegrave from the rack and the gallows. He knew he was keeping silent as much for the sake of his own pride as for the old man. All his life he'd wanted to see Waldegrave suffer, yet now – when he could not only bring that about but perhaps save his own skin in the process by offering up a fugitive priest – he found himself risking all to shield him. It made no sense even to him.

FitzAlan listened without interruption, steadily munching through the pies and gnawing on the chicken bones, only occasionally darting a fierce and intelligent glance up at Daniel as if he hoped to catch an unguarded expression. By the time Daniel's words had died away, little remained on the platters but chewed bones, though the fragments of meat and pastry that had fallen from FitzAlan's mouth, as he chewed, littered the table and hung in his beard.

A heavy silence descended, like snow, upon the little chamber. FitzAlan lifted a napkin, wiped his beard, mouth and greasy hands, and set it down. He regarded Daniel steadily, leaning forward on his elbows, his long fingers curved, his fingertips pressed together as if he was making a cage for some small bird or beast.

'Your story is an interesting one, but I have heard a stranger tale. It seems that, at dawn, the day after you left Bristol, the sheriff sent his men to collect two prisoners, a woman and her father. They were to bring the prisoners to the sheriff so that he might question them about the murders of three men, crimes to which the father had already confessed in the hearing of the watch, but their accounts and pleas had to be officially recorded. When the men arrived, they found the cell empty, but the iron-barred door still locked.

'They naturally dragged the turnkey to the sheriff, who demanded to know why he had released the prisoners. He swore he had not done so. Indeed, he said he had not been near them since he'd taken them their dole of bread and water the previous noon. Gave oath that the key had never left the chain about his waist, and showed that it still hung there. Two prisoners vanishing from a locked, windowless cell, now that is certain proof of witchcraft at work, wouldn't you say, Master Pursglove?' FitzAlan paused, a triumphant smile hovering on his thin lips.

'Not witchcraft, sir, simply human error. Most likely, the turnkey didn't lock the door properly. Later, he returned to lock it and found the prisoners already escaped, but was too afraid to tell anyone for fear of losing his position.'

FitzAlan nodded sagely, as if that explanation had not occurred to him. He picked up one of the discarded bones and twisted it between his fingers. '*Human*, I will grant you. *Error?*' He paused. 'I'm not the fool you take me for. The turnkey swears that he left a man talking to the prisoners that very afternoon, which is why he took great pains to ensure that door was securely locked. But we both know there is one man in England who has the skills to pick such a lock, release the birds and lock the door again. Is that not so, Master Pursglove?'

His heavy lids flicked up and he stared straight into Daniel's eyes. 'Buxom, was she, this lassy? Warm your bed herself, did she? She'd have to be a rare beauty to make a man risk all for her. After your incarceration in Newgate, you must be well acquainted with the penalty for helping murderers escape justice. And not merely a murderer, but one who likely burned a ship and endangered His Majesty's port. A less benevolent Sovereign than our King James might consider that treason. And I trust you remember the punishment for helping a traitor, Master Pursglove? You'll recall the fate of the gunpowder plotters? First, they were hanged and cut down alive . . .' There was a sharp crack as he snapped the chicken bone in half. 'Then their privy members were cut off, their entrails drawn out and burned before their eyes.' He held the splintered ends of the pieces of bone in the glowing charcoal, where they sizzled and spat.

'Finally, decapitated and quartered,' FitzAlan pronounced slowly. 'Their flesh nailed up for the ravens to pick at as a warning to others.' He tossed all the bones into the brazier. A shrill scream emanated from them as air was driven out in the heat and they blazed up in yellow flames. 'It seems you are in danger of losing more than merely your hands, Master Pursglove.' He wiped his fingers on his napkin.

He looked up at Daniel again, his tone light and brisk. 'But I could, of course, persuade the King that this woman bewitched you. Love – or shall we call it infatuation? – is, after all, a form of enchantment.

'You see, Master Pursglove, you would do well to remember that, whatever you may consider just and right, there is ultimately only one true justice in this land and that is the King's justice. What would you have me tell His Majesty, Master Pursglove, that witchcraft was at work in Bristol? It would explain much, and since this little witch has flown far away on her besom, it is unlikely that she will ever be questioned. It would mean that the King could convince his councillors that there is no need to look for a Jesuit plot in that city, no need to search for aged priests who might be hiding there. They could be left to live in peace . . . for now.'

Daniel felt himself grow hot, then icy cold. FitzAlan knew about Waldegrave. At their last meeting in that very gaol, FitzAlan had warned him that the King had spies everywhere. And so, it seemed, did the King's most trusted adviser.

FitzAlan drew a small object wrapped in cloth from his doublet and placed it on the table. Then he rose from his chair, drained the goblet and stood for a moment warming his backside at the brazier, from which an acrid stink of burning bones and chicken flesh filled the small room.

'You're free to go, Master Pursglove, but do not go far. And for the good of your health and limbs, see that you find yourself another occupation, one that does not involve opening locks without keys or conjuring crosses to miraculously turn by themselves.'

'Free?' Daniel couldn't trust his own ears.

'Aye, for now. But the time may come when you'll think you were safer off in here. You've two powerful enemies in London. Your interrogator Sir Henry Molyngton thought he'd discovered a sorcerer, and was not pleased when you proved him a fool. He wanted to see you suffer as a common felon, a trickster and faker of magic. He'll be in a rare rage when he learns you're not to be brought up on charges at the next assizes, for he'd have made certain you would have been found guilty. You demonstrated your conjuring tricks before a room full of witnesses. So, I'd advise you to keep on your guard, Master Pursglove. Sir Henry will not have done with you yet.

'But it's my belief that the King will find you useful in the months to come, provided you've learned from this. A loyal heart is not enough to keep a man from the gallows, unless that heart is ruled by a sagacious mind. A bird has eyes either side of his head, so that it may look two ways at once, but man's eyes are on the front of his face. He cannot look behind him and in front at the same time, and if he tries, sooner or later, he'll trip and fall. You'd do well to decide if your fate lies with men of the past, or of the future. Choose, and choose very carefully. Remember I entrusted you with a task, Master Pursglove. That has not ended; it has only just begun. I want Spero Pettingar found.'

'If he exists—' Daniel began.

'He exists, Master Pursglove, I've proof of that. And he thinks himself safe. But there is a cell ready and waiting for Spero Pettingar in the Tower, and you will put him in it, unless you wish to occupy it yourself.'

Daniel hadn't seen the elegant stick, hidden behind the table, until FitzAlan lifted it and banged it heavily on the stone flags. After a few moments, there was the sound of footfall on the stairs outside. The door was opened by the same man who had visited Daniel in his lodgings the night before. The visitor briefly glanced at him, with that same amused smile, before bowing deeply to FitzAlan. And now, Daniel knew where he had seen that face before. It was the mention of Molyngton which had made the connection. He'd seen those blue eyes, that smile, that auburn hair, not on a man, but a woman, the woman who had laughed and smiled during his interrogation. Daniel stared at the figure, but he . . . *she* was already moving swiftly to stand in the shadows on the other side of FitzAlan.

Leaning heavily on the visitor's shoulder, FitzAlan limped from the room, with an odd sideways gait, one foot twisted, as if his legs were not strong enough to bear him up unaided. At the door FitzAlan turned.

'I didnae mention the second man you'd best be on your guard against, did I? I think you'll recall him, too. It would seem Lord Richard Fairfax has a powerful hatred of you. Now why is that, di ye think?'

As the door closed behind them, Daniel seized the flagon and poured a measure of the dark wine into the goblet FitzAlan had just drained. He was trembling so violently, he had to grasp it in both hands. That twisted foot . . . that strange crab-like gait. He took a long, deep draught from the goblet, knowing then that he was drinking from the same goblet which, only minutes before, His Majesty King James of Scotland and England had raised to his own lips.

His gaze fell on the small bundle FitzAlan had placed on the table. He lifted it and unwrapped the cloth. There in the palm of his hand lay a fragment of carved stone – an eye, the same eye that Waldegrave's note had been wrapped around. The same eye that Daniel had hidden in his chamber in the Salt Cat.

Remember, the King has spies everywhere.

Epilogue

LONDON

Now that he was alone in his bedchamber, Lord Salisbury read the letter for the second time that evening. The names were in code, of course – but not numbers, as he had used to correspond with King James before Queen Elizabeth died. James had invented that system himself. It was the sort of childish puzzle that amused the King, but it was not reliable. It was all too easy for the wrong number to be written in error. There was no memorable link between the person and the number assigned to them, which was both its strength and its weakness. Cecil preferred to use the names of stars, or even beasts – easier to remember, especially if the cypher reflected the personality of the person, like the author of this letter, John Smith. *Father* John Smith as he had been before Cecil had him released from prison in exchange for a promise of good service.

And Smith had lived up to his promise; his service had been remarkably good, far better than even Cecil had dared to hoped. Thanks to his persuasive tongue, many recusants had turned from their faith and had offered up other names as proof of their new-found loyalty to the Crown. As an ex-priest, Smith was worth his weight in gold, and he damn near got paid it, too. But Cecil still despised him, as he did any turncoat, even though he had turned the priest himself. The cypher Cecil had obliged Smith to use was entirely fitting: *Anguis*, the snake that sheds its skin.

But what of that other name in this letter? Was it, too, a true reflection of the man upon whom it had been bestowed? Smith seemed convinced of it, but Cecil wasn't so sure. He searched for the passage again, running his finger beneath the black spidery letters in the firelight, until he found the phrase – 'devourer of the dead'. Yes, that was him, the priest they called the *Yena*.

Acknowledgements

This novel is the first of a new series set in Jacobean England, and I would like to express my heartfelt gratitude to Mari Evans, Managing Director of Headline, Frances Edwards, Commissioning Editor at Headline, and my agent, Victoria Hobbs, Director of A. M. Heath, for all the many hours of discussion, support and ideas they all put into helping conceive and shape this book and the series, and for their endless patience and encouragement. I'd especially like to thank my editor, Frances Edwards, for her untiring enthusiasm and her willingness to read all the drafts, and for all her many ideas and suggestions. My thanks to all those at Headline who have worked on typesetting, proofreading, design, sales and publicity. It takes the skills and talents of many people to get a book into a print, and the author is only a small part of that big team.

I would also like to thank all staff at the museums in Bristol, especially The Red Lodge Museum; Bristol Museum and Art Gallery; and the M Shed, for their assistance in my research on Jacobean Bristol. And to Richard Lloyd Parry, author of the astounding book *Ghosts of the Tsunami* about the 2011 disaster in Japan. It was a book that my agent, Victoria Hobbs, introduced me to and which proved to be such an inspiration during the writing of this novel.

A novel remains unfinished until it is read. An author can only ever write half of a book, the other half is created by the reader who brings their own unique experiences and imagination to each page. So, finally, my grateful thanks go to you, the reader of this novel, for all that you have brought to this book.

Behind the Scenes of this Novel

I can't always be certain of the moment when a novel is conceived; often it comes from an incident or landscape that has been simmering away in the back of my mind for months or years, until another idea collides with it and creates the magic spark of life. But with this novel, I knew from the moment I stumbled on the broadside that it would become the core of a story. 'Lamentable News', printed in 1607 and quoted at the beginning of this book, was probably written a few weeks after the incident and is a dramatic account of a great flood which had swept up the Bristol Channel, devastating the south-west of England and part of the Welsh coast, leaving over 2,000 people missing or dead. I have to confess, at first, I thought the report was somewhat exaggerated, because so much of what was printed in the seventeenth-century broadsides was what today we would call 'fake news'.

Broadsides were the tabloids of the day, consisting of a single large sheet of paper, which, in the eighteenth century, gave rise to the broadsheet newspapers. They were widely distributed from the mid-sixteenth century and used for news, public information, announcements of forthcoming events, and open letters of ridicule or complaint about people in authority, such as the Royal Court, the town council, or rivals in politics, religion and business. They were also often used to print topical and satirical ballads. Broadsides were commonly sold at public executions, giving a lurid account of a felon's criminal history, trial and confession, the latter being, at best, third-hand gossip, or invented by the broadside writer.

Nearly thirty different broadsides describing 'monstrous' births or conjoined twins, both human and animal, still exist from the sixteenth and early seventeenth centuries, though there were clearly more accounts published that did not survive. They were usually illustrated by a crude woodcut of the baby, often from two different angles, though it is unlikely that the artist had actually seen the infant. Even where the 'unnatural' or wicked behaviour of the mother was held to blame, the fact that 'God had permitted' the child to be born meant that the birth itself was still regarded as a sign that something was seriously wrong in the nation, or was seen as an omen or warning of a momentous event about to be unleashed.

So, perhaps I could be forgiven for initially mistrusting the writer of 'Lamentable News'. But then I turned to historical records and modern research papers, and I soon realised that though the imagery might be flowery, the writer had not exaggerated the horrors of the disaster. In late January 1607 a huge wave did indeed flood the coasts of the Bristol Channel and the low-lying regions of Devon, Somerset, Gloucestershire and South Wales. Some old documents and plaques on buildings marking the height of flood level record the year as 1606, because they were still following the old calendar, as I have done in this novel. More than 2,000 people were believed to have drowned, along with thousands of animals and livestock. Ships were carried far inland. Buildings and even entire villages were swept away, and around 200 square miles of farmland lay under water, wrecking the local economy along the coasts of the Bristol Channel and Severn Estuary. The coast of Devon and the Somerset Levels were flooded as far inland as Glastonbury Tor, which is 14 miles from the coast. Worst affected was the Welsh coast from Laugharne to Chepstow. The flood was recorded in a number of broadsides and chapbooks written shortly afterwards, such as the one entitled 'God's warning to the people of England by the great overflowing of the waters or floods'.

The cause of the flood has since been widely debated. Theories range from a storm surge to a tsunami produced by an underwater landslide off Cornwall or an earthquake under the sea near Ireland. It was noted at the time that the sea receded a considerable distance before a dazzling wall of water surged back, which is consistent with a tsunami. And many of the details which the broadside writers report are remarkably similar to those given by modern eyewitnesses to recent tsunamis. One account of 1607 notes details such as bells ringing in towers some hours prior to the wave striking, which might indicate an earth tremor – or might, of course, be an 'omen' added in hindsight, since several writers record experiencing an earth tremor several months later, in May. But all are agreed that the speed of the wave appears to have been faster than any normal storm flood. Eyewitnesses claimed the wave travelled 'with a swiftness so incredible, that no greyhound could have escaped by running before [it]'. And this seems to be confirmed by recent scientific analysis.

Whether it was a storm surge or a tsunami, there is no doubt that the funnel shape of the Bristol Channel helped to create the dramatic increase in the height and speed of the wave, in the same way that it produces the phenomenon known as the Severn Bore. In the open sea near the coast of North Devon, the wave was just under 13 feet high, but as it entered the Bristol Channel and the Severn Estuary, the wave increased to 16 feet and was over 25 feet high, by the time it reached the Monmouthshire coast. The speed is estimated to have increased from 27 mph along the North Devon coast to 38 mph when it hit Monmouthshire.

The second element of this book, and indeed the whole Daniel Pursglove series, is the repercussions of the failed Gunpowder Plot. This emerged from my long-held fascination with Father Henry Garnet and his alleged role in the gunpowder conspiracy, which was first aroused by the sale of an old book at an auction in Doncaster, South Yorkshire, at the end of 2007. It was a seventeenth-century volume entitled 'A True and Perfect Relation of the Whole Proceedings against the Late Most Barbarous Traitors, Garnet a Jesuit, and his Confederates'. The book was printed by the King's printer, Robert Barker, in 1606, and in a truly macabre twist, it was bound in skin, *human* skin, reputed to be the hide of the executed Jesuit leader himself. It was not usual to bind books in the skin of executed felons, but to have used the skin of such a revered priest to bind a book detailing his crimes against the Crown does seem to be a particularly malicious act of retribution, though no doubt his enemies thought it amusing. In a strange postscript to this tale, just as it was claimed in the seventeenth century that an image of the head of Henry Garnet appeared on a bloodstained straw taken from the site of his execution, so some people examining the book in 2007 said they could see the image of Henry Garnet's face emerging from the skin which bound this book.

There were numerous conspiracies and plots to overthrow the reigning monarch in both the Tudor and Stuart periods, but the one that continues to dominate public imagination is the Gunpowder Plot. One reason is that King James was determined it should be remembered. Until the Act was repealed in 1859, the 'Thanksgiving Act', or 'The Observance of 5th of November 1605', required that ministers in every cathedral and parish church read out the Act in full during a special service each year on the anniversary. Every person in the land was required to attended, and the day was marked by the ringing of church bells, bonfires, special sermons and prayers of thanksgiving for God's mercy in delivering the King, and indeed England itself, from her 'enemies'. But another factor in its enduring fascination is that, even today, there are still elements of the plot which are yet to be uncovered. Who knew what and when? Did Robert Cecil know about the conspiracy before the anonymous letter tipping him off?

But one of the most interesting puzzles for me is the identity and role of the shadowy figure known as Spero Pettingar, a mystery which has yet to be unravelled by historians. Most of the gunpowder conspirators wisely used a variety of assumed names, even among themselves. Robert Catesby called himself Mr Roberts when visiting Jesuit priests. Father Oswald Tesimond was known as Father Greenway when working as a missionary from Hendlip Hall. Anne Vaux, who often sheltered up to sixteen Jesuits at a time, including Henry Garnet, posed as his widowed sister, calling herself Mrs Perkins and Father Garnet, Mr Meaze. Even King James, when corresponding with Robert Cecil about the plans to secure his succession to the

English throne, referred to all the players using numbers. James called himself 30 and Robert Cecil 10.

But Spero Pettingar seems to have existed, at least in name, before the Gunpowder Plot, being mentioned in passing in a letter written in 1599 from Henry Cuffe in Ireland to the secretary of the Earl of Essex. Spero Pettingar is reported as being at a meal with some of the key gunpowder plotters on 24 October 1605, a meeting which was overheard and reported after the plot was uncovered, but he does not seem to match up with any of the known conspirators. So, was he one of the plotters or was he an agent provocateur or intelligencer who had somehow managed to worm his way into the inner circle? And if so, who was he reporting to? An intriguing mystery for both historians and novelists, and one I shall enjoy exploring in future novels in the Daniel Pursglove series. I hope you will join me.

Glossary

BAT-FOWLING – stealing from a shop by distraction. A common method was to strike when the light was fading, but before the lamps were lit. Thieves would target a shop where only one person had been left to serve, often an apprentice. The decoy thief, usually a girl, woman or elderly man, would pretend to have dropped something small and valuable in the street outside and ask the apprentice to go and light a lamp or candle for them to see by. The thief would either grab what they could while the light was being fetched, or would wait until the apprentice returned and beg them to come outside to help look, keeping them occupied, while their accomplice sneaked into the shop.

BATTLE ROYAL – a particularly vicious and cruel form of cockfighting in which a number of gamecocks armed with steel or silver spurs were all placed together in the cockpit and fought until all but one were either killed or disabled. The victor being whichever bird was left standing at the end.

BOUSY or BOWSY – *inebriated*. First used in the thirteenth century, deriving from a Dutch name for a type of drinking vessel. By the sixteenth century it had become a popular street term, meaning *drunk*. By the eighteenth century, the word had evolved to *boozy*.

BRISTOL CASTLE – at the time the novel is set, many of the professional criminals, beggars and villains in Bristol occupied the semi-ruined castle, which was owned by the Crown; because it was a royal property, the civil authorities in Bristol had no jurisdiction over it. In 1602, Sir John Stafford had been appointed constable of Bristol Castle, but in March the same year the mayor petitioned the aged Queen Elizabeth for Stafford's removal on the grounds that he had delegated all responsibility to a vicious and corrupt deputy, who had permitted 49 families, around 240 people, to take up residence in the castle, from where they preyed on the townsfolk. But nothing was done and the castle continued to be used by beggars and robbers, because the town constable had no authority to enter.

CAPOTAIN – or *copotain*, sometimes known as a *sugarloaf* hat, was a tall hat worn by both men and women, tall-crowned with a narrow brim, similar to those hats pictured in illustrations of the Pilgrim Fathers, but without the buckle on the front. Later in the century, the capotain was favoured by Puritans, but during the reign of King James it was worn by most fashionable people, whatever their religious beliefs.

CHAPEL – a printer's workshop was known as a *chapel*, perhaps because it was a development of the monks' scriptorium where manuscripts were once copied by hand. The name might also have arisen because in the early days of printing many of the books duplicated in the printer's chapel were religious, especially Bibles and prayer books, which had to be produced in sufficient quantities to furnish every church, and after the Reformation were increasingly bought by laypeople for use in their homes.

COCKENTRICE – not to be confused with the mythical monster the cockatrice. The cockentrice was a roasted meat dish popular with the wealthy, where a skilful cook sewed the upper body of a suckling pig to the lower body and legs of a capon. It could also be served the other way around, with the head and torso of the chicken sewn to the hindquarters of a piglet.

CONEY – an adult rabbit over one year old. Until the eighteenth century, *rabbit* was the name used just for baby or immature conies.

CROSSBITER – an archaic word for a trickster, sometimes applied to those who fleeced the gullible with the age-old three-cups trick, known then as *thimblerig*, or more elaborate scams such as faking the conjuring of spirits.

DICING FLIES – con artists sold tiny boxes containing bees or flies to gamblers who would smuggle them into cockfights, card games, etc. The insect was supposed to be a familiar spirit or imp who would tell the gambler which way to bet or could influence the outcome. Latin phrases, Hebrew letters or magical signs inscribed on the box were used to convince the customer the seller had trapped a 'spirit' in it. To consult with spirits was forbidden and carried a possible death sentence. But in the 1570s, Adam Squier, Master of Balliol College, Oxford, had a profitable sideline in supplying these flies to the gullible, a fact that only came to light when three of his victims were foolish enough to lay a charge against him with the local magistrate, complaining they had bought a fly from him to go dicing and, far from being assisted by it, they had lost heavily.

GAFF – a steel or silver spur, spike or sharpened knife used in cockfighting. There were two different sizes – a short gaff, which was one inch in length, and a long gaff that was around two and a half inches. The metal gaffs were fastened by means of leather bracelets around the gamecock's legs where the bird's natural spurs would be.

GEE-HOES – sledges used to transport heavy goods all year round in Bristol. These were low to the ground, making the loading and unloading of barrels and crates easier. But the main reason for using them was the fear that the vibration caused by iron-rimmed cart and wagon wheels trundling over the roads would shake the cellars and passageways beneath the city, affecting the wine that was stored there as well as risking the collapse of the vaults themselves. At the time of this novel, carts, wagons and gee-hoes were all used in Bristol, with carts and wagons frequently getting wheels stuck in the open sewers and locking together due to the V-shaped camber of bridges and roads. Half a century later, in 1651, an Order of the Common Council prohibited the use of carts and wagons in Bristol city for fear of damaging the cellars below the streets. Any iron-rimmed cart found within the city would have its wheels confiscated.

GENTLEMEN PENSIONERS – were an elite troop of fighting men, all sons of nobility. The Honourable Band of Gentlemen Pensioners was originally known as the Troop of Gentlemen when they were formed in 1509 by King Henry VIII to act as the King's personal bodyguard in battle and on ceremonial occasions. They were mounted and armed with lance and spear until 1526, when these were replaced with battleaxes. They last fought as a troop in battle in the English Civil War, but continued to serve as the Sovereign's 'closest' bodyguards until 1834, when they became Her Majesty's Body Guard of the Honourable Corps of Gentlemen at Arms. They still provide protection to the Queen on ceremonial occasions including the State Opening of Parliament. During the reigns of the Tudors and Stuarts they were under oath to reside within 12 miles of the King and worked in shifts, with around 20 Gentlemen Pensioners in attendance on the King at any one time.

GONG FARMER – someone who dug out the human excrement from privies, cesspits and public lavatories, known as *houses of easement*, and took it to an official dumping site, or *laystall*, outside the town, from where it was transported to be used as a fertilizer for crops. *Gong* meant both the privy itself and what was disposed in it.

GOWK – Scottish and northern English dialect word, meaning *simpleton, fool, idiot*. It comes from the Old Norse *gaukr*, meaning *a cuckoo*.

HALBERD – (or *halbard*, *halbert*) was a two-handed weapon used by foot soldiers in warfare, mainly in the fourteenth and fifteenth centuries. It consists of a long wooden shaft, around 5 feet or 6 feet long, surmounted by an axe blade for slicing, topped with a spike which could be used like a pike or spear to pierce armour. On the back of the axe blade was a hook for dragging riders from their mounts. Civilian watchmen and guards were required to bear a halberd at all times on patrol, but its length meant that it was awkward to carry and cumbersome to wield in winding, narrow streets or when passing through low archways. It was useless against firearms and, as the seventeenth century progressed, town watchmen increasingly ignored the law and stopped carrying them except for ceremonial occasions.

HOBBLERS – men who towed the big ships up the River Avon from the Bristol Channel, starting from the Somerset village of Pill. There the tidal difference can be as much as 40 feet, the second highest in the world. As each tide flows in, huge volumes of water are driven up the river from the Channel. Ships had to be towed upriver on the rising tide and safely moored before the ebb a few hours later, when they would sink on to the thick mud of the river bed. The hobblers towed ships into Bristol using rowboats, and the journey from Pill to Bristol could take several days. Later, smaller ships were towed by horses walking along a towpath, and these were eventually replaced by steam-driven tugs, but hobblers still work out of Pill today performing the same job.

HUTCH TABLE – today often called a *monk's bench*, probably because the decorative carving often depicted religious images, but there doesn't seem to be much evidence that these were originally used in monasteries. It is a bench or settle, where the bottom part is a chest with the lid forming the seat. The back of the settle swivels forward to a horizontal position, so converting the seat into a table. In bedchambers these could be used to serve breakfast, which, in Jacobean times, a wealthier master and mistress often ate in their bedroom. In smaller, poorer houses, the hutch table might be the table for the whole family, and when the top was swivelled back, the bench could be used as an extra bed, with bedding and a thin mattress being stored in the chest below.

IHS – often found on old graves, this is sometimes taken to stand for *In Hoc Signo*, which is translated as 'in this sign', or *In Hac (cruce) Salus*, meaning 'in this (cross) is salvation'. But it is usually simply read as 'Jesus' (*Iesus* in the Greek) or *Jesus Hominum Salvator* – 'Jesus Saviour of Mankind'. In the sixteenth and seventeenth centuries, the I and H were frequently merged to form a single letter, with three vertical lines, the middle one being longer than the other two.

JADING OIL – skilled blacksmiths and horse charmers knew ancient recipes for two oils: a *jading oil* that would make the horse refuse to take another step forward, and a second known as the *drawing* or *calling oil*, which would attract and calm horses. They would soak dry chicken bones in each oil, putting the jading oil bone in one pocket and the drawing oil bone in the opposite one. To control a strange horse and make it either come towards them or retreat, they would conceal one of the bones in their fist and hold out their hand towards the horse, so that it appeared to obey their command without even being touched. Using the drawing oil would help someone catch and bridle a skittish horse running loose in a field, as the smell carried a long way. Jading oils or powders could be covertly sprinkled on the ground or on an object such as a fence, causing a horse to stop dead when it approached that spot or to veer aside. If someone passing close to a horse and rider covertly wiped their hand coated in the oil on the horse's flank, the poor creature, maddened by the smell, would bolt and keep galloping, trying to escape from it.

JAKES – the street term for a lavatory or privy.

LICKER – sixteenth-century underworld slang meaning a *ruffian* or 'muscle' in a criminal gang who beats people up to obtain money, or to force them to do something. From *lick*, meaning *to defeat* or *thrash*.

LUCERNARIUM – also called *Lucernalis* or *Lucernaria hora*, this was the Christian evening service of the 'lighting of the lamps or candles'. This is one of the most ancient rites of the Christian Church, descending directly from the Jewish tradition of lighting candles in the evening to separate day from night, and to mark the beginning of Shabbat and the festivals.

Prior to the rule of St Benedict (written around 530–43CE), the Catholic Church symbolically lit all the candles and lamps in the church at the beginning and end of the Sabbath, which was usually done after the sun had set on Saturday evening and again on Sunday evening. But St Benedict's rule created two evening services: *Vespers* at sunset, which meant the candles didn't need to be lit as it was still daylight, and a later evening service, *Compline*, conducted just before the monks retired to bed, by which time the candles had already been lit in the church. The symbolic lighting of candles as the key element in the service therefore ceased, though the two services were together still referred to as *Lucernarium*, with the emphasis shifting to Christ himself being the light. Although the ceremonial lighting of candles at dusk was, and is, still carried out once a year as one of the high points of the Easter vigil.

MAINS – another name for matches in cockfighting. A main was a series of fights between an agreed number of pairs of gamecocks. The winner of the main was whoever had the greatest number of victories overall.

MERCHANT'S TOLZEY – or *Tolsey* was a recognised meeting place or commercial exchange in a town where business deals could be settled. In Bristol, there was one in Corn Street, built in around 1550. It took the form of a covered colonnade. Between 1621 and 1631, nine brass tables known as 'the nails' were erected between the columns, on which contracts could be signed, sealed and witnessed and money exchanged. When the Merchant's Tolzey was demolished in 1782, four of these 'nails', or tables, were moved to the front of the Exchange, which was built on the site, and they can still be seen today.

MUMPER – a fake beggar. Someone who feigned disability or hardship to obtain money. Mumpers usually begged aggressively and became violent if they were refused.

NAVENS – a variety of turnip, generally chopped and added to mutton or other meat stews, as an alternative to carrots.

NIP – professional cutpurse, often a young boy, who would be trained by older gang members to cut purses or pick pockets by practising on bags which had been stitched with bells and hung up on hooks, until they could steal the contents without making the bells ring.

PEACHER – an informer. Someone who 'peaches' or secretly informs on others, while continuing to live or work with them. Used in criminal slang since the fifteenth century.

PRIGGER – sixteenth-century underworld slang meaning a *horse thief*. A common trick was for thieves to steal a horse, dye it and then sell it back to the same unsuspecting owner who, of course, as they knew, was now in need of a mount.

SKIMMINGTON – otherwise known as a *rough music* or a *charivari* or *shivaree*, in which a crowd collected after dark outside the house of someone they wanted to punish and made as much noise as possible by beating metal tools, bells, pots and pans, shaking bird scarers or whirling bullroarers. The victim or victims might be dragged out and paraded through the village or town in a cart or sitting on the back of an animal facing its rear. They were mocked, pelted and might be ducked in a pond, beaten or even forcibly expelled from the parish boundaries. If the crowd feared reprisals or merely wanted to deliver a warning, they instead paraded an effigy in front of the wrongdoer's house, on which they vented their anger, often ending by tossing it on a bonfire, as was done in the years after the Gunpowder Plot with an effigy of Guy Fawkes. This unofficial form of community punishment has been documented since the fourteenth century but is undoubtedly much older.

There are numerous local terms for this custom, including *riding the stang*, *lewbelling* and *ran-tanning*. But *skimmington* is often used in the West Country and may derive from a large ladle used in cheese-making, which became the implement depicted in satirical medieval art with which a woman would berate her husband for arriving home drunk or kissing the maid.

It was erroneously believed by many ordinary people in England that if a skimmington had been declared, the perpetrators could not be held liable for any damage to property or person they inflicted, even if the victim died. Of course, in law, anyone taking part in the disturbance and assault could be arrested, but in practice they usually got away with the crime, because the terrified victim had either fled or refused to bring charges. And if he had been maimed or killed, it was almost impossible to prove who in the crowd had struck the fatal blow, especially if no one in the community was prepared to talk.

THRAWN – a method of torture unique to Scotland, whereby a rope is tied around the victim's head and jerked violently, which was said to cause agonising pain. This was commonly used during the Scottish witch trails.

TOUCHMARK or TOUCH – the mark stamped on quality pewter to show which master craftsman or workshop had made it. It was often stamped near the rim or on the lid of a vessel rather than on the base, so that it could be instantly seen. Throughout the Middle Ages the craft guilds encouraged their members to stamp their own marks on quality pewter, but in 1503 this became compulsory by law in England, though French pewter makers had been legally required to mark their wares since around 1304.

The medieval craft guilds had very strong links with the Church, endowing guild chapels within churches and processing to them on the feast days of the patron saints of their guild, as well as other religious festivals. It is hardly surprising then that, like the merchants' marks, many master pewterers used or incorporated Catholic symbols in their touches. This meant that the touchmark also functioned as a kind of talisman. Many had been registered when England was a Catholic country and since touches were registered by being stamped on huge lead touchplates or 'counterpaynes', kept at the guild headquarters, the design of an individual craftsman's touch could not be changed, even when England became a Protestant country. So, throughout the reigns of Elizabeth and James, the authorities did not regard a touchmark with a Catholic symbol in it as any indication of the religious beliefs of the craftsman who used it.

UNCUSTOMED – in the port record books of the period, when goods were seized, the ship impounded or the ship's master arrested, the reason often given was that certain goods such as wine had been 'landed uncustomed', or raw silk, wax and wheat had been 'laden for export uncustomed', meaning the customs duty hadn't been paid on the goods being imported or exported through the port. This was usually a deliberate attempt to smuggle the goods in or out to avoid paying the tax, rather than an oversight.

VERJUICE – a sour juice made from tart fruit such as crab-apples, gooseberries, sour grapes or cooking apples, often used in meat dishes to add piquancy. For example, aloes (slices) of veal or mutton would be baked in an oven in a dish of butter and covered with soft fruits including barberries and currants, then after cooking a little verjuice would be added to the dish and it would be returned to 'seethe', before serving.

WARD and WATCH – citizens were obliged to help keep the peace and protect the town under the direction of the constable. Usually a dozen or so men would patrol the streets in pairs. The day shift was known as *the ward* and the nightshift *the watch*. At night, it was the duty of the watch to challenge anyone on the streets after the curfew bell had been rung, but in practice, noblemen or wealthy citizens were allowed to pass unhindered, not least because most of the watch feared offending men who had great power and influence in a town and considered it wiser to ignore their violations of the curfew.

WATKIN'S ALE – a bawdy and somewhat explicit Elizabethan street song, which recounts the story of how a naive maiden is seduced into losing her virtue by a lad who tells her they are just playing a game called Watkin's Ale.

WHITTAWER – a maker of leather saddles, horse tack and harnesses.

WITCH'S BRIDLE – used commonly in Scotland. The prisoner would be chained to the cell wall by means of an iron bridle with four sharp prongs that were forced into the mouth. Two spikes pressed against the tongue, the other two into the cheeks. This was often used as part of a regime to 'break' the victim by preventing them from sleeping for days at a time.

YENA – the old name for a group of animals which included the hyena. They were believed to live in tombs and dig up graves to feast on the dead. They were said not to be able to turn around, because their spines were rigid, but they were able to change at will from being male to female. They lured their prey, humans and dogs, from their homes by imitating the sound of a human vomiting, as dogs were known to eat human vomit. If hunting dogs crossed the yena's shadow, the dogs would be unable to bark to alert the hunter. If a yena walked round an animal three times it could not move. The beast was said to carry a stone in its eye, also called a yena, which if placed under a human tongue would enable that person to foretell the future. In his *History of the World*, 1614, Sir Walter Raleigh maintains that they were not one of the animals carried on Noah's Ark, because only pure-blood creatures were saved. He believed the yena or hyena appeared after the flood and were the offspring of dogs mating with cats.

BONUS MATERIAL

The Business of Trickery

In the Middle Ages, the supernatural was regarded as part of the natural world. Magic and a belief in demons and angels were an integral part of religion and scholarship. But by the Elizabethan period, the two had separated. The Churches, both Catholic and Protestant, fiercely decried practises such as casting of spells and the summoning of spirits, condemning not only the magic intended to cause harm, but even the charms made by cunning women as cures. But Church, Crown and commoners had not stopped believing in magic – far from it. The laws passed by Henry VIII in 1542 and Elizabeth I in 1563, making the practise of witchcraft and consulting of spirits punishable by imprisonment or death, and King James's Act of 1604, which linked witchcraft to 'a pact with the Devil', reveals that many people – from kings to peasants – believed in the reality of magic and feared it. You don't bother legislating against something, if you don't believe it exists.

For all kinds of motives, a number of people in the sixteenth and seventeenth centuries claimed they had been harmed by witches. Others discovered it was a good way to make money. In 1621, Katherine Malpass from West Ham in Essex was examined by no less a person than King James himself. She claimed she had been possessed by a demon sent by the two witches she accused. Her stomach would swell up before the onlookers' eyes. Her bones could be heard crackling through her skin and her mouth appeared to move to the side of her face. She attracted an ever-increasing stream of visitors who were asked for 'donations' to help the possessed girl. It was later revealed that an older woman had taught her how to fake these tricks, and both were making a very good living from it.

There were many lurid reports in the broadsheets of the day about the birth of 'monstrous' babies, which both fascinated and horrified the public. Throughout the reign of both Elizabeth and James, women, or those managing them, cashed in on this by claiming to have given birth to a variety of animals, including kittens, cats, toads and serpents, some of which could be seen writhing in the women's bellies beneath their skirts, then emerging from under their shifts covered in a suitable quantity of fake birthing fluid. The astounded visitors flocked to see these 'abominations' and paid well for the entertainment. Even as late as 1728, Mary Toft of Godalming, Surrey, claimed to have given birth to a litter of fifteen rabbits and pieces of rabbit over several days. A claim that so intrigued King George I that he sent his court physician to investigate. Mary and the male midwife, John Henry, then petitioned the king for lifetime pensions, and might have succeeded had not several villagers admitted that they'd supplied rabbits to her at the time of her confinement.

In these scams, the women posed as victims of witchcraft. But some people saw there was money to be made precisely because the practise of magic was illegal. Anyone sucked into a scam involving spells or divination couldn't complain to authorities when they discovered they had been duped for fear of finding themselves prosecuted for taking part in a crime. And there were many ways this could be exploited.

In *The Drowned City*, some of those wagering on fighting cocks use dicing flies trapped in nutshells, which they are conned into believing are imprisoned spirits who will tell them which birds to bet on. But it wasn't only the uneducated who could be persuaded that magic would help them win. In the reign of Henry VIII, a young nobleman, Henry Neville, had managed to run up considerable debts in gambling dens and brothels. So, when Ninian Menville, a family servant on his father's estates, told him there were men who could fashion magic rings that would make him win at dice, Henry was tempted. After all, even gamblers today use lucky charms, rituals or lucky numbers.

Lord Henry was wary, but like modern scammers, Menville reeled him in slowly. Menville didn't know any sorcerers himself, but said that he'd heard whispers that one of Henry's personal servants did. The servant and Menville were a good double act. The servant claimed it was too risky, even consulting a sorcerer could get you executed. But Menville assured them it would be fine just so long as no one found out, thereby ensuring Henry dared not confide in anyone.

The 'sorcerer', Gregory Wisdom, whom the servant brought to the house, was very well dressed and charming. And Menville did exactly what a modern scammer would do, urged Henry to act quickly – this professional man would not hang around for long. Gregory Wisdom told Henry that what he was asking of him was dangerous, and therefore he would only do it for trusted friends. The ring's powers would come from angels not evil spirits, and would earn Henry as much as three thousand pounds in a few weeks. As payment, Wisdom demanded twenty pounds a year for life. Henry wasn't entirely naive. He offered a pension of ten pounds a year, but only if the ring worked, and the pension would start only when his father, Ralph, died and Henry came into his inheritance.

The ring was made and Henry was delighted to win thirty pounds at dice in a game that was undoubtedly rigged to ensure he won. He gave the magician a modest cut of his winnings. Elated with his success, Henry was easily convinced to finance another spell that would turn him instantly into a virtuoso lute player. We may wonder at his gullibility, but millions of pounds today are spent on products that promise instant weight loss or super-toned muscles without having to exercise. Wisdom said the spell could only be performed on St Stephen's day and dressed a room with luxurious cloth, altar, candlesticks, and elaborate robes for himself and Henry, all at Henry's expense. But the casting of the spell was interrupted when, by arrangement, a neighbour came knocking. And Henry was told he'd have to wait a full year before they could try again.

The disappointed Henry consoled himself with a visit to a gambling house with his magic ring, and lost all he'd wagered. He returned in furious temper, but the magician told him he must have looked lustfully on a woman during the evening, which had angered the holy angels who'd broken the spell. Despite this, Menville and Wisdom managed to extract more money from Henry through another scam in which Wisdom claimed that a spirit, conjured in a crystal, had revealed that a fortune lay buried beneath a cross on Henry's father's northern estates. Needless to say, that was also a hoax.

The whole sorry story finally came to light when, in October 1546, Henry was imprisoned in the Fleet, charged with the attempted murder of his wife and father by witchcraft to obtain money. He blurted out the whole tale, claiming Wisdom had cast the murderous spells without his consent. Fortunately for him, the King died three months later; Henry was pardoned and went on to become a Privy Councillor.

Wisdom and Menville had paid others to help them dupe Henry and many scams of this nature depended on teams operating together. Dishonest innkeepers, chamber maids, thieves and fortune-tellers often worked together in cities such as London and Bristol to defraud visitors. The landlord or chamber maid would set out to learn some personal information about a guest and would make it easy for a thief to rob him by, for example, leaving a door or window unlatched. Then they'd advised the guest to consult a fortune-teller who'd convince him she had the gift of second sight by revealing information that had been fed to her by the staff. He'd pay her to 'divine' where his stolen possessions were, usually in the hands of a fence, who would sell them back to him. And it was not merely the naive traveller who was duped. During the reign of Edward VI, Seymour, Lord Protector of England, paid for the services of a sorcerer to summon a spirit to find a missing silver plate, and, of course, the magician was able to reveal its location since he had ensured it had gone 'missing'.

The crimes of a notorious con artist were published in a booklet in 1613. Alice West, assisted by her husband, John, began her career as a fortune-teller, who claimed to receive her knowledge directly from Oberon and Titania, the Fairy King and Queen. In fact, she'd built a hiding place in her cottage so that she could listen to whatever her customers said to the person answering the door, before they were ushered in for their consultation. She could keep some clients returning for weeks with promises of what she could reveal until she had taken every last penny they had.

She told one hapless goldsmith's apprentice that Titania was in love with him and convinced him to bring four silver-gilt servers to a secret rendezvous at night where they would be magically turned to gold. Instead of a fairy queen, he found a gang of burly robbers waiting for him. A maid was persuaded by Alice to sit naked in a garden one winter night, clutching a pot of earth, which, by cock-crow, would turn to gold. Instead, the maid was robbed of her clothes and life-savings. Alice convinced a wealthy woman she was genuine when she magically turned two shillings into two sovereigns beneath a napkin. Alice told the woman to lock the sovereigns in a strong box where the royal fairies would double them in a week. The coins doubled. The lady was then persuaded to put in one hundred marks of her own money, a huge sum then, but instead of doubling, it vanished into Alice's pocket.

The scam, which eventually got Alice arrested, was perpetrated on the Moores – a couple from Hammersmith. They were persuaded that Titania and Oberon planned to make them rich, but only if they performed a costly ritual to honour the fairies, and told no one. They were to provide a lavish banquet and a room decked out with the finest linen for the fairies to use. The Moores were led into the chamber in which two people, dressed as Titian and Oberon, surrounded by others dressed as elves, showed them what appeared to the bags of gold with their names on, but they were not yet permitted to take them.

As the cost of the rituals Alice demanded rose, the Moores began to have doubts, but various tricks and illusions always convinced them to continue. Alice recruited their maid to persuade them to part with another huge sum for expenses. And then she fled. Alice was subsequently caught, flogged, pilloried and flung into prison. Her ultimate fate is unknown.

That same trick – providing costly furnishings for a room in which to perform summoning spells for spirits, or receive the royal fairies – had been used by other villains before, and the householders usually returned to the chamber to discover it had been stripped of all they'd been instructed to buy.

What is common to most of these scams is that the victims were told to tell no one, their silence was ensured, unless they were arrested by the Witchcraft Acts that made any form of magic illegal. The other common factor is that few, if any, of these fraudsters operated alone. There was a well organised team behind them, specialising in different parts of the operation, from obtaining personal details of the victim to stealing the goods, with a front-person doing the persuading. In fact, all the same ingredients of scams of today.

For more details and discussion of some of these crimes, I thoroughly recommend *The Sorcerer's Tale*, OUP, 2008, an excellent book by Alec Ryrie.

Daniel Pursglove will return . . .

TRAITOR
IN THE
ICE

Coming spring 2022

Prologue

BATTLE ABBEY, SUSSEX

He should have turned back before the blood-red sun began to sink. He should have hurried away before the rooks descended like ragged witches upon their night roost. He'd been a fool to walk all the way out there to the holy spring at that hour and he would live long enough to curse himself for it . . . *just* long enough. We fret and sweat over the choices that seem certain to tip the balance of our fortunes, but in truth it's not the crossroads of our lives that determine their lengths. It is the unseen thorn which poisons our finger, the forgotten key we turn back for, the single careless step. It is these tiny pismires in our fragile lives that will ultimately cut them dead.

The bitter cold had savaged every field and forest, byre and barn. The wolf's bite they called it, for the beast had sunk its sharp teeth deep into the heart of the land and nothing would make it relinquish its prey. As the cold sun sank behind the black bones of leafless trees, the man could feel the breath of the ice wolf on his skin. He stamped his feet as he trudged over the frozen leaf-mould, trying to force feeling back into numbed toes. He had stuffed his boots with raw sheep's wool, torn from the hedges, but the frosted air sucked every last drop of heat from his limbs.

A crack echoed through the wood. He spun round, but nothing was stirring, not even the withered brown bracken, each frond encased in its own ice coffin. Sense told him he should be holding his staff at the ready, for darkness was closing in and with it the foul creatures of the night, both animal and human. But he had tied his staff to the pack on his back for it was more of a hindrance than a help on the iron-hard ground. Now he was too weary and stiff to wrestle the pack to the ground. Besides, all he wanted to do was to reach the blessed heat of a warm room and a blazing fire as quickly as his frozen legs would carry him.

With clumsy fingers, he pushed the scarf he'd tied around his face higher up his nose, breathing hard through the cloth, though that was now stiff with ice from his breath. He quickened his pace. For the second time that evening, he cursed himself for not having started back an hour since. If he had, he'd already be warming his numb feet at the hearth, his belly full of hot mutton stew, his fingers wrapped around a steaming beaker of mulled ale. He slipped in one of the ice-filled ruts on the path and his shoulder crashed into a tree trunk. He growled in pain and annoyance.

He stood for a moment, trying to regain his breath. It was almost dark now. Only a faint grey breath of light ghosted between the black trunks. The first stars glittered in the devil-dark sky. No animals scuttled through the crust of fallen leaves; not even the owls called to one another. The only sound in the stillness were the crackles, like ice popping in water; the branches were splintering in the cold.

He strode forward again, suddenly aware now of the echo of his own footfalls as his thick boots crunched over the frozen ground. He had never heard an echo in woods. The icy air must be playing tricks on his ears, just as it was on his eyes, making the stars seem to creep between the tangled branches. He stopped, but the echo did not. It quickened. It was no longer an echo of his footsteps, for his own feet had taken root in the earth. He sensed, rather than saw, the movement behind him, felt, but did not hear, the great crack on his skull. He fell to his knees and was already insensible before his face crashed down on to the glass-sharp leaves.

*

He thought he was lying in a deep well, fighting up through the heavy, back water, struggling to reach the light and air above. Only the sudden explosion of pain in his head convinced him that he wasn't trapped in a dream. He tried to open his eyes and thought for a moment that his lids had frozen shut, until he painfully twisted his head and glimpsed three needlepoints of silver light that he realised must be stars far above him and by their faint light he saw the jagged spars of a broken roof.

It was only as he tried to move he understood that his numb and gloveless hands were bound tightly behind him. His legs . . . did he have legs? The searing pain in his bare feet told him they must still be attached to him. The throbbing of his head and limbs was so all-consuming that it was only as he tried to cry out, he found he could barely draw breath. The cloth which he had used to mask his face from the cold had been tied tightly across his mouth, smothering any sound. He was cold, so cold. His coat was gone. He lay on the icy earth, clad only in his shirt and breeches.

He heard footsteps crunching over the leaves, ponderous, heavy, coming closer and closer. He turned his head. Someone was standing over him, staring down. Relief flooded through him. He wriggled and mewed through the gag, trying to show his rescuer he was alive but bound. It was too dark to see the figure's face, only a dark mass, a smudged outline, the whites of eyes shining in the starlight that pierced the broken roof. He caught the smell of tobacco and a sickly fetid stench. He knew that foul odour. He had smelled it before. But his head was aching so much, the cold gnawing so deep into his thoughts, that he was struggling to put a name to it.

The figure heaved up something large and heavy, holding it in both hands, seeming to take aim at the helpless man lying trussed beneath him. Relief turned instantly to terror. The man tried frantically to roll away. He was pleading, praying, calling out to Christ to save him, but his desperate words were smothered by the thick gag. A shock of icy water cascaded down on his head and back, snatching the breath from his lungs and momentarily arresting his heart so that he feared it might never beat again. He lay shaking violently, jerking back and forth, as if he was in the grip of the falling sickness.

For a long moment, the figure stood over him, watching him silently, then it turned and trudged away without word. The man on the ground was dimly aware of the footsteps fading away into silence in the woods beyond the hut. They did not return.

He had gone beyond shivering. His sodden shirt had frozen to his skin and to the hard earth beneath him, but the agony in his hands and feet had melted away. He felt hot now. He was at home, sitting far too close to the fire. The air was stifling. He couldn't breathe. He was burning up. He was dragging off his clothes, running out through the door, trying to reach the pump or the river, desperate for cold water.

But as quickly as he'd grown hot, he was suddenly chilled to the marrow of his bones again. It was dark, so dark. Where was he? What was he doing out here? How had he got there? He was sure he could remember if he tried, but he was too tired to think now. He was sinking down and down into the soft oozing mud of sleep. Briefly he turned his face towards the jagged hole above. Three eyes were peering down at him, glittering like little fish in a brook, or were they candles? Had they come to light his way home?

The pale pink light of dawn washed through the trees, sending sparks of light shivering across the frost that lay thick on the broken spars of the old hut. A spider's web hung from the corner, each hair-thin thread gilded in silver and spangled with a thousand tiny diamonds. The black spider who had spun this exquisitely lethal trap lay as dead as the husks of the flies beneath it.

A hungry rat, driven by desperation from its hole beneath the ruined hut, gnawed on a blackened fingertip of the corpse. Why should worms feast while rats starve? The trees beyond did not hear the scrabble of sharp claws on the man's frozen skin or the rasp of yellow teeth on bone. They stood peering down in wonder at the rust-red puddles and the scarlet pools frozen at their feet, red as the blood of the ten thousand men once slaughtered in this place. Proof, they say, that the earth rejects the blood of the innocents, as water rejects the bones of a witch. Our corpse will not want for company among that great army of the dead.

Chapter One

Out of the darkness, cannon fire roared across the river, reverberating off the buildings around Charing Cross. Shutters and doors rattled, and an old barrel set on top of the teetering pile of firewood, towering almost as high as the Eleanor Cross itself, crashed to the ground, exploding into a shower of splinters and dust. But the crowd gathered around only roared with merriment when those close by fell over their own feet as they scrambled aside. Another round of cannon fire answered the first, and the night sky was suddenly lit by a red and orange glow as bonfires all along the banks of the Thames, and in every patch of open ground in the city, burst into flames. In Charing Cross, two men dashed forward to the heap of wood, brandishing burning torches, trails of smoke and fire streaming behind them in the chill breeze. They thrust the torches deep into the base of the bonfire. The rush and crackle of flames as they swept up through the pyre was drowned out by the roar of the crowd.

'Traitors! Traitors! Death to all traitors!'

Two small boys ran up, their arms full of broken wooden panels that looked as if they had been newly torn from the shutters of a house. Whooping, they hurled them on to the fire, their gleeful, dirty faces aglow in the flames. Judging by the assortment of wooden clothesline poles, stools and pails, many goodwives in London would be cursing the gunpowder plotters anew as their tenements and yards were ransacked for anything that passing lads could carry off to burn on the bonfires.

A man, squeezing between the houses and the back of the crowd, found himself momentarily trapped as the mass of people drew back from the stinging smoke pouring from tar-covered timbers and green wood that had been heaped on the pyre. A volley of shots rattled across the river, as men in the boats fired their pieces at the squibs exploding in the night sky, as if they were shooting at firebirds. Everyone seemed determined that this year's celebrations should be even wilder than the last.

Church bells had been ringing out across London for most of the day, and the regular congregations had been swollen to bursting by those crowding in to listen to the thanksgiving sermons and the prayers of deliverance from the Jesuit plot two years earlier, which had threatened to blow the King, his family and every member of Parliament and the House of Lords into millions of bloody pieces. Attendance at church on this day was compulsory and few men or women, Protestant, Catholic or Puritan, would dare to absent themselves from the services when the Act of the Observance was read out from every pulpit in the land. There were eyes and spies on every street and any man's neighbour or goodwife's maid might be willing to report such an absence to prove their own loyalty, or for the temptation of a fat purse.

But the man trying now to extract himself from the press of people was one of the few exceptions, though you would not have guessed as much merely by observing him. He was clad in plain brown and olive-green riding clothes and leather boots. He had left his heavy riding cloak at the inn where he had taken lodgings for the night and replaced it with a short half-cloak fastened across one shoulder, which left his dagger arm free for swift defence, should it prove necessary. His dark hair, neatly cut, grazed his shoulders, but he sported no curled lovelock, and his beard, which had also been newly trimmed, was unfashionably full and long. Together with the high white collar of the shirt, they mostly concealed the scarlet firemark that encircled his neck like a noose from all but the keenest stare.

Daniel Pursglove, which was not, of course, his real name, but the most recent of many he had adopted over his thirty years, had not attended church that day, nor had he any intention of doing so. He had ridden into London late that afternoon, and now he had only two things on his mind: food, and the message he had received three days before, summoning him to the tiny hamlet of Rotherhithe on the banks of the Thames the following morning.

Obliged to spend the night in London, he had avoided the cheap taverns of Southwark; not that he had money to waste, but he had frequented those places when he had worked the streets entertaining the crowds with his tricks of legerdemain, before those same conjuring tricks had got him arrested on charges of sorcery, and he could not risk running into old friends – or enemies.

Daniel extracted himself from the crowd and started up the street away from the bonfire behind him, but before he could turn the corner, he heard shouts and boots pounding up the street behind him. He whirled round, his back pressed against the solid wall of a house, his knife already in his hand. A dozen or so youths were running towards him, stout sticks and iron bars in their fists. Daniel braced himself, but they didn't give him a second glance as they rushed by, slowing only when they reached some houses further ahead. The group had divided, so that they were now running along each side of the street, beating on doors and shutters with their cudgels, and gouging the plaster on the walls of the houses as they passed. A woman foolishly opened a window in the one of the upper rooms, shouting at them in broad Scottish accent to 'leave folks be'.

'We'll leave you be, when you leave London,' one yelled up at her. Another started a familiar chant and the others joined in high-pitched parody of the woman's voice:

'Hark, hark, the dogs do bark,
The beggars have come to town,
Some in rags and some in jags
And one in a velvet gown.'

It was a dangerous mockery of King James and his Scottish courtiers, for no one in the city could mistake who the last line of the verse referred to, but it was one that Daniel had heard chanted with increasing boldness over these past months. Resentment of the Scots was growing by the day and rumours swilled through every street and village that all of the money raised by the fines on the English Catholics was being sent north of the border or lavished on the King's Scottish favourites, the latest of which, if the broadsides were to be believed, was the dashing young horseman, Robert Carr.

The woman in the upper window vanished for a moment, then reappeared with a pail, which she emptied on the men standing below. They leapt back as vegetable peelings, mutton bones and chicken guts slithered out and tumbled down. Their clothes were splashed as the soggy mess plopped into the mud, but they only laughed and jeered, scooping up handfuls of it from the street and hurling it back, splattering the walls as they tried to lob it through the open casement. The woman hastily slammed the window. The men beat on her stout front door with their iron bars, denting and splintering the wood.

They seemed hell-bent on staving it in and would probably have continued until they had succeeded, had not a young man turned into the street ahead of them. With a howl like a pack of wolves, the 'Swaggerers' ran at him, their cudgels and iron bars raised high. The man stared at them in a moment of frozen alarm, then turned and fled. Daniel knew if they caught him, he would be lucky if he could crawl home. Many Scots had taken up residence in Charing Cross and Holborn, banding together for protection and support from their hostile English neighbours. The Swaggerers knew their hunting grounds well and they seemed to have developed an instinct for spotting a Scot even at a distance.

A boom from the canons rang across the city, probably from a ship making its own loyal salute to God and King. It was followed by another wild burst of shot as men fired their own pieces with reckless abandon. It was to be hoped that no one got killed this year as the ships' crews tried to outdo each other by producing ever louder explosions, determined to make as great a bang as the gunpowder plotters had intended.

As the sound of the cannon died away, a blast of pipe, lute, cymbals and drums rolled out from the archway ahead, with cheers and good-natured yells. The music, if you could call it that, was coming from the courtyard of a tenement inn where a play – a comedy, judging by the shrieks of laughter – had just ended. Men and women hung over the balconies tossing coins down upon the motley group of players below who, between deep bows, scrambled to scoop them up and make their escape, darting anxious glances at any new faces that appeared through the archway. Either they were not licensed to perform by the Lord Chamberlain, Daniel thought, or the play was one that might land its authors in the Tower for sedition, as the authors of *Eastward Hoe* had discovered to their cost. And the players had good reason to be nervous, for every informer and intelligencer in the pay of Robert Cecil or the King would be abroad among the crowds this night, listening for talk of plots, unrest or treason.

Now that the play was concluded, trestle tables were being dragged forward and those who had been in the balcony were already clattering down the wooden staircases, drawn by the smell of roasting pig and crab apple sauce that wafted out tantalisingly from the kitchens. Daniel's belly growled. But he marched on passed the inn and drew back into the recesses of a dark doorway, from where he could watch the street without being seen. Behind him, a broad shaft of light spilled out right across the road from the lanterns and torches that had been lit in the courtyard of the inn to illuminate the players. Anyone walking past would have to pass through that cone of light and would, for a few moments, be clearly visible.

Daniel had been on his guard ever since the message from Charles FitzAlan had arrived, sure that his journey into London was being tracked and that FitzAlan would already know where he was lodging and would have someone trailing his every step. But none of those who strolled through the shaft of light seemed to be following him. No one quickened their pace as if they had lost sight of their quarry or pulled hoods lower over their faces as the light struck them.

He forced himself to wait a little longer, then made his way back to the courtyard, seating himself in the corner beneath the overhang of balcony above, from where he could watch all who came and went through the archway. The pork proved to be every bit as succulent as it smelled, the skin crisp, honey-sweet and spicy, glistening red-gold in the lamplight. The musicians continued to play bawdy songs on fiddle, lute and pipe which a few customers joined in singing, but most were occupied with the serious task of eating and drinking, while others wagered on games of Maw or Hazard, their muttered conversations punctuated by shouts of triumph or groans as they won or lost on the roll of the dice or the card in their hands.

The inn was evidently a popular one, especially on this night when every man and woman in London seemed to be abroad, determined to make the most of the revels. No table or bench remained empty for long, as those pushing out through the archway were quickly replaced by those shoving in, seduced by the savour of sweet roasting meat and the familiar tunes of the musicians. Those who could not find places to sit had gathered close to burning braziers, for though the courtyard was sheltered on three sides by the buildings, with the coming of darkness the air had taken on a sharp winter chill and a snide wind from the river made even those highborn enough to be wrapped in fur cloaks draw them tighter.

A furious yell made Daniel glance across to the far side. Two men had risen from a dicing table and now appeared to be confronting four others who had just entered the courtyard. Both the men who'd been gambling were clearly of some wealth, if not standing. Their hair was long and curled over stiff lace ruffs, plumes were fastened to their hats by jewelled broches, and by the weighty hang of their velvet cloaks, they were fur-lined. The shorter of the two men sported a long drop earing in his left ear, which gleamed red like a clot of fresh blood in the lamplight, swinging and dancing with the smallest movement of his head.

The four men who'd entered were more plainly clad, their hair shorter, their beards spade-cut, and wore long collars of soft linen in place of stiffened ruffs. As they advanced, they flicked back their woollen cloaks, three of them revealing long daggers on their belts, the other a wickedly slender stiletto, the assassin's weapon. Although they had not drawn their blades, the threatening gestures were unmistakable. Customers began to back away. Those who had been playing with the two men swept up their dice and coins, and rapidly vacated the benches. Those seated at nearby tables also scrambled up, some slipping out through the archway, others lingering to watch. The innkeeper, alerted, perhaps, by one of the serving girls, came hurrying across the yard, frantically signalling to the musicians to play louder, as if the music might sooth the inflamed tempers. But though it drowned out the words, it was evident to all it had not calmed the men, for judging by the obscene and threatening gestures, taunts and insults were flying freely on the chill wind. All the time, the two parties were edging closer to each other.

One of the four newcomers lunged towards the pair, grabbing the earing that had been winking and flashing so provocatively in the light and tearing it from the man's lobe, ripping the flesh away with it. The man yelped, pressing his hand to the wound. Blood ran from between his ringed fingers, splashing down on to the white lace ruff. The musicians' notes faltered and died as they retreated. The assailant brandished the jewel aloft in a clenched fist, whooping in triumph and punching the night sky with it, while his three companions rocked with exaggerated guffaws of laughter.

'Whoreson Scots!' a man close to Daniel snarled. 'Been snatching earrings all over London. Some've had their whole ear slashed off.'

'Aye.' His neighbour shook his head 'So, you'd think those popinjays would have more brains than to walk around wearing them if they're not looking for trouble.'

'And why should any true Englishmen be forced to change what he wears in his own city by those foreign barbarians?' his wife retorted.

Her husband opened his mouth to argue but was cut off by a screech of rage. All craned to see what was happening. One of the serving girls came flying out from the kitchens like an avenging fury, yelling curses at the Scots. She pulled the wounded man down on to a bench, cradling his head against her breasts, and attempted to staunch the copious flow of blood with the stained and grubby cloth she used to wipe the spills from the table.

His companion unfastened his cloak clasp with one hand as he drew his rapier with the other. The cloak fell to ground and he advanced on the Scotsman, who had his back to him and was still waving his prize aloft, jeering and laughing. His fellow countrymen, catching sight of the weapon, yelled a warning and pulled out their own daggers. The ringleader whirled round and tried to unsheathe his stiletto, but he was not swift enough. The rapier flashed as the Englishman thrust it forward in a deadly strike. The Scotsman swerved aside, but though it missed his heart, the blade went right through his shoulder with such force that the steel, glistening with scarlet blood, protruded a good three or four inches out the other side. The Englishman twisted it, trying to drag it out, while the Scot, his face contorted in agony, kicked out at his stomach, attempting to knock him backwards and wrench the weapon from his hand. After a moment's hesitation, the other three Scotsmen darted into the fray, their daggers drawn, while another man vaulted across a table and savagely struck the Englishman's sword arm with an iron ladle, so that he lost his grip on the rapier hilt. But the crowd around were not standing for that. Brandishing stools, knives and even wooden trenchers, men and women alike charged at the Scots.

For a moment, little could be seen or heard except for shrieks and yells, the crash of overturning benches, and the clatter of falling pots and jugs as the knot of people pushed and shoved. Then, with a howl of fury, the gang of Swaggerers that Daniel had seen earlier came running into the courtyard. At the sight of them, two of the Scotsmen tore themselves free from the fight and, unable to escape through the archway, charged towards the doorway of the inn, slashing out wildly with their daggers as they ran. The man who had snatched the earring staggered after them. He had evidently managed to wrench the rapier from his shoulder, but blood was streaming down his arm, leaving a wet glistening trail on the flagstones behind him. The fourth man lay slumped on the ground, his face battered and bleeding. The Swaggerers charged after the fleeing men. The Englishman, pausing only to snatch up his rapier, sprinted after them. As they hurtled towards the parlour door of the inn, they came within touching distance of Daniel.

Up to then, the face of the man wielding the rapier had been largely in the shadows, but now Daniel saw him clearly. He was in his thirties, tawny blond hair, his cheeks clean-shaven and a beard trimmed into a short, sharp point. Those eyes, pale and green as spring grass, were only too familiar to Daniel. In fact, he knew them better than he knew his own, for he'd spent most of the first fifteen years of his life studying, sleeping and eating in this man's company. Together, they had learned to ride, to dual, to fight. Together they had grown from boys to men. They had been raised as if they were brothers, but they were not and never could be. Richard Fairfax!

He had already reached the door, charging straight past Daniel, so intent on hunting down his quarry that he hadn't even looked in his direction, still dismissing all those around him as not even worthy of a glance. Daniel's dagger was in his hand before he was even aware of it, the blade pointing straight between those shoulder blades framed in the doorway. One swift thrust, that was all it would take. He had done it before. Killing a man was easy; forcing himself to lower the dagger was not. Daniel pressed himself back into the shadows, as more men crowded through the open doorway behind Richard. Then he turned and walked out through the archway, his fist still gripping the knife.

TRAITOR
IN THE
ICE

Winter, 1607. A man is struck down in the grounds of Battle
Abbey, Sussex. Before dawn breaks, he is dead.

Home to the Montagues, Battle has caught the paranoid eye
of King James. The Catholic household is rumoured to shelter
those loyal to the Pope, disguising them as servants within the
abbey walls. And the last man sent to expose them was
silenced before his report could reach London.

Daniel Pursglove is summoned to infiltrate Battle and
find proof of treachery. He soon discovers that nearly
everyone at the abbey has something to hide – for deeds far
more dangerous than religious dissent. But one lone figure
he senses only in the shadows, carefully concealed from
the world. Could the notorious traitor Spero Pettingar
finally be close at hand?

As more bodies are unearthed, Daniel determines to
catch the culprit. But how do you unmask a killer
when nobody is who they seem?

Available to order

REVIEW